A MOMENT OF TIME

A MOMENT OF TIME

Jilaine Tarisa

INSPIRED CREATIONS LLC

Author's Note

A Moment of Time is the first volume of the series *The Red Rose Way*.

The Office of Special Projects is a fictional agency within the United States Department of Justice. Passing references are made to historical figures and events, to businesses, books, motion pictures, theatrical performances and songs, and to theories and findings from various fields of study. The author has researched these subjects and has attempted to accurately convey the matters addressed, but the details provided are neither comprehensive nor current, and the information is used in the context of a fictitious story; therefore, readers should not assume that a literal or factual statement or interpretation is intended. (The controversy over the vaccine preservative thimerosal, for example, was investigated in a series of Congressional hearings, and the author read hundreds of pages of hearing testimony concerning potential health risks related to thimerosal, including the suspected link between childhood exposure to thimerosal and the development of autism. No causal relationship between thimerosal-containing vaccines and autism spectrum disorders has been scientifically demonstrated. The time frame for this story is 1996-1998; in 1999, the U.S. Public Health Service and the American Academy of Pediatrics (AAP) issued a Joint Statement recommending removal or reduction of thimerosal from vaccines. The AAP retired the recommendation in 2002 and now recommends retaining thimerosal in the global vaccine supply.)

Readers are advised to explore the many resources available concerning the topics mentioned in *A Moment of Time*, and to reach their own conclusions after further investigation.

PART ONE

IRELAND

∞ 1 ∞

"You were born at a precise moment in time for a reason," said the male voice. "And so shall you be again. Ponder on this."

"Please return your seat backs and tray tables to their upright and locked positions," said the female voice. "We will be landing in Dublin shortly."

Caitlin Rose yawned and stretched to rouse herself. She removed the sleep mask from her eyes and lifted the shade on the window by her seat.

Clouds.

She turned away and gripped the armrests, bracing herself. Landings made her nervous.

As the flight attendant walked down the aisle one last time, Caitlin looked at the passengers around her, wondering who had told her to ponder the reason she was born. *Sounded like something Kimo would say,* she thought. *Strange.*

She settled back into her seat and tried to relax. Focusing her thoughts on a positive outcome often helped her get through a rough patch. She closed her eyes and inhaled, imagining how exhilarated she'd feel walking off the plane. Exhaling slowly, she visualized Kimo greeting her with a welcoming smile.

She didn't mind hiring a taxi, she'd told him, but Kimo was adamant about meeting her at the airport. As much as Caitlin appreciated the gesture, she knew she would need some down time before she would feel like socializing.

Kimo was endearing but not at all the sort of man Caitlin wanted to date. She didn't find his long hair, earring, and gypsy-style clothing attractive and usually kept him at a safe distance, meeting him occasionally for a Saturday lunch or a game of tennis. In Washington, she worried what her colleagues would think if they saw her with him, but in Ireland raised eyebrows would threaten no consequences. She hoped Kimo understood that she considered him a friend, not a romantic prospect.

"You realize this doesn't, like, 'mean' anything—about us, I mean," she'd said when she agreed to meet him in Ireland.

"Everything means something," he'd said.

Ordinary conversations frequently turned philosophical as Kimo found hidden significance in everyday language, events, and circumstances. Caitlin often felt discombobulated and off-balance around him. Traveling together for three days was going to be . . . *interesting.*

Of course, she didn't have any proof that he wanted to date her, either, Caitlin reminded herself; maybe she was reading too much into his eagerness to be with her. She didn't waste time with guessing games. Her job was all-consuming. This vacation would be her first in the five years she'd been working for the Department of Justice and she was only taking time off now because her boss, Neil Morton, insisted.

Now there's a man who knows how to go after what he wants.

Neil's actions didn't leave any doubt about his intentions, but he pursued his aims without regard for Caitlin's wishes—or anyone else's, as far as she could tell. She had risen to the upper echelons of a male-dominated profession through aggressive pursuit of her goals, but when it came to love, she needed to be courted and won.

She opened her eyes as the wheels of the plane touched down on the runway. Maybe the pop psychology books were right and she was looking for a father figure.

Where important matters were concerned, Charles Rose had been the unquestioned ruler of his household and Caitlin learned early to accept his decisions without complaint. But she also learned that, on most occasions, her father was amenable to persuasion and she became adept at the art. Now she sought a man who, like her dad, cherished her and cared about her happiness—but didn't try to dominate her. Neil wasn't the type of man who cherished anyone or anything, and he tried to dominate everyone.

Cherishing something, Caitlin thought, *requires seeing its value.* Neil saw only short-term gains and losses, measurable results, surface qualities, and how a thing—or a person—could serve his agenda.

As the plane taxied toward the gate, Caitlin relaxed her grip on the armrests. She peeked out the window, recalling her father's words the morning the family left Olathe, Kansas, for the first of many vacations in the Ozark Mountains.

"It's a soft day," he'd said.

At the age of seven, the start of a new adventure interested Caitlin more than the weather. Still, the remark had stayed with her all these years. She wasn't quite sure what it meant until she gazed out at the light gray sky above Dublin.

Her eyes brimmed with tears. Her father had been gone for more than four years, but waves of grief still overcame her at times. She reached for her handbag and pulled out a handkerchief, but the emotion subsided as quickly as it had surfaced.

She brushed back her hair and allowed her hand to linger for a moment on her bare neck, remembering the necklace her father had given her for her sixteenth birthday. As he clasped it around her neck, he said, "This belonged to my granny and then to my ma. Now I want you to have it. And never forget: it's Irish blood that runs through your veins."

The necklace was too old-fashioned for a sixteen-year-old to appreciate; Caitlin never wore it after that first day. She didn't even know where it was anymore. The summer of '79 was so long ago. Before college, and law school. And Jayson.

Caitlin neatly folded the handkerchief. Its monogram reminded her of the weekly after-school lessons in embroidery and needle-point she'd endured, back in Kansas, with her maternal grand-mother. If the afternoon was bright and sunny, Caitlin's mind invariably wandered to the field outside her grandparents' house and her eyes soon followed. Grandmother Clayton never failed to notice the lapse in attention. She would clap her hands loudly and declare, "An idle mind is the devil's workshop!" and motion for Caitlin to resume her task.

Caitlin sighed. These days, daydreaming was a luxury she couldn't afford and tears were an indulgence she wouldn't allow. She put the handkerchief in her pocket. *Grandmother Clayton would be proud.*

When the cabin door opened, she gathered her belongings and followed the line of passengers to the terminal. Stretching her legs felt good after the long flight in cramped quarters. Next time, she decided, she would fly first class—and choose an aisle seat.

After retrieving her luggage, Caitlin waited near the baggage claim area. Kimo seemed more responsible now than when she'd first met him, but Caitlin still doubted his reliability. If he didn't show up, she would manage. Her job required frequent travel and she was accustomed to finding her way on her own.

If she were traveling solo, she would skip the tourist attractions and focus on finding the place where her father's grandmother, Katie Moran, had lived; next, she would uncover as much informa-tion about Katie's life and times as she could during her brief stay. With Kimo involved, sticking to a plan would be harder. Caitlin had learned to expect the unexpected.

She advanced the time on her watch five hours, then looked up. Kimo was walking toward her, wearing a goofy expression. How could she not like someone so affable?

"Good flight?" he asked.

"Great." She smiled. "Just the way I imagined."

They exited the terminal. Caitlin's carry-on bag, with its built-in wheels, glided easily over the pavement. Kimo carried the larger suitcase by the handle.

"It does roll, you know," Caitlin said.

"What, this? It's fine."

Caitlin shrugged and shook her head. Pointing at a diminutive car they passed in the parking lot, she giggled and said, "That would fit inside one of my shoeboxes!"

The notion of the tiny car surrounded by boxes of designer shoes inside the spacious walk-in closet at her townhouse in Alexandria, Virginia, was amusing but Caitlin's mirth was short-lived; Kimo opened the trunk to a car just like it. When he placed her luggage inside, it nearly filled the small compartment.

"What about your stuff?" she asked.

"It's at the hostel."

"Where will we put it?"

Kimo closed the trunk. "I don't have much." He looked into her eyes and calmly said, "It's not a problem."

"Hmm," Caitlin said, unconvinced. Heading for the car door, she bumped into Kimo. "Oh, right—other side." She walked slowly around the car and paused by the passenger door. "We could get an upgrade. I'll pay the difference."

"Nah, this is great for these narrow roads. Look at this," Kimo said, pushing on a side mirror until it collapsed inward. "Those extra inches make all the difference in a tight spot."

Caitlin held her tongue. Kimo was the driver; she wouldn't argue. She waited for him to open her door.

"It's open," he said, and climbed behind the wheel.

Caitlin took her seat and buckled the seatbelt.

Kimo started the motor. "Amazing, isn't it?"

"What—that it started?" The toylike car looked better suited to an amusement park than a highway, Caitlin thought.

"That, too," Kimo said with a sheepish grin. He made a sweeping gesture with his hand. "All of this. Being here. Isn't it great?"

"The airport?"

"Ireland!"

Kimo paid the fee and exited the parking lot. Caitlin was impressed by the way he adeptly shifted the manual transmission with his left hand and smoothly navigated the roundabouts that led to the M1 motorway, but her right eye felt irritated. She lowered the visor above her head, hoping to find a mirror, but the economy car lacked even basic amenities. She flipped the visor up, glad that she had made the arrangements for their lodging outside of Dublin.

Kimo would have chosen some rustic lodge with a leaky roof and peat for heat, advertised as "authentic Ireland."

He had already arranged to stay at a hostel downtown when Caitlin decided to meet him in Dublin. She wanted more comfortable lodging and reserved a room at a guesthouse recommended by her travel agent. A converted convent, The Abbey House was famous for its gourmet breakfast.

"Do you know how to get to the guesthouse?" Caitlin asked.

"Yep. Everything's under control," Kimo said as he drove toward the west side of town.

"Good, 'cause my brain is going on vacation," Caitlin said. She had worked a full day on Monday before driving to Dulles International Airport to catch the evening trans-Atlantic flight and had slept little on the plane.

"It takes two weeks of extra work to get away for a week," she said, adjusting the seat to give herself more legroom. "I think I met all the immediate deadlines and diverted the impending disasters."

She leaned back and closed her eyes, wondering what crisis she would find waiting for her when she returned to Washington.

"*Crisis* means turning point," Kimo said.

Caitlin opened her eyes and stared at him. Sometimes she wondered if he could read her mind.

"Take an apple." As if by magic, Kimo produced two rose-colored apples. He held one out to Caitlin. "It starts as a flower," he said. "The fruit grows slowly, in its season, until finally—it's ripe and ready. Its moment has come."

Warily, Caitlin took the apple. "Good thing my name isn't Eve."

Kimo chuckled and rubbed the other apple against his cotton shirt before taking a bite. The sound of his teeth piercing the juicy flesh made Caitlin's mouth water, but her irritated eye demanded attention.

The tears found a way out after all, she thought, and reached into her pocket for the handkerchief. Still needing a mirror, she searched her handbag but didn't find one there, either. Finally, she gave up and contemplated the apple in her hand.

"Ripeness applies in law, too," she said, dabbing at her tearing eye with the handkerchief. "It's one of the tests for determining whether to file a lawsuit. Not all disputes are ready for a courtroom. If a controversy isn't ripe, the judge will dismiss the case. But what has ripeness got to do with crisis?"

"A crisis is an opportunity for transformation. It's the crucial moment when something shifts. A change from one state to another."

"Does one country to another qualify?" Caitlin asked after glimpsing a highway sign written in both Irish and English.

Kimo took another bite of his apple. "It's a process, ya know? Change can be imperceptible. On the surface it seems like nothing is happening. Then, suddenly you realize: you're at the summit of the mountain. You're harvesting the fruits of seeds you planted in the ground. The babe in your arms is now a full-grown adult. Most so-called overnight sensations have been honing their craft for some time before they get noticed. Even a prodigy like Mozart needed guidance and tutoring for his natural talent to reach its full expression."

"Your point being?"

"Explain it however you like—fate, destiny, the planets aligning in some rare formation—when conditions are right for something magical to occur, a window opens. There's no telling what might emerge out of the mist. Doesn't the air feel portentous?"

"Feels like rain," Caitlin said.

"This is Ireland. It always feels like rain."

"You've been here, what—two days? Already you're an expert on the climate?"

"I learn fast." Kimo sped up the car as if to emphasize his point.

The mention of Irish mist reminded Caitlin of the crazy stories she'd heard since childhood about her great-grandmother, Katie Moran. In her time, Katie was known throughout County Cavan. She tended her garden as lovingly as she ministered to the people who came to her for healing. An herbalist, she also served as midwife of birth, and death. According to family lore, she once delivered a child with fuzzy, pointed ears to a pale woman who appeared, seemingly, from out of the mist.

As puzzling to Caitlin as these tales were, she was equally mystified by the casual manner with which the Roses related them. No one seemed embarrassed—or fearful of being locked up—when they spoke of Katie's unique talents.

They always were a colorful bunch, Caitlin thought, kicking off her shoes. They talked about the weather with the same relish as a Celtics game, and an innocent remark could start a brawl if one of them was in a fighting mood.

Caitlin first met her Rose relatives during a trip to Boston when she was nine. Her father was the second son, she learned, the first child born in America. His parents named him Charles after a Rose ancestor from Scotland. Always unpretentious, the formal name never suited him. Soon, everyone called him Charlie.

Charlie's sister Maureen was still living at home. She took Caitlin to the neighborhood movie theater, ice cream parlor, pizzeria, and bowling alley. Caitlin loved the attention and wished she could stay longer.

Her father, she knew, had left home at his earliest opportunity, eager to escape an environment that was too stifling for his ambitions. With three younger siblings underfoot, the house was noisy and crowded. Provisions were meager and Charlie was restless to strike out on his own, free from worries about family obligations. He wanted to travel and hoped a career in journalism would give him the opportunity. He thought he was on his way when he accepted an internship with a newspaper in a small Midwestern town, but the train ride to Kansas City was the most he ever did see of the United States. A dalliance with a local girl turned him into a reluctant father and husband.

He stayed on with local newspapers, and his assignments kept him close to home. Eventually, he turned to teaching at the local junior college. After Caitlin's mother divorced him, Charlie retired to the lake house they'd found on that first trip to the Missouri

Ozarks. Retirement brought the freedom to travel, but a back injury soon confined him once more.

He could still dream, though. During Caitlin's last visit to the lake house, her father said he wanted to visit the land of his ancestors. Caitlin didn't attend his funeral, but she vowed to go to Ireland on his behalf. She hoped his spirit would find vicarious satisfaction through her travels.

Kimo stopped the car in front of The Abbey House and turned off the motor. Caitlin grabbed the rearview mirror and located the errant lash in the corner of her reddened eye.

"We could go to Phoenix Park," Kimo said, studying a map. "It's near here. Seventeen hundred acres—it's the largest park in all of Europe."

Caitlin coaxed the eyelash onto her handkerchief and wiped away the mascara that had smudged around her eye. "I'd like a couple of hours to myself, if that's okay."

"Yeah, sure," Kimo said. "I'll go to the park alone." He folded the map. "I'd rather take you to Trinity College. The *Book of Kells* is worth seeing. I was there yesterday."

Caitlin slid her feet into her shoes and opened the car door. "Whatever." She had not come to Ireland to tour famous landmarks but she was prepared for some give and take. Researching the Rose family tree was her priority. "Thanks for the ride," she said as she exited the car. "I'll see you back here—when?"

Kimo shrugged. "In a while." He carried her luggage to the entrance of the guesthouse and left.

Caitlin rang the bell. The door opened and a portly woman greeted her.

"You must be Miss Rose," the woman said. "I'm Mary Brady."

Caitlin hadn't been called "miss" in years and bristled at the title. She lugged her suitcases inside and followed Mrs. Brady to the registration desk. The hostess slowly waddled along, wincing and moaning as she soothed her right hip with her hand. After Caitlin signed in, Mrs. Brady handed her a room key and summoned "Mr. B" to help carry the luggage up the stairs.

"American?" Mr. Brady asked as he led the way to Caitlin's room on the second floor.

He was lithe and wiry and moved with alacrity, a stark contrast to his plump wife's plodding manner. Caitlin guessed he was about the same age her father had been when he injured his back.

"Yes. How did you know?"

"Ah, well, don't we get plenty of Americans stayin' here. Tracing their family hist'ry, a lot of 'em."

"My father's family came from County Cavan."

"Is it to Cavan you're headed, then? Why, that's grand," Mr. Brady said. "You're likely to find a few Bradys in them parts."

"I've never been there."

Caitlin watched anxiously as Mr. Brady hauled the larger of her two suitcases up the stairs. She knew she had overpacked, but she wasn't quite sure what to bring on this trip and she disliked being caught unprepared.

"It's your first time, is it?" Mr. Brady asked when they reached the landing. He slowly straightened his thin frame and fumbled with a set of keys before opening the door to "Saint Anne's Room."

"In Ireland, you mean?"

"Aye."

Caitlin nodded and scanned the room. The quilt covering the queen-sized canopy bed looked handmade, as did the needlepoint wall hanging. The large claw-foot tub in the corner was clearly not a holdover from convent days, though the crucifix on the wall could have been.

"You'll see a bit of the country, then. Myself, I'd be content in a little cottage by the sea. But, I married a Dublin girl who dreamed of running an inn. So there ye have it."

Caitlin reached into her purse to find Irish money for a tip. She pressed a five-punt note into Mr. Brady's palm and said, "Thank you."

His eyes widened as he smiled and tucked the bill inside a shirt pocket. "Be sure an' let us know if ye need anything."

Caitlin closed the door and unlocked her luggage. She hung a silk blouse and two dresses in the closet, turned on the faucets of the tub, and sat on the edge of the bed nibbling a scone she found on a serving tray. When the tub was almost full, she stripped off her clothes, sprinkled lavender oil into the water, and eased into the hot bath.

"Ahh!" she murmured as the tension melted from her shoulders. Maybe lying on a pristine beach or lounging by the pool at a spa resort would have been a better choice for a relaxing vacation than trudging around the Irish countryside in search of elusive clues about her heritage. Working at nothing but a suntan would be appealing—for about a day. Before long, she'd probably be organizing fellow vacationers into a dream study group or encouraging the staff to demand better wages. She laughed at her restless nature. If the pace of her life was too hectic, she had only herself to blame.

Reaching for the soap, she caught a glimpse of the crucifix and shifted her position in the tub. Many people considered the image of Jesus as Savior a comforting one; he'd died for their sins and offered the promise of redemption if they followed the rules of their religion. For Caitlin, the image of the man in agony was unsettling.

That there were differences among various Christian denominations had been evident to her since childhood, though she hadn't studied the history or doctrines enough to reach any conclusions about her own views. Protestants, Catholics—they were all Christians, weren't they? Followers of the same Christ? Caitlin thought of the large sassafras tree outside the lake house in Missouri. As a child, she liked sitting in the "V" where the tree branched in two directions. Fed by common roots, the divergent limbs were part of the same tree.

Caitlin remembered the evangelical church in Olathe that she and her brother, Bobby, had attended along with the rest of the Clayton family. The Claytons had been members of the congregation since pioneer days. Built in 1870, the building was turned into a playhouse by a local theater group a hundred years later, after church attendance dwindled. Caitlin's mother, Martha, sometimes took Caitlin to performances at the theater. Caitlin was never sure whether her mother really liked plays or simply wanted to visit the place where she and Charlie were married, but her love of musical theater began with the first show she saw there—*Bye Bye Birdie*.

Caitlin's father didn't care for religious or theatrical performances, and once remarked about the artifice of both. He preferred stories about real people and current events and believed citizens should stay informed about the issues facing their communities and the actions of their elected officials, so important for a vibrant and healthy democracy.

As she lathered her body with soap, Caitlin realized that her father hadn't ever joined the Claytons at their church. He did, however, take his family to the Catholic Church in Boston where he'd been baptized. The stained glass windows, fragrant incense, solemn rituals and priestly vestments aroused a feeling of reverence Caitlin had never experienced in her mother's church. After Mass, the whole Rose family gathered to celebrate the first Communion of Caitlin's cousin, Ginnie. Food, alcohol, music, laughter, and stories flowed into the night. Caitlin even talked her father into giving her a sip of his Scotch whisky. The strong liquor burned her throat but the taste wasn't bitter like the black coffee her mother once let her try.

In the years since her father's death, Caitlin had grown closer to her Aunt Mary. The elder of Charlie's two sisters, Mary had undertaken a similar journey to Ireland when her mother, JoAnn Moran Rose, passed over. Mary told Caitlin about the old Moran homestead in County Cavan and asked her to bring back a rose from Grandma Katie's rose bush, something she wished she had done when she had the chance.

"That's our family crest," Mary said. "No coat of arms on the wall could capture the spirit of life—of love and beauty—like a living rose."

Caitlin was eager to get to Cavan but first she needed rest. Next, she would explore Dublin's treasures with Kimo. She rinsed off the soap and dried herself with a fluffy white towel. Noting the time on the clock by the bed, she nestled between crisp sheets for a catnap.

An hour had passed when Caitlin looked at the clock again. She dressed quickly in a skirt and matching top, brushed her hair, and unpacked a pair of sandals. She picked up the apple Kimo had given her, dropped the room key into her purse, and closed the door.

Before descending the long staircase, she bit into the apple. Juice dribbled down her chin.

Yep, she thought, *it's ripe,* and wiped her face with the back of her hand.

∽ 2 ∽

Outside The Abbey House, Caitlin found Mr. Brady teaching Kimo the pronunciation of *Brú na Bóinne,* the Irish name for a prehistoric complex of tombs and standing stones in the Boyne Valley, an hour's drive northwest of Dublin. Kimo planned to stop there the following day, on the way to Cavan. One of the tombs, Newgrange, was designed to align with the sun's rays at the winter solstice, he'd told Caitlin, but he hoped to discover something about the nature and location of summer solstice rituals as well.

Mr. Brady set down the shears he was holding and opened the car door for Caitlin. She smiled and settled into her seat. Mr. Brady closed the door, waved, and resumed his landscaping work.

Kimo maneuvered the car down the narrow street. Driving on the other side of the road seemed to come naturally to him, Caitlin thought. She appreciated his willingness to drive, but still wished they had a bigger car.

"Where's the air conditioning?" she asked, examining the knobs on the center panel.

"Um . . . The windows roll down."

"Great. Remind me to buy a hat."

Kimo reached for a cap on the back seat and handed it to her.

"Guinness," she read. "I'll be a walking advertisement." She gathered up her long auburn hair and stuffed it under the cap. "I don't even like beer."

"The beer here is different," Kimo said with a devilish grin. He ran his fingers up her arm. "It's alive!"

Caitlin laughed, surprised by Kimo's boldness. He was an enigma. Perhaps that was what drew her to him—she was still trying to figure him out.

She held onto the cap as the wind rushed through the open windows. The reality of having to negotiate with Kimo the thousand decisions that get made in the course of a day started to sink in. They were so different. Would they be able to agree on anything?

Kimo and Caitlin strolled down Grafton Street, pausing to listen to street musicians while Caitlin sipped a cup of coffee. Next, they headed to the campus of the College of the Holy and Undivided Trinity of Queen Elizabeth. Reading from his guidebook, Kimo told Caitlin the school was built on the site of a former monastery.

"In 1592, the land lay south of Dublin's city walls," he said, closing the book. "Now, four centuries later, it's in the center of the city."

They entered the Old Library building and paid the fee to see the *Book of Kells*, the most famous volume in the library's renowned collection. The Latin text of the Gospels, embellished on vellum calfskin with elaborate illustrations and artistry, was believed to be the work of eighth-century monks. The jeweled cover was long gone, but the book had survived theft and burial and Viking raids.

When their turn came, Kimo and Caitlin approached the glass case in the center of the small room. The *Book of Kells* lay open, displaying a page with the traditional representations of the four evangelists, Matthew, Mark, Luke, and John, as man, lion, ox, and eagle.

"Look at the detail," Caitlin said, admiring the rich ornamentation. "I wonder how long it took to illustrate this one page."

"Look at the symbols," Kimo said. "They represent the four elements and the four fixed signs in astrology—Aquarius, Leo, Taurus, and Scorpio."

"No way," Caitlin said. "The Church opposes such things."

"Religions tell people what to believe. But if you know otherwise, are you going to recant under pressure? That was the dilemma facing scientists and alchemists for centuries. The Church condemned Galileo for suggesting the Earth moves around the sun, in contradiction to Church teachings. Centuries earlier, the Greeks taught that the planets rotate around the sun, but much of their knowledge was lost when the Pagan centers of learning were closed down. Astrology was an integral part of those traditions."

Caitlin stared at the distinctly Celtic designs. "Aren't there twelve signs in the zodiac?"

"Yes, one for each month. The Bible, you'll notice, speaks of twelve tribes of Israel and twelve sons of Jacob. In Greek mythology, the twelve Titans were the offspring of Gaia and Ouranos, Earth and Sky. There were twelve apostles, of course, though the names of the twelve vary in the different gospel accounts. Other disciples wrote gospels, too," Kimo said quietly, "but Irenæus, an early bishop in Lyons, decided there should be four—no more, no less. There were four winds and four directions, he reasoned—there ought to be four pillars of the new faith. After Christianity had the backing of the emperor—"

"That was—" Caitlin snapped her fingers in vain. Her memory for history was weak. Given a case name, though, she could recite the facts and holding like a law professor.

"Constantine."

"Right."

"—the early 'fathers' decided which doctrines would be part of the new church they were forming," Kimo explained. "Over time they adopted traditions, right down to names and dates and rituals—from other religions, from Pagan lore—in order to gain acceptance in different regions. Gradually, traces of the old ways disappeared—the mystery schools, the sacred writings of groups like the Gnostics. The orthodox have always detested those who seek to know for themselves or who claim to have special knowledge. They think it's arrogant and heretical."

"So they destroyed evidence of contrary views."

Caitlin scowled. The courtroom was her temple, and the rituals that occurred therein were sacred. Jury tampering, lying under oath, concealing evidence—these were crimes tantamount to sin within the religious schema. Laws, rules, agreements—these were the hallmarks of civilization that kept the social order intact.

"They destroyed everything," Kimo said as they exited the

building. "Libraries . . . temples . . . people. Documents were edited—
or created—to strengthen the Christian agenda and to refute opposing views."

"In the name of God!"

"Religions are powerful. Throughout history, the head of the
church was often the head of state. Some Roman emperors insisted
on being worshipped as divine. For Christians, Jesus was the divine
king."

A familiar knot tightened in Caitlin's abdomen. Long ago, she'd
strayed from the pat answers provided by her mother's religion and
put aside theological matters to focus on jurisprudential ones.
Questions about morality, ethics, values, and laws concerned her
more than notions of an eternal afterlife, and she didn't find the
minutiae with which most religions concerned themselves illuminating. Still, nagging doubts plagued her at times.

"Grandmother Clayton used to tell me I'd burn in Hell if I didn't
temper my willfulness," Caitlin told Kimo as they walked the cobble-
stone streets in Dublin's trendy Temple Bar district.

"I wouldn't worry too much about it," Kimo said. He held open
the door to a popular pub. "Hel was the Norse goddess of the underworld, you know."

"Norse?"

They sat at the bar and waited for a table. Kimo signaled the bartender and ordered a pint of Guinness.

"Four of our weekdays are named for Norse gods and goddesses,"
he said. "The Romans were good with architecture and engineering,
but much of their culture and philosophy they adopted from the
Greeks. The Greek god Hermes became the Roman god Mercury;
Aphrodite became Venus, and so on. The Greeks learned a lot from
the Egyptians, and the Jewish kabbalists probably got some of their
ideas from the Chaldean Magi during the Babylonian captivity. The
wisdom of the Magi may have originated in Tibet and India."

India! How'd we get there?

Caitlin's head ached. She was ready for a hot meal. Someone
dropped a tray; the clatter made her cringe. She tried to concentrate
on the menu, but Kimo was intent on continuing the conversation.

"Buddhism spread into many lands during Asoka's reign in India," he said. "He joined a Buddhist order while he was emperor and sent out missionaries, east and west. Which brings us back to Ireland." He raised his mug and took a drink.

"It does?"

"Mmm," he murmured.

Foam clung to his upper lip like a moustache. Caitlin stifled a grin.

Kimo reached for a napkin and wiped his face. "Classic Buddhist symbols like those found in dharma wheels appear in pre-Christian Celtic designs," he said. "Some people think the teachings of druids and Buddhists paved the way for Christianity in Western Britain and Ireland. The druids practiced ritual sacrifice, but they didn't use violence as a means of conflict resolution; they relied more on reason and intellect. They opposed Saint Patrick, for example, when he arrived in Ireland in the fifth century, but they didn't persecute him."

"And Buddhists?"

"Buddhists don't impose their views on others by force or use conquest as a means of expanding their influence. The Buddha taught compassion for all sentient beings and methods for achieving liberation from suffering."

"How does that relate to the coming of Christianity?"

"Jesus's teachings about love and forgiveness would have found a ready audience among people who already embraced a similar philosophy."

"Principles like 'do unto others,' you mean."

"Confucius expressed a similar view six centuries earlier," Kimo said. "The teachings attributed to Jesus were known in many lands as the perennial philosophy or ageless wisdom. The truths are universal. Masters are teachers who realize the truth and point the way to others."

"So Ireland's conversion to Christianity wasn't a hostile takeover, is that what you're saying?"

"That's one way to put it," Kimo said. "Ireland was so isolated from Rome that Christianity developed in its own way, for a time.

The new religion blended with the old. Instead of praying to the Irish goddess Brighid, people prayed to the Christian saint, Brigid of Kildare. Christian missionaries brought Latin and writing, which opened up a new world of ideas and principles that would have appealed to poets, bards, and the like. Some druid priests even joined orders and became monks."

"So they could learn to read and write?"

"In part. The new learning included not only the teachings of Christianity but also Plato and other classical texts," Kimo said, pausing to decide on his order. He closed the menu and continued. "That's not to say that prohibitions were not imposed. As the Church gained influence, practices like human sacrifice were abolished."

"Thank God for that!"

"For Christians, Jesus's death atoned for human sin, ending the need for sacrifices to the gods. You know, Jesus wasn't generally shown hanging on the cross until the seventh century. Before that, the lamb was a commonly used symbol."

"The crucifix again," Caitlin mumbled. She felt her forehead. Could she have a fever? She hardly ever got headaches.

"The cross was an ancient symbol, found in many lands, each with its own distinctive style," Kimo said. "It was here in Ireland long before Christianity came ashore. The equal-armed cross was a symbol of life in many traditions, but the crucifix emphasized Jesus's death and resurrection. The medieval Church, especially, endorsed a worldview of sinners in need of salvation and, hence, in need of the Church."

"You've got to be carefully taught," Caitlin said.

Kimo grinned. "I think you're taut enough," he said. "Sorry—I couldn't resist." He finished off the last of his beer.

"Yeah, yeah. It's a song from *South Pacific*." Caitlin sang a few lines from "You've Got to Be Carefully Taught" but clammed up when she saw Kimo's amused look. "I played Nellie the nurse in high school," she explained, and then cleared her throat. "Your version of history doesn't sound like anything I was taught," she said, straining to read the menu without her reading glasses.

"The conquerors write the history books," Kimo said. "They leave out the parts they disagree with. That's as true in religion as it is in politics."

"So how can we know the truth about what happened if no evidence survives?"

"Myth. Legend. Tradition. You have to learn to read between the lines, to look beyond surface explanations. Surely you do that when you examine witnesses or decide if a source of information is reliable."

"Yes," Caitlin conceded.

The complex cases that landed on her desk nearly always required investigation; rarely was the solution as simple as finding a court decision that was exactly on point. In the real world, defendants lied, informants had faulty memories, and documents got shredded or hidden. Finding the true story often required a combination of common sense, intuition, persistence—and luck.

"Evidence often does survive, if you know what to look for," Kimo said. "The city of Troy was considered a legend until ruins were unearthed that fit Homer's description in *The Iliad*. The Dead Sea Scrolls have revealed a lot about the teachings and practices of the ancient Qumran community. Who knows what mysteries await revelation in the pyramids or the Sphinx—or the ocean?"

Caitlin was silent. She thought of Socrates, whose unorthodox views and annoying questions stirred up trouble in ancient Athens. He refused to honor the established gods, claiming to be guided by a personal spirit that he called a *daimonion*. Was that what Kimo meant when he said the orthodox oppose those who claim to know for themselves? Caitlin shuddered. Other religious groups besides Christians had eliminated heretics from their midst, just as political dissenters were not tolerated in totalitarian regimes.

Caitlin closed the menu. "Why don't we sit outside?" she suggested, hoping the fresh air would clear her head.

❧ 3 ❧

Caitlin moved to a table in the pub's garden courtyard while Kimo placed their orders at the bar. Her head was spinning from his tour of the ancient world. Maybe that was why she had a headache. Looking around, she wondered how her life would have been different if she'd been born in Ireland rather than America.

At thirty-two, she had already achieved many of her career goals. She worked in an elite branch of the Justice Department and knew that, with perseverance, she could advance to a supervisory position or become an administrative judge. Her salary didn't match that of associates at high-priced Washington law firms, but her income afforded her a comfortable lifestyle.

She'd recently purchased a new BMW—because she wanted to and she could. Fine clothes and furnishings and good food and wine were earned through hard work, and regular trips to the salon for facials, manicures, and massages helped her feel pampered and attractive—all the more important for her well being now that Jayson was gone. If she had to go it alone, she was determined to go in style. At least now no one was looking over her shoulder—or her credit card statements—and criticizing her spending habits.

Still, she realized how easily opportunity and privilege could be taken for granted in prosperous times. Would she hold different values if she had grown up during the Depression, or in a country the size of the State of West Virginia? Would she have become a lawyer, or might her life have taken a different course?

Long ago, she had dreamed of a career on the stage. She'd starred in high school productions and in college she minored in theater, but when the time came to choose a career, she submitted to her father's wishes and pursued the practical path: law. He knew what it meant to struggle. He'd worked as a bricklayer while earning his degree in journalism, and warned Caitlin not to waste her keen mind.

She wasn't complaining. Once she began her studies, Caitlin never questioned her choice. How could anyone find stability in life or in love if they were always questioning everything? She was determined to rise as far in her profession as she could, and that required staying the course.

Maybe her father knew her better than she knew herself. When Caitlin was a teen, Charlie covered the Kansas legislature for the paper and moved the family to Topeka, the state capital. Even then, Caitlin was more interested in worldly affairs than domestic concerns. At Thanksgiving and other Clayton family gatherings, she wandered into the living room to listen to the discussions among the men—and avoided the preparations going on in the kitchen. All those trivial conversations about babies and recipes gave her fits. She couldn't wait to escape the confines of Topeka and go off to college. The University in Lawrence wasn't far, but until she had her own wheels, it might as well have been on the moon.

Kimo arrived at the table with another pint of Guinness. "Hey, the bartender told me James Joyce used to come here!" he said.

"We just missed Bloomsday. I'm sure the place was packed."

"Do tell."

"My dad was a Joyce fan. Of course, he was a fan of pubs, too. June sixteenth was a key day in *Ulysses*; it's commemorated every year with a pub crawl."

"I'm surprised I didn't know about it."

Caitlin grinned. "So am I."

A waiter delivered bowls of the potato-leek soup they both had ordered, along with the tasty brown bread that would be served with nearly all of their meals for the next three days. Soon, the main courses arrived. Caitlin savored each bite of a trout so delicate it practically melted in her mouth. Kimo devoured an assortment of grilled vegetables and pushed aside his plate.

He had toured Dublin the day before and wanted to share what he'd learned about Irish history. Caitlin had heard enough lectures for one day, but Kimo either failed to notice her glazed expression or else he didn't understand that she was too tired to care about unfamiliar events from someone else's past.

Like Eliza Doolittle in *My Fair Lady*, Caitlin was tired of words. Lawyers needed to be thorough, but the good ones understood the concept of relevancy. Kimo seemed to float along whatever stream was running through his consciousness. Caitlin listened with half an ear.

It's only a few days, she reminded herself, and quietly finished her meal.

A waiter cleared the plates from their table. Nearby, a few musicians were setting up their equipment. Caitlin turned her chair around for a better view when the band started playing a traditional tune. A keyboard and acoustic guitar soon joined the fiddle, bodhrán, and tin whistle for a lively, contemporary sound.

Kimo shouted to be heard above the music. "Did you know the Brits outlawed bagpipes and tartans in the eighteenth century?"

Caitlin continued watching the band. "How come?" she shouted back, then immediately regretted encouraging another demonstration of Kimo's encyclopedic knowledge.

"Same reason Native American dances were forbidden in the American West, and chanting and hula were restricted in Hawai'i in the nineteenth century. Conquest requires destruction of a people's cultural identity. Forbid the old ways, install new gods. Teach children how to talk and think like the conquerors."

Caitlin smiled and nodded politely. She enjoyed the music and forgot about the headache. When the band took a break, Kimo headed "off to the jacks"—Irish slang for the men's toilet, he told her.

Emotions swirled as Caitlin listened to the conversations around her. Without her father, she felt alone in the world. Her grandparents were all gone. Bobby lived in Sydney now with his Aussie wife, and Caitlin had stopped speaking to her mother when Martha married Ray Johnson soon after her divorce from Charlie. With no family ties to encumber or sustain her, connecting to her Irish roots seemed all the more vital.

By the time Kimo returned to the table, Caitlin had calculated her share of the tab and was noting the amount in a small notebook she'd brought to track expenses. They left the pub and walked to the rental car. Caitlin appreciated the opportunity to glimpse a bit of Dublin's night life, and now that her headache was gone, she was glad for Kimo's company. When he wasn't chattering incessantly, he was a pleasant companion.

Back at The Abbey House, Caitlin quickly fell asleep. She dreamed of a barefoot young girl wearing a white pinafore dress. The girl carried a basket and tossed rose petals as she walked, smiling, along a path strewn with rocks.

In the morning, Caitlin lingered at the long breakfast table with other guests. A woman from Prague was visiting her son, who worked for one of the global companies that had recently moved its European headquarters to Dublin. An American man was in town on business; two English sisters were on holiday. The breakfast itself was the main topic of discussion—everyone was impressed by the food.

Unaccustomed to a large meal so early in the day, Caitlin was reluctant to budge. When Kimo arrived, she excused herself to finish packing. She turned in her room key and thanked Mrs. Brady for an enjoyable stay. The breakfast, she told the hostess, was memorable. She wouldn't hesitate to recommend The Abbey House to others—and she wouldn't need to eat again until supper.

She listened to music while Kimo drove to the Hill of Tara. After a quick tour of the site, they continued on to Newgrange, a structure estimated to be one thousand years older than Stonehenge. The ancient sites interested Caitlin for a time, but the appeal of mounds of dirt and piles of stone was limited. Kimo, however, seemed to have found his natural habitat. He talked to guides, meditated, and looked around for Caitlin knew-not-what. Finally, when the Visitor Centre was about to close, they left.

As he drove away from the site, Kimo talked about the Battle of the Boyne. The defeat of the deposed Catholic King James by William of Orange helped ensure Protestant and British supremacy in Ireland for the next four hundred years, he said.

Caitlin reached for her portable CD player. Living alone these past four years, she'd grown accustomed to doing what she wanted to do, when she wanted to do it. Sometimes she needed to tune out the world and tune in to her own thoughts. She listened to a Mozart CD through headphones for the remainder of the drive to Cavan. After reading about "the Mozart effect" on brain function, she was curious to see if listening to the CD each day would produce any noticeable results. Anything that helped keep her in peak form for the long hours her job required was a welcome practice—especially if it gave her some down time in the process.

They arrived in Cavan in time to enjoy a late meal in the dining room of the small hotel where Caitlin had reserved two rooms. The hostess led them to a table overlooking the garden. With the summer solstice only two days away, the dusky twilight lingered long into the evening.

Kimo scribbled in a notebook after deciding on his order. He'd been traveling in Europe for several weeks, searching for traces of the mystery schools that had flourished prior to Christianity's domination of the Western world. He was keeping a journal about his discoveries, he said. Caitlin gazed out at the remains of a tomb that had been preserved on the property, wondering what the stone monuments symbolized to the people who had built them. The notion that some secret knowledge had been lost or hidden was, she had to admit, an intriguing one.

After dinner, Kimo agreed to drive out to the old Moran homestead. Following Aunt Mary's directions, they found the place with ease. The thatched roof had been replaced, but little else about the whitewashed cottage had changed, Caitlin somehow knew. She knocked on the door and found the owners at home; they said it was fine for her to look around.

She thought she had come to Ireland on her father's behalf but as she walked toward the garden Caitlin realized that a deeper need had drawn her there. She, too, was searching for something that was lost long ago. Like Kimo, she wasn't entirely sure what it was, but something vital was missing from her life and had been for some time.

She found Katie's rosebushes right where Aunt Mary had said they would be. Using Kimo's pocketknife, she cut two yellow blooms, one for Mary and one for herself. A sudden wind whipped past her. Looking around, she almost expected to see Katie coming toward her to show her the proper way to cut roses.

"It's in the blood, Catie," Charlie had said one evening when Caitlin returned home late from a high school dance. He was sitting on the porch, smoking a cigar and sipping whisky. Whisky was all he drank. Caitlin remembered the familiar sound of ice cubes clinking against glass. "It's all in the blood."

Caitlin never knew what that remark meant, either, until she stood on Katie's land. She'd never met her great-grandmother, yet they were connected by an invisible thread. How far back did that thread reach—and where else would it lead?

∽ 4 ∽

Kimo returned his room key after packing the last of Caitlin's bags in the car. He would have preferred to stay at one place and use it as a base for exploring the area but Caitlin wanted to sample different accommodations. If she ever returned, she said, she'd know exactly where to go.

If he ever returned to Ireland at midsummer, he would go to the Hill of Tara. Tara was the coronation site of Ireland's ancient high king and prominent in myth and legend as an entry point into the nether world. While there, Kimo heard a rumor that neo-druids were planning a solstice ritual somewhere in the vicinity. He'd been tempted to tell Caitlin to go on to Cavan without him but knew their budding friendship would be at an end if he did, a risk he wasn't willing to take—especially when he didn't even know where the group would meet.

He left Caitlin at the genealogy research centre in Cavan and wandered into Brady's Pub. Ireland's public houses were much more than places to imbibe alcohol, and Kimo liked the convivial atmosphere of the traditional pubs. He ordered a bottle of spring water and sat at the bar, happy to find water bottled in glass. Glass was easily recycled, and it didn't emit potentially harmful chemicals like some plastics.

Kimo's rejection of many conveniences that Westerners deemed normal seemed radical to people who hadn't researched—or even considered—the invisible costs of mass production. Modern life was complicated enough; people struggled to get by and keep up without ever questioning where they were being led, or by whom. They were more concerned about cost and convenience than how food was grown or packaged, or whether the materials used in building their homes and offices emitted toxic vapors. But the price of ignorance was usually greater in the long run, Kimo thought.

He unfolded a map that came with his guidebook. A patron sitting nearby leaned toward him and asked if he needed help finding his way. He was disappointed he hadn't found any holy wells along his route, Kimo told the man.

"You'll be wanting a visit to the Shannon Pot, then," the man said. "It's over in Leitrim, so it is."

The Shannon Pot was the source of the Shannon River, Kimo learned. He wrote directions on a napkin as the man spoke, and then signaled the bartender.

"A pint for my friend."

The man patted Kimo on the back. "That's a good man," he said. "The name's Gerry." He held out his hand for Kimo to shake.

Kimo enjoyed an absorbing conversation with Gerry about Ireland's history and politics—subjects Caitlin had shown little interest in—until she arrived and tapped him on the shoulder.

"Oh, hey! How'd ya know where to find me?"

"Luck of the Irish," she said, flashing a tantalizing smile.

Kimo was beginning to realize that Caitlin was naturally flirtatious and that he shouldn't read too much into her displays. She probably wasn't even aware of how much she flirted—but he was. He felt his jaw tighten whenever he watched her working her magic on other men. Her charm was an asset she held in reserve and drew upon as circumstances required, but Kimo wished she would reserve it all for him.

Was she manipulative? Probably. But he didn't mind. He was putty in her hands. When she trained those sparkling eyes with their luscious, long lashes on him, he was a willing victim. It all happened so fast—the dazzling teeth framed by moist, red lips; the hair toss. Add the lilting laugh and a whiff of perfume and he was lost. Enamored.

He introduced her to Gerry and offered her his bar stool, but she chose to wait outside.

"Too smoky for me," she said.

She was right, of course, but Kimo had made so many bicycle trips through D.C. traffic, he figured a couple of hours of second-hand smoke wouldn't do much more damage to his bronchial tubes. Tobacco was sacred in some Native American traditions; maybe the smoke would chase away any evil spirits that had been attracted to the alcohol.

After saying goodbye to Gerry, Kimo stepped out of the dark pub into a gleaming world. Gone were the rain and gloom that had blanketed the island since his arrival. He breathed deeply to clear his lungs and looked around.

Ireland was beautiful, even in the rain, but now the Emerald Isle sparkled like a jewel, as if sunlight striking millions of droplets of water created infinitesimally small rainbows everywhere, each one imperceptible but collectively forming a shimmering, resplendent aura across the land. Kimo was reluctant to blink, afraid it all might vanish. He cherished every moment. Soon, he'd be on a plane back to Washington. He'd been away long enough. His earnings from a part-time job as a courier for a law firm barely covered tuition and expenses. He needed to get back to work.

Caitlin smiled and waved the papers she was holding. A ray of sunshine touched her hair, illuminating red and gold highlights. Her eyes danced with a vibrancy that had gone missing these last few years. Kimo had often been struck by the many shades of green that he could see in Caitlin's expressive eyes. Logic told him that changes in lighting caused the effect, but he liked to think the changes in her mood had something to do with it.

Despite his concerns about money, he didn't object when she wanted to eat lunch at the town's nicest hotel. He had learned to indulge her taste for fine dining and he let her choose the lodging. If she slept poorly or didn't like the menu, it wouldn't be his fault. Her urbane tastes struck him as extravagant but he kept his opinions to himself. The day was too perfect to spoil by worrying about finances. He could always take out another student loan to cover costs if he needed to.

At lunch, Caitlin shared what she'd learned about her family and showed Kimo the copies of baptismal and marriage records she had obtained. She offered to buy his lunch, but he wouldn't allow it. They had agreed from the outset, they would each pay their own way and share common expenses, like the rental car. He left the final accounting to her. They could settle any discrepancies after they returned to the States.

Kimo was eager to get outside and enjoy the fine day but he waited patiently while Caitlin browsed through local shops for gifts and keepsakes, unable to fathom how she could distinguish among the selections of Irish linen and crystal that filled every shop. Still, he admired her exceptional style, and she seemed to have a knack for finding a bargain. He bought a book on Irish mythology and stood by the car reading until she finished shopping.

In the afternoon, they checked into the farm guesthouse where Caitlin had made a reservation. Their rooms came with a view of sheep grazing on the hillside. Kimo asked the owner, a retired Yank, about local activities and learned that a popular dance band would be playing nearby that evening.

Caitlin yawned when Kimo suggested they go. "Well . . . maybe for one dance," she said.

She was on her feet the entire evening.

"Is it over already?" she asked when the musicians started packing their instruments.

Back at the farm, Kimo spread a blanket on the soft grass at the edge of the property. Caitlin scanned the sky for a star to wish upon.

"Oh, look! Over there."

Kimo gazed at her, lying on the blanket beside him. His wish hadn't changed since the day he met her.

In the morning, Kimo nearly collided with Caitlin when they both stepped out of their rooms at the same time. They stood, laughing nervously, towels in hand. He told her she could use the shower first and watched her glide down the hall in a skimpy silk robe, envious of the water that would soon be caressing her skin.

At breakfast, he ate a generous helping of bacon rashers and fried eggs. He sampled the black pudding as a novelty, but declined the sausages. The boxty, a kind of potato pancake, was a special treat and Kimo requested a second helping. He watched with a bemused smile as Caitlin cut a scone lengthwise and carefully spread home-made marmalade on one half and butter on the other half. Would she eat each half separately or sandwich them together?

The hostess came to the table offering coffee refills. Caitlin held out her cup. Smiling radiantly, she told the hostess that she hadn't slept so well in years. The hostess looked pleased. The magic worked on women, too.

Caitlin added cream and sugar to her coffee, stirring it with a spoon before taking a sip. "My father's mother, JoAnn Moran Rose, worked at an inn in Ballinamore before she married. Will we be near there?"

Kimo checked the map and found the town in County Leitrim. "We could stop there on our way to the Shannon Pot," he said, liking the sound of "we" and "our." He put aside the map and watched Caitlin bite into the half of the scone topped with marmalade.

"Okay," she said, licking her lips.

Kimo wanted to tell her how pretty she looked without makeup but he wasn't sure how she would respond. She might wander off by herself, leaving him to hunt for the Shannon Pot alone, and finding it wouldn't be near as much fun without her.

The hostess returned with another plate of boxty. Kimo paused to appreciate the moment before digging in. *Potato pancakes in Ireland with Caitlin. What could be better?*

∽

They spent a quiet morning exploring the farm and then Kimo drove Caitlin to Ballinamore. She picked up postcards at the only inn in town and addressed them during lunch at a pub down the street. After stopping at the post office for stamps, they returned to the car.

Kimo drove to the overlook where Gerry had said he could leave the car. From there, his notes were sparse: "turnoff"; "trail"; "half mile." He'd figure it out as he went.

"This is part of the Cavan Way," he said. "It's got a forest and stone monuments and ancient tombs. If we had more time, we could walk the whole Way."

Grinning, Caitlin sang a line from an old Peter Frampton song, "Show Me the Way."

"If only you'd let me!" Kimo muttered.

Carrying daypacks, they set out along the country road near the southern slopes of Cuilcagh Mountain. Caitlin complained about blisters on her feet from new hiking boots. Kimo thought the silly shoes she'd worn dancing the night before were more likely at fault.

The atmosphere felt charged; electric. Kimo remembered watching lightning storms from the back seat of the family station wagon when his parents crossed the Plains States at the end of a summer stock theater season. Even then, he yearned to understand the laws of nature.

What is electricity? Scientists name things so we can talk about them, but that doesn't solve the mystery. It doesn't mean we really know.

They encountered a short, stout man on the road, poised like a guidepost near the turnoff for an unmarked path. The man carried a walking stick in one hand and a pipe in the other. His long side-burns, tweed hat, and plain style of dress belonged to a lost era. Kimo hurried to greet the man, eager to ask if the path led to the Shannon Pot. Caitlin continued walking at her own pace.

Kimo inquired about *Log na Sionainne.* He'd been practicing the Irish name for the Shannon Pot all morning.

The man rubbed his chin and frowned, and then gestured toward the hills. The directions he gave meandered like a country road and his brogue made much of what he said unintelligible. Kimo politely thanked him and stepped onto the trail. For a moment, he felt a thrill of anticipation. Then Caitlin spoke.

"I wonder if he's senile."

Kimo sometimes wondered what Caitlin thought of *him*, now that he was sober, steadily employed, and enrolled in a professional course of study. She didn't share much about her feelings. She'd been trained in confidentiality and worked with classified information, but Kimo suspected that something in her past had caused her to shut down. He hoped she would learn to trust him. In order for that to happen, he knew he needed to stop dominating their conversations and allow her to blossom.

He was about to mention the irony of her joining his search for the Pot but quickly realized that reminding her of the circumstances that first brought them together, five years earlier, would tarnish the new image he'd worked hard to cultivate. He wasn't ashamed of his past, but he wasn't proud of it either.

To him, growing marijuana and selling small quantities to friends and associates was a harmless and lucrative sideline. The legislature had different views on the matter and branded the offense a felony. After he was busted, Kimo spent a night in jail until his partner, the landowner, posted bond.

The attorney who showed up at the jail seemed clueless about drug offenses. Kimo learned that the funds of the Commonwealth were allocated in favor of the prosecution: Virginia's compensation rates for court-appointed attorneys were among the lowest in the nation. He decided to explore his options after he was released.

He arrived at the Legal Aid office with no expectation of finding real aid, legal or otherwise. The staff were mostly women, the kind who wore sensible shoes and pulled their hair straight back in a ponytail. No frills justice.

Kimo signed in. He filled out the necessary forms and sat in a chair in the small reception area until a woman called his name. The placard on her desk said her name was Annie. She assembled Kimo's forms into a neat file and verified his income. By omitting the profits from marijuana sales, he easily met the guidelines for indigence.

Annie was young and sweet and looked a little confused—just the sort of girl Kimo usually liked to flirt with. He was too tired. It was after noon when he'd crawled out of bed and he hadn't had any coffee yet. Annie sent him back to the reception area to wait for the next available attorney.

Kimo thought about what he wanted to say to a judge. He was considering pleading not guilty and challenging the drug laws on constitutional grounds. He could proceed *pro se*—without an attorney—if necessary, but he wanted someone to advise him about his options.

The Commonwealth of Virginia was doing its part in the "war on drugs" but Kimo thought the government's paranoia about marijuana was archaic and misguided. Marijuana was a beneficial plant that had been used therapeutically for thousands of years in China and India before Napoleon's forces brought it to Europe. Alcohol and tobacco products arguably caused more widespread societal ills; those were regulated—but not banned. Many American colonists, including George Washington and Thomas Jefferson, had planted fields of hemp, and they used the plant to make cloth, rope, and paper.

A hefty linebacker appeared and introduced herself as Penny Nichols. Kimo followed her through a maze of cubicles, refraining from making any jokes about her name. The desks they passed were all cluttered with an impossible number of files; Penny's was no different. Subsistence living didn't afford the luxury of space. The small apartment Kimo shared with his girlfriend looked pretty much the same.

"I'm sorry," Penny said when she read the case summary Annie had written in the notes. "Annie's new. She should have told you— we only handle civil matters."

"Great, I'll remember you next time I have a spat with my landlord," Kimo said. He got up to leave, but instead of showing him the exit, Penny told him about an attorney in the office who sometimes handled criminal cases by court appointment.

"She's starting a new job soon at the Department of Justice, so she may not want to take any more cases," Penny said as she led

Kimo to the desk of Caitlin Rose. "We've been lucky to have her for two years. The DOJ has their pick of qualified applicants. She wasn't here because she had to be."

Let's go see what's so great about Caitlin Rose.

Kimo expected to find a pasty-faced brainy type whose idea of fun was watching C–SPAN. People who were good at memorizing data and taking exams didn't necessarily know about life.

When he first saw her, she was talking on the phone, laughing. It was an intimate laugh, the sweet sound a lover makes when tickled. She looked up when she saw Penny. They exchanged signals and Penny handed her Kimo's file. Penny gave Kimo an encouraging look before returning to her desk.

Ms. Rose gestured for him to sit in the chair by her desk while she finished her conversation. He approached but found the chair occupied by a plush lion, so he stood nearby and waited. Looking around, he knew everything was going to work out all right. The stacks of files and papers on Caitlin's desk were neat and organized; the display of greeting cards and framed photographs added a personal touch. The sense of order was refreshing. Kimo decided to eliminate clutter from his life. Its effects were disorienting.

Caitlin jotted an address on her legal pad. With her head bowed, her hair draped across the side of her face like a veil. "Okay, 6:30," she told her caller. "See you then."

She swiveled her chair around, brushing her hair aside with one hand and picking up Kimo's file with the other. After putting on her reading glasses, she glanced at her watch, as if calculating whether she had time for another case, before reading the case summary. "Sit!" was the first word she said to him.

Kimo picked up the lion and handed it to her.

"Oh!" She smiled and set the lion on top of a filing cabinet. "Birthday present. From the staff," she explained.

"Happy birthday," Kimo said as he sat down—the first words he ever said to her.

That was original, he thought. He looked back to make sure she was still following him. She'd fallen behind, but she was still visible. She seemed as lost in her thoughts as he was in his. He stopped to wait for her to catch up. Maybe someday he would ask her what she remembered about their first meeting.

"First offense?" she'd asked.

He nodded. *"I'm not a criminal,"* he wanted to say.

"No DWIs, petty thefts?"

"Nope."

"Employed?"

"Huh?"

Her beauty muddled his thoughts. She was a splendid flower blooming in a neglected garden.

She looked up. "Do you have a job?"

"Oh, uh—no. Not at the moment. Why?"

"Another source of income would make you a better candidate for rehabilitation. You'd be less of a risk for continuing to deal drugs. Steady employment would help your case if you want to plead to a lesser charge."

"I'm no dealer!" Kimo said. "I have a college degree, I just—"

"I'm just telling you how a judge is likely to evaluate your situation," Caitlin said, removing her glasses. "What was your major?"

"Philosophy," Kimo mumbled and then slouched down in his chair. The conversation reminded him of visits to the guidance counselor's office in high school.

Maybe she felt sorry for him. Whatever her reasons, Caitlin agreed to take his case. She told him she had zero time to talk to him that afternoon; he should come back early the next morning. Together, they would decide on his best course.

He was cocky in those days, Kimo recalled, and ambled along without much planning or forethought. He'd probably been stoned too long to fully consider the potential gravity of his situation. If convicted as charged, he could have been fined up to $10,000 and awarded a prison term of "not less than five nor more than thirty." Years.

From the start, he trusted Caitlin's capabilities. Sometimes he listened to the musicality of her voice rather than the words she spoke. He could tell a lot about people from what they didn't say. People who proclaimed their greatness were usually just good at self-promotion. Caitlin, however, radiated integrity and a certain naiveté. He doubted she *could* tell a lie.

She had just turned twenty-eight, arriving there two and a half years ahead of him. At first, Kimo directed his efforts toward eliciting that intoxicating laugh. When his attempts at humor fell flat, he resorted to his second-favorite approach, the one that usually worked well with brainy women—showing off his knowledge. He knew a little bit about a lot of things, enough to appear knowledgeable about a wide array of subjects, as long as no one probed too deeply beneath the surface.

He proudly educated Caitlin about the federal agenda to outlaw a plant that was safely used as an analgesic in the United States until 1937, when the first tax laws were applied to marijuana. By 1942, *cannabis* compounds had been removed from the *Pharmacopœia of the United States* as "approved therapeutic agents." Now, the Drug Enforcement Administration denied that marijuana met the "currently accepted medical use" standard.

"What a great tactic," Kimo told Caitlin. "Declare something illegal, then justify the failure to legalize it again by the fact it hasn't been in use!"

What was worse, he said, was that the Food and Drug Administration had approved a synthetic version of THC, the psychoactive substance found in marijuana, for nausea caused by chemotherapy and AIDS-related wasting. Caitlin wrote notes on her to-do list as he spoke. To her, he was only another client, but that didn't stop him from trying to get her attention.

"The ultimate in greed and hypocrisy! What better way to ensure profits from sales of the patented product than to ban use or even possession of the natural substance? If there's money to be made by some pharmaceutical company, just watch as the FDA lines up behind it!"

He was fired up at the time about the FDA's campaign to restrict consumer access to herbs and vitamins, which couldn't be patented by any company or controlled by requiring a prescription from the medical establishment. Clearly, safety alone could not explain the distinction between natural and synthetic versions, he told Caitlin.

"Look at the list of side effects accompanying most prescription drugs," he said.

Yet the manufactured product was approved for human experimentation, while nature's pharmacy, grown on his buddy's farm, was strictly off-limits.

Caitlin explained that attorneys don't make the laws. Her job was to come up with convincing arguments about how the law applied to the facts and to anticipate the strategy of opposing counsel so she could counter with a better reason why the judge should rule in favor of her clients. Policy arguments, she said, did not work well for tax evasion and probably would not work for marijuana violations either—especially when Kimo's circumstances did not fit the limited categories that had been proposed for the legal use of marijuana as a medical palliative. The best she could do for him was to work out a favorable plea agreement with the prosecutor's office, preferably without jail time.

She didn't simply dismiss him, though, and Kimo loved her for that. She heard him out. He thought she was brilliant, and he willingly followed her advice. She wasn't like the women he had an easy way with. He couldn't win her affections with boyish pranks or play helpless and expect her to rescue him. She wasn't one to coddle or cuddle. Deprived of his usual tactics, he didn't know how to act around her. She was more than out of reach; she belonged to a world he had criticized from a safe distance and could no longer reject outright—because she was part of it. But what did she know of his world?

As Caitlin drew near, Kimo pulled a travel guide from his backpack. He walked backwards so he could face her.

"Legend has it that if you drink from the Shannon Pot you will attain immortality. Or perhaps speak Leprechaun." He grinned.

"I suppose you'll want to kiss the Blarney Stone, too," Caitlin teased.

Her smile made his heart glad. "No, it's the philosopher's stone I'm after," he said, turning to walk forward.

And your kiss.

He read from the guidebook: "'Flowing 214 miles to the Atlantic, the Shannon River was used as a means of transportation and commerce for centuries. Shifting shape along its course, it feeds lakes and tributaries, expanding to nearly ten miles wide and narrowing to a few hundred yards.'" Kimo closed the book. "The river of life carries us ever onward," he said.

Caitlin sang a few lines from "Take Me to the River," exaggerating the punk style of the new wave band Talking Heads. But she was laughing too hard to continue.

Kimo smiled. He was happy to see her silly side emerging. Away from Washington, she was beginning to relax and have fun. He was surprised, however, by how readily he became the serious and responsible one when she surrendered the role.

"Change is the only constant in life," he said. "Dynamic flux. Molecules perpetually in motion."

"Sounds like chaos."

"Don't underestimate the power of chaos. Everything in the universe follows laws, even if we don't understand them. Order is lurking within seemingly random events. Something new being birthed. The dark tunnel might feel like a death, but it's the only way to new life. Forces are set into motion and propel us along. The more we resist, the more difficult the journey."

"So we need to be more fluid."

"*You* need to be more fluid," Kimo said, pointing a finger at her. Caitlin had little tolerance for disorder and uncertainty. *Too much control*, Kimo thought, *stifles creativity, imagination, intuition—flow.*

"Are you saying I'm controlling?"

"I didn't say that. But you'll never know what you might become if your vision is limited by what you think you already are."

"Huh?"

"In physics, shifts between solid, liquid, and gaseous states happen when the necessary temperatures and pressures are reached. A substance in liquid form could change to a solid under other conditions, but it retains the potential to be a gas. Defining the substance by the phase it's in is, ultimately, meaningless. It's all relative."

"You mean it has an identity crisis?"

"I mean identity itself may be an illusion."

"So I might turn into a bird and fly away?"

Kimo laughed. "I see you more as a butterfly."

"As long as I'm not a moth."

"Conditions change for people, too. The shift from one level to another requires the ability to withstand heat and pressure. Our response affects the outcome. If we don't let the pressure build, the process is aborted. There's not enough energy to complete the transformation."

Caitlin stopped to adjust the laces on her hiking boots, and then unscrewed the top from her canteen. "Does that mean we shouldn't let off steam?"

"It's more about developing the ability to withstand discomfort without feeling the need to do anything about it—to change anything, blame anyone, or even complain about something that's not to our liking."

"How many people can do that?"

"Not many. That's why a spiritual discipline is called a practice. Changing the way we habitually react to events can take years of conscious effort. Committing to a spiritual path doesn't make life easier. In many ways, it's harder."

Caitlin took a long drink from her canteen. "Are we almost there?"

"I don't know," Kimo said. He leaned forward to examine a hazelnut forming on one of the bushes alongside the trail. "I read that the druids planted the hazel bushes. They made an elixir from the nuts and used it in their ceremonies."

He cocked his head and listened to a faint cry. His senses were always on high alert when he was with Caitlin. Absorbed in her own experience, she often seemed to miss the beauty around her. Her inattentiveness awakened Kimo's innate gift for observation, and he considered it his sacred duty to share with her the everyday miracles that abounded.

"Hear that?"

Caitlin listened to the call of a cuckoo bird and nodded her head.

"Okay, then," she said, putting her canteen back in her pack.

"Let's get there before this day is transformed into night."

Kimo turned away from the hazel bush.

She probably thinks I'm nuts.

≈ 5 ≈

Sweaty and tired, Caitlin wished she could turn back. Blisters were forming on her feet, making walking painful. She didn't want to spoil Kimo's plans, though; he had been patient while she researched her family tree. She would try to be a good sport so he could enjoy his little jaunt. She had no idea where they were going, but she was willing to follow the yellow brick road, for a while at least, to find the wizard behind the curtain. She'd be careful, though, and watch her step, lest she fall into a rabbit hole.

Kimo's description of the spiritual path didn't sound very inviting, and finding fault was an essential part of Caitlin's job. Still, the constant conflict was wearing her down. She hadn't realized how much strain she'd been under until she took some time off.

She had entered law with idealistic notions about improving "the system." In reality, keeping up with the workload was all she could manage, and her ideals had given way to practical considerations like paying the mortgage on her townhouse. A skilled negotiator, she possessed all the attributes of a good trial attorney—impeccable instincts, solid research skills, a charismatic oratory style, and dogged persistence. She had mastered the rules of procedure and evidentiary objections, and was at the top of her game. Her achievements were recognized and rewarded, but professional success came at a price. The job that had been such a wonderful opportunity five years earlier was beginning to feel like a prison.

Maybe "no man is an island," she thought, recalling John Donne's words, *but I've done a good job of cutting myself off from everyone lately. And I'm not just any island; I am Alcatraz.*

Prisons had been on her mind a lot lately, ever since her boss, Neil Morton, instructed her to file an *amicus curiae* brief on behalf of the U.S. Bureau of Prisons in a class action lawsuit pending in district court. State prisoners claimed that transfers to "Supermax" facilities required due process procedures like notice and an opportunity to be heard. Supermax units were designed to segregate the most dangerous prisoners from the general prison population, and conditions were sometimes more restrictive than on death row. Confined in a small cell twenty-three hours a day, inmates never saw the sky and rarely heard a human voice.

The U.S. Bureau of Prisons operated two facilities that were similar to the state prison that was the target of the lawsuit. If the judge ruled that the inmates had a protected liberty interest, federal prisons would also be required to afford due process protections. Caitlin knew that prison officials and other bureaucrats didn't take kindly to having their policies dictated by judges. But after researching the issue, she agreed with the inmates' claim.

"Issues of humane treatment aside," she'd told Neil, "transfers to Supermax are only required to be reviewed annually. A person could languish there unjustly for a whole year."

Predictably, Neil sided with the Bureau of Prisons. "The costs of taking greater measures to guard against inappropriate transfers would be burdensome," he said. "By definition, prison curtails liberty. Prison officials, not courts, are the proper agents to decide who belongs where."

Caitlin wondered if Neil was as callous and indifferent to the suffering of other human beings as he seemed. True, the U.S. Supreme Court had ruled that the Constitution did not create a liberty interest for inmates who were transferred to more severe conditions of confinement, as occurred with a move from a low-security facility to a maximum-security prison. But a recent Court decision indicated that a liberty interest could be found in state policies or regulations.

Sending prisoners to Supermax for indefinite periods, without any limits except the length of their sentences, was a fundamentally different scenario from sending inmates to solitary confinement for thirty days as a disciplinary measure, Caitlin reasoned. She'd hoped to convince Neil—and the district court—that recognizing a liberty interest would require only minimal procedural protections.

"The impact on federal prisons would be negligible," she wrote in a memo that she attached to her draft brief.

In the end, the court agreed with her; prisons would, indeed, have to follow due process procedures before assigning inmates to Supermax units. But Neil was still her boss. When he told her to rewrite the brief, clearly stating the Justice Department's position that the transfer of inmates to Supermax facilities did not violate any constitutional rights, Caitlin complied. She filed the eviscerated brief, urging the judge to rule against the inmates.

Losing a case for the right reasons didn't bother her, but she disliked the tension with Neil. When he learned that the judgment was in the inmates' favor, he blamed Caitlin. He accused her of being careless and said she must have overlooked something—that she could have won the case if she'd wanted to.

Caitlin knew she wasn't careless. She mentioned the recent Supreme Court decision and explained why temporary transfers to solitary confinement were different from indefinite placements in Supermax. Neil didn't want to hear about it, and Caitlin didn't want to jeopardize her favored position in the office hierarchy by pressing the point. When he told her to take some time off, she reluctantly agreed.

For nearly five years, she hadn't missed a day of work. She wasn't quite sure what to do with free time, but she didn't have to wonder for long. The next day, Kimo called and told her he was going to Europe soon. When he suggested she join him in Ireland, his last stop, Caitlin didn't hesitate. She had procrastinated long enough.

There were reasons for the delay, just as there were reasons she hadn't attended her father's funeral. Charlie's death had been sudden and unexpected, and Caitlin had just transferred to the Office of Special Projects. Her first trial was looming and important issues were at stake. How would it look if she put personal interests ahead of professional responsibilities? That was exactly the kind of reasoning that had been used to keep women out of positions of power and influence for far too long—concerns that hormonal fluctuations would affect their reliability, or they would disappear to attend to relationships or family matters.

Technically, the transfer was not a promotion, but OSP was the select corps of attorneys within the Civil Division and Caitlin was determined to distinguish herself as a top litigator. If she'd requested time off to attend the funeral, she might never be given important responsibilities again. She would have been relegated to the minor, insignificant cases that no one else wanted to handle. With one chance to prove herself, she wasn't about to blow it. Getting the job done was what mattered, not how she felt about it. At least, that was what she believed at the time.

The trail passed through a pasture and along the edge of a dark wood. Following Kimo's lead was a nice change. With no pressing thoughts requiring her attention, Caitlin allowed her mind to wander. From the other side of the Atlantic, she was able to view her life in Washington with greater detachment. But she was still brooding about the prison case. Why was Neil suddenly so eager to send her away? Normally, he didn't like her to be gone for more than a day.

She adjusted the cap Kimo had loaned her, grateful that her face was shielded from the hot sun. *Should have brought sunglasses. Hard to think of everything.*

The green surroundings felt cool and peaceful. Caitlin turned and looked behind her. The Shannon Pot was clearly not a high-traffic tourist destination; she and Kimo were the only people around.

Her sore feet tortured her, but with each step, worries about work faded. Thoughts of the previous night's dancing brought a smile to her face. She hadn't had so much fun since . . . she didn't know when. Slowly, she was rediscovering her sense of humor and other qualities of a person she once was and only dimly remembered. So much had changed in the last five years. *She* had changed. And she wasn't entirely happy with the direction her life was heading.

Maybe Kimo was right; she needed more magic and mystery in her life. More friends, more—dare she think it? *Love.*

After her engagement to Jayson ended, work provided a good distraction from painful memories. Caitlin had proven her abilities and her career had benefited, but she had withdrawn from nearly everyone in the process.

When she worked at Legal Aid, she'd had good friendships and an active social life. Now, her only friend besides Kimo was Patrice, another attorney at OSP. They mostly talked about work-related matters but Patrice listened to Caitlin's tales as avidly as she might follow a soap opera and after Jayson's indifference and neglect toward the end of their relationship, Caitlin appreciated Patrice's genuine interest.

She also valued Kimo's friendship. When they first met, she dismissed him as a party boy. His visit to her office in Washington, three years after she'd handled the marijuana charge for him at Legal Aid, surprised her. His desire to improve his life seemed sincere. Caitlin made a few phone calls on his behalf, but she never could have guessed that two years later she would be roaming around Ireland's peat bogs with him. Life had taken her down some unexpected byways.

She was startled out of her reverie when Kimo suddenly resumed their earlier conversation.

"What's really interesting is that, at the moment of transformation, the distinction between the two states disappears," he said. "You can't tell if it's a liquid becoming a gas or a gas becoming a liquid."

"Like the twilight zone," Caitlin said.

"It's the liminal state," Kimo said. "On the threshold."

"Is that what 'liminal' means—'on the threshold'? I guess that makes sense; motions *in limine* are made at the start of a trial. A judge has to decide whether the jury can hear potentially prejudicial evidence—even before it's presented. Some things are hard to forget once you've heard them. They change your way of thinking."

"That's it exactly!" Kimo said, waving his hands around. "Crossing the threshold changes you—like in the ancient myths!"

Caitlin couldn't help but smile; Kimo's enthusiasm was one of his most appealing characteristics. But after three days of listening to his stories, she was beginning to feel more like a captive audience than a willing participant in a two-way conversation. The stream of information could start flowing with little warning or provocation. The Shannon Pot was their last stop; after one more day together they would fly to London, where Caitlin planned to meet some of her Rose relatives and Kimo would board a plane back to Washington. Any longer and Caitlin would have been forced to address the issue—delicately or bluntly. She was capable of both, as the situation required.

"The Sumerian myth of Inanna's descent is one of the oldest recorded myths," Kimo said. "Wanna hear about it?"

At least he asked this time, Caitlin thought.

"Sure, why not," she said.

She didn't know a thing about Sumeria, but she'd enjoyed Greek mythology in school.

"The goddess Inanna left her heavenly temples and her earthly throne and descended into the underworld. She had to pass through seven gates in order to reach it. At each threshold, she was forced to surrender a symbol of power—her crown, her robe, her jewelry. In all these descent myths, the initiate must enter naked and endure trials."

"No due process protections in those days," Caitlin said.

"They relied on divine intervention," Kimo said. "Eventually, Inanna reached the queen of the underworld—her sister. After the queen's council, the Anunnaki, passed judgment on Inanna, the queen cursed and killed her. Her corpse was hung on a spike like a piece of meat for three days."

"Why three days?"

"That's how long the moon looks dark or full to the naked eye and the sun appears to hover at the solstices."

"So it's about the heavens?"

"In those days people could actually see the sky—it wasn't a blur from pollution and city lights. Early astronomers learned to connect cyclical occurrences on earth, like the monsoon season or the Nile's flooding, with recurring signs in the heavens. And, indeed, Inanna was rescued by an emissary from above who sprinkled her with the water of life."

"Sounds like a baptism."

"Baptism was a sacred rite long before Christianity adopted it. Many of these stories are saying the same things, with cultural variations. In Inanna's story, when she ascended to the upper world, her powers were restored—she was resurrected."

"After three days. Like Jesus."

Kimo was quiet for a moment. "There's no denying some of the parallels between Jesus and other figures in the ancient world."

"Does it really matter? It all happened so long ago."

"In our time, we have a tremendous amount of information about the world available to us. We can examine the cells from inside our bodies and send probes out into space. But we're still asking many of the same questions today about religion, philosophy, psyche and soul that people debated two thousand years ago."

"We're still asking who Jesus was," Caitlin said.

"Christianity took an ageless story and turned it into a historical occurrence that happened in one time and place. The Church said it could only happen to that one man because he was different from the rest of us," Kimo said. "But what if we each have the potential to reach the same state?"

"Then Jesus showed the way to the kingdom of heaven."

"Through our own efforts, not because he died to save us. That's a huge shift in thinking for some people. In the ancient myths, the journey into the darkness of the underworld brought confrontation with death and rebirth into new levels of awareness. The Greek descent story had Persephone and Demeter; in Egypt it was Isis and Osiris. Conquering death is still the only route to wisdom and immortality."

"So you're saying the stories contain wisdom, but they're not true."

"It's a different kind of truth. Facts speak to the mind; myths speak to the soul. Over centuries, the line separating history and myth tends to blur. Real people become mythologized."

Kimo strained to see past the trees. "I think it's up ahead, on the other side of that bridge."

They walked to the center of a worn wooden bridge and stood

listening to the sound of the wind blowing through the trees. Caitlin tossed a coin into the stream below.

"Just what are you expecting to find here?" she asked.

After a long pause, Kimo replied. "Answers."

As loquacious as he could be when spouting off ideas and opinions, Kimo kept his innermost thoughts and feelings to himself. Caitlin respected his privacy and didn't inquire further. She resented probing questions when they were directed at her. Perhaps she didn't really want to know what lay across the threshold. She was content to stay within the known universe.

Still, she did wonder: *Answers to what?*

∽ 6 ∽

When he reached the Shannon Pot, Kimo found a circular pool about fifty feet in diameter. A thicket of trees blocked most of the light, but patches of blue sky were reflected on the surface of the water. The humble scene wasn't exactly what Kimo had expected.

But, then, what is? Everything has to begin somewhere.

At the first mention of the Shannon Pot, he knew he had to come. The healing properties of water had long intrigued him, and he hoped some mystery might be revealed to him here. He removed a bowl from his backpack and crouched down to dip it into the water. Pure water was so important to life, and it was becoming scarce.

Lifting the bowl to his lips, he took a welcome drink. He passed the bowl to Caitlin and then sat on a patch of grass. Caitlin knelt down and splashed her face with the cool water.

"In the ancient world, water figured prominently in many religious festivals and ceremonies," Kimo told her. "Temples were built near sacred wells and springs. Among the Mandæans, baptism had to be performed in a flowing river—*yardna*. It means 'living water' and translates as 'Jordan' in English."

Caitlin swatted at a fly. "Who were the Mandæans?"

"A Gnostic sect in ancient Mesopotamia. Their sacred books speak of a baptizer named Iuhana, or John. The Mandæans survived into modern times in Iraq and Iran. Some of their legends parallel those of surrounding cultures, like Nu and the flood, or Adam and his descendants. In their version of the Exodus story, the waters of the Sea of Reeds stayed parted for Moses, but not for Pharaoh, because Moses waited for all his people to cross safely before he passed to the other side. Pharaoh put himself first, so his followers all perished when the waters closed over them."

"Don't you mean the Red Sea?"

"A mistranslation," Kimo said. "At one time, all the Mandæans were believed to be *naṣuraiia*, the pure and powerful who possessed secret knowledge and wisdom. Due to repeated persecutions over the centuries, much of their secret knowledge has been lost. They followed strict rules about purity, but they didn't circumcise like the Jews. A baptism ritual was part of their weekly holy day celebration."

"So that's the connection to the Jordan River?"

"Possibly, though the name could have been symbolic. Saying John baptized in 'the Jordan' meant he baptized with the living water, truth. Still, 'as above, so below' is a well-known principle in alchemy, so the heavenly river that is the source of light and life has a parallel in earth's waterways. Waters that are believed to possess healing or purifying properties always attract hordes—like the springs of Lourdes, or the river Ganges."

"So the water itself isn't any different but it's considered holy?"

"Well, life depends on water so it makes sense that good sources are revered," Kimo said. "But certain spots on earth do seem to have special qualities, and strong energies can linger in the atmosphere. If you visit a battleground, you may notice scars upon the land, both physically and etherically, if you're sensitive that way. A place of prayer feels calm and serene because of the accumulation of positive forces."

Kimo positioned himself directly in front of Caitlin and said, "Our thoughts and words are more powerful than most people realize. Feel the effect my words have on you if I say, 'You bitch, I hate you!' or, 'You are so beautiful, I love you.'" His gaze lingered a little too long, and Caitlin moved away.

"Very different," she said, "but that's because the words have meaning to me."

"The intention underlying the words has its own power," Kimo said. "One force is destructive, the other is healing. I could create the same effects using only sound." He paused for a moment, then hurled a loud "hah" at her, followed by a soothing "hoo."

"Yes, I felt the difference," Caitlin said, rummaging through her pack. "The first felt like an attack. The second was more like a warm embrace."

Kimo looked past her to the willow tree hanging gracefully over the Shannon Pot. Like people, some trees emanated an indescribable quality, a presence.

"I wonder what this tree might have witnessed here."

"Why don't you ask it?" Caitlin teased. She found her camera, said "I'll be back," and walked to the bridge.

Kimo watched her walk away. Sometimes he felt as if he had spent lifetimes waiting for her to notice him—waiting for the day when she would walk *toward* him. He recalled his appearance at the Arlington Courthouse on a sultry August day in 1991.

Under the arrangement Caitlin had worked out with the Commonwealth's Attorney's office, Kimo would pay a fine, complete forty hours of community service, and desist from further illegal activities. The felony charge would be dropped, and the prosecutor would not seek jail time if Kimo pled guilty to possession, a Class I misdemeanor, at the sentencing hearing. Of course, the judge was under no legal obligation to approve the plea bargain, Caitlin told Kimo, so he should be on his best behavior.

And what did he do? He leaned forward and waved at Caitlin until he caught her eye. Then he winked and grinned. When Judge Armstrong removed his eyeglasses and frowned, Kimo guessed that the judge had seen his display. Caitlin looked embarrassed, not amused, by his antics and, for the first time, Kimo felt self-conscious. His attire was neat and clean, but his long hair and Birkenstock sandals were out of place in the solemn courtroom.

Long the defiant outsider, he'd once enjoyed deriding society's staid conventions. When the spotlight was on him, however, he felt like a fool. His choices had landed him in jail. The prosecutor probably only agreed to the deal because of Caitlin. She was well-liked and treated everyone with courtesy and respect.

"Well, at least you have good taste in attorneys," Judge Armstrong remarked before raising the community service requirement to fifty hours. Humiliated, Kimo accepted the sentence.

The judge wished Caitlin success at the Department of Justice and thanked her for the quality of her representation in his courtroom. His job was easier, he said, when attorneys were prepared and didn't waste his time with frivolous motions and unfounded objections.

As for Kimo, the judge warned, "Don't let me see you back here again. You won't get a second chance." He waved the thick eyeglasses in his hand for emphasis before banging his gavel and adjourning for the day.

Kimo knew he wouldn't get a second chance with Caitlin, either. The timing had to be right.

She returned from the bridge and pointed her camera at him. He grinned while she snapped a picture, and then placed his hands over his heart.

"You've captured my spirit," he said dramatically.

Caitlin smiled and set the camera on top of her pack. "I'm going to pee," she announced, and then walked past him toward a copse of trees.

Her earthy manner always surprised him; her direct speech was a sharp contrast to her sophisticated airs and graceful movements. Her hair was never mussed and her outfits looked like something out of a magazine. Whether they met for lunch or a bike ride, she always wore jewelry and a touch of makeup—never gaudy, just enough to accentuate her delicate features.

Kimo picked up a twig and scratched at the ground. Maybe

Caitlin had the right idea, searching for family roots. *Perhaps it's my own Source I'm seeking,* he thought. The trace of Native American ancestry on his mother's side was the only part of his heritage that interested him. He appreciated the simplicity of the old ways, the tribal ways, the natural ways, but he didn't glamorize the past.

He studied the trees around him. He'd long felt an affinity for trees. Youthful birch and aspen, mighty oak—each variety had its own personality. As a boy, Kimo saw faces in the patterns of the bark. In his teens he'd enjoyed hiking among the majestic redwoods of Northern California. The great banyan he'd found in Hawai'i was like a little fortress, with dangling roots and hidden trunks and crevices inviting exploration. Some Native Americans referred to grand old giants as "the standing ones" and had dedicated the white pine as the tree of peace.

Kimo reached for his backpack and pulled out a small pad and pen. *Trees provide so many beneficial gifts,* he thought. Shade. Beauty. Edible delights, like the sweet sap from maple and aromatic spice from cinnamon bark. Useful products, like latex rubber. Beautiful amber that forms from hardened resin. The paper in his pad.

During his travels in Europe, Kimo had sketched train stations, street cafés, and city plazas. Drawing required him to see his environment with greater depth and attention to detail; it reminded him that he was constantly selecting which features to emphasize and which to ignore. Art, like life, was a subjective experience.

Kimo admired the way the willow tree seemed to surround the Shannon Pot like a guardian. He'd read in his mythology book that willow was the tree of enchantment. He sketched an outline of the scene and then checked his watch; a quarter of an hour had passed since Caitlin had left. He put down the pad and looked around.

"Caitlin?"

The only reply came from the bleating sheep that were grazing on a nearby hillside.

Kimo removed his shoes and stretched out his long legs. Using his backpack as a pillow, he leaned back and stared at the sky. Watching the cumulous clouds drift slowly by, he imagined reading poetry to Caitlin while she massaged his feet. He laughed aloud at the unlikely prospect of her sitting still long enough to submit to his fantasy, and sat up quickly when he heard a rustling sound in the bushes.

Caitlin appeared, out of breath.

"Kimo!" she said, panting. "Come with me!" She grabbed her camera but left her pack lying on the ground. "You've got to see this!" She turned and headed back into the bushes.

∽ 7 ∽

Caitlin led Kimo to a grove, where they crouched behind bushes and trees, hidden from view. Twenty people, wearing animal costumes and covered in body paint, were gathered in a clearing. Mesmerized, Caitlin tried to fathom what was happening. She studied their outfits. *Deer. Fox. Badger. This is no picnic in the park.*

No one seemed to be in charge, yet everyone was busy. Several people were starting a bonfire; a few others were preparing food. A tall man planted four spears around the site, marking off the boundaries of a square. When he had finished, he placed a burning torch atop each spear.

A young man blew a horn and the group formed a large circle within the square. Then, a woman with long, graying hair raised her arms to the heavens and murmured some strange mumbo jumbo. She drank from a crude chalice that she passed around the circle before taking her place tending the fire.

All eyes turned toward a short man wearing a feathered headdress.

"He must be the master of ceremony," Caitlin whispered to Kimo. "Not very impressive-looking, is he?"

"He looks like a shaman," Kimo said. "I've read that they can induce a trance simply by beating on their drums."

The man's garment appeared to be made from some kind of skin or hide, like the others, but his headdress commanded Caitlin's attention. Fashioned from brightly colored feathers, it contrasted sharply with the blackness of the bird perched on his right shoulder.

The shaman beat rapidly on his drum; soon, other participants joined in with flutes, rattles, bells and horns. Gradually, the discordant sounds fell into a unified pattern. People chanted and swayed and moved their feet. As the flames from the bonfire reached higher, ominous shadows crept over the landscape.

Caitlin hardly noticed the passage of time as the color of the sky changed to a darker hue. Trancelike, she snapped a couple of photographs, then cried out when a large hand suddenly grabbed hold of her hair. "Ow!"

Yanked from the safety of the trees, she was thrust into the center of the circle. Kimo stood beside her, rubbing his shoulder and looking bewildered, as if he'd just been awakened from a deep sleep.

The instruments stopped. Everyone stared at the two intruders. At the shaman's signal, two members of the group moved toward them and held out two costumes. Caitlin glanced at the hulk-of-a-man who had seized her. He stood, immovable, with his arms crossed. Red symbols covered his granite face, but Caitlin didn't dare look at them long enough to try to decipher their meaning.

The women swarmed around her and tugged at her clothes. She tried to push them away, but they overpowered her and smeared her face with paint. Soon she was naked inside the skin of a feline with the animal's head covering the top of her head. She wanted to scream and run but, paralyzed by fear, she could barely speak.

She was led to the center of the circle and placed with her back to Kimo, who was wearing the hide of a bear. Looking down at her furry attire, Caitlin imagined Hallowe'en traditions evolving from such a scene.

Maybe Kimo arranged all this. He'd been talking about Pagan ceremonies and rituals; he probably signed them up while she was researching her family's history in Cavan—that was when he first mentioned the Shannon Pot. He hadn't seemed too surprised when they met that man on the road. In fact, the shaman bore a strong resemblance to the dotty old man!

"What is this?" she asked Kimo.

"Looks like a lynx."

"I meant—"

"Welcome to our celebration," the shaman announced loudly while beating a slow rhythm on the drum.

Glowing red coals from the fire were carefully laid out, first in a path in front of Caitlin and, next, before Kimo.

Caitlin glared at the man with the headdress. His voice was eerily familiar. Laughing nervously, she turned her head toward Kimo.

"You set this up, right?" she asked faintly, sweat pouring out of her.

"Me? You're the one who led me here!"

"Silence!" the shaman commanded.

He circled, like a vulture preparing to swoop down on its prey. Hypnotized by the drum beating in rhythm with her heart, Caitlin struggled to stay focused.

"Who *are* you?" she asked when the shaman moved in front of her. "What gives you the right—"

"Caitlin—" Kimo whispered.

The drumming ceased; hushed murmurs and gasps spread through the crowd. The shaman walked close to Caitlin and stared into her eyes. Her knees went weak as she stared back. What was this strange power he had over her? Feeling trapped and powerless evoked an odd mixture of fury and fascination; a need to protest, a desire to flee—but not before learning this peculiar man's secrets. She leaned against Kimo as the shaman bent toward her.

"It is you who do not have the right," the shaman said as he peered into Caitlin's face. His English was flawless. "Why concern yourself with who I am when you do not even know who you are?"

Spear-man handed Caitlin the chalice and motioned for her to drink. Reluctantly, she took a sip. The thick, rooty mixture made her gag. The man shoved the cup closer; Caitlin drank a bit more. The cup was passed to Kimo, who swallowed the remainder in one gulp. The man refilled it before handing it to the shaman.

Caitlin inhaled sharply as her body stiffened. An electric current passed through her like a lightning bolt from the sky, and she was certain she felt roots growing out of the soles of her feet, extending into the ground and binding her to the spot. She held her breath.

What if I've turned into a tree?

The pulsating energy reversed its direction. A fiery tingle traveled up Caitlin's legs and spine, as if a fuse had been lit beneath her feet. Energies swirled around her and Kimo, forming a pillar of light; sparks and flames seemed to shoot out the top of the column they formed. Caitlin couldn't see Kimo, but she could feel him behind her. His steadiness was reassuring.

Caitlin exhaled and watched, warily, as the shaman walked over to one of the spears. Chanting all the while, he passed the cup over the flame of the torch, lifted the cup to the sky, and then slowly poured the contents onto the ground, tracing a circle around Caitlin and Kimo.

Caitlin gasped. *Dear God, they're not going to set us on fire, are they?*

Kimo said the ancient druids sacrificed humans in their rituals. These people didn't look like druids, but their primitive attire and odd behavior suggested they followed practices that fell outside the bounds of polite society—to say the least.

The shaman stood near Caitlin and extended his right arm; on cue, the black bird hopped onto it. With eyes closed, the man began to speak:

> By golden sphere of day
> and silver orb of night
> unchained we are now free
> to set our souls aright
>
> Beneath the churning sea
> erupts a fiery light
> that burns the tender reed
> when passion's flames ignite
>
> Illusions still remain,
> clouds upon our sight
> Prepare now for a change,
> Create a future bright

Trials prove our strength
opponents test our might
Seek not to escape
the battles you must fight

The angels of the road
sing praise as they take flight
Await the fateful day
when lovers reunite!

When he had finished, he swung his arm upward. The bird cawed and took flight. Transfixed, Caitlin watched as it soared out of sight. Part of her spirit seemed to follow.

She lowered her gaze and saw a big cat skulking along the periphery of the circle. It moved stealthily and stopped directly opposite her. Her sight was hazy, but she recognized the distinctive tufted ears of a lynx. Its eyes locked on hers as it prepared to pounce.

Caitlin's eyes widened when the cat lunged at her. She tried to scream but couldn't utter a sound.

This can't be happening!

The shaman's deep voice sounded in her ears: "Don't resist! Surrender to the spirit that claims you!"

The voice sounded far away and near at the same time, as if the shaman was speaking from inside her mind. Caitlin knew now why his voice seemed familiar—she'd heard it when she was high above the clouds, before the plane even landed!

The drumbeat resumed, and when the other instruments joined in, the pressure inside Caitlin's head became unbearable.

"Be the cat!" the shaman said.

Caitlin felt a surge of energy and, suddenly, she *was* the cat. The group broke into frenzied shouts and movements as she bounded over the gleaming carpet of hot coals and plunged into a circular pool at the end of the path: the Shannon Pot.

Am I dead? she wondered as the cold water jolted her senses.

Deeper and deeper she sank as images filtered into her awareness. An eighteenth-century pirate stood in the rain on the deck of a ship, surrounded by men awaiting his orders. She stood before him wearing a long, coarse garment, her blond hair gathered into a loose braid. Looking down, she saw that her feet and hands were in shackles, her garments torn. She'd been raped.

"Throw her overboard," the pirate sneered. "But first—cut off her hair!"

She cried out as the men sheared her hair with a blunt knife. They tossed the braid to their leader and shoved her toward him. She landed in a heap at his feet.

"We'll hang it from the mast," he said, clutching the braid in his grimy fist. "As a warning."

"Why?" she asked, her eyes pleading for understanding if not salvation. She was about to go to her death and she had no idea why she was the victim of this man's vile intentions.

He glowered and came closer. His breath reeked of alcohol. She recognized him: Neil.

"You think you're so superior," he said. "Well, look at you now."

He folded his arms and spat on her. "I despise your piety."

With a wave of his hand, the men hauled her away and threw her overboard. Again, the murky stillness enveloped her. She fell deeper through the currents of time. Was she here, or there? She heard the shaman's voice.

"Follow the light!"

She looked up and saw a light shining from above. Her arms and legs no longer in shackles, she swam upward. Reaching the surface, she gasped for air. She was in a vast ocean. The night was black with pelting rain. The searchlight of a helicopter flying overhead cast its blinding beam her way; someone was trying to rescue her. A rope ladder dropped from the chopper. She reached for the rope but lacked the strength to hold on and slipped into the depths once more.

Molten lava spewed from a volcano; smoke and ash burned her face and lungs. She ran, but the river of fire was close at her heels, destroying everything it touched. Then she fell, and everything went black.

The image of a temple in a desert appeared before her. A bulky man stood guard at the outer gate, like a bouncer posted at a barroom door. Foreign troops stormed the entrance, tossing the man aside as they streamed inside.

They invaded the inner sanctum, desecrating the carved symbols and smashing the large feline statues that adorned the temple. *Her* temple. The other priestesses screamed and scattered, but she stood firm as the sacred cats were rounded up. She heard their cries as they were brutally destroyed.

She turned toward the man she knew now as Kimo; so often, she had found solace in his serene eyes. His face was sullen. The beauty they had worked for years to create was destroyed.

The commander came toward her, looking smug and satisfied. Neil again; her nemesis. His men restrained Kimo and led her away from him. She glanced back one last time, heartbroken. Side by side, they had served the temple, never expressing their human desires.

Now it's too late, she lamented as she sat shivering on the floor of a dark, stone cell, wondering what they had done with him.

She refused to eat the worm-infested slop her captors brought twice a day, leaving it for the rats. She had no hope, no reason to live. Her will was broken. They had won.

Finally, her life force left her. "I loved you," she whispered before her body slumped over, dead.

PART TWO

BECOMING

✑ 8 ✑

Caitlin awoke with a gasp when the radio turned on. She quickly sat up.

Where am I? she wondered, her eyes darting around the room.

The cover of the cushion for Grandmother Clayton's old bentwood rocker was decorated with Caitlin's embroidery; the familiar floral pattern on the bedspread matched the drapes and wallpaper.

Home.

She rubbed her eyes and breathed a sigh of relief.

"The time is six o'clock," said the National Public Radio announcer.

Caitlin turned her head toward the clock on the nightstand. Her heart skipped a beat when she saw the photograph she'd set there the night before. Taken in front of Edinburgh Castle, it was the only picture she had of her and Dru.

She reached over and picked up the photo, then flopped back down on the bed, giggling. She would much rather think about Dru than the wild dream she'd been having—or the lecture she expected to get from Neil Morton. When she extended her vacation to be with Dru, she was, briefly, absent without leave.

AWOL.

Gazing at the photograph, Caitlin remembered the rush she'd felt when wrapped in Dru's embrace. They'd met in London, when

69

Caitlin wandered into a Piccadilly art gallery. She hadn't planned on going to an art gallery that day; she hadn't planned much of anything, other than meeting Miranda for lunch and doing a bit of shopping. Miranda suggested Simpsons for English apparel and a stop at Fortnum & Mason, the store that had supplied the gentry with edible delicacies for centuries. She also suggested a walk past the Shaftesbury Memorial Fountain and its statue of Eros in the center of Piccadilly Circus. The statue was famous for being among the first in the world to be cast in aluminum, she said.

Inspired by the god of erotic love, Caitlin had skipped the shopping and walked, instead, toward the colorful banners hanging outside the Royal Academy of Arts building. She passed through the entrance gate but left after seeing the sculptures in the courtyard. She wasn't in the mood for a crowded exhibit and wandered down a side street, where the open door of a small art gallery beckoned. Standing in the entrance, Caitlin saw about a dozen patrons milling about. Curious, she went inside.

As she stood admiring the sensual lines of a marble stallion, she overheard a conversation behind her. The award-winning sculptor, Dru McAlister, was talking to another man about his work.

"It's an interactive process," he said.

After examining a block of wood or stone, he waited until he sensed the potential hidden within it. His task, as he saw it, was to liberate the soul of a piece by first acknowledging its essential character. That required accepting the raw material as he found it. Next, he cut away all that was extraneous to his vision. Characteristics that at first glance seemed like flaws and imperfections became distinct and unique features in the finished piece.

"Every subject," Dru said, "is like every moment—filled with unlimited potential, only some of which will ever be realized. The point of art—well, mine, anyway—is to capture a moment, a feeling, a memory, an idea—whatever—and give it expression. But it's still my interpretation—my view of the world."

When he finished speaking, Caitlin turned and looked into his eyes. She longed for someone to see her inner beauty and call it forth. When he smiled at her, her heart leapt.

She watched as the two men moved from one work of art to another. As Dru spoke, the other man scribbled notes on a small pad. Finally, the men shook hands—and Dru was alone.

Seizing the moment, Caitlin approached him and asked if she could photograph him next to her favorite piece, a relief sculpture of a fishing boat being tossed upon the waves of a stormy sea. Dru smiled for the camera and then, in a beguiling Scottish brogue, asked Caitlin where in the States she was from. He'd been to America once, he said, to New Orleans, and dreamed of a show in New York City. Caitlin took a chance and invited him to join her for tea.

"I'd be delighted," Dru said, "but I'll have to wait until the crowd thins a wee bit."

He winked at her, sending her heart fluttering.

While Caitlin waited, she studied Dru's sculptures—and Dru. Tall, slim, and muscular, Dru's physique was as attractive as his art.

He'd make a good model, Caitlin thought. She imagined him posing nude for a class of art students. Or . . . for her.

Dru's presence, and his art, aroused all her senses. She looked again at the fishing boat, wishing she could breathe the sea air and watch the fishermen returning to shore, safe from the storm. And the marble stallion—she could practically hear its pounding hooves as it ran wild through a field. But unlike the subjects of his sculptures, Dru was right there, in the flesh, and Caitlin longed to run her fingers through his thick, dark, wavy hair.

When he was ready to take a break, they left the gallery and walked to St James's Restaurant in Fortnum & Mason. Caitlin wanted tea the way she imagined real Brits enjoyed it, in an elegant setting complete with scones and clotted cream and preserves. After perusing the menu of classic and rare teas, she selected the Royal Blend. Dru ordered coffee, black.

Caitlin asked him about his work. He had experimented with bronze, wood, stone, and metal, he said, creating figures of people and animals, and abstractions patterned on nature. His latest interest was bas-relief, like the sculpture Caitlin had singled out for special praise. Principles of composition were similar for painting and relief sculpture, Dru said; some painters even used bas-reliefs as models.

When he talked about his home and studio in Edinburgh, Dru's face relaxed. He no longer sounded like he was answering questions in an interview. Caitlin noticed the change immediately, and she relaxed as well.

Dru's manner was easygoing; his gaze, soft and amiable. His blue eyes didn't bore into her like Kimo's stares. If anyone was staring, it was Caitlin: at the dimple in Dru's chin . . . the tuft of hair poking out from under his collar . . . the way he licked his lips after sipping his coffee. She guessed from his tan that he didn't spend all his time locked up in a studio. He seemed, at once, restless and content, and both qualities appealed to Caitlin.

When he mentioned different sculptors, ancient and contemporary, who had influenced his work, Caitlin admitted that she didn't know a lot about sculpture. Dru offered to meet her at the National Gallery the following afternoon to show her some of the works he found inspiring. Caitlin didn't tell him she was scheduled to fly to Washington that day. They agreed on a time, and Dru left.

Caitlin felt uneasy about his abrupt departure, but she understood that he needed to get back to the gallery for a reception. Still . . . couldn't he have invited her, or asked if she was going in the same direction?

She paid the bill and lingered at the store to shop, picking up an assortment of preserves for Miranda and a tin of chocolate truffles for herself. After returning to Miranda's flat, she called the airline to change her flight. When Miranda came home from work, she told Caitlin she was welcome to stay on a few days. Caitlin was grateful, though, after that evening, she scarcely saw Miranda.

Breezing through the National Gallery together the following day, Dru didn't object when Caitlin slipped her arm through his. Afterward, they strolled hand in hand around Trafalgar Square. Suddenly, sculpture was everywhere Caitlin looked. She read the inscription by a statue of George Washington and learned it was a gift from the State of Virginia. She asked Dru to photograph her next to one of the bronze lions in the square before they moved on to their next stop, Westminster Abbey.

They ate dinner at a magnificent French restaurant in Covent

Garden and attended a play in the West End. Late at night, Caitlin returned to Miranda's ground-floor apartment in Dolphin Square, removed her shoes, and tiptoed quietly toward the small bedroom that doubled as a home office. After booting out the resident cat, she closed the door and went to bed.

Caitlin realized that distance would be a factor if she entertained any ideas about a long-term relationship with Dru; nonetheless, her affection for him deepened after he willingly spent an afternoon atop a double-decker bus—an activity he clearly considered bourgeois—because she wanted to tour the city. She guessed he felt something, too, when he asked if she could, possibly, come to Edinburgh with him for the weekend.

"I know you need to get back to your busy life—"

Caitlin touched her fingers to his lips. "I'd love to," she said before kissing him.

And lovely it was, Caitlin thought as she lay in her bed hugging a pillow. Perhaps she'd acted impulsively, but what was the worst Neil could do—fire her? She didn't intend to give him the chance. She'd tasted pleasures that had been missing in her life for far too long. On the flight home, she'd made up her mind: all Dru needed to do was ask and she would be on a plane to Scotland. She'd been alone long enough. She was ready to risk her heart again.

She softly sang a tune from *Brigadoon* and smiled, recalling her two short days in Edinburgh, when Dru showed her his favorite spots around town. *But the nights . . . mmm.* At night, Caitlin showed Dru some of *her* favorite spots.

He had occupied most of her waking thoughts since she'd met him. After the confusing time she'd spent in Ireland with Kimo, Caitlin appreciated Dru's straightforward manner. Strange things happened when she was with Kimo—things she could neither comprehend nor explain. She'd been able to put questions about the night of the solstice out of her mind, but the intensity of the morning's dream made the connection difficult to ignore.

They'd fallen asleep by the Shannon Pot. When Caitlin woke in the early morning, her head throbbed with vivid images of wild animals and chaotic dancing. She looked around and saw Kimo tending a small campfire. For the first time, she felt a desire to expand the bounds of their friendship. But when she walked over to where he was sitting, he didn't look up; he just stared into the fire. Caitlin noticed wafers of bread neatly arranged on a plate on the ground.

"May I?" she asked, gesturing toward the plate.

He glanced over at her. "Sure—you brought them," he said, and then tossed a stick onto the fire.

"No, I didn't."

"Hmm," was all he said.

Caitlin placed a thin wafer into her mouth. It had little taste or substance and melted quickly, but she felt alert and energized after eating it. She wondered what it was made of; a healthy snack would come in handy during a trial or on a long flight.

She walked around the site, trying to recall what had happened the night before. Had she done something she might regret? She remembered a bonfire and felt vaguely uneasy. Did something intimate occur between her and Kimo?

Why can't I remember?

Only one time, in college, had she experienced a similar feeling—when she drank too much at a fraternity party and woke up in bed with a guy she hardly knew. She crept out of his room before dawn and avoided him thereafter, too ashamed to ask what, if anything, had happened that night. She was older now and more capable of raising her concerns with a man, but she had also learned to wait for an appropriate moment. Kimo wasn't usually so withdrawn, but she'd never spent an entire night with him before. Maybe he hadn't slept well.

Searching for evidence that a group had gathered at the site, Caitlin walked again to the copse of trees where she'd gone the previous day. At least, she *thought* it was the previous day; she had no way of saying for certain. For all she knew, she could have been there for a week!

The thought terrified her. What did she know about Kimo, really? Could he have slipped some hallucinogenic drug into her canteen? When they first met, he'd expounded the virtues of marijuana.

Caitlin dismissed the idea that Kimo would resort to such a ploy and tried to recall what he had said about the shift from one state of awareness to another. She wished she had listened more closely to his rambling. She stopped moving when she realized she was pacing around a large circle.

Where was the line between the dream state and the one normally considered "reality"?

Two facts were apparent: they were traveling in a remote part of a foreign country, and Kimo had the keys to the car. Caitlin was totally dependent on him; she had no choice but to trust him.

Eager to return to civilization, she hurried back to the Shannon Pot, where Kimo was dousing the fire. They followed the trail back to the main road and walked briskly to the car.

Breakfast was still being served when they arrived at the guesthouse. After eating a quick meal from the buffet, they went to their separate rooms to shower and pack, and then headed for Dublin.

They didn't speak much during the ride to the airport. Caitlin thought about the images she remembered—the pirate, the lava, the temple. Perhaps her dreams were trying to tell her something important. She had kept a dream journal for a while in college, when she had time for such things.

She and Kimo were booked on the same flight to London. They sat together on the plane and talked about the weather, Caitlin's work—anything other than what had happened at the Shannon Pot. At the terminal, Kimo scanned the airport monitor for information about his flight to Washington.

"I'll call you when I get back," Caitlin said.

"Yeah, okay."

Caitlin paused for a moment, expecting a hug or other parting gesture. Receiving none, she shrugged, said "bye," and went to the baggage claim area to find Miranda Smythe, the cousin who had offered to host her during her stay in London.

Like Caitlin, Miranda was a great-granddaughter of Katie Moran. Miranda's grandmother, Kathleen, was Katie's namesake and the older sister of Caitlin's grandmother, JoAnn. Kathleen married Albert Smythe and left Ireland for England soon after JoAnn married

Bernard Rose and moved to Boston. Now in her nineties, Mrs. Smythe lived with Miranda's parents in a town about forty miles north of London—a short train ride away.

Miranda had arranged a Sunday brunch at her favorite restaurant in London with her brothers and their families. One of the brothers dropped Caitlin and Miranda at the station afterward, and they rode up to visit Miranda's parents. In the evening, they all sat around the living room, getting to know each other and sharing stories and photographs. Caitlin had brought a gift: the wall map of the United States that Charlie had bought when he was twenty. Made circa 1950, before the territories of Alaska and Hawai'i became states, the vintage map was in good condition and a collector's item. It was also easy to carry.

Caitlin enjoyed learning more about the family's history and wished she had brought along a tape recorder or video camera. Mrs. Smythe contributed little to the conversation, but smiled and nodded as the others reminisced. Frail and hard of hearing, she tired easily and retreated to her room after supper.

On Monday, Miranda borrowed her parents' car and showed Caitlin around the area where she'd spent her childhood. They returned to London Monday night.

The next morning, Miranda handed Caitlin a packet of brochures, maps, and transit schedules before leaving for work. Caitlin dropped two rolls of film at a shop in Victoria that offered three-hour processing for an additional charge. She met Miranda for fish 'n' chips before meandering to Piccadilly and the art gallery.

When she returned to pick up her photos later in the day, Caitlin could scarcely contain her excitement. She ripped open the envelopes and searched for the pictures of Ireland. She thought she remembered a show or ritual the night of the solstice and hoped the photos would help her piece together the jumbled images in her mind.

The only clear picture was the one she'd taken of Kimo lounging by the Shannon Pot; the rest were overexposed, as if a bright flash of light had obliterated all detail. Dazed and disappointed, Caitlin ordered a copy of the photo for Kimo, stuffed the envelopes into her Fortnum & Mason shopping bag, and walked back to Miranda's flat.

Had she imagined it all?

She hadn't spoken of the Shannon Pot to anyone—not to Kimo, not to Miranda, not to Dru. What could she say about it, when her memory was so hazy? Psychological treatment, drug use, and foreign affiliations were all viewed with suspicion by the security specialists who approved and monitored access to classified information, and Caitlin wasn't about to give anyone reason to question her mental stability and jeopardize her security clearance.

She remembered a date with an attorney who worked at the National Security Agency. The man was forever barred from speaking about his work and seemed to look for hints of untrustworthiness in Caitlin's conversation. She declined the offer of a second date, thankful her job didn't require Top Secret authorization.

Oh, right—job.

Her bed felt so nice and cozy after her travels, she wished she could linger a while longer.

Vacation's over, she reminded herself and slowly got out of bed.

Someday, she would ask Kimo what he remembered about their last night in Ireland. But now she had to prepare to face Neil's wrath. He wasn't going to be happy about the changes the trip had set in motion. He had come to rely on her, confide in her, plan strategy with her. They were a good team, and that had been enough to satisfy Caitlin, for a while. She'd been able to forget all that she was missing. But now, some dormant part of her psyche was beginning to stir. She was weary of the lawyer persona; so many other characters within were clamoring for expression.

She felt a *calling,* something she doubted Neil would understand. She didn't completely understand it herself.

∽ 9 ∾

Kimo phoned Caitlin again before he left for work. Again, he was greeted by the recording on her answering machine:

"I'll be back in time for the fireworks!"

He glanced at the calendar hanging on a wall in his bedroom:

Monday, July 1, 1996

The fireworks were only three days away. *Where is she?*

They'd left a lot unsaid when they parted ways at London's Heathrow Airport. How could he begin to tell her all that was in his heart? He knew he needed to try.

"Caitlin, are you awake?" he asked, hoping she would pick up the phone if he kept talking. "We should talk about what happened in Ireland." He paused, waiting for a response.

Caitlin always kept him guessing. Their friendship had developed in spurts and was punctuated by gaps; more than once, he'd had to just let her go. She was a lesson in non-attachment.

"It was a blue moon last night," he said.

Full moons bring illumination, he wanted to say. They shed light on things that previously remained hidden.

"Be careful out there in the urban jungle," he said, and then howled playfully. "Ow-oooh!"

He hung up the phone and walked into the kitchen. Melody had left his bagged lunch on the counter.

She must be in the shower.

Kimo stuffed the brown bag into his backpack and exited through the back door. He retrieved his bicycle from the garage, strapped on his helmet, and wheeled away. The black lab from across the street ran alongside him, tail wagging. Kimo pedaled slowly until the dog fell behind and then picked up speed.

The morning ride gave him time to think. He remembered his efforts to kindle a friendship with Caitlin after their attorney-client relationship ended. Following the sentencing hearing, he offered to buy her a drink to thank her for her help.

"That's not necessary," she said as they left the courtroom. "All part of the job."

He noticed a diamond ring when she lifted her left hand to press the call button for the elevator. How had he missed that? Was it new? He stared at her during the ride down to the main floor, wondering if he would ever see her again.

When they stepped out of the elevator, she turned to face him. "Good luck to you, Karl," she said, extending her right hand.

She knew him by his legal name, Karl Marx Owen. He hated that name. "Marx" was a family name and evoked comparisons to the comedic quartet or *The Manifesto*. Granted, he was a bit of a joker, and some people might call him a socialist. His parents' influence did little to discount either association. Veteran small-time entertainers, they had seen their friends blacklisted during the McCarthy era because of leftist political leanings. After settling in California when Karl was fifteen, they became vocal activists and protesters. Now, he appreciated his parents' courage and conviction in speaking out against what they thought was wrong. But back then, he sought to forge an independent identity. On a surfing trip to Hawai'i, the name "Kimo" stuck.

"My friends call me Kimo," he told Caitlin, his hand clasping hers.

Caitlin gave him a strange look and tentatively repeated the name. When a man called to her from across the lobby, she abruptly withdrew her hand and spun around toward the sound.

"Jayson!" she said, as if remembering an appointment.

The man approached and kissed Caitlin's cheek. "Car's all packed," he said, ignoring Kimo. "Ready for some Maine lobster?"

"How soon can we be there?" Caitlin asked as they walked off together.

The man put his arm around her. Kimo stood and watched.

Claiming his property, no doubt.

Caitlin turned back to glance at Kimo, and then she was gone.

He walked to the Metro station, brooding.

New job, vacation in Maine—nice life.

The guy even looked like a lawyer. And a jock. Clean-cut, good-looking, successful—Kimo knew the type. He couldn't compete; he had nothing to offer a woman like Caitlin. He looked ridiculous in her eyes. And *that* had to change.

His mandatory community service at a juvenile detention center exposed him to kids whose childhoods had been far more dysfunctional than his own. His home life had not exactly been stable or normal, but the stories he heard about abuse, neglect, poverty, and homelessness made him feel fortunate, even a little guilty. He could blame circumstances and make excuses to justify wasting time, partying his life away. Or, he could take steps toward becoming the kind of man Caitlin would be proud to know.

He joined Alcoholics Anonymous. As he worked the twelve steps, he faced the painful truths he'd sought to escape by getting drunk or high. The shame he felt fueled his determination to change his life; he knew he could do better.

And he *had* changed in the five years since he first met Caitlin, Kimo thought as he pedaled along Arlington's streets. It hadn't been easy, but he'd felt okay about how things were going.

Until Ireland.

The route to work was familiar now. The Custis Trail bike path ran along Interstate 66 into Rosslyn; from there, the Key Bridge would lead him into Georgetown. Once he arrived in Washington, the pace would quicken until his last delivery of the day.

The thought of applying for a courier job never would have occurred to him. He didn't even own a bike until his license was revoked for six months as a consequence of the marijuana conviction. Caitlin had arranged the interview.

Kimo had gone to her new office in Washington after Melody's second arrest for drunk driving.

"Still growing weed?" she asked as she filled boxes with files.

At least she remembered him. It was a start.

"It's not about me," he said. "It's my girlfriend."

Kimo felt helpless watching Melody sink into the nightmare of addiction. If he could help her stay out of jail, he thought he'd feel better about ending their relationship. He cared about her, but he wasn't in love with her. He went to Caitlin's office that day in March 1994 hoping she still carried influence with local prosecutors.

"Sorry, I don't keep up those ties."

She was on the road half the time, she said, handling cases all over the country. *Perpetually in motion,* Kimo thought. He noticed she wasn't wearing any rings.

"And the other half?"

"Getting ready to go on the road."

"What's that do for your marriage?"

Caitlin paused before responding. "No marriage."

With her face turned away, Kimo couldn't read her expression. He wrote his name and number on a notepad on her desk—in case she ever wanted to reach him.

"I've changed," he said when she turned toward him.

He'd been accepted into a professional training program to become a doctor of naturopathy, he told her. He could start in the fall, but he needed a part-time job to cover expenses.

"That's great," Caitlin said. She wished him luck and left the office carrying a box of documents.

She didn't sound sincere, Kimo thought as he left the building. Why should she care what happened to him, or to Melody? They meant nothing to her.

He was surprised by a call the following week from one of the top law firms in Washington. At first, he balked at the idea of becoming a delivery boy. But because Caitlin had set it up, he showed up for the interview, and after meeting Jake Liggett—the attorney she knew at the firm—he decided to give it a try. For now, the job was perfect for him. The hours were flexible enough to fit his schedule at school, the pay was decent, and the work steady. Kimo discovered he liked biking and adopted it as his primary means of transportation.

He also learned that doing his job well satisfied his soul in a way that making a quick buck never could. Selling pot didn't really provide a service, though no one could have convinced him of that at the time. The bad-boy image had been appealing for a while, but continually breaking the law was slowly eroding his self-worth. His relationships suffered, too. Worried about getting caught, he'd stopped trusting people. He was ready to grow up and find his place in the world, and holding a steady job was part of his plan to create a new life.

When he called Caitlin to thank her for the referral, she accepted his dinner invitation. Later, she agreed to meet him for lunch; another time, for tennis. Kimo was careful not to make demands on her time or affections, allowing a friendship to develop organically, free from the protestations her mind undoubtedly would have invented if she worried about forming an attachment to an iconoclast like him. He provided comic relief from the weighty matters that occupied her thoughts; she inspired him to make something of his life. He suspected that beneath her cool demeanor beat a wounded heart. Someday, he would penetrate the walls she hid behind. But first, he had to get his own life in order.

He'd made a lot of changes these past few years. He started eating organic food and learned to cook. He took classes in martial arts and developed new interests. He leased a drafty old house in Arlington and rented rooms to several housemates, including Melody, when she was in town. She'd gone to Santa Fe and cleaned up her addictions, and now they enjoyed a solid, supportive friendship.

Kimo planted a few herbs in the yard—the legal kind—and enjoyed having friends over for potluck dinners. He always invited Caitlin; she always declined. It had become a ritual of sorts. He knew she appreciated being asked. He also knew she dismissed his crowd—social and environmental activists, holistic healers, artists, and musicians; their unconventional lifestyles didn't interest her any more than her fancy friends interested Kimo. But she interested him, and by working at the firm, he'd taken a step closer to her world.

He'd hoped that traveling together in Ireland would help them forge a deeper connection—that if they got away from Washington, maybe Caitlin would come to see him as more than a former client or a struggling student. Maybe she could get beyond her *idea* of him and discover his strengths and talents.

Kimo paused to appreciate the beauty of the morning before crossing the Francis Scott Key Bridge into the District of Columbia. It hadn't actually gone that way, he knew. He left Ireland with more questions than answers, and he still felt haunted by the images he'd seen during the solstice ritual. He was beginning to sense that maybe *she* held the answers to some of the secrets of his soul.

∽ 10 ∽

Caitlin sang along to the soundtrack of *My Fair Lady* while she showered. Though she was no longer performing, she still loved the theater—especially musical theater. On a recent trip to New York, she'd attended a production of *Rent*, the latest sensation. At home, she sometimes passed a Friday night watching videos of her favorite movie musicals while eating pizza from a nearby Italian restaurant.

The courtroom provided a different kind of stage, one where she could move an audience to care about her clients. At her best, Caitlin added pizzazz to otherwise dull hearings, though she was rarely given routine cases any more. She was advancing rapidly through the ranks and had every reason to look forward to a long and successful career at the Justice Department. But that had never been her dream. The move to Virginia was Jayson's idea.

They'd met in law school. Caitlin knew on their second date that Jayson was the man she wanted to marry. After graduation, she clerked for a justice on the Kansas Supreme Court while he completed a master's degree in public administration. He wanted to work for a public policy institute, but those jobs were highly competitive and usually went to graduates of Ivy League schools. He accepted a position as counsel for a trade association in Old Town Alexandria, a good opportunity for a Midwestern chap. The job was a start—a place to plug into the Washington legal community. Caitlin agreed to go along, with the understanding that they were planning a life together. They packed up a moving van and drove east, stopping in the Ozarks to visit Caitlin's father. There, at the lake house, Jayson proposed.

Soon after, they were living in an expensive townhouse near Jayson's office. Caitlin was sworn into the Virginia Bar and qualified for a waiver into the District of Columbia Bar, making her eligible to practice law in both jurisdictions. She took a job with the local Legal Aid office and considered her long-term career objectives.

Associates at most law firms worked long hours, and she and Jayson wanted to start a family in a few years. Work schedules were more manageable with government jobs, but Caitlin was too energetic and outgoing to sit at a desk all day shuffling papers; she needed to be in the thick of the action. Litigation seemed the best match for her talents. She had the right qualifications, and the right temperament.

Before long, she set her sights on the United States Department of Justice. Applying the thoroughness and discipline she brought to all her tasks, she researched the various divisions at DOJ, developed a timeline for completing each step toward her goal, and listed activities and resources that could help her achieve her objective. Then she methodically carried out her plan, involving herself in D.C. Bar Association functions and committees, and attending networking breakfasts and fundraisers to make the right connections.

Her ready acceptance of pro bono cases won Caitlin recognition from the Virginia State Bar: the Young Lawyers Conference awarded her the Young Lawyer of the Year award. She didn't volunteer because she sought awards—she'd been raised to pitch in and help others however she could. Still, her demonstrated willingness to do more than what was asked of her surely helped her win a coveted position with the Justice Department.

During an interview for an opening in the Civil Division, Caitlin learned that Neil Morton had recently been named Director of the Office of Special Projects, a small agency within the Civil Division that was in a class by itself. Caitlin had never heard of OSP, but she had known Neil in law school. The news that he would be at Justice gave her a new aim, and within a few months she had clawed her way onto his staff.

Attorneys in the Office of Special Projects handled matters that required special attention or fell outside the normal channels of case processing and distribution. High-profile and politically-sensitive issues were the norm rather than the exception, as Neil frequently reminded his staff. He bore final responsibility for what happened on his watch, and he kept a close eye on Caitlin, his rising star. Her prodigious output earned her responsibilities normally reserved for more senior attorneys, but her enthusiasm won her few friends at the office. With families and other interests, her colleagues worked the requisite hours and left the job behind at the end of the day.

That had been my plan too, Caitlin thought as she stepped out of the shower and wrapped her wet hair in a towel. She loved the battle of wits, but the feeling of conquest when she won a case was a poor substitute for the feeling of belonging. Somewhere along the way, she'd lost the sense of mission and purpose she'd felt at Legal Aid; it had all become a game to her. Busy-ness and ambition had taken the place of love and meaning.

Heartbreak has a way of numbing a person.

She stared absently at the array of suits in her closet before selecting a floral print dress. The scrabbling sound of a squirrel on the roof reminded her of the gerbils she'd kept as pets when she was a child. Day and night, the rumble of a gerbil running in its wheel emanated from the cage.

No wonder they call it a rat race, Caitlin thought. *The road leads nowhere.*

After drying her hair, she coated her lashes with mascara and checked her makeup in the mirror. What did Dru see when he looked at her? Was an American a novel departure from the women he usually dated, or did he think her spoiled and selfish? Was an attorney a good match for an artist, or were mutual attraction and admiration all they shared?

Caitlin decided to tell Dru how special their time together had been for her. *I wouldn't want him to think I make a habit of going home with strange men!*

She was always amazed by the divergent views people held about her. Though Kimo denied it, Caitlin suspected that he considered her controlling—probably because his life was so *un*structured. Her mother thought she was too impetuous—maybe because Martha *was* so controlling. Both views contained an element of truth. She could be rash and impulsive at times, especially when someone—or something—provoked her ire; in other ways she was, perhaps, overly cautious. Her schedule was structured because if she didn't impose some measure of order and control on her life, it would soon be overrun with meaningless tasks and she would accomplish little. But that didn't mean she couldn't act spontaneously.

She walked to the alcove off the kitchen that she used as a home office and selected personalized ivory stationery from a desk drawer. After writing a short note to Dru, she sifted through the stack of photographs that chronicled the development of their relationship: Dru working in his studio, Dru frolicking in the yard with his collie, Juniper, and the photo that started it all—Dru standing next to the bas-relief of the fishing boat at the gallery. Caitlin planned to find a nice frame for that one.

Guessing that Dru probably had enough pictures of himself, she chose a photograph that he had taken of her. She was holding a paintbrush, and grinning. They'd had fun painting a small mural on one of the walls of his studio. Caitlin sighed. With Dru, it had all been fun.

She rummaged around for an envelope large enough to hold the photo. She found a pink companion to an old Valentine's Day card never sent and addressed it to Dru McAlister, 12 Hartman Place, Edinburgh, Scotland, before licking the stamps that were left over from corresponding with Miranda.

While she was at her desk, Caitlin typed a resignation letter. During the long flight home, she'd thought a lot about what she wanted to say, and now the words flowed easily. She printed a copy and signed it.

After carefully packing one of Katie's rose blossoms in a sturdy box for Aunt Mary, Caitlin went to the kitchen and looked in the refrigerator. Empty. She opened the door of the pantry. Not even a can of tuna to slap together a sandwich. She would have to eat out for lunch.

She selected a morsel from the tin of chocolate truffles on the kitchen counter, tossed it into the air and caught it, open-mouthed—a trick she and Bobby had practiced during their summers at the lake house. They usually used grapes or bing cherries, competing to see who could catch the most. Martha fretted that one of them might choke, so they waited until they were away from her watchful eye. Caitlin chuckled at the memory and wondered if Bobby had also retained the skill.

She picked up her briefcase and headed for the garage. After backing the car out, she decided to bring along a few compact discs to listen to during the drive to the office. She left the car running and hurried up the stairs at the front entrance of the townhouse.

Running on heels—now there's a talent to include on my resume.

Inside, she accidentally brushed the statue of Lady Justice that stood guard over the entry, causing the scales that hung from the Lady's left hand to wobble. Caitlin grabbed the *Carousel* and *Funny Girl* CDs and slithered past the statue on her way out, carefully avoiding the sword in the Lady's right hand as she passed by. She closed the door firmly behind her, and tensed when she heard the clatter of the metal scales crashing against the marble tile.

Driving down the street, Caitlin noticed the flags hanging outside several neighbors' townhouses and made a note to buy herself a new one. Jayson had kept theirs when they split up.

Independence Day was always a lively time in the nation's capital, and Caitlin had planned her travel so she would be back in Washington for the celebration. Something about the mix of people from different cultures all celebrating the birth of freedom in a common land made her feel happy—and hopeful. She was an idealist at heart, but after seeing, up close, the internal workings of the government, she doubted that the current system really provided liberty and justice for all. Ideals were just that: standards to strive for. They were not always attainable, and the obstacles sometimes seemed insurmountable.

Once upon a time, Caitlin had envisioned a rosy future for herself. She'd chosen a career and a mate—wasn't the rest supposed to fall neatly into place? She recalled an old joke: "Wanna make God laugh? Tell Him your plans."

Is God a trickster who likes to keep us guessing and stands ready to foil our best-laid plans? Is there a Plan—Divine Will—that we mortals have a choice to cooperate with, or suffer?

How could she know? Now was not the time to think about something so grand as God and His plans—or even her hopes and dreams. Immediate concerns required her full attention. She'd have to hurry if she hoped to get her letter onto Neil's desk before he arrived at the office.

Eager to try out her new car phone, Caitlin dialed the number for Neil's secretary, Betty.

"No, he's not in yet," Betty said.

"Did he get my message—about returning late?"

"I've got to tell you, Caitlin, he was not amused."

Working with Neil Morton was like handling hazardous material; the consequences of a misstep could be severe. Caitlin had learned not to push too hard or test the limits of Neil's patience. "Safety first," she reminded herself whenever he tried to goad her into losing her composure. She needed to stay alert for danger signs, protect herself, and if her early warning system failed, get out of harm's way as quickly as possible.

"Hey, Betty, do me a favor and find out the postal code for Edinburgh, Scotland. The address is 12 Hartman Place." Caitlin knew that much by heart.

Betty grumbled and placed the call on hold.

Caitlin set the cruise control just over the speed limit and headed north on the GW Parkway. The leather steering wheel of her new BMW coupe felt smooth to the touch, and the ride was just as smooth. Sunlight streamed through the open sunroof; the *Funny Girl* soundtrack played in surround sound. Caitlin sang along with Barbra to "Don't Rain on My Parade."

She turned off the music when she heard Betty's voice, and pulled out a pen to write the postal code for Dru's address on the front of the envelope.

"Thanks, Betty. You're a dear."

As she approached the Arlington Memorial Bridge, Caitlin gazed across the river at Washington's famous landmarks. Was she prepared to leave the familiar landscape of her life and begin anew somewhere else?

"In a heartbeat."

Stately, magnificent structures filled block after block of the capital's streets. *Some of the most important decisions in the world get made in these halls of power.* But to her they were just buildings—concrete, steel, and stone. And the windows didn't open.

How unnatural our lives have become, Caitlin thought as she prepared to return to working in a secure building with artificial lights and recirculated air.

Midway across the bridge, traffic slowed to a standstill.

Caitlin banged impatiently on the steering wheel. "C'mon, c'mon, c'mon!" She wouldn't miss rush hour traffic, either.

While she waited for traffic to move, she pulled open the mirror on the visor, covered her lips with a rosy shade of lipstick, and smiled at her reflection.

"A girl's gotta have a mirror!" she said playfully, remembering her travels with Kimo in the midget rental car.

She closed the mirror and glanced to her right. A suntanned man driving a convertible was watching her, and grinning. Caitlin giggled and advanced her car forward a few feet.

A news helicopter hovered over the bridge. Caitlin listened to a traffic update on the radio. The slowdown was caused by the huge vans carrying sound equipment for the annual Fourth of July Concert on the Mall, the announcer said.

Caitlin usually looked forward to the event—a free party, with vendors and live music, on the West Lawn of the Capitol. Fireworks topped off the evening, launched over the Lincoln Memorial Reflecting Pool. As traffic inched forward, Caitlin glanced over at the Lincoln Memorial.

If only Dru were here . . .

When she finally arrived at the Justice Center, a satellite complex separate from the Justice Department's main offices, Caitlin parked her car and walked to the mailbox near the front entrance. She pulled on the handle, prepared to deposit the pink envelope she held in her hand. She paused for a moment and held her breath.

Following her dreams felt scary. Doing the safe and sensible thing was easier.

That's why most people never test their wings and find out whether or not they can fly.

Caitlin wanted to know. She released the envelope—and her breath—and turned toward the building.

One more letter to deliver.

Inhaling deeply, she threw back her shoulders and marched inside.

✑ 11 ✑

Neil Morton read the letter and tossed it onto his desk. He was counting on Caitlin to play a supporting role in his plans. If he didn't act swiftly to thwart a potential onslaught of lawsuits against vaccine manufacturers, his stocks would soon be worth about as much as Confederate currency.

Neil had powerful friends and he protected their interests, secure in the knowledge that his efforts would be rewarded. He was part of a network of leaders who were well-positioned throughout government and industry. Known simply as "the Club," its members were the new breed of players in Washington. They dubbed themselves "the Capitalists." These were the men who made the news and negotiated outcomes behind the scenes. They knew who they were.

Membership in the Club was by invitation only. A handshake was as good as a signed contract—they would never violate a confidence. They supported each other's initiatives, much as other groups formed to support charitable or community causes. They all profited, or they all suffered. Usually, they profited. They made sure of it.

In his early days at the Food and Drug Administration, Neil was new to the Club and eager to impress. Some of the members had invested in a foreign pharmaceutical company that was threatened with a lawsuit after a number of consumers in the U.S. were allegedly harmed by a contaminated lot of one of the company's prescription drugs. Inspections of the manufacturing facility had revealed significant deviations from current good manufacturing processes, resulting in noncompliance with federal regulations. Warnings were issued, but the company failed to remedy questionable practices. Controversy erupted when investigation revealed that Neil's inertia had delayed a response from the FDA that might have prevented the contaminated lots from being admitted into the United States before any harm was caused. Neil was forced to resign—but no one in the Club disapproved of his actions.

After he left the FDA, Neil found new ways to participate in the Club's enterprises. Along with several other members, he designed a grand scheme to streamline the process of getting vaccines from laboratories to consumers. The first step was an overhaul of the National Childhood Vaccine Injury Act of 1986.

Because vaccines were deemed essential to the public health and welfare, Congress had granted vaccine manufacturers liberal protection from lawsuits. A no-fault compensation system was funded by a surcharge on vaccines; damages were allowed if a vaccine covered by the Act caused harm. Claims were filed in the U.S. Court of Federal Claims, and awards were capped at $250,000 per claim. But manufacturers could still be exposed to class action suits in civil court, where tort remedies threatened potentially devastating consequences to the companies—especially if punitive damages were included.

One such lawsuit was pending in a federal district court. The plaintiffs alleged that some of the children who had received vaccines containing the preservative thimerosal had suffered neurological damage and other adverse reactions. Neil was confident he could quietly dispose of the case, but he worried about the avalanche of similar claims that was sure to follow. Legislation granting vaccine manufacturers total immunity was needed, and soon.

Neil convinced key members of the Club—including an influential senator from Tennessee—that manufacturers needed insulation from liability for *any* harms resulting from FDA-approved vaccines.

He sought passage of legislation requiring all claims concerning vaccines to be processed through the U.S. Court of Federal Claims. His bill, as he thought of it, would put an end to pesky lawsuits and judicial oversight of matters best left to officials responsible for public health and safety matters. He also made a case for granting the Secretary of Health and Human Services additional authority and resources to form partnerships with the private sector, reasoning that such a move would facilitate the development of new drugs and vaccines. Fewer obstacles meant fewer delays and less red tape holding up the introduction of new products into the marketplace.

During Caitlin's absence, the bill moved quickly through the Senate Subcommittee on Public Health and Safety. Neil didn't want the pending court case attracting the attention of anyone who might want to stir up controversy and endanger the bill's passage. He arranged for the case to be transferred from the Civil Division, where he had little control over how it would be handled, to OSP. He planned to bury the case alongside the fossils of extinct species—with a little help from Caitlin Rose.

Caitlin approached law like a sport and Neil gave her plenty of opportunities to prove her prowess. As long as she received accolades, she was content. As long as she served his interests, so was he.

Caitlin was smart and capable but she didn't show much interest in the political power plays that motivated so many of the attorneys and lobbyists who flocked to Washington seeking personal gain. For those reasons, Neil trusted her with highly sensitive matters. She was seasoned enough to understand that complex issues required careful weighing of the competing interests at stake; he was skilled at creating an appearance of agreement.

Playing *devil's advocate is very different from* being *the devil's advocate,* he thought. The best strategists didn't make strenuous objections and dramatic gestures; they quietly carried out their aims with a minimum of fuss.

Neil usually refrained from opposing Caitlin purely for argument's sake. He listened closely when she expressed her ideas about an issue; occasionally, she even gave him a good suggestion. He discussed with her the ramifications of different possibilities and then quietly steered her toward the desired outcome. He liked watching her carefully consider the situations he presented to her; she was so serious about it all. The way she tore into an issue or problem reminded him of a circus lion being thrown a slab of meat. And he was the ringmaster.

Caitlin paid attention but she also demanded attention. Her presence was seen and heard and felt. When she wanted something, she persisted until she got it. She had a sense about people; she could spot their weaknesses. Neil had seen her cajole information out of the most recalcitrant witnesses. She tossed them about the way a cat plays with a mouse before striking the lethal blow.

The way he played with her, it occurred to him. He too had a serious side, but unlike Caitlin, his energies weren't invested in creating a better society for his nonexistent grandchildren or pursuing some abstract notion of justice. He didn't need to wonder whether his efforts would have an effect in some future utopia; his actions brought prompt results. And when his course required correction, he made the necessary adjustments without a lot of fanfare.

Still, Caitlin's nature was similar to his own—more so than any other woman he'd known. Perhaps that explained their intuitive understanding of each other. Like predators of different species, they regarded each other with cagey respect. They observed territorial boundaries, but neither of them lost awareness of who was boss. Neil wasn't sure if their similarities or their differences fed their sizzling chemistry, but what did it matter? It was undeniable and ever-present—ever since law school, in Kansas City.

Neil's uncle was a generous benefactor and a former member of the University's Board of Regents; the school's Morton Arena bore his name, and Neil arrived on campus with instant clout. Securing a spot on the law review, however, was up to him.

Membership on the law review was based on class standing after final exams. A write-on option was available after grades were submitted and ranks determined, but few students bothered to expend the energy necessary to research and write a journal-quality case note after surviving the ordeal of first-year law school. Neil had no trouble persuading a brilliant-but-hungry senior law student to write a case note for him. The senior paid off a few debts, and Neil achieved his aim.

Caitlin was invited to join the law review staff the usual way, by ranking in the top ten percent of her class at the end of her first year, and her case note was accepted for publication. Neil was her editor; he saw her capabilities. Caitlin worked hard, but Neil had trouble taking her seriously at first. She was too sweet and innocent. Once she understood the rules of the game, however, she developed a tough hide, and she excelled.

It was during the spring semester of Caitlin's second year—Neil's last—that they debated and joked and worked late together in the law review's offices in the basement of the administration building. Neil liked the way he felt when giving Caitlin advice and direction. He was certain that she also felt the heat between them, smoldering amidst the demands of law school and injecting some vitality into their caffeinated, sleep-deprived existence. But she was already with Jayson.

She was still with Jayson in the fall of 1991 when she started working in the Civil Division. Neil's connections had recently landed him the role of Director of OSP. He watched Caitlin's progress at the Civil Division for several months before inviting her to join his staff.

His ability to read people made Neil a good administrator. He knew that, beneath her hard shell, Caitlin was still a girl from the prairie who would never approve of his shenanigans. He used her conscientiousness to his advantage. The likelihood that she would stumble upon a connection between the vaccine case in district court and the bill pending in Congress was slim, but Neil took no chances. He didn't want her keen sense prying into *his* affairs. He came down hard on her about losing the prison case so that she would take some time off. No one could have won that case, he knew. The vaccine case, however, must never get as far as trial.

"You've got all this leave accumulated," he'd said. "Do something nice for yourself. Why don't you get out of town for a while? See a bit of the world. Haven't you been talking about going to Ireland? Here's your chance."

Neil glanced again at the resignation letter. *She must have had a good time.*

He picked up the phone to make a call. Entering into negotiations fully informed just made good sense. He wasn't afraid of unpopular choices, but he didn't like surprises. He knew what needed to happen and he knew how to get the job done. He had no more need of a conscience now than he did in law school. It would only get in his way.

∽ 12 ∽

Patrice Kowalski walked briskly toward the break room, eager to see if Caitlin would show up. For over a year the two of them had been meeting on Monday mornings, the only time they could both count on being available. The weekly staff meeting convened in Neil's office at eleven o'clock, and everyone was expected to be present. Patrice kept the morning free of engagements, using the time to catch up on paperwork and phone calls until she met Caitlin at nine thirty. One of them arrived early to make coffee; the other brought muffins from a bakery around the corner. Even bomb scares and fire drills hadn't disturbed their appointed time—they simply found a private spot outside. As of Friday, though, no one had seen Caitlin; her whereabouts were a mystery. Disappearing without warning wasn't like her.

Patrice scanned her memory for clues Caitlin might have dropped before her trip to Ireland. She had started teaching piano to an autistic boy, Patrice recalled. Her research on autism for a case she was investigating indicated that musical interventions were sometimes effective for higher functioning autistic children, and Caitlin was curious to see if piano lessons would benefit her young friend. She also appreciated the opportunity to help someone in a more personal manner than her work typically afforded her.

"Besides," she added in her insouciant way, "I don't have any other men in my life."

Patrice had heard the rumors that Caitlin and Neil had once had an affair. His marriage ended about the same time Caitlin and Jayson broke up, spawning speculation. Caitlin never gave any indication of an association with Neil outside of the office, and Patrice had never asked. She sometimes noticed an edge in Caitlin's interactions with Neil—she spoke to him in ways one wouldn't dare address a boss unless they had a special understanding—but that didn't justify gossip.

Patrice knew that Caitlin relied upon her for updates on the latest office scuttlebutt, but she refrained from sharing the worst of the rumors. Her protectiveness was probably unnecessary. Most of the time, Caitlin seemed oblivious to what others said and did; she simply tuned out what didn't interest or concern her. Patrice suspected that she filed all the information away for use at a future time when she would, undoubtedly, occupy some powerful position. If such a day ever arrived, Patrice hoped Caitlin would still consider her a friend. Though she didn't relish the thought of having any enemies, she certainly didn't want Caitlin to be one of them.

Caitlin had her share of detractors, but she had won at least as many supporters among people like Patrice who could see into the heart of her character and chose to overlook the more self-serving manifestations of her success. Patrice, more than anyone, knew that Caitlin usually spent weekends in her office or at the gym. She saw the sacrifices Caitlin made for her career and encouraged her to get involved in a hobby or activity where she would meet new friends, but Caitlin set her own course and didn't complain much.

In any other setting, Patrice thought, Caitlin never would have noticed her. Caitlin had probably been one of those popular girls in high school. They never sat next to Patrice on the bus or at basketball games or in the cafeteria; they didn't invite her to their parties. At OSP, however, age and gender made her and Caitlin likely companions. Most of the other attorneys were older than them—and male.

"Women need to stick together," Caitlin had said on more than one occasion. "Especially here."

When Caitlin was around, the spotlight was always on her. Patrice didn't mind; reflected light was softer. She knew her work was satisfactory—all the attorneys at OSP were highly qualified or they wouldn't be there. Still, Neil Morton never stopped by her office to chat. He didn't ask her to accompany him to Congressional hearings. He didn't seek her counsel.

Lately, though, he'd been prowling the halls more than usual. He even poked his head into Patrice's office to see if she knew anything about Caitlin's plans. He looked a little lost. Or was he furious? Patrice didn't know him well enough to read his moods, and his face revealed little. His neutral expression remained constant whether he had just fired someone or closed a deal. Patrice remembered his announcement at the holiday party. After more than a year of persistent lobbying, Neil had achieved his goal: expanded jurisdiction for OSP. He raised his glass of cider and said, "Cheers, everyone. Happy holidays." Cool as ever.

When she arrived at the break room, Patrice used the gourmet coffee she and Caitlin reserved for Monday mornings. The rest of the time they drank the office brand.

This was Caitlin's week to bring muffins. Patrice set out two disposable plates and was reaching for a mug when Caitlin burst into the room. Patrice smiled. Caitlin's exuberance spilled out in all directions. She wasn't very good at hiding her feelings and opinions, and that made her an easy target for criticism. She set a box of doughnuts on the counter, chattering all the while.

"I was already running late and then there was a delay by the Lincoln Memorial—so I stopped at the coffee shop downstairs and bought a dozen doughnuts. I hope that's okay. I figure, if we cut them in half, we can each sample several different kinds and then take the rest to the staff meeting." She took a knife from the drawer and starting slicing the doughnuts.

Before Patrice could respond, Caitlin said, "I loved doughnuts when I was a kid, but I haven't had any in years! My mom used to get an assortment from the bakery when she had friends over for bridge. The ones with white frosting and colored sprinkles were my favorites, though jelly doughnuts were a close second. Maybe I got

inspired by the tea and scones I had in London. Of course, my companion was also very inspiring! His name is Dru and—oh, here I am
going on and on and I haven't even given you a proper hello."

"I never interrupt a woman who has a knife in her hand," Patrice
said.

Caitlin laughed and set down the knife before hugging her friend.

"Welcome back," Patrice said.

They each selected several doughnut halves and carried their
plates and drinks to the table.

"So you met this guy Dru, and?" Patrice asked, eager for details.

"And . . . it was good!" Caitlin said, blushing. "He's an artist.
Scottish. Single."

"That's always a plus."

Caitlin sparkled as she showed Patrice the pictures from her trip
and told her all about Dru's charms and the places they'd gone.

One photo stood out from the rest. "He's cute," Patrice said, "in
a bohemian sort of way."

"That's Kimo."

"The guy you defended when you were at Legal Aid?" Patrice
knew that Caitlin sometimes went cycling with a former client, and
was fascinated by their association.

"Mmm," Caitlin murmured as she sipped her coffee. "He was in
Ireland and wanted to find the Source of the Shannon."

"The what?"

"Don't ask. I was researching my Irish roots. We met up for a few
days."

"How you got to be friends with a drug dealer is beyond me,"
Patrice said, shaking her head. "And in your line of work!"

Patrice's taste in friends was more conventional—dull, even. She
enjoyed a steady relationship with John, a golf and tennis instructor.
She admired Caitlin's spunk, but she valued simplicity and ordered
her priorities differently. Caitlin seemed to thrive on challenge and
hadn't shown any signs of slowing down in the time they'd known
each other.

"He gets migraines and was growing marijuana for medicinal
use," Caitlin said. "There are worse crimes."

"Did he have a prescription?"

"No. Maybe that's why he wants to be some kind of natural doctor. Then he can write his own."

"Oh, great. A quack."

"He's harmless," Caitlin said, reaching for a napkin. "And he doesn't smoke pot anymore. He told me acupuncture and herbs were so helpful to him after his arrest that he wanted to help other people find healing through natural methods. He's enrolled in a professional program. But why are you so interested in Kimo when I finally met someone who takes my breath away?"

Patrice picked up a photo of Dru and set it next to the picture of Kimo. Dru looked rugged and sexy. His hair was tousled and he was laughing, playing with a dog. But something about Kimo was intriguing, in spite of his ponytail and Patrice's wariness about his past. His eyes had a soulful quality. More important, though, was the way Caitlin sounded when she spoke about him: solid and steady.

Patrice looked over at Caitlin, who was waiting for a reply, and suddenly realized that love and romance might be more confusing for those popular girls she'd envied in high school, especially the ones who lacked a strong sense of identity. Did they fall for false promises and flattery? Were they distracted by status and charm? Did the attentions of so many men make it harder for them to identify a suitable partner? Maybe Caitlin couldn't distinguish infatuation from compatibility. Maybe she really did need a friend like her.

Patrice stood up. "Dru's safely tucked away in Scotland," she said before tossing her plate into the trash. "Kimo's right here—I'd say that's a desirable quality in a man. Unless you're thinking of moving to Scotland!"

When Caitlin didn't refute her remark, Patrice sat back down. She reached over and grasped Caitlin's arm. "You're not thinking of that—are you?"

The door opened and Neil entered the room, papers in hand. "I thought I might find you in here," he said to Caitlin.

Patrice watched Caitlin calmly bite into a jelly doughnut before replying. "I guess you found my letter."

"I'll see you later," Patrice said to Caitlin. She quietly placed her mug by the sink. "Good morning, Neil," she said as she slid by him.

He nodded to her. "Patrice." To Caitlin, he said, "Can I see you in my office, please?"

Patrice looked back and saw Caitlin salute as she took a swig of coffee. "Sure, boss. Be right there."

"Now."

Caitlin rolled her eyes but put down the mug and dutifully followed Neil down the hall.

Patrice watched them for a moment before turning toward her own office. "Oh my," she said softly.

∽ 13 ∽

Neil closed the door to his office and stood in front of his desk. He held up Caitlin's resignation letter.

"What's this about?"

Caitlin plopped down into an overstuffed leather chair. "Welcome home, Caitlin. How was your trip?"

"Yes, of course, it's good to have you back." Neil gave her a thin smile. "But not for long, it seems. Did you get a better offer?"

Losing Caitlin would affect him more than he cared to admit. She wasn't like most women, but he had her pretty well figured out. His biggest concern was that she would jump ship for some other agency or, worse, for private practice, taking all her institutional knowledge with her. That's what he planned to do, eventually.

Caitlin responded with a silly grin. "No, but I'm hoping to," she said breathlessly.

Perhaps she was like other women in some respects, Neil concluded as he watched her twirl her hair in a flirtatious manner, feel the empty ring finger of her left hand, and chew on a fingernail. He recognized that glow, though it had been a while since he'd been the cause of it.

"Look, Cait, we've known each other a long time," he said. "I think I can speak frankly. Your record has always been exemplary, but your behavior lately . . ." He searched for the right words that would communicate his concern about her actions and forestall further disruption of his plans.

Caitlin rose to her feet. "It was only a few days."

"That's not the point," Neil said coolly. "You extended your leave without prior approval. I can't condone that kind of behavior. It undermines my authority, and that's something I won't stand for."

"Under the circumstances, you won't have to!" Caitlin said, glancing at the letter in Neil's hand.

Her face was flushed, he noticed.

"Look, I've given my life to this job," she said, "and I don't regret that. But I need more in my lap at night than a computer. And I intend to have it!" She folded her arms defiantly, as if expecting opposition.

He wanted to suggest she get a dog, but he knew that sarcasm would only antagonize her. True, he had wanted her out of the way while the subcommittee considered his bill, but he had no intention of letting her go—not when she could be utilized so readily, unaware that she was being manipulated.

He moved toward her and touched her hair, lowering his voice in an attempt to sound seductive. "You know, Cait, if it's a little action you're looking for, you didn't need to look far."

"Don't be crude!" she said, turning away.

Neil drew back. "Maybe I should let you go. Then you can't use our work relationship as an excuse for avoiding a more personal one."

Caitlin's eyes locked on his. "You can't be serious."

Did she consider him unworthy of her affections? He dropped the pretense of charm and circled behind her.

"I play to win; you know that. First it was Jayson, then—" He chose his words carefully. "I've been patient," was all he said. He stood facing her.

Caitlin glared at him. "You're getting very close to a line you don't want to cross."

Neil's eyes narrowed. Was that a threat? From her? That was laughable. He flicked a finger under her chin and retreated behind his desk in a show of authority.

"What are you gonna do—cry harassment? It'd be your word against mine, and don't kid yourself who'd win."

Hired guns, attorneys. She should know better than to play games with him. How far did she think she'd get on her own, without his support?

"You think it's your brilliance that wins all those cases? You've got the backing of this whole Department—the resources of the United States Government available at the touch of a button, a phone call away. You're just a mouthpiece. A cute one, but disposable."

"And all this time I thought I worked for *justice,*" Caitlin replied. "Call me naïve."

Neil liked her feistiness. Her honesty was a refreshing change from cowering fools who agreed with him outwardly and then quietly undermined his initiatives. With Caitlin, he didn't need to question her authenticity. He could take her at face value.

"That's part of your appeal," he told her. "You really believe in baseball, apple pie, and the American Dream. It is just a dream, honey."

Caitlin walked to the window, clearly annoyed by his remark.

"So, what's your plan?" Neil asked. "What will you do when you leave here in—" he glanced at the resignation letter "—thirty days?"

"I don't think that's any of your concern."

"It is if I make it my concern," Neil said as he shot rubber bands at various targets around the room. "What are you gonna do—run off and paint daffodils?"

He knew that she often doodled—flowers, feathers, crescent moons—in staff meetings, on phone calls, and during other absent-minded moments of boredom. He also knew that the fact he had noticed this about her would further irritate her, which might throw her off balance. She would be more likely to reveal something in an unguarded moment.

People are so predictable.

"You'd be bored inside a week." Neil picked up a stainless-steel letter opener and pointed the blade at Caitlin. "You and I are a lot alike, you know. We've both got that killer instinct. We enjoy the thrill of the hunt."

"Don't presume to speak for me," she said.

He knew she would resent any assertion that they were alike. Caitlin's haughty demeanor was going to get her into trouble someday, Neil had often thought. She liked to think she was morally superior. After their one-night stand, she acted as if he were the devil, luring her into sin.

Her tone softened. "Something changed. On this trip—I experienced something. A taste of a life I forgot even existed. Outside of books and courtrooms." She stared out the window. "Why does everything always need to be so carefully planned?"

She seemed to be asking the question more of herself than of him, Neil thought; he offered no reply.

Caitlin turned away from the window. "Get good grades so you can get into the right college, so you can get good grades to get into the best law school, which looks good on your resume so you can get a good job. That's the game, right? Then what do you get? Answer me that, Neil. Then what? Is this all there is? Because it's not enough. Not for me."

One thing about Caitlin, Neil thought, she kept him on his toes. This notion of leaving wasn't just about a man.

"You do important work that affects the lives of a lot of people," he said with all the sincerity he could muster.

Caitlin was unmoved and Neil had no strategies left to induce her to stay, other than to remind her of basic considerations she might have overlooked in her idealism.

"You've got a promising career here. Not to mention health insurance. Why would you want to throw it all away?"

"How about if I took a leave of absence? Say, for a year?"

Neil slit open an envelope and removed its contents. He had Caitlin right where he wanted her. "Can't do it," he said. "You play a key role in this office. I'd have to replace you."

Caitlin silently considered her options.

"Look, you just got back," Neil said, his tone now almost indifferent. He held out Caitlin's resignation letter, saying, "Here's my advice. Give yourself a couple of weeks to think it over. If you still want to leave, I'll write you a glowing letter of recommendation."

She glanced from the letter to Neil. He could see her brain calculating the possible outcomes, like a chess player.

"All right," she said, grabbing the letter. "You win. This round."

She started to walk away, but his next remark stopped her in her tracks. "And if things don't work out with Dru, my offer's still good."

She turned to face him, hand on her hip. "How do you know about Dru?"

Neil leaned back in his chair. "I have resources at my disposal, too," he said calmly. Now he was in complete control.

Caitlin shot daggers at him and grunted, then flung open the door and stormed out.

Neil laughed and rested his feet on his desk.

All right, then. Now we can move on to more serious matters.

∽ 14 ∽

Caitlin repeated her mantra all the way back to her office: "Hazmat. Hazmat. Hazmat." *Don't let him get to you!*

Neil thought he had wooed her onto his staff; he never suspected that she had maneuvered herself into his arena. Was she being weak, allowing him to talk her out of leaving?

She was embarrassed to admit she had no plan—especially to Neil. Until now, she'd always had a plan, even if she decided to deviate from it. She'd been taught that her future happiness depended upon her actions in the present. Being a responsible adult required patience and restraint, the ability to delay gratification and work steadily toward goals. That's what she had believed—until her father died. He never had much opportunity to enjoy his retirement, the supposed payoff at the end of a long career. Caitlin knew the statistics: mortality rates within five years of civil service retirement were alarmingly high. Was there an alternative to the struggle to get from "here" to "there" that no one was telling her about? What about her present unhappiness? Failing to prepare for the future was risky— but so was putting off living.

She reached into the stash of chocolate bars she kept in a desk drawer. The fix was temporary, but the distraction was usually enough to help her regain her composure. She took a bite and chewed furiously, as if the chocolate were a drug she wanted to ingest quickly. With the next bite, she felt calmer; her shoulders relaxed as she enjoyed the feel of the creamy substance dissolving in her mouth.

Chocolate is surely a gift from the gods.

She closed her eyes and inhaled, savoring the aroma the way a wine connoisseur assesses a bouquet.

Bitter sweetness . . . like life.

She wasn't sure what upset her more: that Neil had traced her whereabouts, or that he was stirring troubled waters. Caitlin was incensed about the former; the latter forced her to remember one of the worst regrets of her life.

When she received news of her father's sudden death in January 1992, Caitlin was shocked. For weeks, her feelings alternated between vulnerability and anger. She wanted someone to hold on to; she wanted to be left alone. The stress of her first big trial for OSP weighed heavily on her mind. At the time of the funeral, she was in Cincinnati for a pre-trial conference. With teams of lawyers involved, rescheduling was not an option. The case settled soon after, and Caitlin returned to Washington—exhausted.

If ever she needed Jayson's support, it was then. He seemed distant. Their schedules conflicted; they hardly saw each other. Caitlin hoped they would share a quiet evening together on Valentine's Day. She went home early, but Jayson said he needed to return to his office to work. Caitlin's anguish escalated. She went to the office to distract herself—the first of many attempts to bury her pain in a mound of papers.

Neil was still at the office, and Caitlin consulted him about a case. He surprised her by ordering takeout Chinese food and a bottle of plum wine from the restaurant down the street. She didn't ask why he wasn't at home with his wife. She didn't care. She was lonely. Being with Neil felt comforting. His presence brought reminders of a more hopeful time, when she was still protected by the incubator of school and eager to enter the practice of law.

As the snow fell gently outside, Caitlin and Neil turned up the heat inside Neil's spacious office on the third floor of the Justice Center. It was after midnight when they fell asleep. Neither of them wanted to traverse the capital's slick roads, only to return a few hours later. A mere dusting of snow was enough to shut down the government; during real snowstorms, timid Washingtonians abandoned their cars on highway exit ramps.

Disturbed that a man so wrong for her could arouse her desire so strongly—and easily—Caitlin had refused to discuss the incident with Neil ever since. It wasn't just the illicit nature of the act that had tinged their encounter with excitement; she and Neil were linked in some inexplicable way. Sometimes she could *feel* him wanting her. To her dismay, her body responded, as if the cellular memory of ecstasy drew her toward him, trancelike. Her better judgment overruled any thoughts of a repeat performance. She'd learned her lesson, the hard way. Her indiscretion had cost her Jayson, and she didn't care to be reminded of the loss. Even in law school, she thought that Neil wanted to come between her and Jayson. He'd finally succeeded.

Caitlin put away the chocolate and moved to the chair by the door, hoping the change in perspective might bring her some new insights. She enjoyed the privilege of a scarce window office. Perhaps she ought to take more time to really see what was around her. Too often, she was absorbed in crisis management.

What was it about Neil Morton that affected her so strongly? He was not unattractive; he always dressed impeccably—his shoes were shined; his dark hair was trimmed; his nails were manicured. But Caitlin didn't love Neil any more than he loved her. She didn't even respect him. Still, something about him fascinated her.

Maybe it's his passion, she thought, looking through the window to the world outside. Neil lived large. He commanded his life.

Caitlin glanced at her watch; the staff meeting would be starting soon. She took a deep breath to center herself. Going to Scotland with Dru was the first spontaneous thing she had done in a long while—and she had no regrets. Being in a foreign land, far from her usual roles and responsibilities, freed her to act differently. After a taste of adventure, her old life seemed stifling. Her newfound spirit was diminishing rapidly, but caution and sensibility dictated that she wait until she had a plan—or at least until she heard back from Dru.

She picked up a legal pad and a pen and walked toward the conference room. Maybe she would ask Patrice to join her for a quick lunch after the meeting. Talking to a friend might help her decompress after the morning's drama.

✑ 15 ✑

After Caitlin left his office, Neil put the word out that he was looking for an expert to testify before the Senate Committee on Labor and Human Resources.

"Maybe someone with experience in the Gulf," he told a Club member who worked for the Central Intelligence Agency in Langley, Virginia. "That's likely to be a hot spot again."

Neil hoped to convince committee members that current regulations constrained the development and production of new vaccine formulas; he'd been assembling a team of experts—and was still one man short.

"The armed forces need to be adequately prepared—before deployment, if possible—for the hazards they will encounter in theater, or the nation's security will be put at risk," he said to a policy maker at the Pentagon.

Neil knew that the surest way to incite action was to create an imminent threat—or the perception of a threat. Building alliances required speaking to the interests of those concerned and gaining their trust and support.

"I don't need to tell you that if we have a bioterrorist attack we need to be able to get vaccines out there, pronto," he told a senior researcher at C–BER, the Center for Biologics Evaluation and Research in Rockville, Maryland.

That afternoon, Neil received a call from Carter Simms, a reliable resource within the Federal Bureau of Investigation.

"I knew a doc during Operation Desert Shield," Simms said. "He was fresh out of residency, but up on all the latest developments in infectious disease at the time."

"I didn't know you served in the Gulf, Carty."

"Reserves."

"Where's this guy now?"

"Somewhere in the Mojave Desert. Twentynine Palms, maybe, or China Lake. He, uh, had an incident and got caught—with his pants down."

"Not very bright, is he?"

Neil stood looking out the window. His corner office afforded a clear view of two city streets.

"Let's just say his judgment in some areas was a little faulty," Simms said.

Can happen to any of us, Neil thought as he watched Caitlin exit the deli across the street. She was with Patrice, laughing and gesticulating. Neil wished she would be that animated and expressive with him.

He turned away from the window. "We don't need a Nobel Prize winner," he said. "We've got plenty of scientists who can testify about vaccine safety and R & D. What we need is someone who understands the military's need for preventive measures. Someone who's been on the front lines and can speak from experience."

"This guy's worth a look."

"Does he have the credentials?"

"A little out of date, but probably good enough," Simms said.

"He was a key part of the immunization program in the Persian Gulf. His team was sent to the area of operations early, to assess risks and hazards. Their efforts resulted in record-low morbidity rates for disease nonbattle injuries during Desert Storm."

"That's impressive," Neil said. "You think he'll cooperate? I need someone who will follow orders. This is important."

"Isn't it always?" Simms chuckled. "I've got an ace in the hole. His midnight escapade never made it into his records. Not many people know about it. I'm sure he'd like to keep it that way."

"Okay. Have him meet me at the Pentagon tomorrow morning. Eight o'clock in the Executive Dining Room. Lounge Three."

"I'll get right on it."

"Thanks, Carty. Always best to work with people we know something about," Neil said. "Oh—what's the guy's name?"

"Burns. Lieutenant Commander Sam Burns."

Neil hung up the phone and opened a desk drawer, looking for a new pencil to sharpen. He derived a strange satisfaction from the ritual: sliding the blunt tip inside the receptacle until contact activated the motor . . . feeling the vibration as the excess wood was shaved away . . . twisting the tool to ensure even contact . . . withdrawing it to check for sharpness—mustn't break the fragile point—and, finally, blowing away the dust.

He located a virgin pencil and thrust it toward the blade.

∽ 16 ∽

Caitlin felt distracted throughout the staff meeting and was glad to get out of the building for lunch. She stopped at the post office to mail the rose to Aunt Mary, and then met Patrice for lunch at the delicatessen across the street from the Justice Center.

She couldn't share her concerns directly with Patrice, but knowing she had a friend at OSP—someone who understood the challenges of working with Neil—helped her get through the rest of the day.

By late afternoon, she'd finished clearing her desk of the memos, mail, and phone messages that had accumulated during her absence. She stretched and looked around her office. A framed movie poster from the Disney film *The Lion King* hung on the wall. Caitlin knew that her colleagues called her "the Caitlion." She didn't mind, really. After all, her astrological sun sign was Leo, symbolically represented by a lion. Over the years, people had given her a variety of lion images and figurines.

She shared a birthday with Carl Jung, the Swiss psychiatrist who founded analytical psychology. Caitlin had studied some of Jung's theories of dream interpretation when she was in college. The research-oriented psychology departments at most state institutions, she discovered, were not very interested in Jung's ideas about personality, myth, synchronicity, and symbolism. The course Caitlin took was in the religion department, the traditional place for inquiry into meaning and transcendence.

The morning's dream lingered at the edge of her awareness. She didn't remember much—a feeling, mostly. Wasn't there something about a wild cat? She made a mental note to stop at a bookstore over the weekend and look up the significance of cats in dreams.

Jayson had called her "Cat" sometimes. He teased her because she liked to laze in the sun, and she was territorial about her space. She could be playful, generous, and affectionate—when she wasn't focused on work. But she wanted what she wanted, on her terms.

Lions need to be in charge. Don't try and tell us what to do.

She had called Jayson "Jaybird" because his bright blue eyes reminded her of a blue jay. He did most of the cooking and took an active role in decorating their nest. But he pecked at disagreements she preferred to let lie. Their final conflict, she knew, was a serious one. Still, she had hoped he would get over it and continue with their wedding plans. Instead, he flew away, leaving Caitlin to lick her wounds.

She put on her reading glasses and sifted through the stack of files awaiting her attention until she found the Jacobs case, a class action filed in U.S. District Court. Caitlin opened the file and reviewed the notes she'd written before leaving for Ireland.

The class members lived in four different states. They had developed symptoms of autism and other disorders after being vaccinated, and alleged that thimerosal, a vaccine preservative, had caused their injuries. Some researchers suspected a link between exposure to environmental toxins and the development of autism spectrum disorder. Thimerosal was derived from mercury, which was known to be toxic to humans and, especially, to developing brains. Parents of the lead plaintiff, Myron Jacobs, sued on behalf of Myron and others who had suffered an adverse reaction to any vaccine that contained thimerosal.

In researching the Jacobs case, Caitlin learned that policy makers expected some adverse reactions to vaccines but believed that the public health interest served by widespread immunization outweighed the risks to the relatively few individuals who might suffer admittedly tragic consequences from vaccinations. Congress had established the Vaccine Injury Compensation Program to help shield the companies that manufactured vaccines, and the doctors who administered them, from liability. The measure was deemed necessary to ensure enough vaccine supply remained available to meet demand.

The National Childhood Vaccine Injury Act required claims for compensation to be filed in the U.S. Court of Federal Claims; damages for injuries from vaccines were awarded if the statutory requirements were met. The special masters who served as judges in the "Vaccine Court," as the Claims Court came to be known, were accustomed to handling the kinds of questions that arose under the Act. A petitioner who was unhappy with the Vaccine Court's final decision could file a lawsuit in civil court, but the difficult burden of proving causation discouraged many would-be plaintiffs from going forward. Nonetheless, if a case could survive the challenges that defense attorneys would surely raise, the remedies available in federal district court were more favorable to injured parties than in Claims Court.

While Caitlin was away, the attorney for the vaccine manufacturers had filed an answer to the plaintiffs' complaint. Caitlin reviewed the answer, well aware that the task of deciding whether or not the Justice Department would intervene in the case to protect the integrity of the Compensation Program fell upon her. She removed her reading glasses and rested her head in her hands, palms covering her eyes the way a stress reduction expert had shown her.

Images of severely injured children had haunted her since she read the plaintiffs' individual accounts. Vaccines, after all, were expected to have a beneficial and protective effect; parents believed they were doing the right thing, ensuring their children received the recommended vaccinations. Knowing the case would require her immediate attention when she returned to Washington, Caitlin thought about it from time to time while she was away. On the way to London, she told Kimo she was researching vaccines. He told her about a doctor named Edward Bach who had lived in London a century earlier.

Doctor Bach specialized in bacteriology and developed a theory about intestinal pathogens as the root cause of disease. To test his theory, he injected mild vaccines into patients with various chronic disorders. After he learned about homeopathy, the principle of treating "like with like," he experimented with oral doses of the pathogens he had identified. Standard homeopathic procedure required dilution of the original substance many times over until only the pure essence, or vibrational pattern, of the original tincture remained.

"In Western medical theory, such an approach would be absurd," Kimo said. "There is no scientific basis for explaining how or why one molecule—or less—of any substance could be effective, other than as a placebo. But the homeopathic remedies worked better than the vaccines—with virtually no side effects."

"That's interesting," Caitlin said, "but this case isn't challenging vaccines. It's the preservative. Something called thimerosal."

"I know about thimerosal," Kimo said. "It's used in contact lens solutions, nasal and throat sprays—dispensers that have multiple uses—to prevent the spread of bacteria. Problem is, it's not all that effective, and the potential for harm far outweighs the benefits.

It was developed in the 1920s, before the FDA was established."

"So it wasn't tested for safety."

"Not to the degree it would be scrutinized now."

Convenience and cost-effectiveness, Kimo said, guided most medical practices. Vaccines were typically administered in multiple-dose vials that could be used repeatedly. Single-dose preparations didn't need a preservative, but the cost was higher.

"Medicine is big business."

Kimo believed in strengthening the body so the immune system could effectively deal with whatever assaults it encountered. He also believed that natural medicines, gentler than the pharmaceutical varieties, could address almost any ill. Caitlin had never tried most of the healing modalities he talked about—acupuncture, herbs, homeopathy, energy healing. She didn't even take vitamins. Thankfully, she was healthy—except for allergies that could result in life-threatening asthma attacks with prolonged exposure to cats. She ought to ask Kimo if he knew of a remedy that would help alleviate her symptoms.

She put on her reading glasses and sifted through the pleadings, weighing the options. If she filed an amicus brief as a "friend of the court," she would have to recommend that the judge dismiss the case. The judge was not required to follow the Justice Department's recommendations, but the position taken by the governmental agency affected by the outcome of a case was usually given weight in such matters, and the Vaccine Injury Compensation Program was administered jointly by the Department of Health and Human Services (DHHS) and the Department of Justice (DOJ).

Attorneys in DOJ's Civil Division normally handled the claims filed in Vaccine Court; they had more experience with the kinds of issues raised by the Jacobs case. Caitlin decided she would talk to some of her former colleagues and find out their views. Recalling Neil's accusations about her handling of the prison case, she vowed to show him just how thorough she could be. Nothing would get by her this time. She would become versed in all the issues related to vaccines, even the matters that were merely tangential to this case.

But why was he keeping tabs on her? Was he still obsessing

about her unwillingness to agree to an ongoing affair? She wasn't that stupid, she'd told him at the time. Not only was he her boss—at best an unwise choice for involvement—he was married. After Jayson, she needed time to sort out her life. Now she was clear: getting involved with Neil again would be a very bad idea.

Caitlin was writing herself a note to contact Dan Fielding, an attorney she'd worked with during her brief stint with the Civil Division, when she heard a voice in the corridor outside her office.

"Oh, the Caitlion is back," Jim Jenkins lamented. "Guess that's the end of candlelight dinners with the wife. Hello pepperoni pizza!"

Yes, it's true, Caitlin thought. *I'm a workaholic.*

She and Jim sometimes collaborated on larger cases where co-counsel was needed, and Caitlin always pushed him to work late. A nearby Italian restaurant made deliveries after hours; Caitlin usually ordered a large pepperoni pizza and shared it with the marshals on duty at the Justice Center's main entrance.

Jim stepped inside Caitlin's office. "Hello, Jim," Caitlin said. She put down her pen. "Missed you at the staff meeting."

"Emergency dental appointment," Jim said, holding his hand to the side of his face. His eyes moved to the large file on Caitlin's desk. "Who's this week's prey?"

Caitlin waved away the question, too tired to explain. "Don't get me started."

Jim took the cue and changed the subject. "Going to the concert this year?"

In past years, many of the attorneys and staff had gathered for an unofficial picnic at the Fourth of July Concert on the Mall. In contrast to the enormous size of the Department of Justice, OSP was a small agency, and the staff worked together in close quarters. The office party in December and the picnic in July provided the main opportunities for socializing with co-workers and loved ones.

Caitlin's schedule was typically booked six weeks in advance, yet she hadn't even thought about weekend plans—and this was already the First of July.

"I'm not sure just what I'm going to do," she said, glancing down at the Jacobs file. She looked up at Jim. "Are you going?"

"Oh, yeah. They've got a great lineup this year. And my kids love the fireworks."

"Well, if I make it, I'll look for your friendly face in the crowd," Caitlin said, envious of Jim's seemingly normal family life.

He waved before departing and flashed a crooked smile, his face still numb from his visit to the dentist. "Smile and the world smiles back!"

No matter what crisis they were in the midst of, Caitlin thought, Jim maintained a light and easy disposition. She smiled and waved back.

Following Jim's lead, Caitlin packed up for the day. She phoned in an order to an Italian restaurant in Old Town Alexandria and headed for the elevator.

After dropping her clothes at the dry cleaner, she picked up her takeout lasagna and went home. When she arrived at the townhouse, she saw the blinking red light on the answering machine alerting her to messages, but she didn't have the energy to attend to one more thing. She'd slept little while in Scotland. All she wanted to do now was eat and go to bed.

Scotland.

Caitlin sighed and unzipped her dress. She'd only been back for one day and, already, Scotland felt worlds away.

✑ 17 ✑

On Tuesday morning, Caitlin listened to Kimo's message. He, too, wanted to talk about their experience in Ireland. Maybe he could shed some light on what happened the night of the solstice or, at least, explain why he acted so strangely the following morning. Right now, though, researching the vaccine issue was foremost in Caitlin's mind.

She spent the morning talking to the attorneys in the Civil

Division who regularly represented the Department of Health and Human Services in Vaccine Court. The system Congress intended to be streamlined and nonadversarial was, in practice, quite cumbersome. The Justice Department's policy was to litigate rather than settle; claims sometimes dragged on for years because of government requests for information that many families had difficulty providing.

In order to receive an award of damages, a claimant had to show that his injuries were caused by an adverse reaction to a vaccine listed in the applicable table. Recovering damages was easiest, Caitlin learned, when the side effects were among those already recognized as potential reactions to the specific vaccines identified in the regulations. The Secretary of Health and Human Services narrowly interpreted which medical conditions created such a presumptive injury, thereby narrowing the field of claimants for whom recovery would be swift and certain.

Without the presumption, claimants faced the more difficult task of *proving* that a particular vaccine caused their injuries—a feat that usually required scientific data. Many families, already stretched thin by their ordeal, had neither the energy nor the money to pursue a full-blown trial. Parents of children who'd been harmed by vaccines often declared bankruptcy, lost jobs, divorced, and deprived their other children of attention because they were overwhelmed with the needs of their afflicted child and the never-ending search for effective treatments. Most of the children who were part of the Jacobs class would never lead normal lives.

Caitlin realized that if a preservative as widely used as thimerosal were found unsafe, the implications would be far-reaching. Vaccines were mandatory for school enrollment in most states, and the CDC added new vaccines to the recommended immunization schedule with alarming frequency. How many of those were administered from multiple-dose vials? Caitlin wondered.

Overwhelmed by the massive amount of information she'd gathered throughout the morning, she headed for Dan Fielding's office. Of all the attorneys in the Civil Division, Caitlin expected Dan to be the most candid in answering her questions. She wanted to talk to him last, when she was well versed in the issues, and had arranged to meet him for lunch. She knocked on his open door. When he stood up to greet her, she noticed he'd put on weight.

Dan was one of the nicest attorneys Caitlin knew, but he had often seemed a bit lonely, and she'd suspected he had a crush on her. Married now, he seemed content.

"Marriage agrees with you," she said.

Dan suggested they walk to a nearby restaurant so they could talk more freely than in the DOJ cafeteria. Caitlin noticed that he turned the lights off when he left his office—a practice few people at OSP bothered to follow.

While they waited for their meals, Dan showed Caitlin photos of his wife and son. Caitlin knew that marriage didn't make men immune to flattery and charm; she gushed about how beautiful his wife was and how healthy his son looked.

"I always knew you'd make a great husband and father."

"I'm sorry things didn't work out with you and Jayson," Dan said. "How's life in the big leagues? Did they make you Division Chief yet?"

Caitlin giggled and pushed playfully on Dan's arm. "Naw, we don't have divisions at OSP!" she said. "Though maybe we should."

She enjoyed the work, she said, but the demands were stressful at times. Staying with the Civil Division might have been a wiser choice. At OSP, every case required learning about a whole new field. She couldn't develop expertise in any one area and always felt a step behind.

"Like now," she said as she picked at a chef's salad. "I've got this case about a vaccine preservative. What do I know about vaccines or preservatives—or about the FDA's approval process, or how much approved products are monitored?"

"What would you like to know?" Dan asked before biting into a cheeseburger.

She'd read the act that established the Vaccine Injury Compensation Program, Caitlin said, and had familiarized herself with procedural and statutory requirements. But she hadn't found any regulations that addressed the safety of preservatives like thimerosal. Dan said he wasn't aware of any, either.

"So there aren't any recognized injuries related to thimerosal or other additives because no one is regulating the cumulative effects from repeated exposures?" Caitlin asked. "Hasn't anyone done any studies on this stuff?"

"That would be up to agencies like the CDC and NIH," Dan said. "Adverse reactions are supposed to be reported to the VAERS, and the VSD monitors select HMOs—"

"Whoa, whoa—slow down, cowboy! I need a manual to decipher all those acronyms!"

"Sorry. Suffice it to say, somebody could run the numbers if they had a reason to."

Caitlin asked Dan for his impressions about how well the Compensation Program was working. He told her there had been some controversy over the administration of the fund from which claims were paid, though he couldn't—or wouldn't—elaborate. Critics of the system wanted greater efforts to inform parents about the availability of the Compensation Program before their children were vaccinated. Public health officials didn't want to create fears where none were warranted, so publicity had been scant—parents might overreact and refuse to subject their children to a risk, resulting in increased incidence of diseases that had been brought under control. Dan's remarks echoed Kimo's: the pharmaceutical industry had a powerful lobby and could be a formidable foe.

Caitlin thanked Dan for his help and left enough money on the table to cover the bill plus a generous tip. When she stood up, she saw Neil sitting at a table in the corner with several other men in suits. He was staring at her, expressionless. She met his stare and then left the restaurant.

When she returned to her office, Caitlin pulled out the box of documents pertaining to the Jacobs case that she'd packed up before leaving for Ireland. Something was missing. Caitlin checked the contents against the index. The copies of two depositions from a related case were gone. The experts' testimony, though based on anecdotal evidence, supported the assertion that the amount of mercury in thimerosal was sufficient to cause serious harm to a susceptible child, with multiple vaccinations resulting in mercury levels far in excess of the amount the Environmental Protection Agency had deemed safe.

Caitlin checked the box again. Had she misplaced the depositions?

She was baffled. She couldn't possibly remember every detail from before her trip; too much had happened in the intervening time. She felt like she'd been transported into some other reality and then dropped back down into her old life. Everything looked the same; nothing was the same.

God, could Neil be right—am I getting careless?

She searched the stacks of papers and files on her desk, and then looked through her filing cabinet. Those last few days before leaving had been hectic; in her rush to get out of town, she might have been less careful than usual.

She returned to her desk and wrote a note asking a paralegal to sort through the other boxes to see if the files had been returned to the wrong place. When she looked up, Neil was lurking in the doorway.

"I read your memo on the vaccine case," he said, entering Caitlin's office.

Before she left for Ireland, Caitlin had given Neil a status report summarizing her active cases. "Jacobs," she said. "I've talked to some of the parents whose children suffer from developmental disabilities, allegedly as a result of the preservative."

"Kill it."

"What? I'm still investigating—"

"There's no credible evidence that thimerosal causes autism. And there's already a procedure in place to handle vaccine-related injuries. These people can file in the Vaccine Court like everybody else."

Neil picked up the copy of *Washington Lawyer* that was lying on Caitlin's desk and sat in the chair by the door.

"This is hardly a routine claim," Caitlin said. "These families don't have the resources to mount a scientific expedition to try and prove causation in Vaccine Court. The whole question of whether mercury-derived preservatives are linked with autism is something medical researchers and clinicians disagree on."

"Then it's not a question for the courts. Talk to your representative if you don't like the law. As for this case, argue failure to exhaust administrative remedies and move for dismissal."

Neil flipped through the pages of the magazine, but Caitlin knew he wasn't actually reading anything. Was he avoiding looking at her, hoping she would go along with his pronouncement and turn her attention to something else?

"The suit is against the manufacturers, not the Department of Health and Human Services," she said. "It's up to the defendants to move for dismissal."

"You know what I mean. Write up the reasons in your brief. I'm sure the judge will agree and the whole matter will quietly disappear."

Caitlin eyed him surreptitiously. *Why is he so sure?*

She knew that Neil had worked at the Food and Drug Administration before OSP. Was he covering up for someone? Did some inside arrangement make dismissal a foregone conclusion? Caitlin didn't doubt that Neil—or his contacts—had the ability to pull it off. She didn't doubt that such things went on at times, covertly, behind the scenes.

While Neil pretended to be absorbed in a magazine article, Caitlin collected her thoughts. Claims covered by the Compensation Program did have to be filed first in the Court of Federal Claims, and Congress had given the Secretary of Health and Human Services broad deference in matters pertaining to vaccine safety. The need for uniformity in carrying out the intentions of the Act could, arguably, require DHHS and the Vaccine Court to determine the legal implications of a potential hazard with a preservative before getting state and federal courts involved. Judges and attorneys were not necessarily any more competent than bureaucrats when matters concerning science and medicine were at issue. Attorneys at DOJ frequently consulted a panel of renowned doctors—who often had their own career interests and grant funding to protect.

But what if the government's whole approach to the topic was part of a systemic problem—would anyone within the system be able to recognize a fundamental flaw in how these matters were handled when they all shared the same beliefs and assumptions?

Einstein recognized that problems don't get solved at the level on which they are created, Caitlin recalled. *Sometimes we need to appeal to a higher authority.*

The plaintiffs had brought this suit in federal district court because they could not find adequate relief in the manner provided by the Compensation Program. Wasn't that why OSP was handling the case rather than the Civil Division? And wasn't federal court the appropriate forum for challenging actions of the executive branch—and interpreting the laws passed by the legislative branch? What Neil was asking her to do would foreclose the plaintiffs' opportunity to bring their complaint before a judge—an outcome Caitlin felt compelled to oppose.

"It doesn't make sense to wait until so many lives are ruined that the harm can no longer be ignored," she said calmly. "There has to be some independent oversight of these matters if the government is going to mandate that citizens be treated like lab rats. Besides, the plaintiffs aren't arguing harm from the vaccine itself, but from the preservative. Claims against manufacturers of 'components' don't have to be filed in Vaccine Court."

"The preservative is part of the manufacturing process, so it is part of the vaccine," Neil countered.

Caitlin was glad she'd done her homework. "Preservatives are not necessary to the efficacy of vaccines," she said confidently. "Single doses are available. They just cost more."

"Just because something can be done doesn't mean it has to be done—or even should be done," Neil argued. "The FDA requires products distributed in multi-dose containers to use a preservative. If the vaccine formula calls for a preservative and the formula's safety has been approved, then the preservative has also been approved. You can't seriously contend that manufacturers should be liable for something the government required in the first place."

"That's a circular argument that protects both government and industry from any liability for harm caused by products the manufacturer profits from and the government requires. Do you seriously contend that the burden should fall on families who followed the rules and thought they were doing the right thing in having their kids vaccinated?"

Caitlin noticed her voice rising and realized she felt genuinely passionate about this issue. She had no intention of backing down.

"Even if the plaintiffs could prove thimerosal caused the injuries, the Compensation Program might not cover most of them," she said coolly. "The statute of limitations bars claims that aren't filed within three years from the date of actual injury. As I'm sure you know, the Justice Department, as well as the Department of Health and Human Services, has consistently resisted efforts to toll the statute of limitations, which would allow claims to be filed after the *discovery* of the injury, which can easily exceed three years."

Autism, Caitlin had learned, isn't diagnosed until other possible causes are ruled out. By then, parents had often missed the deadline for filing a claim, and many of them were uninformed about the Compensation Program. A waitress at a local café had recently told Caitlin that her son wasn't diagnosed until he started first grade— well over three years from the time his symptoms first manifested.

"If they're not covered, then there's nothing to discuss," Neil said.

"The whole system is a labyrinth," Caitlin said, tossing aside her pen. "It's no wonder there's such a huge trust fund accumulated."

Money that could have gone to needy families was instead diverted to government litigation expenses, including teams of medical experts hired to disprove the families' cases. Where was the sense in that?

When Neil suddenly stopped leafing through the magazine, Caitlin realized she had said too much. Leaning forward, she watched him closely. Did he have some interest in the trust fund? Perhaps she was overly suspicious of his motives, but Neil was far more attuned than she was to the political implications of various litigation strategies where controversial matters were concerned. Suddenly, he threw down the magazine and stood in front of her desk. Startled, she instinctively pulled back.

"You going soft on me? Got a bleeding heart all of a sudden?" He leaned toward her. His bushy eyebrows and dark eyes made his stare seem all the more intense.

Caitlin averted her gaze. Allocations of federal funds didn't normally concern her; the system was what it was. Something about this case, though, engaged her heart and her mind. She felt compassion for the victims, and she was unwilling to be a pawn in Neil's scheme, at their expense. Traits she had once appreciated about herself were resurfacing, and she refused to shut them down in service of getting the job done. She liked the person she was becoming.

"I think the allegations have merit, and the plaintiffs deserve a chance to be heard," Caitlin heard herself saying. She stood up. "Why can't the government ever admit its mistakes? We experiment on our troops, because almost anything can be done in the name of 'national security,' and then we deny culpability when something goes wrong—until the evidence is undeniable. It doesn't matter whether it's Agent Orange or strange symptoms afflicting veterans of the Gulf War; the priorities are never about discovering the truth, just covering someone's behind!"

She was surprised how nervous she felt taking a stand with Neil. *Why not* say what she really thought? If she was serious about leaving law or, at least, her present job, what did she have to lose?

Neil scoffed. "You think? Who cares what you think?"

He pointed a finger at her for emphasis.

"Your client is the Department of Health and Human Services, and your client's views on the matter *will* get heard—and listened to!"

Visibly shaken, he turned to leave. He paused long enough to say, "You know, if you're not going to be a team player, maybe it would be better if you took a hike."

"And which team is that—your FDA cronies?"

Caitlin regretted the jab as soon as she'd said it. She knew how to push Neil's buttons, but inciting his wrath would only complicate matters.

He reached across the desk and grabbed her arm. "What was it you said earlier? 'You're getting close to a line you don't want to cross.'"

Neil released his grip and abruptly left the office. Caitlin rubbed her arm and sat back down, stunned. How had things taken such a bad turn so quickly? Had she stumbled onto something that threatened Neil's interests? Was that why he'd been following her movements? She had witnessed his insensitive treatment of others, but this was the first time she'd been on the receiving end.

With Neil's backing, she had helped fight abuse and corruption in government and industry. She'd thought they were on the same side. Now she was alone in her battle against injustice, and her adversary had a familiar face.

✒ 18 ✒

Neil leaned against the wall of the empty corridor around the corner from Caitlin's office. He removed a handkerchief from his pocket and dabbed the beads of sweat that had collected on his brow.

He'd assured all the interested parties that this thimerosal case would be disposed of promptly. One didn't get put into a position of power so early in a career without owing somebody something. His promises had come due.

He walked slowly to his office. Caitlin was proving more naïve than he'd supposed.

It's not love that makes the world go around, Catie darling—that's just something people without power say to make themselves feel better. Power is the ultimate aphrodisiac, and money is a form of power.

Everything worth having could be readily obtained with money and power, and Neil was determined to have his share of both. Conquest, possession, ownership, and control were the aims, whether the objective was land, women, or nations.

I might not be cut out to play football, Neil thought, *but that doesn't mean I can't own the team.*

He reveled in capitalism, celebrating the freedom to compete and the opportunity to profit, and embraced risky ventures that allowed him to demonstrate his shrewdness and cunning. He was proud of his ability to spot a good investment—and to exploit any situation to best advantage. The Almighty Dollar was his idol, and not because of its inscription, "In God We Trust." More accurate would have been, "in trusts we place our god"—and in stocks and bonds and offshore accounts. The Declaration of Independence could have listed rights of "life, liberty, and the pursuit of power," he'd once said while toasting a success at the Club.

That's the great thing about America. We all share equal rights.

Neil had no sympathy or respect for those who lacked the gumption, intelligence, resources, or will to succeed. The choices, mistakes, and hardships of others were not his responsibility; he was not his brother's keeper. In the natural order of things, hierarchies and pecking orders were established as a matter of course. The strong preyed upon the weak; the fittest survived. Jungle law.

When he reached his office, Neil closed the door and removed his jacket. Loosening his tie, he stretched out on his burgundy leather couch and reviewed in his mind the morning's meeting with LCDR Sam Burns. Burns had been up most of the night, traveling across three time zones to get to Washington in time for their meeting in the Pentagon's Executive Dining Room. As he watched Burns devour a hearty breakfast, Neil evaluated the doctor's suitability to represent the Club's interests.

Neil wasn't too concerned about the offense that never made its way into Burns's records. Operation Desert Shield had commenced on short notice and confusion abounded. In some cases, Carter Simms had said, both Marine Corps and Naval commanders had been responsible for the provision of medical services in theater. Burns had been part of a specialized team; that allowed for some laxity in following the rules. His transgression was minor, as long as the damage was contained. If rumors had been allowed to spread, Burns would have been perceived as a liability to the team. The easiest path was to make him someone else's problem.

He was shipped to the remote Mojave Desert, a hardship post for any man who loved the sea. After completing a three-year tour of duty at the branch medical clinic at the Naval Air Weapons Station,

China Lake, he was assigned to a Marine base near Twentynine Palms, where he currently headed one of the Naval Hospital's clinics.

Not the most impressive credentials in terms of cutting-edge research, or even policy and decision-making authority, Neil thought, but other considerations weighed in. Burns's expertise would be sufficient to get the testimony of a practicing, active-duty military physician into the record. As an administrator, Burns no longer saw many patients, but he oversaw the base immunization program that served military personnel as well as civilian spouses and dependents.

Neil never trusted a man who wouldn't look him in the eye, but Burns didn't flinch when he said that after five years in the desert, he was eager to get back in the game. Divorced, he only saw his daughter two weekends a month. He had time and energy for greater responsibilities than treating the wives and children of Marines stationed at the Marine Corps Air Ground Combat Center. He was thinking of leaving medicine entirely once his military commitment ended; he was interested in covert operations and had made some inquiries. He was too old, he knew, for the rigorous training required by the Navy's elite commandos, the SEALs, but perhaps he could be useful in another capacity.

Neil saw something of himself in Burns: the hunger to be a player. He decided to give him the opportunity.

"We could put you on the ACCV after the hearings are over," he told him. "The Advisory Commission on Childhood Vaccines—it's the oversight board that makes recommendations to the Secretary of Health and Human Services about the operation of the National Vaccine Injury Compensation Program. Not one of the medical seats, though; that would be scrutinized too closely. Three seats are for members of the general public. Two of those have to be filled by parents or guardians of children who've suffered a vaccine-related injury or death. We'll put you in the third."

"Is it vacant?" Burns asked as he prepared to eat the last bite of sausage on his plate.

"It will be," Neil replied matter-of-factly. "Oh, and one other thing."

Burns carefully laid his silverware across his plate and looked directly at Neil.

"You don't know me," Neil said. "If we cross paths at a congressional hearing or, hell, even in the john. We've never had a conversation. Don't ever call me or come to my office."

"Understood," Burns said.

Neil extended his right hand in a gesture of welcome and said, "You're in."

The doctor hesitated a moment, smiled, and firmly gripped Neil's hand in agreement.

Burns was probably still in town, Neil thought as he lay on the couch, drops of moisture collecting on his brow; he could probably still catch him, if he acted quickly.

His breath whistled between his teeth as he let out a long sigh. He was in deep this time. How far was he willing to go? He wiped away the perspiration with his shirtsleeve and covered his eyes with his forearm. He stayed that way for several minutes before reaching a decision. Then he stood up, walked to his desk, and called Burns at his hotel near Washington's National Airport.

The call woke Sam from a nap.

"If you can stick around another day," Neil said, "I have an assignment for you. Unofficial business."

༄ 19 ༄

Caitlin left the office and went to the gym for a workout. Staying in shape was essential for maintaining the high output her job required, and regular routines helped keep chaos at bay. Lifting weights strengthened more than her muscles; her resolve to fight for the children and families who could not negotiate the maze of governmental rules and regulations on their own also grew stronger.

Her mind wandered as she pedaled the stationary bicycle. In a flash of insight, she understood why she had accepted so many pro bono cases while working at Legal Aid: she liked helping others. Sometimes, people's lives improved as a result.

Kimo was a good example. After Caitlin represented him in court, he stopped hanging around with the party crowd and started pursuing a career that would allow him to put his talents to good use. Sure, he was still a fringe dweller, but—as far as Caitlin knew—he wasn't breaking any laws. And what would happen if he did get arrested on another marijuana charge—or if he wound up in jail as part of an environmental protest? Would she support him in a different way now than she had before?

Five years earlier, she had advised him to plead guilty to a lesser charge, but answers to questions about right and wrong no longer seemed starkly evident to her. Laws were not always just, and rulers throughout history had done some horrendous things to people. Patriotic citizens rushed to defend their country against imagined threats from an "evil empire" but remained dangerously ignorant about the duplicity of their own government.

Caitlin headed for the treadmill. She didn't want to become paranoid, but she didn't want to stick her head in the sand, either. She would have to stay vigilant if she intended to challenge Neil. She couldn't allow him to gain an advantage. He knew how to find the chink in her armor.

Carl Jung had called the disowned parts of a person the "shadow" self, Caitlin recalled. Maybe nations also had a shadow side.

Are nations subject to the same maladies as individuals? she wondered as she ran a mile on the treadmill. Governments, after all, were designed and run by people. *Maybe the avoidance mechanisms that people use—denial, escapism, projection—get magnified into group pathologies when no one is brave enough to publicly acknowledge the emperor's nakedness.*

History had shown that the whistleblowers and watchdogs who called attention to situations that endangered the collective good were usually considered pests before they were acknowledged as heroes.

Would we be a stronger nation if we were willing to listen to all voices, even the disenchanted ones? We shut away the mentally ill, criminals, and others in institutions, keeping them out of sight so we don't have to think about the darker side of life—the crushed dreams, the dying, the frail, the deviant. Shouldn't we try to help people break destructive cycles before we condemn them to a life of isolation and neglect?

The politicians and policy analysts Caitlin knew seemed to function from a purely intellectual vantage point, forgetting that real people were affected by their dealings.

If a system is only as strong as its weakest link, we all need to be concerned about the outsiders as well as the superstars—the full spectrum of humanity.

Caitlin thought again about Kimo. She'd been keeping him at arm's length, his ideas too strange and unsettling. She winced. She might not understand all the things he talked about, but she was willing now to hear what he had to say.

No, she thought, *not just willing. Interested.*

As sweat oozed from her pores in the steam room, she realized that her lifestyle also deviated from the norm. Her days were occupied with ideas and ideals, laws and principles, procedures and logistics. Her concerns were broader than changing diapers or mowing the lawn, but the simplicity of the ordinary activities she had once viewed with disdain was becoming increasingly attractive.

She had wanted to stand out; to be special, and live an extraordinary life. Her job at OSP provided many benefits and opportunities, but living from home to car to office to airplane to hotel room to courthouse wasn't very fulfilling. She was beginning to understand that life's ordinary tasks could be meaningful, too. Social rituals were not mere obligations; they wove a person into the web of community. Caitlin knew the importance of a positive attitude, but she'd never before seen so clearly how much her thoughts influenced her experience. And thoughts could change.

Her drive to make a name for herself had dissipated; she had nothing left to prove. Fighting for something she believed in was more important to her now than keeping Neil happy. He held no power over her, and his opinion no longer mattered. She welcomed a test of her capabilities. If she succeeded, she would leave OSP knowing she'd made a difference—and stood her ground. Sure, she'd won other cases—lots of other cases—and the outcomes mattered, to someone. The Jacobs case she would win for the right reasons, and she would reclaim her integrity in the process. Maybe this was her destiny; the reason she had entered law; the moment all her legal training had propelled her toward. If she failed—well, she couldn't afford to think about that. Once she decided on a course of action, she must not allow doubt to enter her mind.

She rinsed off before changing into her swimsuit, and then plunged into the deep end of the pool, determined to double the number of laps she usually swam at the end of her workout. She needed to build endurance for the battle ahead.

After a long shower, Caitlin dressed in a t-shirt and shorts and left the gym. Driving home through the streets of Alexandria, she recalled how much she had liked living there when she and Jayson were together. When they split up, Caitlin moved out and bought a townhouse nearby. With all the changes going on in her life, she didn't want to change neighborhoods as well.

Early on, she and Jayson sometimes crossed paths—shopping at the local grocery store or running in the park. Once, they were both waiting at the Metro station at the same time—odd, she'd thought, since they both drove almost everywhere. They engaged in polite conversation until the train arrived, and then sat separately for the commute into Washington. That was probably the last time she had seen Jayson, Caitlin thought as she drove her car into the garage.

Since moving into her own place, she hadn't made any effort to get to know her neighbors, and she felt no sense of community. The townhouse was a residence, but it wasn't a home. Caitlin was rarely there; she made sure of it. She had invested so much of herself in the relationship with Jayson and the home they were creating. She missed scouring the flea market with him for unique furnishings and exploring options for wedding and honeymoon sites. She even missed the inevitable disagreements that arose when she wanted to buy something he didn't like or considered too expensive. She'd sometimes pouted for days when she didn't get her way.

How silly, she thought as she entered the dark kitchen. *Fighting about a chair or a table or a bedspread.* Those petty arguments seemed so inconsequential now. She turned on the light and looked around. She could choose whatever décor she wanted; no one would object. But she no longer cared. The townhouse was a place to eat and sleep and change clothes.

Caitlin stared at the empty shelves in the refrigerator. *Well, sometimes it's a place to eat.* She trudged up the stairs, undressed, and crawled into bed without dinner.

In the morning, Caitlin woke before the alarm. After a quick shower, she drank a cup of coffee and left home an hour earlier than usual. She wanted to wrap up her research and write a recommendation so she could enjoy the Fourth of July holiday. Maybe after work she'd have time to buy some groceries. Today, she would pick up a sandwich at the deli across the street and eat lunch at her desk.

During the drive to the office, she planned her strategy. She would phone Kristof, her journalist pal, and alert him that the government's handling of the thimerosal matter might be worth investigating. Media attention could bring pressure for reform, even if this case got dismissed.

She needed to call Kimo as well. He understood her in a way Dru never would. She and Kimo had been joined together in some meaningful way, in Ireland—or earlier.

That night at the Shannon Pot, Caitlin had seen images of the past. Whether they were imagined or real she couldn't say, but the experience had changed her. Perhaps spending three days around Kimo had initiated the change—or listening to the Mozart CD, or a confluence of circumstances. Whatever the cause, she no longer looked at life in the same way.

Did the currents in her life reflect dynamics that had been manifesting for eons with Kimo and Neil—and others? Were souls drawn to each other to play out cosmic dramas in the human sphere? What law of physics could explain *that?*

By going to the office earlier, Caitlin avoided much of the traffic congestion she usually encountered during her morning commute, making for a more relaxing drive. Her thoughts drifted beyond the mundane concerns weighing on her heart and mind. Eternal questions loomed large. She desperately wanted to understand her life's meaning and purpose. Where could she go for answers?

She recalled, with little affection, the pastor of her hometown church. He'd told Martha that Caitlin had "a wild imagination, that one" after she inquired about the transmigration of souls.

"Study your Bible, Catie," the pastor advised. "It contains everything you need to know."

"But if a soul gets a body once, and the soul is eternal and lives on after the body dies, why can't the soul get another body?" she asked precociously. The pastor just laughed and shook his head and told her to "run along and play now." That was the moment when Caitlin turned away from her mother's religion.

Why were the selected prophecies, traditions, understandings, and events of the particular times and places described in the Bible considered superior to other times and places—didn't the teachings of other cultures and other religions also contribute to human understanding? Were the prophets all confined to the past? Where were the modern oracles? And what was the link to Ireland? Was some magic still alive there, though long gone from other lands? Had she been led there by something more than curiosity about her ancestors and a vague wish to pacify her father's soul?

Caitlin glanced at the dried, yellow rose blossom dangling from her rearview mirror. After she'd cut it from Katie's rosebush, Kimo told her that roses emanate a very high vibrational frequency—the highest of any of the plant essences that had been measured. He was studying something called "vibrational medicine." He said it was part of a paradigm shift that signaled the dawn of a new understanding of the human experience in the cosmos, an evolutionary leap in consciousness.

"Energy is the wave of the future," he'd said on the way to Newgrange. "Everything has a frequency, or rate of vibration. People, plants, organs—diseases even. Dead food, pollution, and negative thinking lower people's frequencies. Then they're more vulnerable to getting sick or depressed." Healing, he said, entailed finding the proper vibration to restore balance and harmony.

In the sixties, the Beach Boys sang about "good vibrations," Caitlin thought. People often spoke of someone giving off good or bad "vibes."

Maybe we're sending and receiving subtle clues all the time. Maybe we know more than we realize. If only we could tap into that knowledge!

She hadn't retained much from high school physics, but she recalled that water molecules vibrate less when the water is frozen than when it is liquid, and the molecules in solids move at a much slower rate than the molecules in liquids and gases.

Even solid matter is not as fixed as our senses perceive it to be.

Could emotions get stuck and frozen? Thoughts certainly could—she knew narrow- and closed-minded people who refused to consider new ideas. Some people were plagued by obsessions; others repeated the same litany of complaints the way she replayed her favorite songs—over and over.

What would a spiritual rut look like? she wondered.

She returned her attention to the road and prepared to exit the parkway. Washington's traffic circles and diagonal streets, laid out in an elaborate geometric pattern by Pierre L'Enfant, may have been innovative two centuries earlier, but they were no boon to modern travelers.

Caitlin thought of the garden maze Kimo had discovered in Ireland. Following him through twists and turns, she watched as he sensed which direction to choose. He looked for opportunities to develop his intuitive faculties, he said, and explained that certain practices help raise a person's frequency to a higher level—a state in which healing and so-called miracles become commonplace.

"As consciousness unifies and clarifies," he said, "the understanding of universal principles is enhanced."

Caitlin had made some smart remark. *That was before the Shannon Pot,* she thought. Before reality turned upside down. Now, she wanted to remember every word Kimo had said.

"The journey from spirit into matter and back to spirit is a function of consciousness moving into the dense and slow vibrations of the material plane by inhabiting a physical body and then ascending into the lightness of pure being."

Kimo saw life as an interconnected web, a continuum of energies pulsating at different rates, much as the colors of the rainbow are distinct yet remain inseparable and emanate from the same source.

"People are like colors," he'd said. "Different colors forming one rainbow."

Caitlin thought of Kimo's pale blue eyes, expansive as the sky, encompassing her. Stopped at a red light, she reached up and lightly touched the dried blossom.

What color would I be, if I were a rose?

She glanced at her image in the rearview mirror. The scarlet lipstick she'd applied before leaving the house was her favorite shade.

Surely, she thought, *a deep shade of red.*

The light turned green. It was time to go and finish what she'd started.

∽ 20 ∽

Sam Burns munched on a cheeseburger at his listening post while he waited for his target—"rabbit" in surveillance lingo—to make a phone call. Being idle gave him too much time to think. At least he was away from the hospital for a couple of days. Out of the desert. Back on the East Coast. Closer to the seat of power.

Administrative tasks were never-ending since his promotion to Lieutenant Commander and head of the Family Medicine Clinic. He'd chosen military medicine because he wanted adventure, but a multiple-vehicle pileup on the base was the most excitement he'd seen in recent years. Ten casualties were sent to the hospital's ER; Sam rushed over to triage and treat patients. A taste of the high-intensity activity that emergency rooms at urban hospitals regularly encountered made him all the more restless for change.

The stability of routine duties at a base hospital had been all right for a while. After his daughter was born, Sam appreciated being close to home. But that situation quickly deteriorated once the baby's developmental delays became apparent.

Yvonne had complained about their desert exile from the start. She'd married a Navy doctor, and she expected to share in the perks of his career. *Or maybe she just needed a way to stay in the States*, Sam thought as he spread ketchup over his fries.

A native of France, Yvonne was a gorgeous and exotic exchange student when Sam met her. His determination to impress her spurred him to excel, and he ranked high in his class at the F. Hébert School of Medicine. Part of the federal government's Uniformed Services University of the Health Sciences, the medical school in Bethesda, Maryland, accepted both civilian and active-duty applicants, but not everyone was suited for a career in military medicine. The specialty required skills in trauma management, behavioral sciences, environmental medicine, and tropical infectious disease as well as knowledge of military medical intelligence. Sam was competent in all. When he proposed marriage, his future looked bright.

He'd chosen a career in medicine because he was fascinated by the delicate link between the body and its animating force; by the tenacity of the human spirit when met with adversity, and the body's ability to muster forces to repel an invasion of pathogenic intruders— or not. He'd chosen infectious disease as a specialty because he wanted to help eradicate the undesirable conditions that affect large numbers of people throughout the world. He'd thought maybe someday he would formulate policy or develop his leadership abilities—even work for the World Health Organization or some other international program. When he was a pre-med student, he'd imagined himself as the hero who saved the day by warding off a pestilence that threatened the safety of whole cities, towns, and villages.

He had hoped the military life would help him again experience the *esprit de corps* he'd known in junior high school when he was part of Father Brandon's gang of altar boys. Sam's first exposure to cigarettes, alcohol, and porn magazines came during the Saturday night card games the priest organized at the rectory. Brandon's distorted mixture of sacred and profane was seductive. He rode a motorcycle and seemed to have the best of both worlds—serving God while satisfying his own desires. Sam wanted to be like Brandon and begged his parents to send him to a Jesuit prep school at the start of ninth grade. He promised to work hard at his studies to justify the expense.

All those years, Sam never knew that, one by one, each boy served his turn on Brandon's private altar. The pain was too great, the psychological trauma too severe, to divulge to anyone at that tender age when beliefs about the world were still forming. Each boy lived with his secret shame; never telling the others, never daring to ask. Gradually, each one fell away from the group, replaced by an eager young face not yet marred by the initiation ritual.

But manhood wasn't what the priest was introducing. Brandon had preyed on Sam at his most vulnerable time, after his father's sudden death. The loss of two important father figures devastated him. He left the parochial school at the end of tenth grade, finishing out his last two years at the public high school near his mother's house in Southern California. He never made any friends there. And he wanted nothing more to do with religion.

Sam had forgotten about the darker side of the boys' club—pushed it out of his mind—until he was alone in the Gulf with Conrad Jones, the young preventive medicine technician who drove him from one medical treatment facility to the next. The Navy had deployed its team of experts in August of 1990, early in Operation Desert Shield, to initiate a disease surveillance system. They monitored water, sewage, and food supplies for possible hazards. A sophisticated lab was established in Saudi Arabia to identify infectious disease or biological warfare threat agents peculiar to the region. As the junior member of the team, Sam collected samples for the lab to analyze. Weather conditions, equipment breakdowns, and communication difficulties sometimes delayed him and his driver for days as they waited for an opportunity to move to the next site.

Life anywhere in the U.S. is Edenic compared to the hardships of service in the Gulf, Sam thought as he sat in the small, stuffy office

waiting for some activity on Ms. Rose's phone line. Adequate supplies had been hard to come by—ordinary disinfectants like bleach
and chlorine were unobtainable through standard supply sources.
Lack of trained personnel hindered all activities, and communica-
tions were limited by inferior equipment with insufficient power to
meet range requirements. On top of all that, poor coordination
between the Navy- and Marine Corps-assigned surgeons hampered
joint planning. Sam had trained long and hard to become board-
certified; he was ready to serve and coped as best he could. While
traveling with Conrad Jones, he found some of the camaraderie he
had longed for.

Jones wasn't much older than he had been the last time he saw
Father Brandon, Sam suddenly realized. What's more, Sam was
about the same age in 1990 that Brandon had been at the time of
their encounter.

He'd gone over the episode with Jones many times in his mind,
wondering why it had turned sour; who had ratted on him. *In
strange conditions, people act strangely*, he concluded.

Out there in that foreign wasteland, he'd felt dependent on the
enlisted man. They shared a tent—or whatever sleeping quarters
were available. Jones had been a willing participant in Sam's experiment. It was too easy. It was the one time Sam had acted on his
"compulsion," as he thought of it. But he was found out—and home
by November. He agreed to get counseling to keep the incident out
of his records, but the disgrace of the exposure had been almost as
bad as the initial insult by Brandon.

At first, Sam thought he had sabotaged his career; he couldn't
blame anyone. Therapy helped him see that he had also been a victim. He blamed Brandon. When his marriage failed, he blamed
Brandon for that, too. After nearly two years of alimony and child
support payments, his bitterness about the divorce had turned into
animosity. The house in the California desert hadn't felt like a home
since Yvonne left with Jacqueline, but Sam's leave went unused.
Where was he going to go, alone?

Now, six years into his seven-year service requirement, he was
thinking about a career change. He needed an outlet for his energy.

Neil Morton had promised to open doors for him if he spent the day listening in on some attorney's phone calls. Caitlin Rose was working on an important case, Neil said—one with potential ramifications for the vaccine market. Neil wanted to find out what Ms. Rose knew about his ties to the pharmaceutical industry. He reminded Sam that he would be compensated for his testimony before Congress with shares of pharmaceutical stock and instructed him to be on the alert for anything that could damage their interests.

The listening device notified Sam of calls to and from the attorney's office phone. It was programmable—Sam could monitor and record calls from his hotel room or any phone selected. Neil had set him up in an unused office at the Justice Center as a matter of convenience. After today, Ms. Rose would be out of the office until Monday. If Sam's sampling indicated a need, Neil would bring in trained professionals to watch her movements. But that wasn't necessary at this stage, and Sam was directed to listen until Caitlin left the office at the end of the day. Neil seemed most interested in knowing if she discussed anything vaccine-related.

Did it have to be vaccines? The subject was an ongoing source of tension with Yvonne. She had accused him of ruining their marriage by poisoning their daughter, but Sam wasn't convinced that Jacqueline's disabilities had been caused by routine immunizations.

He knew that allergic reactions were possible; flu-like symptoms were not uncommon, and there might be some redness around the site of injection or maybe some joint and muscle stiffness. He had received numerous vaccines. He'd never suffered from—or even witnessed—the extreme reactions some people complained about. As far as he knew, the vaccine supply was safe and effective. He couldn't explain those isolated cases. Maybe the individuals in question had some weakness or genetic anomaly and were inferior anyway. Maybe they had been exposed to some pathogen, or a bad batch.

Yvonne had refused to allow Jacqueline to be vaccinated. Tired of arguing, Sam took the baby to the clinic himself. He worked in public health, for God's sake—how would it look if his daughter didn't receive the recommended vaccinations? When Jacqueline became ill, Yvonne flung accusations at him. Sam secretly wondered if she had ingested drugs or alcohol during pregnancy. Maybe the child wasn't even his. In the end, the reasons didn't matter. Yvonne was gone.

Sam sucked the last of his soda through a straw and tossed the empty cup into a trashcan. Listening to attorneys talking about scheduling hearings and depositions made him glad he hadn't chosen law as a profession. Even the desert was preferable to being stuck in some high-rise building poring over boilerplate.

Sam checked the time. So far, none of Ms. Rose's conversations had set off any alarms. Neil had told him to give a summary of any concerns to Carter Simms when he came by the hotel to pay the bill and pick up the keys to the SUV Neil had given Sam to use during his stay. Neil had also given Sam a phone number in case he needed to reach Carty. Under no circumstances, Sam was told, could he contact Neil directly.

He understood about confidentiality. He had his own secrets he wanted kept under wraps. Like Brandon had said, "What goes on in private chambers is nobody's business."

He also understood Neil's desire for information about this Rose woman's intentions. Sam hadn't trusted Yvonne enough to tell her about Brandon—or Jones. He hadn't told her why he'd returned so quickly from the Gulf. She would have found some way to use it against him. He was convinced that his ex-wife, his mother, and his sister all conspired, on an ongoing basis, to make his life miserable. They used whatever damning information any of them could conjure up to make him the bad guy. They would never turn Jacqueline against him, though. She didn't possess the sensibility required for hatred.

Sam slapped his face to stay alert. He didn't mind wasting a day on a meaningless task, if that was what Neil wanted. Neil carried influence in Washington; he was someone Sam wanted to know better. Given the right opportunity, maybe Sam could put his bad luck behind him. He could talk to the FBI or CIA about job possibilities, or even the Defense Investigative Service. First, he had to prove his trustworthiness to Neil.

He rubbed his eyes and stood up. How had he ended up here? His life and career had once been full of promise.

He paced around the small office. He had to find some way to get back on a path to success.

◅ 21 ◅

Caitlin continued reviewing and drafting documents in the afternoon. The Jacobs case had been assigned to her, and she intended to prepare a memorandum detailing her recommendations. Neil said he would not approve any course except dismissal. Would he have her removed from the case? Could she take the matter over his head? Maybe her memo would end up in a file, but she felt compelled to follow the dictates of her conscience.

She had never been particularly savvy about politics. She hadn't majored in political science or run for the student council in college; she wasn't one to join protest marches or campaign for her favorite candidates. She just wanted to do a good job, enjoy the usual rewards in life, and leave the world a little better than she'd found it. She had never expected to find herself on the front lines of a cause, and she wasn't trying to be a heroine. She longed to lay aside the pressures of resolving problems and mediating conflicts, but, instead, she found herself drawn into a controversy the magnitude of which was far greater than she had imagined.

She read the newspaper; she knew corruption existed in government. No one wanted to believe their neighbors were criminals or their loved ones child molesters.

How hard we try to protect our illusions . . .

Facing the truth required courage and the ability to adapt as new information came to light; a fragile identity could easily shatter when foundations that had seemed solid began to crumble.

Caitlin felt the rumblings within her own psyche as she dared to open her eyes to what was going on around her. She remembered a time when her were her biggest concerns were choosing a dress to wear to the prom and deciding whether to cut her long tresses; those days were long gone. How had she gotten so far off the course she had always imagined for herself—marriage, family, career? Was this her destiny all along?

She recalled a line from the prayer of St. Francis that she had recited as a child: "Lord, make me an instrument of your peace." Were larger forces at work in her life?

Perhaps even choice is an illusion.

She scanned the certificates on the wall of her office. For so long, she had followed directions and passed through hoops like a well-trained circus animal. Now she was learning to heed an inner voice, and willing to buck the system. No longer would she refrain from speaking her mind for fear of ruffling a few feathers. Some wild, untamed part of her being was crying out for liberation from the constraints of her well-ordered life. She would leave her mark, not slink away like a sick animal. But she was in new territory. Like Kimo in the maze, she had to learn to sense the right path to take. Logic and reason and hard work could only take her part of the distance.

Patrice stopped by before leaving for the day. "John's taking me to see *Cats* on Friday. Why don't you and Kimo join us?"

"Thanks, I've got a lot to catch up on," Caitlin said. "Besides, I'm allergic to cats."

"All right, but I'm still waiting to hear about the rest of your trip."

"I'll call over the weekend," Caitlin promised.

The office would only be closed on Thursday, but anyone with a spare day of leave would take Friday off as well and enjoy a four-day weekend. Anyone except Caitlin. She liked being at the office when it was quiet.

She removed her reading glasses and leaned back in her chair. She wished she could talk to Patrice—or somebody—about the Jacobs case. Neil had always been her sounding board about work matters. With the boss as her ally—and Patrice to trade secrets with—Caitlin hadn't felt the need to cultivate other relationships at work. Freed from concerns about office politics, she had focused her attention on what mattered to her the most: completing as many cases as she could.

She knew she'd been a great asset—to Neil and to the office— but he was right; her success was partly due to him. He had let her do what she did best, often allowing her to choose the cases she wanted to work on. But he had turned on her, and the damage was irreparable. Without his support, she might as well look for another job.

She picked up the phone to call Jasmine Wells, a waitress at a nearby café. Caitlin had been eating lunch at the café for as long as she'd been working at OSP, but only recently did she learn that Jasmine's young son had been diagnosed as autistic. His story was similar to some of the accounts given by the plaintiffs in the Jacobs case; many of those children had also been diagnosed with autism spectrum disorder.

Marvin's birth and development had been normal, though his weight had been a little low. His saga began after his first birthday— after he received the routine immunizations that were recommended by the Centers for Disease Control and Prevention. He regressed, losing the communication abilities he had attained. He didn't like to be held but cried when he was put down. Jasmine was beside herself. Everything she did seemed wrong; what little confidence she'd had in her ability to be a good parent eroded. Marvin's father had vanished when he learned she was pregnant. Jasmine—who had barely graduated from high school—had struggled to make ends meet even before Marvin showed signs of delayed development.

It wasn't until Marvin entered the school system that Jasmine was finally able to get some answers—and help. Parents of autistic children told her about strategies that had worked for them. Currently, she was experimenting with a gluten-free diet.

Some parents believed immunizations had played a role in their child's deterioration. By the time Jasmine learned about the Vaccine Injury Compensation Program, the deadline for filing a claim had passed. According to the regulations, a petition in Vaccine Court could no longer be brought on Marvin's behalf. And without filing there first, Caitlin had told her, a civil action would probably also be barred.

Knowing the Wellses helped Caitlin see the families involved in the Jacobs case as more than statistics on a page. Caitlin admired Jasmine's determination to educate herself about Marvin's condition and to make a better life for them both. She wanted to help in any way she could. She had promised to give Jasmine updates on the progress of the lawsuit, but she also wanted to find out if music could help Marvin. She'd read anecdotal accounts that described various benefits of music for some children who suffered from autism and attention deficit hyperactivity disorders. Putting words to music seemed to enhance learning, much as "The Alphabet Song," set to the tune of a French folksong, helped children learn their ABCs.

Caitlin had offered to give Marvin some basic piano lessons. With Jasmine's permission, she'd purchased an old piano she found at a flea market and had it delivered to the Wellses' apartment. Jasmine insisted on paying her back. Twenty dollars a week was all she could afford, and that was just fine.

Caitlin had gone to the apartment several times before she left for Ireland. Her conversations with Marvin were mostly one-sided. He was fond of a toy rubber hammer and insisted on having it near him at all times. Sometimes he used the hammer, rather than his fingers, to bang on the piano keys.

Trying to reason with him was futile, and Caitlin frequently felt frustrated. She'd never seen Marvin smile. Sometimes he just sat and stared at the rotating blades of the ceiling fan. Keeping him calm was half the battle—much easier than calming him down after he became agitated. He seemed to find being touched painful, as if the sensory stimulation was too intense. Caitlin wondered if he retreated from contact as an act of self-preservation. She hoped that some of her care and attention would seep into the dark recesses of the narrow world in which he existed. She was not one to give up easily; she intended to resume their lessons soon—as soon as she could think about something other than quashing Neil's efforts to dismiss the Jacobs case.

The phone rang several times before Jasmine answered.

"Hi, Jasmine, Caitlin Rose. I found a report warning that the use of thimerosal could cause problems. It was written by a senior health official in Britain and published in a journal dedicated to adverse drug reactions. Ten years ago."

"You think anyone here knew it was a problem?"

"I think they didn't want to know and have ignored all evidence to the contrary," Caitlin said. "Some researchers are finally starting to add up the trace amounts of mercury being given with each of these vaccines and finding that the cumulative load is toxic. It might be a good idea to pull together Marvin's vaccine records and look into just what he was given, and when."

"I'll try an' find the time. I cain't keep up with everything as it is. We didn't get much sleep las' night."

Jasmine had said that bedtime was particularly stressful whenever Marvin got overstimulated. Caitlin caught herself absentmindedly drawing a flower. She put the pen down.

"Is the new diet helping?"

"It all helps a bit. I don't think there's one answer's gonna fix everythin' but I take any help I can get."

"I'll come by the restaurant soon. Can I say a quick hello to Marvin?"

Caitlin heard Jasmine call out to Marvin. He didn't respond, so Jasmine brought the phone to him and told him to say hello to Caitlin. When Marvin spoke, it was usually in a monotone.

"'lo," he mumbled.

"Marvelous Marv! This is Captivating Cait."

Caitlin's attempts to spark some interest in Marvin brought out the performer in her. She had really hammed it up when she introduced him to the piano, playing bits of whatever songs from childhood she could recall. "Rudolph the Red-Nosed Reindeer," her Christmastime favorite, "The Unicorn," the song about Noah's ark that the Irish Rovers had made popular in the sixties, and "Home on the Range," the official song of the State of Kansas, were a few that came to mind. Marvin didn't seem any more interested in deer and antelope playing than he was in the notes of the scale.

Caitlin tried making the music more personal to him by singing his spelled-out name to the tune of "The Mickey Mouse Club March":

"M-A-R, V-I-N, W-E-L-L-S!"

Marvin just stared off into space. Then Caitlin thought up a tune for herself, a parody of a song from Meredith Willson's Broadway musical, *The Music Man*.

"Well now ya got Caitlin, here in the big city, with a capital C and that rhymes with me and that stands for . . . cool!" she sang, impromptu. Perhaps the effort had no effect on Marvin, but it amused her. She'd been coming up with catchy names for them both ever since.

"Did you miss me while I was away?" she asked. She had no idea how Marvin conceptualized the passage of time. Neither, apparently, did he.

"I dunno," he mumbled.

"Well, I sure missed you. Have you been practicing what I showed you?"

"I dunno," he said again.

"Okay, buddy, I'll see you at our next lesson."

Caitlin could hear Marvin running around the room, yelling, out of control.

Jasmine must have tried to take the phone from him.

When he started banging on the piano, Caitlin hung up.

"Whew!"

She and Jayson had planned to start a family together. With what she knew now, would she expose her children to the risks associated with vaccines?

She reread the lists of symptoms and behavioral problems the plaintiffs had experienced: neurological developmental disorders, attention deficit hyperactivity disorder, speech and language delays, tics, autism, decreased immunity, gastrointestinal disorders—a sympathetic group if the case got before a jury. But that was exactly what Neil was trying to prevent.

Caitlin closed the file and pondered the findings of the studies on autism that she had reviewed. People had proposed various theories to explain why rates were rising rapidly throughout the population. Some investigators considered it entirely possible that vaccine preservatives were causing injuries on a widespread scale, even if the vaccines were otherwise generally safe.

If autism was not a genetic disorder, as some researchers professed, or the result of some parents' approach to childrearing, as old theories had asserted, it could potentially strike any child; the causes were unknown. Mercury, however, was a known neurotoxin, universally recognized as one of the most toxic substances on the planet.

Why would anyone intentionally inject mercury into a human being—or an animal?

The form of mercury found in thimerosal, ethylmercury, was believed to be less destructive than methylmercury, which was sometimes ingested through contaminated fish and other sources. Proponents of the preservative's use in vaccines contended that ethyl-mercury is rapidly excreted from the body. Opponents argued that any exposure would be enough to damage brain cells.

Caitlin wondered why no government agencies were researching the safety of thimerosal. Was it an oversight? Had the preservative been in use for so long that it was presumed to be safe? The public's interest in health and safety warranted closer analysis, she thought; the solution might be as simple as spreading out vaccinations over a greater period of time, thereby giving developing immune systems a chance to adjust.

She dialed Kristof's number. *A reporter's daughter should always have a friend in the press*, she thought as she listened to his recorded message. Kristof was rarely in the office but always got back to her quickly. Caitlin knew Linda, his longtime love, from the Women's Bar Association.

"Kristof! It's Caitlin." She lowered her voice. "Hey, I'm onto something that was supposed to be kept a secret. We should get together—soon. Tonight, even, if you're free. Call me."

Patrice had let it slip when they were at lunch: she and Linda were planning a party at the end of the month for Caitlin's thirty-third birthday. They would kidnap her, if necessary, to pry her away from work.

"That won't be necessary," Caitlin had said.

She missed spending time with friends and was determined to make a greater effort to include people in her life. She loved parties, especially when she was the guest of honor. She wanted to give Kristof a suggestion for the cake—off the record. She wouldn't ruin Linda's plans; she was a good actress. When the time came, she could feign surprise.

She also wanted to tell Kristof to add a name to the guest list. She'd never get over her fear that Kimo wouldn't fit into her life if she didn't give him the chance.

Before leaving the office, Caitlin put photocopies of some of the information she'd gathered about thimerosal into a large manila envelope. She picked up her briefcase and, remembering Dan Fielding's small act of conservation, turned off the light.

∽ 22 ∾

Sam drank the last of a cup of coffee. He groaned when he saw the time. Just how late was this woman going to work?

"Get a life, lady!" he said aloud. After a moment's reflection he muttered, "Who am I to talk?"

She'd called a number with a 202 area code—within the District of Columbia. What medical report was she talking about? Did Neil know about it? Neil wanted to know what Caitlin knew about him—how much did he know about her?

Maybe I could sneak into her office and have a look around . . .

Sam couldn't do that, of course; his task was limited in scope, and he wasn't properly trained. They wouldn't let him see any real action—the risks to everyone would be too great if he botched it.

He cringed when Marvin started screaming. "Aw, hang up the phone already!" he shouted, the way he yelled at the television when his favorite player dropped the ball. He hated being reminded of his daughter's disabilities. She was only three. Undoubtedly, she would require assistance for the rest of her life.

The hassles with Yvonne were ongoing; they fought every time a major decision had to be made. Still, Sam was grateful that Yvonne bore primary responsibility for Jacqueline's care; the little time he spent with his daughter was distressing. He felt so damned helpless and ineffective. He'd dedicated his life to a healing profession, but he couldn't make Jacqueline well.

Sam hated feeling helpless. That was part of why he'd wanted to become a doctor in the first place—so he could help. The goal was embedded in his mind after he witnessed his father's heart attack. One moment his father was selecting a golf club from the bag Sam carried for him; the next moment he was sprawled on the ground. But Sam knew now what he hadn't known as a teen: doctors are not gods. He couldn't save his father, and he couldn't save Jacqueline. His failings haunted him; his deep-seated fears—that he was fundamentally flawed, that God was punishing him for his sins—tormented him.

Too many years of religious indoctrination.

He opened the newspaper he'd picked up in the hotel lobby and checked baseball scores and standings. A beep alerted him to an outgoing call—another D.C. number. The guy's recording said he worked for the *Washington Post.*

Weird coincidence, Sam thought as he scanned the sports section of the *Post.*

When he heard the message Caitlin left, Sam became alarmed.

Wait a minute—the guy's a reporter.

The bitch was going to the papers—soon!

That's just like a woman. Can't keep her mouth shut.

Sam called the number Neil had given him for Carter Simms.

Busy signal—shit. Now what should he do?

Neil had told him to gather information and report anything suspicious; Sam wasn't authorized to do more. But surely they would want him to prevent a leak!

Sam saw an opportunity to show he wasn't afraid to exercise independent judgment under pressure—a chance to again be part of a team with a mission. Maybe he would be welcomed into Neil's inner circle as the hero who saved the day by averting a disaster.

He had to act fast, though. The Rose (as he'd named his target) would soon be in motion. What if she met with the reporter that very night? Would they rendezvous in some dark, secluded spot, like "Deep Throat" in the Watergate leak? Or would she brazenly approach him at his house—or invite him to hers—unaware that Sam was onto her intentions?

He had to stop her. But how? Maybe he should just follow her. The SUV Neil had loaned him was equipped with a state-of-the-art Global Positioning System and other gadgetry. Sam used the computer in the office to look up the home address and phone number for Caitlin Rose on the World Wide Web.

Single women really should have unlisted numbers, he thought as he closed up shop.

He would call Carter Simms again later.

✐ 23 ✐

Caitlin vowed to put aside work concerns over the weekend. She strolled to her car, thinking about what she might do instead. She still wanted to stop by a bookstore and read about cats and dreams; she might also look for a CD about music therapy. She had promised to call Patrice; maybe they could get together for lunch or a movie.

She was considering inviting Kimo over for lunch on Thursday. She wasn't much of a cook, but she could prepare something he would like. She remembered the little Lebanese place where they'd gone the first time she agreed to have dinner with him. The restaurant was in Arlington—a bit out of the way but by now the worst of the traffic should have died down. She could pick up tonight's dinner plus something extra.

Caitlin called directory assistance for the restaurant's telephone number and then phoned in her order. Shawarma, a flavorful mix of spiced beef and lamb, came with rice; the generous portion would be enough for two meals. For lunch with Kimo, vegetarian fare: baba ghanoush, tabouleh, falafel, dolmades, and a serving of those delectable little pastries stuffed with spinach and cheese.

She could also toss a salad, Caitlin thought as she drove toward Arlington, and baklava would be a good dessert—she must remember to add that to her order when she arrived at the restaurant. Passing a Giant grocery store on the corner of Lee Highway and Spout Run Parkway, she decided to stop there for breakfast supplies and salad fixings on the way back. The thought of surprising Kimo excited her. If he already had plans for Independence Day, she would feast alone; she knew that Patrice didn't care for exotic dishes.

Hakim, the owner of the restaurant, greeted Caitlin with a warm smile. He always remembered her, though she went there infrequently. He chatted with her while the cashier added the baklava to her total and a waiter packed up her food. After handing her several bags, Hakim held the door open. Caitlin smiled and thanked him.

When she reached the grocery store, the sky was dark with clouds. She grabbed a box of cereal, a carton of milk, and a banana. The rest would have to wait, she thought as she stood in the express lane; she didn't want to get caught in a downpour. She rushed to her car, anxious to get home.

Traffic was steady, making the left turn onto Lee Highway a challenge. The other exit had a traffic signal; she should have gone out that way. *Too late now.*

She darted across three lanes, slipping into a brief gap in the two-way traffic. Hearing the long complaint of a horn, she looked in the rearview mirror. A black GMC sport utility vehicle had followed her car out of the parking lot, forcing the driver behind the SUV to slam on the brakes.

Amazing how much emotion can be expressed through a simple instrument like a horn!

Caitlin looked in the mirror again. The GMC was following too closely. Whatever happened to keeping a safe following distance? Caitlin signaled and moved into the right lane, ready to turn at the upcoming gas station.

The stormy weather was expected to last into the weekend, but Caitlin hoped the skies would clear for the Fourth. If the weather didn't favor a picnic on the West Lawn of the Capitol with the gang from the office, she could always stop by Chris's place.

Now an environmental lobbyist, Chris had started hosting an open house for Independence Day when he worked at Legal Aid. His balcony in Mount Pleasant afforded a great view of the fireworks. People milled in and out throughout the afternoon and evening; some brought snacks and beverages, others came to see who showed up, and some stayed to "ooh" and "aah" at the fireworks display. Caitlin had gone to Chris's gathering twice—once with Jayson, and once without him. The holiday might be a good time to reconnect with old friends, she thought as she filled the tank with gasoline.

She continued driving along Lee Highway. She wasn't very familiar with this part of Arlington, and the interchanges at Rosslyn always confused her; unlike the simple grid layout of a town like Topeka, the old colonial routes meandered in all directions. She would need to watch the signs closely to find the highway that connected to the GW Parkway heading south.

When she glanced in the mirror again, Caitlin was surprised to see a black GMC behind her. Could it be the same SUV that left the Giant when she did?

Her thoughts flashed back to a time in college when a man followed her out of the library. After several blocks—when she was certain she was being followed—Caitlin went to the bookstore where a friend of hers worked; he walked with her back to her dormitory.

But why was she thinking of that now? Panicking, she made a sudden right turn onto a residential street. The GMC continued along Lee Highway.

Caitlin drove into a parking garage beneath an apartment building. She decided to wait there for a while, just to be sure.

I'm being silly, she told herself, and tried to slow her breathing. *Why would anyone be following me?*

She drove a fancy car and wore expensive-looking clothes. Crimes happened all the time; some nut could have spotted her in the grocery store and followed her out.

When her heart stopped pounding, she slowly drove down city streets toward Rosslyn, avoiding Lee Highway until just before the entrance to Interstate 66. The distance from there to the exit for Highway 110 was short, and 110 would lead her to the GW Parkway. If she reached Alexandria without any sign of the GMC, she'd be home safe.

A light rain started falling as Caitlin drove past Arlington National Cemetery. The Pentagon was soon in sight.

Damn! I missed the turn.

No matter; Route 1, Jefferson Davis Highway, would also get her to Alexandria. Route 1 wasn't as direct as the Parkway, but commuter traffic through Crystal City would be minimal now.

As she neared Old Town Alexandria, Caitlin began to relax. The long stretch of highway alongside the former Potomac rail yard in the industrial area outside of Alexandria's city limits was practically deserted. Rain was falling harder now; Caitlin increased the speed of the windshield wipers. A loud clap of thunder startled her. She checked to see if the headlights were on, decelerating when the upcoming traffic signal turned red. On the other side of the bridge that passed over the railroad tracks, Jefferson Davis Highway would become Henry Street. Caitlin's nerves were frazzled and her dinner was cold, but she was almost home.

While she waited for the light to change, she dialed Kimo's number. Three days had passed since he'd left a message on her answering machine; it was time she responded.

"Keep it simple, sweetheart," Kimo's recording advised in his best Bogie impersonation. Caitlin smiled. Kimo changed his outgoing message as often as she changed her nail polish.

"Kimo, it's Cait. I just had the strangest experience."

But what could she say about it, really? She wasn't certain she'd been followed—maybe she was overreacting. After her experience in Ireland, she was no longer sure what was real and what was imaginary.

"Oh, well, never mind; it's over now." She took a breath and continued. "You might be interested in what I've learned about the pharmaceutical industry. Did you know that last year the top pharmaceutical companies showed greater profit than the top auto manufacturers, oil companies, airlines, or media conglomerates? Can you imagine how much money that is? Think how much good those millions of dollars could do if they went to health care or education instead of lobbyists and advertising."

She paused, wondering how long Kimo's tape would allow her to talk before her time ran out.

"And get this: a significant amount of the research needed to develop new drugs is done by taxpayer-funded scientists! Remember I told you I'm working on a case about thimerosal? There's a bill pending in Congress that would virtually wipe out all the current safeguards that ensure vaccine safety—and absolve everyone involved from any responsibility for injuries and deaths that result from adverse reactions to vaccines."

The light turned green. Caitlin checked the rearview mirror before accelerating. Two bright specks in the distance were getting larger as another vehicle approached.

"We can talk about the case later."

She glanced in the mirror again as she rounded the sharp curve onto the bridge. She couldn't tell whether the vehicle was traveling in her lane or the lane to her left, but it seemed to be moving very fast.

With a softer tone, she said, "I'd like to talk about Ireland, too. In pers—"

In the next instant, Caitlin realized that the black GMC to her left was encroaching into her lane. With a cement barrier to her right, she had nowhere to go to escape a collision. She was trapped.

"Oh my God!" she yelled. Time slowed as she registered the hateful look on the driver's face.

The SUV skidded into the side of Caitlin's car, slamming it into the cement barrier. After bouncing off the barrier, the BMW was struck again by the GMC. Finally, both vehicles came to rest on the bridge.

✑ 24 ✑

Kimo returned home later than usual. He'd met his friend Barry for happy hour at a bar in Georgetown, and then Barry drove him home. Kimo knew his bike wouldn't fit into Barry's convertible; he left it at the firm. He would take the Metro to work in the morning.

He checked the messages on his answering machine. He was pleased to hear the passion in Caitlin's voice. He knew she was frustrated by her job; she didn't need to say the words. The last part of her message had been cut off. She sounded concerned, stressed. He called her home number from the phone in his bedroom. No answer.

Kimo had only a vague idea where Caitlin lived; she'd never invited him over. They always met somewhere different when they got together. He figured she had drawn an imaginary boundary delineating how close he was permitted to get to her; he could only find it by trial and error.

Rather like a dog running into an electric fence, he thought as he walked to the kitchen to prepare dinner.

The house was quiet. Kimo and his housemates all followed different schedules and routines. They gathered together about once a month for a dinner or party or house meeting, usually when Jack was in town.

A musician in a bluegrass band, Jack was on the road much of the time. He kept a few things in a room in the basement, where he bunked when he needed to. Lisa was the other feminine presence besides Melody. Lisa liked to eat dinner early; she was usually in her room by the time Kimo got home. Lately, Melody had been spending most of her evenings with a new lover—but she was always back in time to fix Kimo breakfast.

He opened the refrigerator door. After considering his options, he pulled out containers of leftover red beans and quinoa and set them on the counter. For Kimo, cooking was a meditative time. He thought about Caitlin's message while he chopped an onion. He was eager to tell her his views about prescription drugs and the prevailing disease model in modern medicine.

Western science is good at naming syndromes and identifying viruses and bacteria, Kimo thought as he chopped fresh parsley to sprinkle atop the quinoa. High-tech gadgetry had resulted in outstanding research capabilities. *But the allopathic practitioner's understanding of the body as a whole is incomplete.* The treatment of symptoms didn't address the root causes of disease, and quick fixes didn't touch the systemic imbalances that were usually present in chronic ailments.

Educated consumers had begun seeking natural treatments in ever-increasing numbers, and Kimo was confident about the viability of his future profession. He didn't want to alienate people by preaching, but he did want to spread the word that alternatives to conventional medicine were safe and effective. He wanted to nudge people to make needed changes so they could live healthier and more satisfying lives. Getting people to try something new and unconventional often took some convincing, however; they needed reasons, explanations—proof. Words like "responsibility" were not as appealing as the seemingly easier fix of taking a pill, and a ready market existed for every new breakthrough drug.

Kimo knew that the pharmaceutical industry would fight to maintain its dominance in the health care marketplace. Vaccines and antibiotics were the public health agencies' weapons of choice in the battle against infectious disease.

Everything's a war in this country. He tossed the diced onion and a clove of garlic into a pan, added olive oil, and turned the knob on the gas stove.

And it wasn't just here; war had been the way of the world since Cain and Abel. Fearful, angry, unhappy people tended to inflict their misery on others. People who loved—life, themselves, others—had more interesting ways to spend their time.

The world needs more joy, more opportunities for creative expression. More love.

The good news was that people could change their lives—and the world—by changing their thinking.

Kimo remembered how bitter and resentful he had once been. For a long time, he'd felt like an outsider, alone and adrift. He'd separated himself from a culture where he failed to find meaning and belonging. Finally, he had found a direction—*chosen* one. Now he knew that a paradigm shift was needed—and was imminent.

We all need to find a new way of relating. To each other, to our bodies, to the earth. After rinsing tender beet greens, he added them to the sauté.

He wanted to help others move through the transition, and he wanted to start with Caitlin. She had helped him change his life; now he had something to give back. But where to start?

"The scientific model recognizes no difference between chlorinated, treated water and spring water," he rehearsed aloud. "Under the old model, a carbohydrate is a carbohydrate, a calorie is a calorie, and water is water, regardless of the source—regardless of the quality; the taste; the subtle energies."

When everything has a price tag, even genes become commodities. The understanding that the body is a temple of consciousness is lost.

As Kimo cut the greens off the top of a carrot, he recalled his beloved teacher's emphasis on the importance of maintaining a positive attitude while preparing food. The cook's care—or lack of it—was imparted to the food and to those who ate it, his teacher had said. A good cook, like any other artist, concerned himself not only with recipes and techniques, but also with the quality expressing through his creation. Kimo grated the carrot; it would add contrast to a green salad. He continued his imaginary dialogue with Caitlin.

"Nature, it seems, is inconsistent and constantly fluctuating, cycling through seasons and moon phases and taking life forms along for the ride. Trees don't produce uniform or blemish-free fruit. When judged according to an industrial standard, organic products are cosmetically imperfect and therefore less marketable."

Part of the appeal of modern pharmaceutical compounds, Kimo realized, was that the potency didn't change from one pill to the next the way, say, a tea made from roots and herbs did. Synthetic compounds were untainted by the variables that affect plants and living things, and could be widely distributed with the expectation that the substance would behave predictably in the population as a whole.

Kimo moved aside and turned toward where he had been standing. "So what's the problem?" Caitlin might ask.

"The problem," he said, moving back to his original position, "is that humans believe they can improve upon nature's grand design. Companies attempt to imitate the effects of nature's apothecary by manufacturing synthetic versions of substances believed to be effective in treating particular symptoms. But nature's products come whole and complete, with co-factors that scientists may never completely isolate and understand, as well as life-giving forces radiated by the earth and the sun—qualities that cannot be produced in a factory."

Life in a laboratory is sterile, Kimo thought. He stirred the sauté one last time and turned off the heat. After sprinkling sunflower seeds on top of the salad, he added a dressing Melody had made.

He moved back to Caitlin's position. "But synthetic products are unaffected by droughts, depleted soils, and growing seasons. The effective properties found in a plant or bark can be duplicated in a lab and the process patented. Isn't that a good thing—especially when so many plants and trees are disappearing?"

"Wouldn't it make more sense to protect the real thing than to settle for an imitation?" Kimo countered. "The corporate mentality is averse to life. It perpetuates a worldview that acknowledges no difference between natural hormones or breasts or vitamins or neurotransmitters and those produced in a lab. Even the word *antibiotic* means 'against life.' What's *live* spelled backwards? That's right: *evil.* Why are so many species becoming extinct in a relatively short period of time? Industrialization and its byproducts have completely altered the fragile ecosystems that support all life on this planet. Once we accept the imbalances as normal, we gradually forget what 'healthy' even looks like. Lobbyists take over and convince decision makers to do things like fluoridate and chlorinate the water supplies. Government bureaucrats decide what levels of pesticides and contaminants in our food, air, water, teeth, and bodies are safe. And we trust them to monitor these things."

Politicians endorse such practices in the name of "free enterprise," Kimo thought as he spooned food onto a plate. He grabbed some utensils and walked toward the dining room.

But everyone who owns the stocks or buys the products of the offenders encourages and supports them too. As the radicals of the sixties had professed, if you're not part of the solution, you're part of the problem.

Kimo set his plate on the table and retrieved the day's mail from the mailbox by the front door before sitting down to eat.

The day always comes when the evidence of deleterious effects can no longer be ignored. By then, the damage has been done and the profits collected. The penalties and costs to the offenders rarely touch the benefits pocketed, ensuring the cycle will repeat in the next profitable enterprise. Meanwhile, the rest of us are stuck with soaring health insurance costs and increasing rates of disease.

That was what he would tell Caitlin—and anyone else who would listen. He knew that many people would consider his opinions extreme, so he mostly kept them to himself. He could afford to view unsustainable lifestyles and practices with disdain, for he hadn't benefited from the prevailing model; he had no vested interest. With nothing to lose, he didn't perceive change as a threat. He was open to questioning everything in his search for answers. He didn't need to await proof from established medical journals and top scientists. He had experienced alternatives that worked.

Kimo held his hands over his plate and closed his eyes in silent prayer before picking up his fork. Someday, science would bear out the validity of acupuncture meridians and etheric energy fields surrounding the human body, he thought—maybe even the existence of the soul. The real lack, he was convinced, was a spiritual one. People no longer treated life as sacred. Most people's eyes couldn't see the glow emitted by living organisms, and they lacked faith in the Great Unknown. "Invisible" was hard to recognize, much less measure or prove to scientific levels of certainty.

When he finished eating, Kimo sorted through the pile of mail, setting aside coupons and advertising circulars for the recycling bin.

You can sell anything with good marketing.

He had no interest in eating pesticide-laden, genetically modified foods grown by corporations that manufactured products like carpeting. *No matter how sexy their ads.*

He leafed through the latest issue of *Science* magazine. He felt no disdain for the scientific method; he appreciated the role of science in explaining and demonstrating the principles and laws of nature, and when nature's secrets were used in the service of humanity and earth's other kingdoms, he applauded the achievements. The seeds of inspiration and insight that led to scientific discoveries and inventions could often be traced to observation of the natural world or the symbolism of a dream. All too frequently, the fruits of scientific discoveries had been used as part of officially sanctioned efforts to gain dominance over others, but that did not detract from the brilliance of the original work. Inventors and visionaries, by definition, introduced ideas and practices that more conventional types found threatening.

Being different requires strength and courage.

Kimo thought back to his high school days, when he'd flirted with the idea of dropping out; he didn't fit in anyway. Only after many years had passed could he see that he hadn't really been excluded—he had excluded himself. He wasn't interested in being part of the scene around him. Maybe that experience had helped prepare him for his current role. He was still an outsider but no longer a defiant rebel. Now he was a pioneer, a champion of a burgeoning discipline. He didn't waste his energy fighting the system; he was energized by his enthusiasm for building a new model of health and wellness. The distinction was subtle, but it was enough to alter the way he viewed the world and his role in it.

If only Caitlin could see the difference, Kimo thought as he carried his plate to the kitchen. Maybe she would see him in a different light.

He phoned her again from the phone in the kitchen. Still no answer. He would keep trying to reach her until he knew she was all right.

∾ 25 ∾

Martha Johnson fidgeted during the short ride from the airport to the Embassy Suites Hotel on Jefferson Davis Highway. She had come as soon as she could. What more could anyone expect of her? She was thankful Caitlin still listed her as an emergency contact, in spite of their lack of communication in recent years.

A mother is always a mother.

The taxi driver stopped in front of the entrance to the hotel. The next passenger was waiting outside for pickup—a man with his arm in a sling. He opened Martha's door with his good arm and helped her out.

She didn't like feeling rushed. The man was settled in the back seat and whisked away before Martha could pick up the suitcase the driver had deposited at the curb.

People on the East Coast are always in such a hurry.

Maybe Caitlin would be ready to come home soon, to Kansas. She'd had her career, things hadn't panned out with Jayson, and she would need a mother's care when she awoke.

Martha checked into her room and freshened up. It was nearly noon when she summoned another taxi to take her to the hospital. She hadn't eaten anything all morning; she was too upset. Of all the times she had imagined a reunion with Caitlin, she'd never dreamed it would be under such tragic circumstances. She paid the taxi driver and entered the hospital. After a stop at the information desk, she located Caitlin's room.

The sight of her unconscious daughter made Martha gasp. She stifled a cry and turned away. After a few deep breaths and a prayer for strength, she looked again.

Caitlin's head was bandaged. Her neck was in a brace, her left arm in a cast. The visible patches of her face were cut and bruised and swollen. A heart monitor beeped out the pattern of her heart-beat, a feeding tube ran through her nose, and a bag of solution dripped into an intravenous tube that was attached to her right arm.

Martha sat for hours by the hospital bed, holding Caitlin's right hand and singing; she didn't know what else to do. If she could will Caitlin awake, she would.

"He's got the whole world in His hands, He's got the whole wide world in His hands," she sang.

Her eyes moistened when she remembered a young Caitlin, ill with a fever. Martha had sung that song as she rocked little Catie. Now, as then, her baby's life was in His hands.

Finally, the door opened and a doctor appeared. He motioned Martha into the hall and extended his hand. "I'm Jeffrey Stanton."

Martha shook the doctor's hand. It felt cold.

"What can you tell me, Doctor? I hardly recognize her. Her face . . ."

"Her hair was shaved off in the emergency room to facilitate the removal of glass shards from her face and scalp. An intracranial monitor was inserted as a precautionary measure, but there's no sign of swelling so that's been removed." Doctor Stanton flipped through pages of chart notes. "Her left arm was crushed and she suffered a whiplash. Her skull was fractured; that caused some pooling in her brain but probably helped minimize swelling. Swelling can lead to greater complications."

Martha's head swam as she tried to comprehend what the doctor was saying—and what it meant for Caitlin's recovery.

"Her condition was upgraded this morning from critical, so she was moved out of Intensive Care." Doctor Stanton closed the chart and looked at Martha. "Her injuries will heal. Our biggest concern is how well her brain is functioning. We won't know the full extent of damage unless she regains consciousness."

Martha's heart skipped a beat. "Unless? You mean . . . she might not?"

Caitlin was alive. She had survived a horrible collision. Surely she hadn't been spared from death only to lie in a vegetative state for the rest of her life.

"There's no way to tell. There's a lot we don't know yet about coma, or the brain. The body seems to have its own wisdom and timetable. There's no evidence of seizures—that's good. We'll keep checking her vital signs for any changes."

Martha wrung her hands. "Isn't there anything I can do?"

"We have an excellent staff," Dr. Stanton said. "Someone will go over all that with you—what to expect throughout the recovery and rebuilding process. For now, I'd suggest you get some rest yourself." He squeezed Martha's shoulder. "Your daughter is in good hands."

Martha returned to Caitlin's bedside, comforted by the doctor's words. Hadn't she just been singing about His hands? Surely this doctor was the agent of God's will that the Lord had sent to help her Catie through this time of trial. Martha extended her hand toward Caitlin's face. Not knowing where she could touch her without causing her pain, she withdrew it.

"I know you've been angry," she said tearfully. "I thought, given some time . . ." She tightened her reign on her emotions. "But you're so stubborn. Use that stubbornness now—to hang on!"

Martha ate an early dinner in the hospital cafeteria. Walking back to Caitlin's room, she prayed: *Please, dear God, let her be all right. She's been through so much already.*

A white rose was lying outside Caitlin's door. Martha picked it up and sniffed it. How long had that been there? Who would be visiting at this time of day?

She phoned for a taxi. She was still numb from the shock—the news, her fears, the sight of Caitlin all banged up and unconscious. Resting quietly in the back seat of the cab, she held the rose close to her face and breathed in the delicate fragrance. She settled into an uneasy relaxation as the motion of the car rolling down the highway lulled her toward sleep.

Maybe the Good Lord in His wisdom put Caitlin into a deep sleep so she could rest and recover enough to face the long journey ahead.

She would trust in that wisdom.

Somehow, everything will work out for the best.

An explosion of fireworks startled her as the taxi turned into the driveway of the hotel. Martha paid the driver and stood at the curb for a moment, looking up at the sky to see if she could spot a burst of color, or even a star to wish upon. She saw only clouds and the haze of a streetlamp. Disappointed, she turned toward the hotel entrance.

Her daughter was a fighter. That hadn't always been easy on Martha, but at times like these, she was grateful. Caitlin had a fighting chance to fully recover, and Martha would do everything in her power to see that she did.

PART THREE

MOTHERED

✐ 26 ✐

Awareness, yes, but thoughts are different . . . expansive. Images stream by. Brilliant bursts of color in the night sky. Fleeting glimpses of people. They seem familiar, but they drift by so fast . . .

An ancient land. A council; eight men, one woman. She begins to speak but a man interrupts. *Oh, God—Neil! But he looks different. How can he be Neil and yet not be Neil?* Frustration at being silenced is all too familiar to her . . .

The image shifts to Delphi. A ceremony, deep in a cave. She is kneeling. The High Priestess touches her bowed head and declares, "You shall be the next Oracle, the mirror for men's souls!"

No chance to dwell on that image before the next one comes, like a waveform through time that has finally reached the shore of the present.

Is there a present in this dimension of being? Timelessness and spaciousness seem limitless—yet there is movement, as if she is watching a play and acting in it at the same time! Aware of no pain or fear, she observes with detached curiosity.

She is standing on craggy rocks that overlook the ocean. Wait— this one actually feels like *her*, Caitlin Rose. She looks happy, singing a song—but what language?

167

She stops singing when she hears a familiar tune from childhood. It sounds far away but irresistible, like a siren song. She listens closely:

> She's got the whole world in her hands; she's got the whole wide world in her hands.

Mommy. *I want my mommy!*
It all fades again. *No, don't go!*
She reaches out but there is nothing to hold onto . . .

✎ 27 ✎

Martha spent Friday morning at the hospital and then rented a car for the weekend. After checking out of the hotel, she drove to Alexandria to find Caitlin's townhouse. She parked in the driveway, picked up a few newspapers lying there, and then walked around to the fenced backyard and unlatched the wooden gate. The sliding glass door to the lower level of the townhouse was unlocked.

Caitlin never was very careful about locking doors. Martha stepped inside and glanced around. *At least it's tidy.*

Unable to locate a key for the front door, Martha called someone to change the locks. While she waited, she looked around. Nina, the occupational therapist, had suggested that bringing in a few of Caitlin's favorite things might help stimulate her senses. Her lack of responsiveness wasn't unusual at this stage of coma, according to Doctor Stanton. He'd pointed out the lesions on the left side of Caitlin's brain when he showed Martha the brain scan images, but he offered no predictions about her recovery.

Martha chose perfume from the upstairs bathroom and a photo that was propped against a lamp on the nightstand in Caitlin's bedroom. From Caitlin's collection of compact discs, she selected a few favorites—*The Music Man, The King and I,* and *Oklahoma!*

I must ask Ray to bring along a portable CD player when he comes. Thinking of Ray made her smile. *Such a dear man!*

He had offered to drive her car to Virginia so she could get around more easily. Caitlin's car had been destroyed in the crash. Martha could manage all right using Metro trains and buses, but Ray worried about her safety. Martha agreed; having her car was the best option. She disliked driving in an unfamiliar city, but taxicabs were expensive—especially for the distance to the hospital from Alexandria—and renting a car for the duration of her stay didn't make sense. She might be there a while.

Ray expected to arrive on Sunday. He could only stay a few days, he'd said. He was semi-retired and still had commitments. He led an active life—a welcome change from Charlie's reclusiveness in his later years.

After the locksmith left, Martha put Caitlin's things into a tote bag and tried out the new key, locking the front door behind her.

She fiddled with the compact disc player in the rental car and carefully placed *The King and I* disc into the tray. Ray and his son tried to keep her up-to-date with the latest technologies, but Martha still liked listening to her old vinyl records now and then, played on the phonograph she'd kept from the early days of her marriage to Charlie.

Caitlin's interest in the theater must have come from me. For birthdays and special events, Martha had sometimes taken the children to shows and performances around the Kansas City area. She remembered seeing *Bye Bye Birdie* at the old church building—it was one of the few outings that both children had enjoyed. Wanting to be like Conrad Birdie, Bobby later started a garage band; he played lead guitar. Caitlin serenaded anyone who would listen with her rendition of "Put on a Happy Face" for days after the show. Before long, she started pestering Martha to let her audition for a local production of *The Music Man.* Caitlin had recently started taking piano lessons and thought she'd be perfect for the role of Amaryllis, the piano student taking lessons from Marian the Librarian. Martha thought Caitlin was too young for the stage but watched proudly, years later, when she starred in a high school production of *South Pacific.* Even now, the memory brought tears to her eyes.

Martha hadn't ever told Caitlin how precious she was; she might get a big head. That was the thinking in those days: children needed discipline, and parents shouldn't spoil them. Martha's parents didn't spare the rod if any of their children got out of line. In the Clayton household, silence was golden—especially when Father was at home. If the door to his study was closed, he was not to be disturbed.

Martha drove toward the hospital, stopping at a hobby supply store along the way. She selected a plain wooden frame for the photo, a small vase for the rose, and emerald-green yarn for a cap. She'd brought her knitting needles along; she would need something to keep her hands busy while she kept vigil, and Caitlin would need something to cover her head while her hair grew out. The color would bring out the green in Caitlin's eyes, Martha thought as she left the store. She winced at the memory of her daughter's battered face.

After parking near the hospital, Martha turned off the motor and sat quietly for a moment, praying for strength. She was a firm believer in the power of prayer. Before leaving Kansas, she'd asked her church group to add Caitlin's name to the prayer list. She must keep a positive attitude, she reminded herself as she walked toward the hospital—for herself, and for Caitlin.

She took her place in the chair by Caitlin's bed and reached for the tote bag. She dabbed some perfume on her wrist and then pulled out the yarn and knitting needles.

Martha looked at her wristwatch. Could the time really be seven o'clock? She must have been dozing. She put aside the knitting and gently massaged her fingers. Her stomach growled. She would need to stock Caitlin's kitchen with supplies for the coming weeks—or months.

She slowly lifted herself from the chair, her body stiff from sitting too long in one position. Shopping could wait; she'd done enough for today. Ray would probably take her out for a meal on Sunday. For tonight, she'd find a restaurant in Alexandria. She'd noticed an Italian place near Caitlin's townhouse; maybe she would eat supper there.

She stood gazing at Caitlin, wondering where her headstrong daughter had escaped to now. *Oh, Caitlin! There's so much you don't know.*

Being unable to communicate with Caitlin these last few years had been difficult, and Martha had never stopped hoping for an opportunity to resume a relationship. She'd feared that if she pushed too hard, she would only drive Caitlin further away. She had to let Caitlin come around in her own time. *Still.*

When Martha arrived at Caitlin's room on Saturday morning, Nurse Rachel handed her a stack of cards and a yellow rose that had been left outside Caitlin's door the previous evening. Martha rinsed out the new vase in the bathroom sink, filled it with tap water, and placed the rose inside. She set the vase on a small table, next to her Bible, all the while wondering who was leaving roses by Caitlin's door at odd hours.

Martha put the cards on display on top of the dresser. The room was beginning to feel a bit cheerier as it filled with flowers, cards, and balloons from Caitlin's friends and colleagues.

When the staff came to check on Caitlin, Martha asked them about their lives away from the hospital. Did they have vacation plans? Family in the area? Nina, the O.T., was divorced and in the midst of a tense custody battle, Martha learned. Rachel, the nurse with the thick black hair, had once thought she wanted to be a doctor but really liked being a nurse, she said. She made suggestions about stores and restaurants in the area and helped Martha find her way around.

Mari, a widow, was about Martha's age. A licensed massage therapist, she volunteered at the hospital once a week. She showed Martha how to massage Caitlin's feet with oil. She also told her about reflexology points that corresponded to different organs and parts of the body. Martha had never heard of reflexology and knew she wouldn't remember the points Mari showed her, but she found the concept intriguing.

Alone with Caitlin, Martha shared the latest news of family and friends.

"Do you remember Jeannie Davis?" she asked, half expecting Caitlin to open her eyes and utter a tart reply. "Her mother was your piano teacher for awhile. Jeannie just got married. I hear it was a lovely wedding. They're living over in Mission."

Nina had told Martha to assume that Caitlin could hear, and understand, anything said in her presence. "Don't talk about things that might upset her," Nina counseled.

Martha hadn't ever understood her daughter well enough to guess what might upset her. The things that mattered to Martha didn't seem to mean much to Caitlin. They'd had battles over everything from Sunday school to the piano.

For Martha, playing the piano was a relaxing pastime that also brought pleasure to others. She didn't learn to play until after she was married . . . while she was carrying Caitlin, in fact. When she sent Caitlin for lessons—an opportunity Martha had been denied as a child—she was offering a gift she thought would bring Caitlin enjoyment for years to come. She also thought the discipline of a daily practice would be good for Caitlin, whose passions sometimes overcame her reason. But Caitlin complained that she wasn't having any fun; all she did after school was homework and practice. She wanted to be outside riding her bike or climbing trees, like Bobby. Piano, for her, was just another chore.

Martha sighed. Parenting was not an easy business. She'd done the best she could while contending with her own worries and disappointments. Still, maybe she should have listened more instead of always thinking she knew what was best for Caitlin.

She held up the cap and admired her handiwork. A few more stitches along the band and it would be finished.

Rachel came by before taking her lunch break. Caitlin's blood pressure was higher than normal, she said. She asked Martha to leave the room for a while.

Martha bought a sandwich and a bag of chips in the cafeteria and walked to a nearby park to enjoy a breath of fresh air, but the sweltering heat and humidity soon made the chilled air of the hospital more appealing. She ate the sandwich in the cafeteria and then walked the long corridor toward Caitlin's room. A doctor was standing in the hallway, talking to Rachel and scribbling notes in a chart. He turned toward Martha when he saw her approaching.

"Mrs. Johnson," he said, looking up from his notes, "I'm Doctor Tanner, Doctor Stanton's partner. I'll be on call this weekend." He extended his hand.

"Nice to meet you," Martha said, squeezing the doctor's outstretched hand. She glanced at Rachel before asking, "Is anything wrong?"

"There's been a change in your daughter's condition," Dr. Tanner said. "She's responding to some stimuli, which indicates she's entering into another stage. She may be slightly conscious at times—she may moan or cry or open her eyes, but there's still no real awareness of her surroundings."

Martha brightened. "Well, that's good, right?"

"It's an improvement. There's no way to tell how much further she'll progress. If she does regain consciousness, she may suffer from memory loss. She probably won't remember the accident."

"She will know me, won't she?"

Doctor Tanner mustered a polite smile. "Let's hope for the best," he said.

Martha stayed at the hospital until early in the evening, hoping for a sign that Caitlin was emerging from the coma. At times, she noticed a twitch in Caitlin's lip, and she thought she heard a slight murmur. But Caitlin remained lost in some twilight zone. Martha kissed her cheek and left.

On Sunday afternoon, Martha was paging through a copy of *Reader's Digest* when she heard a moan. She looked up and saw Caitlin squinting.

"Caitlin! Oh, I'm so glad you're all right!"

"Wha— Wha—?" Caitlin croaked in a hoarse voice. She attempted to shield her eyes from the bright lights, but the cast on her left arm and the intravenous tube attached to her right arm limited her movements.

"You've been in an accident, honey," Martha said. She moved toward the window to close the curtains. "Don't try to move. Let me call someone." She reached for the call button.

Caitlin strained to lift her head off the pillow. "M-m . . . Ma-a?" she squawked.

"She's awake!" Martha announced when Rachel arrived. She was tempted to add, "It's a miracle!" and get down on her knees and thank the Lord, but decided to wait for a favorable prognosis before counting her blessings.

Rachel quickly surveyed the situation. "I'll page Doctor Tanner."

Caitlin tried to speak but could only whimper.

"Stay calm, sweetheart," Martha said, patting Caitlin's hand. "The doctor will be here soon. Everything's going to be all right."

Martha was elated. For the first time in years, her daughter needed her.

While Doctor Tanner examined Caitlin, Martha called Bobby from the pay phone in the waiting area. He would want to know the latest news, even if it was the middle of the night in the Southern Hemisphere.

Since his marriage to Sarah, Bobby had become more thoughtful and communicative than he'd been during the years he was roaming around with the Coast Guard. Martha and Ray had even been Down Under once to visit Bobby and Sarah after the birth of their son, Derek.

Martha's relationship with Bobby wasn't burdened with unspoken expectations the way her relationship with Caitlin was. Martha had sometimes felt deprived of all the mother-daughter activities she'd hoped to share with Caitlin. Perhaps she had assumed that a daughter would be more like her than like Charlie, and she felt a bit let down. Given a second chance, though, she would do things differently. She would cherish Caitlin's uniqueness.

"Didn' I tell ya she'd be awake in time for her birthday?" Bobby joked when Martha told him Caitlin was out of the coma. "My sister will do anything for attention."

"Oh, Bobby," Martha clucked. "I'll call when I know more." After a small pause, she added, "I love you."

She hadn't heard those words much in her childhood. Her parents didn't share their feelings openly, and Martha could only guess at them. She had often wondered if they were disappointed by her marriage to Charlie, though they clearly loved their grandchildren. It wasn't until she was in her fifties that Martha acquired the grit and confidence to freely express what she felt. Leaving Charlie was a result of that emancipation. She was nearing sixty now, and her parents were gone. She couldn't tell them how she felt, but she could tell her children.

Doctor Tanner emerged from Caitlin's room. Martha hurried over to him.

"How is she, Doctor?" she asked, walking alongside him.

"We'll know more after we run some tests and evaluate her level of functioning," he replied. "Then we can develop a comprehensive treatment program."

His manner was neutral and professional; his tone, neither encouraging nor discouraging. He paused before turning down another corridor.

"It's normal for patients in Caitlin's condition to experience some confusion and agitation," he warned. "Be prepared for mood swings and uncontrollable emotions as her brain adapts to changed circumstances."

Mood swings?

"For Caitlin, that *is* normal," Martha murmured. She returned to Caitlin's room to gather her things.

What a full day! She needed to get back to the townhouse and straighten up before Ray's arrival. She hated being away from him, but this was her chance to rebuild a relationship with Caitlin, and she welcomed the opportunity.

She paused by Caitlin's bed for a moment, smiling at her sleeping daughter. Feelings of gratitude welled up in her heart as teardrops wetted her eyes. She turned in time to glimpse a shadow moving outside the room. She stepped into the empty corridor; a nearby stairway exit door was closing. Looking down, Martha saw a red rose lying on the threshold to Caitlin's room.

She picked up the flower and added it to the vase.

Mystery roses.

❧ 28 ❧

Caitlin adjusted the scarf that Martha had wrapped around her head. The cap her mother had knitted might be nice in winter, but for now she preferred the feel of the smooth, light silk against her tender scalp. Gently, she touched her face. The scabs were slowly healing.

Time had a funny quality, though there wasn't anything about her situation that Caitlin found amusing. Memories of the days prior to the accident were spotty. She remembered a dispute with Neil, and she recognized the man in the photograph by her bed, though she couldn't recall his name or how she knew him. She couldn't recall last week, for that matter.

Martha brought a calendar to the hospital and marked an "X" through the date before she left each night. Caitlin was able to count how many days she had been there, but she had little context for making sense of the rest. Saying "Today is August 17, 1996" didn't mean anything to her. She knew that more than a month had passed since her awakening. The injury itself was only partly to blame for her fuzzy memory—medications played a significant role in her diminished cognitive functioning. Regular times for meals and therapies gave structure to her days.

She used the thumb of her left hand to push a few chunks of carrot onto the spoon she gripped with her right hand. She'd lost the coordination of the right side of her body but, unlike her left arm, her right arm wasn't weighed down by a cast. She paused and tried to remember the name of the occupational therapist who had been teaching her how to feed herself. *Nita?* No, that didn't seem right. Oh well, whoever she was, she'd told Caitlin she just needed patience and practice—and time.

Hungry, Caitlin was determined to move the food from the plate into her mouth. Martha hovered nearby, ready to help. Caitlin hated feeling so exposed. Martha watched every movement and witnessed every failure. Being spoon-fed by her mother was not an option. She *must* succeed.

Carefully, she moved her right hand toward her face and opened her mouth. Her jerky arm movements sent the pieces of carrot scattering around the plate and tray. Frustrated, Caitlin groaned and swiped at the tray with her arm, sending it clattering to the floor.

"I know, sweetheart," Martha said. "Your body needs to find its coordination again. It's not unusual." Martha went to the adjoining bathroom for a towel to clean up the mess.

Martha's placating manner only irritated Caitlin. "Is . . . that . . . sup-p-posed ta . . . help?"

She was tired of hearing about the "normal" stages of recovery. Patience had never been her best attribute, and her usual coping mechanisms were useless in her present condition. She was trapped in a body that felt like an unwieldy burden. The simplest movements took a tremendous effort of will and strength. She felt defenseless and completely incapable of . . . *running away.*

"Wha—wha—what . . . are . . . you . . . doo-ing here . . . anyway?" she asked her mother.

"We're all very concerned about you, Caitlin—Ray and I, and your brother. Bobby's been prepared to fly from Australia on a moment's notice."

Oh, God.

She thought she'd gotten away from all this. She didn't even want to hear Ray's name. And Bobby—well, when had he ever been there for her in her entire life? Energy, including the energy required for thinking, was now a precious commodity. She'd rather not spend her thoughts on her mother's bed partner and her uniformed brother. Or had Bobby left the service? She couldn't remember things the way she used to. That should probably bother her, but maybe her worry brain cells had been destroyed as well.

"So give him a . . . a mead-ow!" she remarked, fascinated by the sound her mouth made when she could clearly picture the image of a medal. Even after weeks of speech therapy, communication was painstaking.

"Listen to me, Caitlin Marie!" Martha said, looking directly at Caitlin.

The inclusion of her middle name succeeded in getting Caitlin's attention. These days, she was easily distracted and lacked the ability to concentrate on more than a few simple thoughts at a time: *I'm hungry; I don't like this food. My neck hurts. This cast is too heavy. I'm stuck here. With her.*

"We're all you've got."

"Do—Don't re-mind me," Caitlin mumbled slowly, avoiding eye contact.

"My God, you can't admit you need help, even now?"

Caitlin sulked. Martha disposed of the carrots that had landed on the floor.

"And it's time you knew the truth about some things—like your father!" Martha said. "Somebody dies and suddenly he's a saint," she grumbled on her way to the bathroom with the towel.

Caitlin closed her eyes, covered her ears, and made nonsense sounds to avoid listening, just as she had done when she was four years old. But she still heard her mother say, "Fine. You'll have to listen someday."

She soon forgot why she was babbling and uncovered her ears. She glanced at her mother; Martha was holding her handbag and sunglasses.

"For as bright as you are," Martha scolded, "you're not very smart about men!"

Caitlin wasn't sure what her mother was talking about, but it was clearly inapplicable to the present moment, so what did it matter? Abstract concepts were too hard to think about.

Martha announced that she was going for a walk.

Caitlin was glad for the peace of solitude. Wasn't some actress famous for saying, "I want to be alone"? Oh, well—there was no one around to ask who'd said it, and it didn't matter anyway.

She remembered a time when she'd wanted to be an actress. Could she have succeeded? Did she have the talent, the larger-than-life presence that people noticed—and remembered? Now she would never have the chance to find out, and comparing her dreams to her reality was depressing. Emotionally spent, she soon fell asleep.

❧ 29 ❧

Martha passed through the exit and walked briskly away from the hospital. She considered herself a patient woman but Caitlin could rile her more than anyone.

Life had been more tranquil these last few years without her daughter's dramatic scenes. The older she got, the less discord Martha was willing to tolerate. Charlie's rudeness and lack of sensitivity were among the chief reasons why she finally left him, even though she'd once been drawn to his forthright manner.

Funny how the characteristics we like about a person can become unbearable over time.

She'd met Charlie after she graduated from high school. Her father had arranged a summer job for her at the local newspaper. Neither of Martha's two siblings had shown any aptitude for schoolwork, so the judge's hope that one of his children would attend college at the University of Kansas, his alma mater, was pinned on Martha.

Her father encouraged her to take an interest in the affairs of the day and expand her knowledge of the world. Martha did want to expand her horizons, but not quite in the way her father had in mind. She wanted to see the world or, at least, something other than the prairie. She'd never been farther east than St. Louis. The streetwise reporter from Boston often talked about travel, and Martha saw an alternative to the path that had been dictated to her. When the paper offered her a full-time receptionist job at the end of the summer, she talked her father into letting her work for a year before starting college. She knew her family wouldn't approve of Charlie, so she didn't introduce him until, having neglected to use birth control, she found herself pregnant.

But scheming didn't bring Martha the exciting life she'd imagined. Charlie did his best, under the circumstances. He took a job in

Kansas City with a larger paper. Martha was often alone while Charlie was off chasing the breaking news. With first Bobby to care for and then Catie five years later, she grew to appreciate the support provided by her family and community. Even now, she baked pies for the church bake sale and brought a casserole if a neighbor was ailing or widowed. The little pleasantries, she knew, were important in sustaining the social web. Her daughter, however, seemed to have acquired Charlie's brash reactions and quick tongue. Perhaps it wasn't too late to teach Caitlin some manners.

Martha also wanted to show Caitlin that she was a new woman—strong and capable and deserving of respect. She could see now that Caitlin would test her at every turn. These were the moments when she wanted to throw in the towel and go home. She wouldn't do that, of course. Caitlin was her only daughter and she needed her mother, whether she admitted it or not.

Martha reminded herself that the shell of a person she was seeing wasn't the real Caitlin—this was Caitlin with a brain injury. Trying to reason with her was pointless, the staff had told Martha; Caitlin didn't have the cognitive ability to respond appropriately. She was often confused and frequently hostile. Martha had no way of knowing how much of Caitlin's irritability was caused by her present condition and how much was due to resentment she harbored about the past. Even before Charlie's death, Caitlin had been angry—because Martha had broken up the family.

She sighed. Caitlin had no idea how hard she'd tried—how long she had struggled to hold the family together. It was a losing effort, and she'd finally given up the battle. The children were old enough to take care of themselves. She wasn't going to be everyone's caretaker forever, and if they didn't like that—so be it! She deserved some happiness too.

She slowed her pace. She was happy now, in her life with Ray. The only thing missing was her daughter. Caitlin had refused to meet her stepfather and had stopped answering Martha's calls.

Feeling calmer, Martha sat on a park bench to rest. One of Caitlin's therapists had suggested keeping comments and questions short and simple; she shouldn't expect Caitlin to carry on a normal conversation, Martha was told. She was supposed to avoid reward-ing inappropriate behavior and instead distract Caitlin by directing her attention away from a problem or source of difficulty. She had failed this time but, fortunately, Caitlin would probably forget all about it, and Martha would have other opportunities to improve in her role as caregiver.

She returned to the hospital and found Caitlin smiling and sway-ing to music from *The King and I,* her earlier tantrum forgotten.

Just like a child, Martha thought as she turned down the volume.

∽ 30 ∽

Patrice walked down the corridor looking for Caitlin's room. The smell of disinfectant was nauseating.

Hospitals reminded her of her mother's agonizing ordeal with cancer. But, as Caitlin's friend, she was the logical office delegate to pay her a visit. Six weeks had passed since the accident, and Caitlin was finally allowed to have visitors other than close relatives. Everyone at OSP wanted to know how she was doing. Would she be able to return to work?

Neil had encouraged Patrice to take as much time at the hospi-tal as she needed. He paid more attention to her now that Caitlin was gone, and Patrice had to admit that she was thrilled with her new status.

The door was slightly ajar; she could hear Caitlin softly hum-ming a tune. Patrice listened for a moment, and then knocked lightly before entering the room.

"It's Monday," she said, holding up a bag from the bakery. "If you can't come to the office, the office will come to you!"

"Pa-Pat-sy!" Caitlin set aside the *Glamour* magazine she'd been looking through. "Ga—good . . . ta see sa— some-one . . . not . . . wear-ring . . ."

She closed her eyes tightly and sounded out the next word: "wa—white." Her shoulders relaxed as she let out a deep sigh.

Patrice hoped her face didn't betray her shock. She glanced down at her formal courtroom attire.

"Oh, uh, yes—if gray counts."

"Maaa-tches . . . my . . . moo—moon—mood."

"I guess you're entitled. I brought something to cheer you up."

Patrice handed Caitlin a large card signed by the attorneys and staff at OSP. Even the U.S. Marshals who guarded the main entrance at the Justice Center wanted to wish her well.

Caitlin smiled and wrote, slowly and carefully, on a small chalkboard: "Thank everyone, will ya?"

Writing, it seemed to Patrice, was as laborious for her as speaking.

"Of course." Patrice pulled a chair closer to the bed and sat down. "Neil said you should let him know if you need the name of a good P.I. lawyer."

"Hah! Sounds like Ne-il!"

Patrice placed two muffins on a paper plate and held the plate out to Caitlin. "Blueberry or cranberry?"

Caitlin pointed to the blueberry. Patrice picked up the cranberry muffin and gave the plate to Caitlin.

"You're so thin," she said. "Is the food here that bad?"

Caitlin laughed but didn't answer.

"Wha—what's new at . . . Ja—Jus-tice?" She carefully sounded out the words before taking a small bite of her muffin.

"Let's see." Patrice thought for a moment while she bit into the cranberry muffin. "The *Watkins* case went to trial. I'm second chair for *Jacobs* in district court—"

Caitlin set aside her plate and scribbled on the board: "The vaccine case?"

"Right."

"The—That was mine," she said. "Who got it?" she wrote on the board.

"Neil's handling it."

"He hasn't been in court in years!" Caitlin wrote.

"He says the allegations are unfounded and is moving to have the case dismissed," Patrice said casually. "Oh! I almost forgot!"

Patrice stuffed the rest of her muffin into the bag and wiped her face with a napkin before showing Caitlin the ring on her left hand.

"John proposed! We're getting married in May. And I expect to see you dancing at my wedding."

Caitlin's face displayed more emotions than Patrice was accustomed to seeing from her friend.

"I—I . . . I'm so hap-py for you—" Caitlin stammered as tears streamed down her cheeks. "Really," she wrote, underlining the word. She kept talking but, mingled with tears, her words quickly became incomprehensible.

"I'm sorry. I didn't mean to upset you."

The nurse had told her to avoid agitating or upsetting Caitlin and here she'd gone and done just that. Maybe she should leave.

"It—it's not you," Caitlin tried to say. "Na—No one's gonna . . . wa-want me now." She reached for a box of tissues and blew her nose. "Le—Look at me." She gestured to her face, with its smattering of fresh scars. "I—I don't even know my-self."

Caitlin's appearance wasn't all that was different; her whole demeanor had changed. Gone was the audacious confidence and, along with it, the sharp tongue and quick wit. Caitlin was clearly frustrated and embarrassed by her inability to speak normally. Her face contorted into unflattering expressions as she struggled to sputter out the words she did manage to find. Still, many of her injuries would undoubtedly heal, Patrice thought, and her ability to function might improve with continued therapy. She was alive, after all, and had every reason to expect a long and rewarding life; it would just be different than the way she'd once imagined it.

Patrice patted Caitlin's hand. "You don't even know how beautiful and special you are. Any man would be lucky to be with you."

Caitlin sniffed and shook her head. "I was on-ly goood at wa-work. And n-now I can't . . . I can't ev-en do that."

Patrice tried to think of something encouraging to say. "You'll be back in the game before you know it. Remember, we've got a block of Redskins seats this year."

She knew she was reaching; the kickoff game was only a few weeks away. Still, it was hard to imagine anything holding Caitlin down for long.

"Du—Don't you get it? I'm . . . I'm not com-ming back!"

Patrice was taken aback by Caitlin's outburst, and by her honesty. Caitlin had always been straightforward—she verbalized thoughts that most people preferred to dance around in unspoken rules of polite conversation: "Don't tread on my sensitivities, and I won't mention your painful, but obvious, failings." Honesty forced people to acknowledge the unflattering realities of their lives.

Perhaps after facing mortality, she's no longer willing to tolerate the bullshit most of us consider "normal."

"My br . . . brain . . . does-n't . . . work . . . right," Caitlin tried to explain. "I fer-forgot a lot. I can't ev-ven talk right."

Yes, well, those things could be problematic for an attorney, Patrice thought, *though surely reasonable accommodations could be made for a disability.* Wouldn't Neil do whatever he could to help her stay, after all she had contributed to the office over the years? Of course, working with Neil might not be the best remedy to speed Caitlin's recovery. He was a shrewd administrator. Would he now view her as a liability to be replaced? Patrice shuddered at the realization that life could change so drastically, in an instant. She shifted in her chair and looked around for a graceful exit.

"You . . . You bet-ter go," Caitlin said.

"Yeah, I need to get back." Patrice wished they could end the visit on a more positive note, but that was probably more for her comfort than Caitlin's.

She picked up the bag from the bakery. Caitlin hadn't eaten much of her muffin either, Patrice noticed.

"Take good care, Cait," she said. "We're all rooting for you."

Caitlin nodded and forced a smile.

Patrice wiped away a tear as she exited the hospital and walked toward her car. She paused to toss the paper bag into a trash can.

Caitlin's intensity was undiminished. She would need to find a new focus for her energies, Patrice thought, or she'd self-destruct.

✑ 31 ✑

Kimo rode his bicycle to the hospital after he completed the day's last errand. He'd been calling every few days, waiting for word that Caitlin could have visitors. He didn't know when visiting hours officially ended, but this was the earliest he could come on a work day.

He'd learned about the crash the morning after it happened. Jake Liggett, the attorney who had hired him, ordered flowers for Caitlin; Kimo delivered them to the hospital. Flowers weren't allowed in the Intensive Care Unit, so he left them at the desk. He returned on Sunday evening, after Caitlin had been moved out of the ICU. He only caught a glimpse of her before someone spotted him—her mother, he guessed. He slipped down the back stairs after leaving a red rose outside her room. From what he could see, she was still unconscious. She looked like she'd been beaten up. Kimo was eager to find out how much she had improved in the last six weeks.

He'd gleaned from snatches of conversation he overheard at the firm that an abandoned GMC sport utility vehicle had been found at the waterfront, a distance of five and a half miles from the accident scene. The passenger side of the SUV was damaged, and its black paint matched the streaks on Caitlin's car. The GMC bore no license plates or identifying VIN number. A canteen in the glove box was the only evidence found inside the vehicle. It contained vodka, suggesting a case of drunk driving.

With subdued voices, attorneys at the firm exchanged stories about Caitlin, describing the gruesome scene, wondering what her life would be like if she survived. For a while, it seemed to Kimo, they were nicer to be around. They left work a little earlier. They said hello to him in the elevator.

For Kimo, Caitlin's misfortune was more than a reminder of life's unpredictability. He regretted missed opportunities, words left unspoken. Aware of the workings of synchronicity, he wondered if the message Caitlin had left him contained any clues. Was the crash really an accident? Did she know too much, or antagonize someone? She wasn't shy about expressing her views. Maybe he'd seen too many Hollywood films about conspiracies, but a nagging feeling in his gut wouldn't let go. He prayed for her daily, thought of her constantly, and was aching to see her . . . to talk to her . . . to touch her . . .

He stood in front of the nurse's station and set his backpack on the floor by his feet. Sweaty from biking all day, he removed the red bandana from around his neck and wiped his upper lip. His sun-streaked hair was pulled back in a short ponytail.

"What room is Caitlin Rose in?" he asked the prim nurse behind the desk.

After giving him a disapproving look, the nurse checked the roster. "She's been moved to another unit. But you can't see her," she pronounced before returning to her desk duties.

"Nurse Proper," Kimo wanted to call her. With her pursed lips and curt manner, she was well suited to enforcement duties—a worthy representative of hospital bureaucracy.

"I don't understand . . . I thought her condition had improved."

"Oh, she's *allowed* to have visitors. She doesn't *want* to see anyone."

"Not anyone?" Surely Caitlin would want to see him, Kimo thought.

The nurse shrugged. "I can give her a message." She set a small notepad on the counter. "Perhaps you'd like to write a note."

No, he didn't want to write a note; he wanted to see Caitlin! He knew he shouldn't blame the nurse but she was getting on his nerves. He disliked hospitals. Sure, they served an important function, especially in emergency medicine and surgeries—even diagnoses and lab work. The doctors there had undoubtedly saved Caitlin's life and for that he was truly grateful. But beyond the initial stages of acute trauma and injury, his approach was so much more effective and healing—for the spirit as well as the body.

He was surrounded by the crumbling structures that constituted the remains of a vast network of interrelated institutions built according to self-serving principles by men of questionable integrity who produced little of lasting value in an age of materialism characterized by waste, greed, and wanton depletion of natural resources. Too many people cared too much about the wrong things. They focused their attention on short-sighted goals and short-term gains when they should be concerned about finding sustainable solutions and resolving urgent problems that would only worsen if they continued to be ignored.

The desire for easy answers and quick returns wasn't wrong; it was just symptomatic of a different mindset. Kimo valued deeper qualities. The satisfaction that came from creating meaning, from developing a soul-filled life, was acquired through struggle and the successful meeting of challenges. Soul couldn't be bought and sold in the marketplace; gloss and finery couldn't cover up a character flaw.

"Just tell her Kimo was here," he told the nurse.

She leaned forward to write on the notepad. "Keemo . . . How do you spell that?"

"Any way you want."

He turned and walked away. The thought of Caitlin stuck in an institution frustrated and saddened him. He wanted to start a clinic where he could put his ideas into practice with people who shared his vision. That was years away. Wishes wouldn't help Caitlin now.

✎ 32 ✎

When Martha arrived in the morning, Caitlin was sitting in a chair by the window, drawing on a pad of paper with a pencil. Remembering the colorful and original paintings Caitlin had brought home when she was in kindergarten, Martha leaned forward for a closer look; the sight of the crude sketch made her want to cry.

"That's great, honey," she said, lightly touching Caitlin's shoulder.

Each day, she challenged herself to maintain a positive, cheerful attitude in spite of Caitlin's negativity. Some days were harder than others.

Martha set her sweater and handbag on a chair and arranged the flowers she'd brought. No more roses had appeared since Caitlin had been moved to the rehabilitation unit, but get-well cards continued to stream in. Martha added the new ones to the others. The only name she recognized was Jayson's; she set that envelope aside.

She'd never understood why Caitlin and Jayson canceled their wedding plans. She didn't have a chance to ask; already strained family relations reached a breaking point when Charlie was found dead at the family's lake house in the Missouri Ozarks.

Martha straightened up the room. "The nurse told me you had a visitor."

Caitlin continued to draw.

"A man with a strange name." Too strange for Martha to remember. "Maybe it's your admirer," she said, grinning. The mystery of anonymous offerings sparked her imagination. "Aren't you curious to know who brought the roses?"

Caitlin scribbled a response on her chalkboard. "Curious what he admires. The haircut? The eloquent speech?"

"Maybe he's not fooled by appearances," Martha replied after deciphering Caitlin's scrawl.

Caitlin grunted.

"Oh, by the way, someone from your office called at the house for information about your condition. Something about processing papers for your disability. She was very helpful," Martha said cheerfully.

Caitlin stared blankly at her mother. "You di-di-didn't!"

"Well, someone has to speak for you, Caitlin. You're certainly not in any condition. They're going to need a doctor's report and documentation."

Caitlin boiled. "What . . . right—argh!" She gripped the pencil tightly and nearly tore the paper with her aggressive strokes.

Martha turned toward the door when she heard a knock. Doctor Stanton entered the room.

"Good morning, Mrs. Johnson." He turned to Caitlin. "Ms. Rose, I have good news. You'll be discharged in a few days. I can send you to a rehabilitation facility or, with home health care and your mother's help, you can continue your therapies on an outpatient basis. It's up to you. Do you think you're ready to go home?"

Caitlin scowled. "I ga-guess."

Doctor Stanton glanced at the drawing. "Drawing and painting are great for relearning fine motor skills—eye–hand coordination and all that," he said. "I'll have your OT set you up with some paints. Adding a bit of color might cheer you up." He patted Caitlin on the back before turning to leave. She didn't look up.

"I know things may seem a little bleak just now," the doctor added, "but given the nature of the collision, you have a lot to be thankful for. Those air bags probably saved your life."

"Yeah, what's left of it."

Martha was speechless. She couldn't imagine a daughter of hers being so rude and self-centered. She looked to Dr. Stanton; he shrugged and left the room. Martha followed, eager to ask his opinion about Caitlin's chances for further improvement. She found him standing next to a desk, dictating notes into a recorder.

"Patient still suffers from apraxia of speech, aphasia, loss of motor skills, and diminished cognitive functioning. Possibly some depression. Continue with OT, PT, and speech therapy on an outpatient basis. Follow up in six weeks."

Martha waited until he had finished speaking before approaching him.

"It's unlikely she'll ever resume her position as an attorney," he replied when Martha asked about Caitlin's prospects for full recovery. The most significant strides were often made in the first six months, he said, but in his years of practice he had witnessed a range of responses as people adjusted to the changes in their lives and their abilities after suffering serious injuries and illnesses. As long as Caitlin followed her treatment regimen, he expected her progress to continue.

"I'm not sure if she'll get better or worse once she leaves here," Martha said. In truth, she was worried about caring for Caitlin full time. Their relationship was still troubled. Living together might destroy it.

"Feel free to call me if you have any concerns," Dr. Stanton said.

That was exactly what Martha had hoped he would say. "Thank you, Doctor," she said, shaking his hand vigorously. "I'm so grateful for all the help you and the staff have given us."

Reassured, Martha returned to Caitlin's room. She sat in a chair and picked up her Bible.

Life is precious, she thought as she opened the Good Book. She turned to the Psalms; they often brought her comfort when she felt troubled.

Everyone gets dealt blows from time to time. Sure, some are worse than others, but it's not for us to second-guess the workings of the Almighty. We have to make the best of what is handed to us.

She put on her reading glasses. She would be lost without her faith, and Caitlin, it seemed to Martha, was very lost indeed.

✍ 33 ✍

Caitlin stared out the window at the steady rain. She dreaded the trip home. Sudden movements caused her pain. With assistance, she could walk a few steps—from the bed to the wheelchair, or the wheelchair to the toilet—but she would never make it up the front stairs of her townhouse; she would have to be carried. She always felt shaken by the experience of being moved, no matter how careful the aides tried to be.

Being with Martha 24/7 was going to be challenging, but it had to be better than going to another facility; at least she would be in her own home. She decided to focus on the destination rather than the painful journey.

Outside, a white van waited by the curb, its motor running. Caitlin was surprised to see Jasmine and Marvin Wells standing under a covered walkway, out of the rain. Jasmine waved to her.

"Hey! M-Mag-i-cal Mar-vin!" Caitlin shouted.

The aide pushing her wheelchair changed direction, allowing Caitlin a moment with the Wellses.

"G-Guess I'm . . . Cwip-*Crip-pled* Cait now."

Jasmine nudged Marvin, who handed Caitlin a small gift-wrapped box.

"We wanted to thank you for your efforts," Jasmine said. "We heard the case got dismissed."

"Yeah. S-sor-ry I wasn't more . . . help-ful," Caitlin said with downcast eyes.

"You did more than most folks." Jasmine nudged Marvin again.

"Thank you for teaching me piano," he said in a monotone.

"You're ver-ry wel-come," Caitlin said. She took Marvin's hand; he abruptly withdrew it, startling them both.

"Ya—You're one spesh—special guy . . . and don't you for-get it!" Caitlin told him.

She carefully removed the wrapping paper and opened the box. Inside was a glass paperweight, the kind that snowed when shaken. Silver frost covered a red rose blossom.

On the verge of tears, Caitlin said, "I . . . I gotta go." She looked to the aide to take her away.

Marvin watched, entranced, as the motorized lift carried Caitlin into the van and out of sight. After opening her umbrella, Jasmine took Marvin's hand and led him away.

∽ 34 ∽

Caitlin looked around the townhouse with new eyes. Everything looked different from a wheelchair. Everything *was* different now. She watched Martha hang their raincoats on the coat rack. Having her mother in her home felt odd.

"I've set up the TV room for you so we don't have to worry about getting you up and down the steps. I've been sleeping upstairs, in your room," Martha said.

Her mother was sleeping in her bed. What private things might she have gotten into? Letters? Photos? Journals? Caitlin hadn't had much time for personal reflection in recent years.

"Whatever," Caitlin mumbled. She winced as she removed the padded brace from around her neck. She must have felt every bump in the road. Dealing with pain was exhausting, she was learning, and healing required energy.

As a small sign of progress, the cast had been removed from her left arm, granting her some measure of mobility without assistance. She'd been practicing navigating by wheelchair in the corridors of the rehab unit and easily maneuvered the chair from the front entry into the living room. She'd never used this room much, as far as she could remember . . .

"Your mail is there, on the table," Martha said. "Looks like you got a card from Jayson. And something from overseas. Scotland, I think."

Martha disappeared down the hall with Caitlin's suitcase. Caitlin wheeled over to the table and searched the stack of mail.

Why didn't she bring this to the hospital?

She found Dru's letter and tore open the envelope. *It doesn't really matter now, does it?* She wouldn't be going anywhere anytime soon.

Tears blurred her eyes. She searched in vain for a handkerchief. Frustrated about being unable to attend to her own needs, she wanted to both cry and scream. Her control over her emotions wasn't much better than her control over her body. She put on her reading glasses and unfolded Dru's letter.

"*I apologize for the delay in responding to your sweet letter,*" Caitlin read.

She could almost hear Dru's voice as her eyes slowly followed his words. The concentration reading required was still a great effort, and she could only manage short passages at a time before needing to stop.

"*I was commissioned to create a small sculpture . . .*"

Caitlin remembered how absorbed Dru became when he was working; he completely gave himself over to a project. When she was with him, she too felt like a work of art, the only thing in his world that mattered in that moment. Perhaps that was why she had fallen for him: he was fully present. He paid attention. She felt listened to, adored. Maybe that was his talent more than her specialness, she thought. Maybe he made a lot of women feel that way. She read on.

"*You know you are welcome to visit anytime,*" Dru had written.

Caitlin vaguely recalled suggesting that they see each other again. Memories of Dru were so faint . . . she couldn't be certain any of it had really happened; what she thought she remembered about their time together could have occurred in a dream—or a story about someone else's life. His letter, though, was proof that something *had* happened.

"*. . . it's only fair to tell you, I'm not looking to settle down.*"

Why didn't that surprise her? Oh, yes. *The airport.*

That part she remembered more clearly. Dru had accompanied her to the gate for one last long, luscious kiss. Before she boarded the plane, Caitlin turned to wave goodbye; Dru was already gone. She was disappointed but didn't think too hard about it. They had shared a wonderful holiday, and Caitlin's mind filled with blissful imaginings of a repeat performance.

She read a bit more of the letter. "*I'm a free bird and I don't have any wish for a cage. Perhaps that's a cynical view of relationship.*"

I guess cats are naturally drawn to birds, Caitlin thought. *And birds sense the inherent danger in the liaison.* She skimmed the rest of the note.

"*I sense your heart longs for a different experience to what I can offer.*"

The bottom line, Caitlin thought. Dru closed with: "*Hoping this finds you well. Always, Dru.*"

Caitlin searched the pile of mail for Jayson's card.

Might as well get this all over with at once.

She knew that Jayson had sent a flower arrangement to the hospital.

His paralegal probably ordered it, she thought as she opened the card with the daisies on the front. *He knows I don't like daisies.*

The handwriting, at least, was his: *"Sorry to hear about your tragic accident. You know I'll always care, and wish the best for you. Warmly, Jayson."*

News of her "tragic accident" must have spread throughout the legal community by now, Caitlin thought. Neil had probably already found someone to replace her at OSP.

She turned her head, aggravating the ever-present ache in her neck. The sharp pain seemed to shoot throughout her entire body. Whimpering, she wheeled her chair over to the fireplace and started the gas flame. After several minutes, the wood log glowed red and ignited. Caitlin switched off the gas. Leaning forward, she opened the wire mesh curtains and held Jayson's card close to the flames.

"Warmly," she muttered as the card caught fire.

I loved you!

She tossed Dru's letter into the fire and closed the curtains. "Cages." She grunted. What did Dru know about cages? She was the one stuck in a wheelchair.

Don't talk to me about freedom.

She held up the glass paperweight that Jasmine and Marvin had given her. When she shook it, glittery flakes fell upon the petals of the rose.

The rose in winter.

Caitlin felt as if she, too, had been shaken up and covered with a layer of frost.

✍ 35 ✍

Caitlin continued with outpatient therapies and exercises as the months churned by and the rain turned to snow. She struggled to coordinate her mind and body. She learned to use a walker, though she still relied upon the wheelchair. Working with a speech therapist, her communication skills improved. An occupational therapist helped her relearn daily living skills so she could function independently in her home environment. Given a goal to strive toward, Caitlin would not give up. When it came to being *seen* struggling, though—when it came to showing vulnerability—pride and vanity interfered, and she retreated into a private world.

Kimo called from time to time; Caitlin refused all calls. During the daytime, she sometimes painted daffodils. The bright colors cheered her, and thoughts of spring flowers helped pass the dreary winter. Mostly, though, painting was another form of self-mastery, a demonstration of progress. Painting required fine movements and attention to detail; it required concentration.

In the evening, when her brain power faded, Caitlin sat and stared vacantly at the fire. After months with no mental or social stimulation, she didn't have much to think about; nothing of interest was happening in her outer world. Maybe this was how her life would be, merely existing. She didn't miss anything in particular—she didn't have the energy or stamina for activity. Reading gave her a headache, and television and films reminded her of all that she could not have or do. Thinking about how narrow her life had become upset her. All her hopes and dreams—all her hard work—for what? More than ever, she questioned the meaning of life. She ate; she slept; she went through the motions of her rehabilitation program.

With Martha, Caitlin was civil but said little. She appreciated her mother's help; she couldn't have managed without her. They didn't discuss plans for the future. Caitlin wasn't ready to think about anything beyond making it through another day. Step by step, it would all lead somewhere. Or not. Did it matter?

By accepting her need for rest and renewal, Caitlin embarked upon an inner journey. Her dreams became more abstract. She felt powerless and insignificant, a small part of a large cycle. Some great shift was underway, and she instinctively knew to bide her time and allow the old façade to fall away.

She was in the bathroom one late-February afternoon when she heard the faint sound of the telephone ringing.

Probably Ray, or one of Mom's friends.

Most of Caitlin's friends had stopped trying to reach her, and she let Martha handle the task of politely thanking callers for thinking of her.

She turned on the faucet. After rinsing and drying her face, she glimpsed her reflection in the mirror. Leaning on the sink for support, she examined her face more closely. Gingerly, she touched a small scar. Her face had healed well. Her new identity, however, was still forming. Perhaps the real Caitlin was still asleep—and waiting to be awakened.

She had no recollection of the day of the accident or the first few weeks out of the coma. Whole chunks of experience seemed to be missing; only fragments remained. Cases that were once in the forefront of her mind were now dim memories. Caitlin sensed that the information was stored somewhere in her brain, but access was denied.

Martha knocked on the bathroom door. "It's Kimo again."

Caitlin sat back down in the wheelchair, exasperated. "Ha—How man-y t-times do I haave to tell you, Mo-ther? I don't want to talk to any-one!"

"I keep hoping one of these days you'll say yes. To life!"

Caitlin opened the door in time to hear her mother say, "I'm sorry, Kimo. Caitlin can't come out and play today. Do check back." Martha hung up the phone.

Caitlin rolled her eyes and said, "Oh, Lord."

"Well, you are acting rather childish," Martha said, hand on her hip. "What do you expect to gain?"

"I'm not la-look-ing to 'gain' any-thing. I just want to be left alone to f-fade in-to o-bliv-vi-on."

Caitlin went to her room to watch television. Her mind was getting sharper, and she was restless for news and ideas beyond her own circulating thoughts; and, the sound of the television would drown out Martha's chatter.

"Be careful what you ask for," she heard her mother say before she closed the door. She was growing weary of Martha's presence. Perhaps that was a good sign. Maybe she was ready to move to the next level of functioning on her own.

✑ 36 ✑

"I can't stay here forever, you know!" Martha shouted down the hallway, though she knew Caitlin probably wasn't listening. "At least when I'm gone you'll be forced to do something different."

Agitated, she paced the floor. She wouldn't stand for much more of this. She'd been away from Ray and her own home for nearly nine months now. She needed some sign that Caitlin was improving. She needed hope, and encouragement.

She picked up the phone. Caitlin was out of hearing, laughing at some inane television show.

At least she's laughing.

Martha dialed the number for Doctor Stanton's office. For weeks, she had been thinking of contacting him. The doctor would call her before the end of the day, she was told.

Martha was preparing dinner when the phone rang.

"She doesn't seem to be getting any better," she said, "and I'm at my wits' end."

As she spoke the words aloud, Martha realized she wasn't just calling about Caitlin—*she* needed a break. She wanted to ask whether some kind of relief care was available; that would allow her to go home for a while. But she knew she couldn't do that. Caitlin hadn't forgiven her. If they ever hoped to have a better relationship, they needed to at least try to understand each other. This was the opportunity they had been given; Martha was not about to walk away. Caitlin would accuse her of abandoning her in her time of need. No, she couldn't leave now; not when they had come this far. Martha smiled at her own stubborn determination. Caitlin had probably acquired the trait from her.

"Physically, she's progressing fine," Dr. Stanton said.

"She's so angry all the time. I don't know if it's just me or . . ."

"People's personalities can change following a brain injury, often without their awareness. They may fail to recognize problems that are apparent to others."

The explanation made sense to Martha. Caitlin needed to prepare for the challenges ahead. She needed to face facts. She'd rejected Martha's suggestion that they return to Kansas together, but she hadn't said what she planned to do instead.

"Isn't there anything we can do?"

"It is possible for the brain to heal. It can take years sometimes."

Martha groaned inwardly.

"I'm not a psychiatrist, but I could put her on a cycle of anti-depressants. Sometimes that's all that's needed to resolve the situation."

"That would be wonderful, doctor. Thank you ever so much."

"Call back in the morning and tell my nurse where you want to pick that up. She'll phone it in."

"You've been very helpful."

The wonders of modern medicine, Martha thought as she hung up the phone. She felt better already.

Late in March, Martha started preparing for the feast of Easter. She planned a special meal for Easter Sunday and wrote out a list of what she would need. While shopping, she spotted a plush rabbit and remembered how Caitlin had loved the story *The Velveteen Rabbit* when she was a child. On a whim, Martha bought the rabbit, a package of multicolored jellybeans, and an Easter basket like the ones she'd left by the door to Caitlin's room when they were both a lot younger. She also bought a dozen eggs and a package of food-coloring dyes.

On Good Friday, the holy day commemorating the crucifixion of the Lord Jesus Christ, Martha baked hot cross buns, as she did every year. While washing the dishes, she thought about which service to attend at the local church she'd been going to on Sundays. Her thoughts were interrupted when Caitlin rolled over to the sink in her wheelchair and nudged Martha to move aside.

"Honestly, Caitlin! I won't be treated like a piece of furniture that's in your way!"

Martha stared at Caitlin, wondering if her daughter's behavior was somehow her fault. Caitlin had been a willful child and Martha had found it easier to let her have her way, as long as she didn't endanger anyone. Martha's mother, Elizabeth, had been strict, but not puritanical the way Martha's grandmother had been. Elizabeth Clayton loved to entertain. As a judge's wife, she was ever concerned about propriety. Martha was raised to "honor thy father and thy mother." If her views differed from those of her parents, she kept them to herself.

Her daughter, however, lived by different rules. Caitlin was competitive and argumentative, like Charlie. Martha's temperament was more placid—passive, according to Caitlin, who'd made no secret of her impatience with Martha's lack of assertiveness. But Caitlin's *sturm und drang* went to the opposite extreme, in Martha's view. Caitlin had yet to learn that kindness does not equate to weakness.

Martha valued domestic harmony; she knew the power of cooperation. Her earliest memories were of her grandparents' farm near Olathe, where the extended family lived together while Martha's father attended law school. Jesse Clayton was a member of the first class of students admitted to the Kansas City School of Law after it merged with the University of Kansas City in 1938, just months after Martha was born. The law school became part of the University of Missouri in 1963—the year Caitlin was born; it would produce more future judges, including Judge Clayton, than any other law school in Missouri.

Martha was in her teens when her father was appointed to the bench. His new status meant stricter rules and greater expectations for the Clayton offspring; keeping up appearances took on new importance, and Martha's mother wasted no time sprucing up the house—and its occupants. But those early experiences on the farm had also shaped Martha's character, and her values. She was a farm girl at heart, she'd realized over the years. The family never completely lost its link to the land, and Olathe, the county seat of Johnson County, remained a farming community until the Kansas City metropolis expanded southward. Life on the farm demanded many forms of strength, especially through hard times when a crop failed or disease spread through the livestock. People learned the value of banding together; neighbors looked out for each other.

Caitlin's lack of sensitivity must have come from Charlie, Martha thought as she watched her fill a glass with water. But maybe she was to blame, too; maybe she'd been too soft on Caitlin. Before Caitlin was born, Martha had suffered several miscarriages. She was overjoyed when she delivered a healthy baby girl. Knowing she would bear no more children, Martha didn't have the heart to scold little Catie. Perhaps if she had set firmer boundaries and enforced them when Caitlin threw a tantrum, Caitlin would have learned to show a little respect.

Caitlin turned off the faucet. "Ga—Good for you, Mo-ther! Stan—Stan-ding up to the Cait . . . Le-Lion." She moved away from the sink. "I don't have much of a roar now. Oh, but you wouldn't know a-bout my rep—repu-ta-tion at . . . work. You weren't around for that chap-ter." She took a drink of water and washed down several pills.

Martha grew agitated. Caitlin's behavior had indeed changed since she started taking the antidepressants, but not necessarily in the desired direction. She had a hidden supply of pain relievers as well, and Martha worried about the interactive effects of combining drugs.

"Didn't the doctor say you should be decreasing your pain medication?"

"Oh, who cares," Caitlin said as she wheeled away. "Whaddo they know a-bout me any-way? I sta-still get head-aches. Docs don't have all the an-swers. Nobody does."

Martha's anxiety blossomed into panic. She followed Caitlin into the hall. "I'm not going to stand by and watch you kill yourself—like your father!"

Caitlin stopped and slowly turned her chair around. "Whaddaya mean, like my fa-fa-ther?

Facing Caitlin's cold, icy stare, Martha lost her nerve and retreated into the kitchen. "Nothing," she said tersely. "Forget I said anything."

Caitlin followed. "No, I won't. Tell me!"

Martha's legs felt wobbly. She sat in a chair at the kitchen table.

She'd been preparing for this conversation for several years but could find no easy way to start it.

"Your father didn't die of a heart attack. Or a broken heart, as you like to imagine." Martha shot an accusatory look at Caitlin before continuing. "He took an overdose," she said. Then she held her breath and waited for the fireworks.

"What? I-I . . . I don't be-lieve you," was all Caitlin said.

"No, of course not," Martha quipped. "I don't have any degrees after my name. What could I possibly know?"

If they were going to air their grievances, they might as well lay them all bare. The tension between them couldn't get much worse.

Still, Martha knew her daughter was suffering; that was the reason she tolerated her abuse. She also knew that Caitlin needed to let go and move on. If Caitlin needed to express her anguish and rage in order to do that, Martha would be there for her. She would listen— even though she thought Caitlin blamed her unfairly.

✍ 37 ✍

Caitlin's mind reeled as she struggled to comprehend her mother's startling revelation.

"But—he . . . he seemed fine," she said numbly, trying to recall her last visits and conversations with her father.

"You were his favorite audience," Martha said. "He adored you. You've never wanted to know the truth about him."

"Tooth—Truth? The fact is: you left. And he nev-ver recovered."

Truth was an elusive subject but facts were hard to dispute. Her mother's departure and her father's subsequent decline were not matters of opinion; they were events that, when linked together sequentially, indicated a causal relationship.

"For once, I acted for myself," Martha said. "I stayed until you left for college. What more did you expect? Bobby was away in the service. I wasn't about to stay a day longer than I had to with that man!"

That man?

Caitlin had never witnessed any rows between her parents; they discussed their differences out of their children's hearing, if they discussed them at all. On occasion, her father had left the house at night and they all knew he was headed to the pub. But the family had always managed, and Caitlin had never suspected the depth of her parents' dissatisfaction. Martha never shared much about her feelings, and Caitlin had long ago stopped looking for the closeness she'd witnessed between some mothers and daughters. It just wasn't that way with them.

"You fic—You fixed it so I had no . . . home . . . to come back to."

Even though she was a grown woman at the time of Charlie and Martha's divorce, the loss of her intact family had a deep impact on Caitlin. Her sense of security—and confidence in her own marriage plans—shattered.

"You always loved the lake house," Martha said. "And you're welcome with Ray and me any time. You've chosen to stay away."

"It . . . It's not the same." Caitlin folded her arms and pouted. Strong emotions of any kind jumbled her thoughts, but anger was easier for her to express than grief or sadness.

"Nothing stays the same, Caitlin, and thank God for that. I'd had enough of late-night calls when the bars were closing. Not knowing if I'd find your father passed out or in a rage. Worrying he'd lose his job, or finally strike me—as he came so close to doing a hundred times."

Caitlin was moved by the genuine distress in her mother's voice. "I—I nev-ver knew," she said softly.

"A child shouldn't have to know such things. After Charlie's back injury, he found he could escape the pain with alcohol and medication. Eventually, he chose to escape completely." Martha rested her face against her hand and stared down at the table.

"Even if it was an . . . an over-dose, you don't know it was in—inten-tion-al!" Caitlin shouted.

Caitlin had her own view of life in the Rose household. Her

inhibitions weakened, she blurted out what she never would have voiced in the past.

"I know why he was ang-ry. Nothing was ever good e-nough for you. You . . . you drove him away—jus . . . just like you pushed me ta be per-fect!"

"Is that what you think? Of course I wanted you to do your best, to live up to your potential. Doesn't every parent?"

"I never felt like you . . . you cared a-bout me—just how well I per-formed so you could . . . shh-show me off!"

"So you want to blame me, too. You are your father's daughter! Prosecutor, judge, and jury! Do you want to hang me or drive a stake through my heart?"

"I *did* wanna be a ju-judge some-day, like—"

"Like *my* father," Martha said, slapping her hand on the table, "who never had time for his own family. Who cared more about his career than his children."

She and her mother were like different breeds, Caitlin thought; they were part of the same species but shared few common traits. She recalled her maternal grandfather as a kind and gentle, reasoned man who had a fondness for his pipe. Reserved and well educated, Judge Clayton was the most cultured of her relatives, and Caitlin aspired to be like him. She, in turn, fulfilled his desire for his progeny to succeed him at his alma mater. By pursuing a legal career, Caitlin went one better. The Judge helped with her tuition and lived to see her graduate from law school with honors.

"I wanted more than—than—than play-ying pi-a-no!"

"My life may not be glamorous, but it's good enough for me!"

"Is it? Or did you lack the ca-ca-cour-age to pur-sue some-thing more than wife and mo-ther?"

Martha laughed. "Oh, I pursued it all right! What I lacked was talent. No, singing in the church choir is all I'll ever be good for. But you—" Martha paused, overcome with emotion. "I wanted you to have opportunities I never had."

"You wanted to live your life o-ver . . . through me."

"I worked two jobs so you could have piano lessons and take ballet classes!"

"Which *you* inst . . . insis-ted upon!"

"Your father's salary got frittered away on gambling and liquor and God knows what else," Martha mumbled.

"Are we t-talk-ing a-bout the same man?"

Martha's portrayal of Charles Rose was completely different from Caitlin's image of her father. Yes, he had a quick temper, but he was hardworking and articulate. Being a reporter, he had an ear for stories and was always abreast of the latest rumors about town. Caitlin imagined him regaling the crowd at the pub with details of the latest skirmish at the legislature, embellishing even politics with enough human interest to add a touch of wit or humor.

She and her father shared a language that neither Martha nor Bobby understood, and Caitlin sorely missed his counsel. Bobby was only interested in playing sports and developing his sturdy physique; subtlety was lost on him. Martha busied herself with home and family and church and friends; her hands were never still, and she could often be found talking on the phone in the kitchen while cooking supper or ironing Charlie's shirts or patching a hole in Bobby's jeans. Caitlin and Charlie were more alike: introspective, passionate, temperamental.

"Whadabout Bobby?" Caitlin asked quietly. "Does he know?"

"Everyone knows, Caitlin," Martha said soberly. "You're always so focused on your own life, you never really notice what's going on with anyone else."

"So I'm . . . I'm the on-ly one you . . . *lied* to?"

Martha fidgeted, but said nothing.

"And you ex-pect me to . . . to trust you now?"

"Not telling you was a mistake," Martha said. "I don't think you've really said goodbye to him. If I had it to do over . . . I just don't know. You were going through so much already with your new job and wedding plans. I wanted to spare you the pain."

Caitlin felt numb.

How could he do it?

How could she believe this about him? She had considered her father a strong man. Was that just how every daughter wanted to view her father? Had she been completely wrong about him? *Was* she in danger of heading down the same road, as her mother feared?

"And . . . And what makes you think I can han-dle it now?" she asked, her voice quivering as she hovered on the brink of tears. She felt let down by her father and deceived by everyone else.

"Because you have to."

Martha's firm and steady tone assured Caitlin that she could recover from this, too.

"I love you Caitlin, and I loved your father, once. That's all that matters. Don't get stuck in what's past."

"That's all I have, Mo-ther," Caitlin said with sad resignation. "The past."

"Where there's life, there's hope," Martha said, leaning forward in her chair. "Part of growing up is coming to terms with life itself. Because it doesn't usually happen on your terms. You don't know what glory God has yet in store for you."

Oh, that religious verbiage again. Martha lost her there.

"You can keep your Sun-day School God, Mo-ther. I'll . . . I'll find my own."

Caitlin turned her wheelchair toward her room. Maybe she had made a mess of her life, she thought, wiping away a tear. Maybe if she'd been willing to learn some of her mother's domestic talents she could have saved her relationship with Jayson. She couldn't change the past or the choices she'd made. But she was more open to examining her life now that she had slowed down long enough to ponder the outcomes. Maybe she had kept herself so occupied with work in order to avoid confronting the difficult feelings that were now surfacing.

There's no escape.

She must face her greatest enemy: herself.

✍ 38 ✍

Rumors about Caitlin died down after she was released from the hospital. People at the firm talked about current events, such as the presidential race and incumbent President Bill Clinton's victory over Republican challenger Bob Dole. Kimo continued to send Caitlin loving thoughts every day. He pictured her smiling and healthy and receptive to his friendship.

She wouldn't take his calls, or so her mother said; Kimo had no reason to doubt her. Caitlin had never mentioned her mother to him, but that wasn't unusual. Neither of them had shared much about their personal lives. They still had time; the contours of their friendship were not fully formed. Kimo respected natural growth cycles. Relationships, like people, go through developmental stages. But Caitlin's unwillingness to speak to him didn't seem natural—not for this long. He had to figure out some way to get through to her. He wanted to send a card for Valentine's Day, but he didn't know her home address. Admiring the blossoming trees on his commute into Washington one fine March day, he recognized the solution: flowers.

Late in the day on Good Friday, Kimo approached Jake Liggett and suggested that another bouquet for Caitlin Rose would be a thoughtful gesture—to show her she wasn't forgotten. He'd be willing to bring the flowers by her house over the Easter weekend, he told the senior partner.

Of course, the flowers weren't really the point; Kimo could buy his own bouquet. He needed to find out where Caitlin lived. He couldn't wait any longer. He needed to see her. If she still rebuffed him, he'd forget her. Forever.

The lawyer removed his reading glasses, quietly studied Kimo, and nodded. Kimo stopped at the desk outside Mr. Liggett's office and waited while his secretary wrote down Caitlin's home address. Then he headed to the flower shop where the firm had an account, riding his bike through downtown streets congested with tour buses, taxicabs, diplomats, and commuter traffic.

A diesel truck spewed a cloud of black exhaust into the air; Kimo coughed to clear his lungs. He longed for a haven he could call his own—a place where he could leave behind the din of traffic and listen, instead, to the birds and the river and the crickets; where he could see the stars instead of the haze of streetlamps; where he could feel the heartbeat of the earth instead of the vibration of nearby high-speed transportation.

How would people know that their lifestyles were leading them down a path of self-destruction if nobody told them?

The information doesn't come from institutions that benefit from keeping people in the dark.

Kimo was committed to educating people about the consequences of their choices. He was tired of being affected by the messes people created because they lacked understanding and awareness: environmental catastrophes, financial disasters, corporate mismanagement, war.

He thought of the ways organisms experience cycles of correction when the balance shifts too far in any direction—in politics, in economics, in ecosystems. In the physical body, imbalances often showed up in the chakras, the interchanges where converging pathways of energy merge in swirling vortices. Unchecked drives for material wealth and status and sex appeal led to greed and wasteful excess, he believed, but the attempt to attain spiritual bliss without first working out one's physical, emotional, and psychological blocks created a split between the spiritual realms and the material world. The pathway to the divine must be found *through* the use of human faculties and personality traits, not in denial of individuality.

Not in denial of anything. Humans are a blend of the animal and the divine. Heaven must be balanced with earth.

Kimo secured his bike and entered the flower shop. He moved amidst the plants and flowers, taking in the colors and fragrances. The system he followed taught that the body's seven major chakras correspond to the frequencies of the colors of the rainbow—the visible light spectrum. Many clairvoyants claimed to see these colors around the chakras. Kimo didn't doubt that some people had the ability, though he did not.

Maybe infrared, below red, and ultraviolet, beyond violet, also emanate from humans' auric fields.

Until someone developed the instrumentation to see those forms of light that were not visible to the naked eye, suggestions that such things might exist would continue to be considered fantastic— or worse—by the conservative-minded.

There will always be visionaries and there will always be doubters

who say "show me." And eventually someone will—if the orthodox fac-
tions don't succeed in stifling all creativity and research.

Kimo selected a bouquet of calla lilies and watched as the clerk
wrapped them. The thought of seeing Caitlin again stirred his imagination. Maybe she didn't remember what happened the night of the
solstice, after the initiation and the cleansing, but he did. He would
never forget it. *Hieros gamos,* the sacred union.

He'd felt shaken by the ritual—by what he'd seen about his past.
Afterward, he sank into depression and had not yet fully emerged.
Yet, wasn't the re-creation of his mistakes partly the point? He'd suc-
cumbed before to darkness and despair; he couldn't allow himself to
fall into the same trap again. It was time to stop brooding and start
putting all his training to the test. Bold action was required. He had
to help Caitlin—if she'd let him.

Learning her address renewed his hope; it confirmed his sense
that he was about to enter a new phase. The waiting was nearly over.
He planned to deliver the flowers on Sunday morning. But would
she admit him to her inner sanctum?

PART FOUR

DIALOGUES

∽ 39 ∽

Caitlin stayed huddled in her room all day Saturday, never changing out of her pajamas and robe. She kept the shades drawn and skipped dinner. Her midsection felt hollow, but she wasn't hungry. Aside from encouraging her to eat, her mother mostly let her be.

A healthy and nutritious diet was important for her recovery, but eating was still a challenge; she needed to eat slowly and think carefully about swallowing each bite. She couldn't recall the last time she'd eaten any chocolate, but she remembered well the pleasure it once gave her. No longer could she use food, wine, shopping, a lover, or even work as a source of satisfaction—or means of escape.

For years, Caitlin's career had given her a reason to get up in the morning. Now, every day was pretty much the same. Sometimes she felt poised at the precipice of a huge abyss that threatened to swallow her up. Along with the loss of income and identity she'd suffered with the end of her career, she'd also lost the confidence that she could take care of herself. The wheelchair was an ever-present reminder of her dependence.

After Martha had gone upstairs for the night, Caitlin made her way to the kitchen for a glass of water. Martha was talking on the phone to Ray, their evening ritual. Caitlin paused for a moment and listened to the cadence of her mother's voice; she sounded happy.

211

Caitlin was glad that her mother had found a loving partner, but a new round of tears flowed when she returned to her room. She set the glass on the table by her bed and turned out the light.

Emotionally spent, she drifted into sleep. In a dream, she wandered through a maze of dark corridors in an underground cave. Was she searching for something she had lost? A pair of eyes watched her from the shadows. They didn't seem human; the thought made her cringe. She turned to see a torrent of water rushing toward her and looked around, desperate for an escape. The deluge threatened to submerge her into the depths; she wasn't strong enough to resist the force of the current. She awoke in a sweat.

Thinking about the dream, Caitlin remembered the vast network of tunnels in the subway system beneath the streets of New York City. Though packed with pedestrians during peak hours, the underground stations seemed sinister when empty. Caitlin had not been timid as a child and, other than a frightening encounter with a neighborhood dog, she'd had little reason to fear anything in her hometown environment. But she first visited Manhattan Island shortly after she and Jayson split up, and she felt particularly vulnerable and alone.

Returning to her hotel late at night after attending a show at an Off-Broadway theater, she got off the train at the wrong stop. Rather than wait in a dirty, smelly, dimly lit and deserted station for the next train, she walked outside and headed in the direction that looked most promising, hoping to hail a taxi. She laughed when she realized she was only blocks from the hotel and walked the remaining distance.

In time, she learned her way around, and the city no longer seemed like an alien planet with potential predators hiding down every alley. Her confidence rebounded, and Caitlin delighted in the variety of museums, restaurants, and theatrical productions.

A tap on the door startled her. "Caitlin? Are you all right?" Martha asked. "I thought I heard you scream."

"I'm fa-fine," Caitlin said, sputtering out the words before another wave of tears overcame her. "Just . . . go away." She wasn't fine, she knew, but her mother couldn't help her.

She groaned as she carefully shifted her body. The hospital bed her mother had rented was adjustable, but finding a comfortable position for sleeping was nearly impossible. She may have to live with some pain for the rest of her life, she was told when she was discharged from the hospital. At least she no longer needed the neck brace.

Lying alone in the darkness, she thought about a conversation she'd had while Martha was out grocery shopping. Reluctantly, Caitlin had answered the phone. The call was from Sandra, a friend from Caitlin's college days. She was in town with her family for the Cherry Blossom Festival. She didn't know about Caitlin's accident, and Caitlin couldn't tell her—because she couldn't stop crying. Her friend had no idea what to make of her outpouring.

"I guess I'm catching you at a bad time," Sandra said.

"Nah, it's okay," Caitlin blubbered. "It's n-nice ta hear from you."

She was glad to know that people thought of her. She was even ready to hear about their lives—their successes and challenges, their families and careers. But she had nothing to contribute. She hadn't seen the latest films, read the best sellers, traveled anywhere, or accomplished anything. She wasn't bored, but she didn't think anyone would find her daily struggles very interesting, and the reminder that others were living full and active lives was sometimes more than she could bear.

"I hope you'll get some help, Cait," Sandra said in closing. "Whatever it is, you don't need to go through it alone."

Caitlin knew her behavior must have seemed a little odd. She *was* psychologically unhinged but, in spite of everything, she felt grateful to be alive. She realized that trying to numb pain also blocked other feelings, like passion for living. Her feelings were close to the surface now, and she wanted to acknowledge them, honor them—*trust* them—and stop judging them.

People seem so afraid of real emotion—afraid they will lose control. But maybe it's the repression of emotion that leads to extreme and unpredictable outbursts.

Still, her well-meaning friend's suggestion that she needed help *did* help. Caitlin realized she didn't need a kind and sympathetic therapist—she'd had all that, and it had brought her this far. What she needed now was something more. She needed greater under-standing about the mysteries of life and death.

She knew that her father was gone, never to return, but her mother's assessment was valid: she hadn't really said goodbye to him. She didn't feel guilty about missing the funeral. Charles Rose was a practical man; he understood about job demands. His career gave his life purpose and structure. Being a journalist suited him. He would have wanted professional success for his daughter as well.

Caitlin didn't regret the sacrifices she'd made for her career; she had done what she needed to do to get where she'd wanted to go. But striving for success in the eyes of the world—or her father—was pointless. She'd chosen a career that met with his approval. Had she also chosen Jayson in order to satisfy her father's expectations?

Lacking a feeling of closure with two important men in her life, Caitlin was beginning to appreciate the power of ritual. *Rituals mark passages. Births . . . weddings . . . housewarmings . . . gradua-tions . . . deaths. Beginnings and endings.*

Free now to "be herself," Caitlin wondered what that even meant. Accepting responsibility for her life and future would require her to establish new rhythms, discover new interests, and make choices based on her own values. She would need to reclaim the parts of herself that she had rejected or denied.

She thought again about the dream. Was there a parallel between the passageways in the dream and the passages of life—the transitions and turning points? Was she wandering in the dark, looking for the light at the end of the tunnel? She had to keep mov-ing; a dam had broken and powerful forces had been unleashed. She must allow the currents of her life to carry her forward. If she resis-ted, she would go under.

At the same time, she needed to accept where she was, right now—flaws and all. If someone else had suffered the traumas she'd endured, she would feel tenderness and compassion. Didn't she deserve the same consideration? She needed to nurture herself and release resentment about all she could no longer do, all she had lost. She needed to grieve. And so, she cried.

When the tears subsided, she sat up and turned on the light by her bed. Maybe she should start keeping a dream journal again, as she had in college. With no place to rush off to each morning, she had time now to become acquainted with the inhabitants of her interior world. She pulled a half-used notebook from a shelf and wrote down what she recalled about the dream. Hadn't Kimo said something once about the river of life? Caitlin could no longer trust her memory. The past had an evanescent, dreamlike quality about it.

Evanescent . . . that's a good word.

Maybe she should also begin a practice of building her vocabulary to exercise her brain. She would try to remember to use the word "evanescent" at least once that day in conversation.

Of course, that meant she would need to *have* a conversation. The next time someone called to speak to her, she decided, she would answer. She still felt timid about talking on the phone. What if she had trouble finding the right words? Busy people didn't have time to wait for her to bungle her way through a sentence. At least, that's how she would have reacted before finding herself in this predicament: with impatience.

She glanced at the time before putting down the pen and turning off the light. Four o'clock; she could still sleep for a couple of hours before her mother would be up and about. She stretched out on the bed and adjusted the pillow beneath her head, amazed by how much calmer and lighter she felt. The simple act of writing out her thoughts and feelings helped clear the clutter from her mind.

She remembered Kimo's stories about the body's ability to heal when it is properly supported. "Too often," he'd said, "people interrupt normal cycles and processes. Like fevers. Researchers have found that certain enzymes function better at higher temperatures. Infection-fighting chemicals are released when the body's communication network alerts the proper cells. Fever is the body's way of raising the temperature so it can rid itself of offending agents. Nature has intelligence. Heck, maybe nature *is* Intelligence."

Caitlin smiled and said a prayer of thanks for Kimo's friendship. His crazy ideas were beginning to make sense to her.

If the whole universe is an interconnected web pulsing with life and intelligence, how can I ever be alone? Maybe separation is an illusion . . .

As Caitlin embraced the silence, a feeling of peace and well-being encompassed her. She no longer felt the need to escape or run or avoid. She didn't feel lazy or depressed or resigned to her fate. For a moment, she felt suspended in time, like pure *being*. She surrendered. No grasping or striving; no struggle or resistance.

It was rather simple, really, now that she was here. She felt . . . still. Purged, cleansed, reborn—all the trite clichés fit. Saved? No, she wouldn't go that far. She wasn't looking for any shining knights to ride by and rescue her, either. This was *her* journey, her quest. And it had only just begun.

∞ 40 ∞

Caitlin fell into a peaceful slumber. Waves of purple light moved toward her like pulsations from a distant galaxy. She read from some Great Book, its pages covered with writing in silver ink. Before she could comprehend the meaning of the symbols, a knock on the door disturbed her sleep. Reluctantly, she left the book and struggled to open her eyes. Kimo was standing in the doorway.

"Wha— Oh, God, what are you do-ing here?" Caitlin pulled the bedcovers over her head.

"Well," Kimo said as he entered the room, "your doorman said it was okay."

Caitlin peeked out to see what "doorman" Kimo was talking about. In the dim light, she saw that he was holding a stuffed rabbit.

"He was on the floor outside your room."

Caitlin retreated again behind the covers. Kimo laughed and set the rabbit on a chair. He sat on the edge of the bed.

"You won't take my phone calls, so you left me no choice but to make a house call." Kimo gently pulled the covers down to expose Caitlin's face and studied her new look.

"Hmm, your hair's grown out."

Caitlin put her hand to her head and felt her hair. It had grown out since when? *The hospital!* Kimo had seen her in the hospital. She sat up and pounded on his chest with her fists. "How do you know?"

"Geez, Cait, is having a bad hair day all you can think about?"

Caitlin pouted, but calmed down.

"I've seen you drunk, hyped up on caffeine, and stressed out over deadlines. Did I mention you can be a real bitch when you haven't had enough sleep? This is just an added dimension to our friendship."

Was this his way of trying to make her feel better? Perhaps she ought to slap his face, like starlets did in old movies. Caitlin doubted that real women ever did that, any more than they demurely lifted a leg when some Valentino kissed them.

"You pa-paint such a . . . pert— . . ." She paused for a moment, as her speech therapist had taught her, to find an easier word that would convey a similar meaning. ". . . *nice* pic—image," she said, and then sank back into the bed.

Kimo affectionately touched her nose. "And, I've witnessed your courage and brilliance and soft spot for—" He pulled out a small glittering box of Belgian chocolates.

"My fa-fa-vor-ites! I haven't ha—"

Caitlin reached out to take the box, but Kimo pulled it away. "Not so fast, princess! We've got work to do!"

She eyed him suspiciously. "What kind of 'work'?"

"Get dressed and find out," he said as he stood up.

"What am I, a Peruvi—no, wait—Pavlov—" She paused and closed her eyes, carefully sounding out the word "Pav-lo-vi-an," then sighed before continuing. "Dog? You think you can get me to . . . sal-i-vate . . . and do tricks for a treat?" she asked slowly, even as she swung her legs around the side of the bed.

"Whatever works."

Seeing the sparkle in Kimo's eyes, Caitlin couldn't help but smile.

"Dress warmly," he said. "It's chilly outside." He closed the door behind him—and took the box of chocolates with him.

Caitlin yawned. Groggy and tired from too little sleep, she stood slowly. Using her walker for support, she made her way to the closet to find something to wear. By eating a healthy, low-fat diet, she'd never regained the weight she had lost while in the hospital, and her old clothes hung limply on her thin frame. She found a pair of old corduroys hidden in the back of the closet; a pair of tights worn underneath would add warmth and bulk. She selected a sweater from a dresser drawer.

Reaching for a pair of earrings, she noticed the bottle of anti-depressants on top of the dresser and realized she felt anxious. She was excited to see Kimo, but did she trust him enough to go on an outing with him? She had no idea where he planned to take her. Still, being confined to the house with only her mother for company was depressing. She felt ready to take a risk. Kimo had brought more than chocolates—he'd offered her an opportunity to emerge from her cocoon.

She remembered her early morning vow to answer a call. What was it Kimo had said? He was making a house call!

Caitlin tossed the bottle of pills into the trash and then wheeled her chair to the bathroom to wash her face and brush her teeth.

⚜ 41 ⚜

Kimo understood now why Caitlin had refused his calls.

It's not about me, he thought as he walked down the hall.

Speaking was difficult for her; knowing Caitlin, she was probably embarrassed. Isolating herself wasn't the answer. More than ever, she needed her friends. Kimo wanted to help, wanted her to need him. She never had before. Maybe now he could earn her trust, demonstrate his caring.

He entered the kitchen and saw a basket of colored eggs on the countertop. Caitlin's mother was at the sink, filling a vase with water. She had changed out of the bathrobe she was wearing when she answered the door. Kimo felt a little guilty about waking her so early. He stood by the kitchen table and tried to think of something to say as he watched her arrange the flowers he'd brought. She carried the vase to the living room and placed it on a table next to a greeting card with the words "He is Risen" emblazoned on the front.

"Do you know how the Easter traditions originated?" Kimo asked when Martha returned to the kitchen.

"I guess with the early Christians," she said, setting a plate of hot cross buns on the table. She opened a cabinet door and offered Kimo a choice of teas. He sat in a chair at the table and told her he'd have whatever she was having.

"The earliest Christians were also Jews," he said. "Of course, the followers of Jesus weren't called 'Christians' until much later. Different groups of people who followed 'the Way' were known by various names—Ebionites, Essenes, Nazoræans. Jesus wasn't called 'Nazarene' because he was from Nazareth."

"No?"

Martha set cream, sugar, honey, and butter on the table.

"There's no reference to a town named Nazareth in any known writings until the fourth century," Kimo said. "By then, pilgrims had started coming to visit the places made famous in the Gospels. After Constantine recognized Christianity as a legitimate religion, councils were convened to decide about the governing doctrines. The Church fathers created a hierarchy and established uniform beliefs and practices. Churches were built, and the likely sites were chosen for events like the crucifixion and the raising of Lazarus based on the descriptions in the Gospels."

"That makes sense," Martha said. "Jesus's disciples were there, after all."

"His disciples were there, but we don't know who wrote the four canonical Gospels. The earliest Gospel we have—by Mark—was probably written after Jerusalem fell to the Romans. That was about three decades after the crucifixion," Kimo said. "Mark didn't have a very accurate understanding of the geography in Palestine; he was probably writing what he'd heard rather than what he knew. Matthew and Luke later drew on Mark's Gospel and possibly other sources for their Gospels, though Matthew was writing for a Jewish audience and he corrected some of the errors."

The kettle started to hiss, and Martha rushed to remove it from the stove before the water reached a full boil. She filled a ceramic teapot with steaming water, added two Earl Grey tea bags, and joined Kimo at the table.

"I would love to go on a tour of the Holy Land," she said. She picked up the plate of hot cross buns and held it out to Kimo.

"Thank you," he said, and selected a bun. He didn't usually eat pastries, but he didn't want to offend Caitlin's mother by refusing her hospitality.

"What does it mean, then, that Jesus was a Nazarene?"

Kimo took a bite of the bun before responding. "He may have been a member of a religious order or sect. A community of ascetics lived on the eastern shore of the Dead Sea long before Jesus's time. We call them Essenes; the more generic term was Nazoræan. They despised wealth and practiced the principles of brotherly love that Jesus spoke about. Nazoræan priests took vows and wore long white garments. They followed strict rules, like fasting."

Martha poured tea into two cups. "Do you want any sweetener?" she asked as she handed a teacup to Kimo.

"No, this is fine, thanks," Kimo said, reaching for the cup. "We tend to associate Judaism of the time with the Temple in Jerusalem, but there were other groups of Jews besides the Pharisees and Sadducees—just as Christianity is now divided into denominations. Jesus aroused opposition from Temple leaders by openly ignoring prohibitions like healing on the Sabbath and by challenging some Temple practices."

"Like throwing out the money changers, you mean?"

Kimo nodded. "One of the incidents recorded in all four Gospels. The Temple was the only place where Jews could offer sacrifices—an essential part of their religion. The animals had to be unblemished and suitable for sacrifice, and the Temple wouldn't accept foreign coins, so trade with pilgrims was a thriving business, especially during religious festivals like Passover. The Christian celebration of the resurrection grew out of the feast of Passover, without all the strict laws like keeping *kosher* and offering sacrifices in the Temple."

"That makes sense," Martha said. "Jesus was the fulfillment of the Hebrew Scriptures. He brought new teaching that didn't require following the old laws anymore."

"That was Saint Paul's interpretation, anyway. Christianity as we know it was not started by Jesus."

Martha added cream and sugar to her tea, then picked up a knife and cut a bun into two pieces. She spread butter on the top half—the part with the cross of icing—and spooned honey onto the bottom half. Kimo smiled, remembering Caitlin's similar ritual in Ireland. Martha bit into the piece covered with honey. Kimo hesitated. Should he tell her that honey wheat cakes were traditionally offered to the Phoenician goddess Astarte? *Better work up to that . . .*

"There was a huge division in the early Church, you know, about whether new Christians had to become Jews first. Paul, in particular, was reaching out to many Gentiles and didn't want his mission to be overly restricted by requirements like circumcision. By incorporating elements of Judaism and Paganism the new religion gained authenticity, but in order to survive as a viable movement, it had to distinguish itself as separate from both. The Jewish Sabbath is observed on Saturday but the Passover date is based on a lunar calendar, so it can fall on any day of the week. Sunday was the Sun God's Day for the Pagans; it became the official day of rest in the Roman Empire when Christianity became the official religion. By ecclesiastical decree, all Christians had to observe Easter on the same Sunday throughout the Empire."

Kimo's studies of comparative religions had shown him that these were the kinds of controversies that still divided churches— not a fundamental belief in God, but disagreements over the acceptability of celebrating the resurrection on a day other than Sunday.

"I wondered why Christmas is always on the twenty-fifth of December but the date for Easter changes every year," Martha said. She took a sip of tea and then ate the other half of the bun.

"Christmas is a fixed feast day, whereas Easter is one of the moveable feasts," Kimo said. "In ancient times, people created their rites in accordance with natural laws and observable phenomena. Nature was sacred to them and they looked to the heavens to guide their movements. The spring equinox was the occasion for a lot of

Pagan rituals, which the Church later prohibited because it wanted to be the only show in town, and because the fundamentalists never have known how to have a good time."

Kimo grinned mischievously but Martha didn't notice, so he continued.

"The spring festivals were sacrifices to fertility goddesses like Astarte—Ishtar in Babylonia, where the Israelites acquired many of their traditions. Easter is celebrated on the first Sunday after the full moon after the vernal equinox, but the Church later decreed that the vernal equinox shall always be the twenty-first day of March—regardless of what's going on in the heavens."

The precise time of the equinox—the moment when the sun crosses the equator—is not a subject that can be debated or decreed, Kimo thought as he drank the last of his tea.

Many ancient cultures had developed systems for predicting cycles and had adopted calendars for keeping track of time. Some Eastern Orthodox churches still used the old Julian calendar, which the West abandoned in favor of the Gregorian. The Mayan calendar extended far into the future from the time when it was calculated, ending ominously in the year 2012. Time streamed onward, the universe expanded, and the sun, moon, and planets continued in their orbits, unaffected by the demarcations assigned by man.

"I knew Passover was often observed around the same time as Easter, but I never really thought about why," Martha said.

"At Passover, the paschal lamb was sacrificed and eaten after its blood was sprinkled—to commemorate the protection of the Hebrews from the plagues in Egypt. Jesus became the Lamb of God who redeemed the world by shedding his blood, a sacrifice commemorated in the Mass. The faithful now symbolically eat the lamb in the Eucharist. But the significance of the symbolism goes beyond that. Important as remembering historical events may be to a people, rituals retain meaning because they represent universal truths. In many ancient initiation rites, people ate the 'bread of life' and drank the 'fruit of the vine' or other intoxicating drink. Common objects can have both a mundane purpose and a symbolic meaning."

Martha rose from her chair and brushed crumbs off the tablecloth and onto a paper napkin. "I suppose bread and wine are standard fare in many cultures," she said curtly, then stepped on the pedal of the trash can to open the lid. She tossed the napkin inside. The lid closed with a bang.

"Sure," Kimo said. "The Essenes' communal meal was presided over by a priest and included a bread-and-wine ritual."

He didn't want to alienate Caitlin's mother and watched her closely for clues about how much information he should share. She seemed to be avoiding eye contact. Kimo looked for a way to bring her back into the conversation.

"Bread represents the harvest of the grain that began as a seed, the completion of a cycle of growth. In agrarian communities, ensuring a good crop was vital."

"I can appreciate that," Martha said, returning to her chair. "I grew up on a farm."

"Really? Where?"

"Near Kansas City." Martha looked up at him. "It was a rural area at the time. Now it's all one big metropolis."

"My parents played at a theater in Kansas City one summer," Kimo said. "I was about nine. I remember it was very flat."

Martha chuckled. "Yes, it is that."

Kimo glanced at a clock, wondering how much more time Caitlin needed. He told Martha about the Pagan origins of traditions like colored eggs and hot cross buns.

"In the Mithraic rites, the neophyte received a small round cake or wafer of unleavened bread—the heavenly host in the shape of the solar disk."

"And the bunny?"

"Hares were symbols of fertility and sacred to Eostre, the Anglo-Saxon goddess of the dawn."

"Hmm," Martha said. "So what do you make of all that?"

Kimo thought for a moment before answering, aware that new ideas could be troubling to old mindsets. "People use myths and symbols to express truths about common human experiences. Popular books and films succeed in capturing the imagination of a whole generation or culture because the themes resonate with basic concerns or emotions we all have, whether the story is set in a future time and distant galaxy, during the Civil War, or in a land like Oz."

"That's different from worshipping idols and believing superstitions and erecting temples to different gods like Pagans did and, I don't know, maybe still do," Martha said.

"Popular culture is superficial. Most people aren't interested in the deeper meaning behind symbols; they tend to look for easy answers and simplistic solutions. That's why mystery schools kept their rituals and teachings hidden and only revealed their secrets to the select few who had been initiated into the tradition and had a basis for understanding the significance of the symbolism. Philosophers and sages in any age seek truth and caution against worshiping outer forms. What you call superstitions may be the empty shells that remain after the original meaning is lost."

A Higher Power may have inspired the original prayer or ritual but, over time, rituals lose their meaning and become empty gestures. Inspiration, though, is limitless.

"But I completely agree with you," Kimo added, "which is why I'm not a fan of religion."

All material forms would eventually give way to newer, fresher expressions. In time, the new forms would be accepted, but initially they seemed unthinkable to conventional believers—much as Christians' radical new views provoked hostility and aroused suspicion in the Rome of Paul's time.

Martha scratched her head and looked puzzled. "Well—I'm not saying all religious people are superstitious. The Jews believed in one God."

"Yes—one that favored them," Kimo said, grinning. *People forget that traditions are developed by humans, not God. And even with the best intentions, humans are fallible.*

"Ideas about God change as people evolve, both individually and collectively. The early Israelites worshipped differently from the Jews after the Babylonian exile. A child's understanding of God is different from an adult's. Maybe God is a force that we've all been worshipping under different names. It's the same spark of awareness in each of us, however we conceptualize that, but our divine nature can't be grasped with the intellect. Divine presence is experienced in the workings of our lives, and contacted in silence."

Martha leaned back in her chair and crossed her arms. "Can't religion play a part in that?"

"I think it's great that people join together to worship and share fellowship—discuss ideas, encourage each other to grow and learn. Some religious people have done a lot of good in the world. But any religion that claims supremacy over others is dangerous and perpetuates division. Ultimately, we're all part of the same human drama. I can't condone teachings and practices that encourage violence and hatred."

"Well, of course not," Martha said. "Jesus taught us to love one another."

"Actually, Paul was the one who emphasized brotherly love, and he was addressing members of his churches. Paul and Jesus both sought to bring people to the spirit of the teachings rather than the letter of the law. They both threatened the established order—like John before them, who was beheaded."

The birth of a new age is never easy, Kimo thought, *and the pioneers usually pay a price.* Throughout history, well-meaning people and ruthless tyrants alike had persecuted prophets and visionaries whose understanding extended beyond the ordinary. *They know not what they do.*

"The Jewish tradition didn't include stories about gods fathering children with mortals, like the escapades of Zeus," Kimo said. "But you may not realize how similar the Christ story is to Pagan mythology. Dionysus, for example, had twelve disciples and turned water into wine. He was the Greek 'god of the vine.' The Christian dying-and-rising god was different from the gods of other ancient mystery religions because God had incarnated in the flesh, as Jesus, to lead his followers to salvation."

"I'd say that's a pretty big difference!"

"If true, then yes. Jesus's disciples didn't believe that, though. The earliest writings in the New Testament are Paul's letters. He never knew Jesus and he didn't talk about Jesus's travels or birth or miracles or parables, like some of the Gospels did. Paul was from

Tarsus, a center of Pagan philosophy. The cities he visited were dominated by the Pagan mystery cults."

Martha removed the teapot and condiments from the table. "He was probably trying to convert them."

"Or *initiate* them!"

Martha stacked the plates and carried them to the sink. "I guess it's a matter of faith."

Kimo smiled, wondering what effect Caitlin's growth process would have on her mother. Religions' faithful followers clung to their dearly held beliefs as if their salvation depended upon reciting the right creed, and religious authorities often discouraged questions about accepted tenets. *Believe, or leave . . .*

"Faith and belief are different," Kimo said. "A person can have faith in life, in people, or in a Supreme Being without believing any particular creed."

Before Martha could reply, Caitlin appeared in her wheelchair. Kimo brightened when he saw her and rose to greet her.

"Ready to go?"

"As ready as I'm gonna be." Caitlin turned her chair around and exited the kitchen. Kimo followed.

Martha walked with them to the door. "It's so early. Where are you off to—sunrise service?"

"In a sense," Kimo said. "The Cathedral is one of my favorite places."

"Really?" Caitlin asked. "When did you get re-reli-gious?"

Kimo smiled. "Who said anything about religion?" He winked at Martha.

"Caitlin, shouldn't you eat something?" Martha asked.

"Nah, I'm not . . . hun-gry," Caitlin said. She sat in her wheelchair facing the door, waiting for someone to open it.

"Don't worry," Kimo told Martha, "I'll take care of her."

"What kind of name is Kimo?" Martha asked.

"It's the Hawaiian version of Jim, but for me it's a nickname." He extended his hand. "Karl Marx Owen. I guess we haven't been properly introduced."

Martha seemed delighted by the gesture and shook Kimo's hand. "Martha Johnson."

"My apol-lo-gies," Caitlin said over her shoulder. "But if we're talk-ing social . . . graces, you're an un-invited guest," she said, point-ing a finger at Kimo.

"Well, then," Kimo said, opening the front door, "I guess I better leave."

Martha held the door open while Kimo pushed the wheelchair across the threshold. "You kids have fun," she said before closing the door.

"We always do," Kimo said.

Caitlin scrunched her face into a puzzled expression. "Karl . . . Marx . . . Owen. I didn't know that was your name."

Kimo was silent, but troubled by the gaps in Caitlin's memory. Her body would heal, no doubt. But would her mind?

✐ 42 ✐

Maybe I should have stayed at home until I can walk on my own, Caitlin thought as Kimo pushed her wheelchair out of the parking lot at the National Cathedral in Washington. They had arrived too late to see the sunrise, but the sight of the cherry trees in full bloom was equally spectacular.

People streamed out of the exits of the second-largest cathedral in the United States. The Cathedral Church of Saint Peter and Saint Paul had been built over a period of eighty-three years. Caitlin had taken a tour with Jayson shortly after they moved to the area. Gazing at the magnificent rose windows, she'd imagined an elegant wedding within the contours of Indiana limestone. After her father died, the Cathedral was where she'd gone to light a candle and pray.

She glanced up at the towers reaching for the heavens, wonder-ing what the view was like from there. The top of the central tower was the highest point in the District, she'd read. Her attention quickly returned to the ground when Kimo pushed the wheelchair off the pavement and onto the grass.

Caitlin gripped the arms of the wheelchair as she was bounced over the bumpy surface. The movement no longer caused her to wince in pain, but it was still jarring and uncomfortable.

Finally, Kimo stopped in an open area, set the brake on the wheelchair, and stood in front of her. After taking a deep breath, he said, "Okay, I've put together a program of some simple exercises that can help you regain—"

Caitlin shook her head. "No. I can't."

"You can," Kimo said gently, "if you start slowly. And trust me."

"Why should I . . . trust . . . you? What do you know about my bo-dy?"

"More than you give me credit for. Look, Caitlin, I want to help. You're making this harder than it has to be."

"No, you 'look.' I didn't ask for your help. I didn't ask—" she paused and took a breath before continuing, her voice faltering—"to be stuck in this . . . chair."

Seeing the wounded look on Kimo's face, Caitlin felt even more helpless and frustrated. The calm acceptance she'd experienced during the night had vanished. In the light of day, she was still confined by her condition. She may have experienced a break-through in consciousness, but transferring new realizations into all areas of her life was going to take some doing.

She had made good progress in therapy but had arrived at an impasse. Her left arm was functional again, though it still ached much of the time. Walking was a challenge; her legs felt wobbly and weak, and she relied on the walker. Her movements were awkward and clumsy. She felt safe in her wheelchair, and vulnerable away from it.

"I feel like . . . like a child, learn-ing how to walk and talk a-gain."

Kimo crouched down to her level and stared at the ground. After a few moments, he stood up and faced her.

"Okay. I have an idea. Close your eyes."

Caitlin hesitated, and then decided to go along. Maybe she did trust him. *Just a bit.* She closed her eyes.

"See yourself as a small child, ready to take your first step. Can you imagine that?"

Caitlin nodded.

"How does it feel?"

How does it feel—a simple question. Why were feelings so hard for her to verbalize? Had she always been this way? She had no way of knowing what she'd been like before the coma; she only knew that now she felt . . . disconnected.

"Scar—Scar-y, but ec . . . ex-citing. There's so much I wanna . . . ex-plore."

"That's good," Kimo said. "What name were you called as a child?"

"Catie."

"Okay," he said, taking her hands in his. "I want you to hold that image of Catie and—keep your eyes closed—stand up and take a few steps, toward me."

Caitlin was skeptical at first and threatened to open her eyes, but with Kimo urging her on, she was willing to try. She stood up and lurched toward him.

Her thoughts flashed to a night scene. She and Kimo were standing together in the center of a circle, surrounded by chanting people wearing painted masks and animal costumes. Kimo was barely recognizable, but Caitlin knew it was him. In her mind's eye, she saw a path of glowing hot coals laid out before her like a red carpet.

Caitlin opened her eyes and fell, disoriented, into Kimo's arms.

Was it a dream, or some kind of vision?

With Kimo's help, she returned to the safety of her chair. "That was w-weird," she said, feeling dazed and confused.

"What?"

"Huh? Oh, it—it's . . . nothing."

"Don't lose heart," Kimo said. "The journey of a thousand miles begins with a single step." He grinned.

Caitlin looked up at him. His eyes were sparkling again. Or was it that her eyes sparkled when she looked at him? She hadn't known how much she'd missed him, until now.

Kimo took Caitlin to a restaurant in Chinatown. She ate a spring roll with her fingers, dipping one end into the hot mustard and the other into the sweet-and-sour sauce, but she used a spoon for the bowl of egg-drop soup. She attempted to use chopsticks to maneuver a prawn onto her plate, but it landed in her lap instead. Flustered, she pouted for a moment before picking up her fork. Kimo either didn't notice or pretended not to notice, and Caitlin was grateful. The aromas were irresistible, and she was hungry.

They compared favorite scenes from books and films. Caitlin relaxed; she could discuss classics that she remembered without feeling embarrassed about not being up-to-date on the latest releases. Most of Kimo's picks were unfamiliar to her, but he was an animated storyteller and she enjoyed listening to him.

After lunch, they played in a park. Kimo gently pushed Caitlin on a swing and slowly spun her around on a merry-go-round. For the first time since Scotland, she felt happy. By the end of the outing, she was practically purring.

"Is the car new?" she asked when Kimo drove her home in the red convertible. She felt timid asking questions about things she might have known before the coma.

"I bought it a few months ago from my friend Barry," Kimo said.

He stopped the car in front of the townhouse and cut the motor, interrupting the Chaka Khan song that was playing on the radio. Caitlin continued to hum the tune as the song played in her mind.

"There's something I need to ask you," Kimo said when she had finished.

Caitlin turned toward him. "Sh-sure, Ki-mo."

"You said earlier you didn't remember my full name," he said, watching her closely.

"That's right."

"You must have seen it on my file a hundred times."

"A long time ago. Guess I for-got."

"What else have you forgotten?"

"If I for-got, how can I say, silly?" Caitlin giggled, and then added, pensively, "What is mem-or-y but the . . . eva . . . eva-nes-cent whis-per of the past?" She grinned, pleased with her growing ability to express herself.

"Who said that?"

"I did."

"I know but—never mind. What I really want to know, I guess, is: Do you remember Ireland?"

"Of course, that's where I met Der . . . Dru," Caitlin said. "No, wait—that was Scot-land. I think . . ." She noticed Kimo's intense stare and realized he didn't know about Dru.

Kimo looked away in grim silence, then unlocked his jaw and asked, "Do you remember the night of the solstice? The initiation?"

"Ini—ini-sh—" Caitlin stammered. "What init-i-ation?"

Kimo let out an audible sigh. "That's what I was afraid of."

"Well—tell me!"

"I can't. I probably shouldn't have brought it up."

"But if I was there—"

"Sorry."

Kimo got out of the car. He removed Caitlin's folding wheelchair and then helped her walk up the stairs. The front door was unlocked. Inside, Martha was sitting on the couch in the living room, reinforcing a loose button on one of Caitlin's blouses. Kimo told her not to get up; he couldn't stay. He handed Caitlin the box of chocolates he'd promised her, said goodbye, and left.

Caitlin sat in her chair in the entryway contemplating the box in her hands. She was frustrated that Kimo wouldn't tell her what had happened in Ireland, but her inability to remember concerned her even more. She laid the unopened box on the table beside the vase of calla lilies and unwrapped the fortune cookie she'd brought from the restaurant.

"He seems like a nice young man," Martha said.

"Yes." Caitlin had little energy left for the effort that conversation required of her.

"Where did you meet him?"

"Umm . . ." No longer having a ready answer for everything, Caitlin was beginning to dread questions. "At the kil—clinic, I think. Where I worked af-ter l-law school. I help—I helped him get a cour-i-er job . . . with a law firm."

"He must be very grateful."

"Yeah, I guess. It wasn't a big deal. I just called some . . . con-tacts."

"Having someone who believes in you *is* a big deal," Martha said.

"It can change your life." She rose to take the blouse to Caitlin's room. "Supper's almost ready."

After working with lawyers for years, Caitlin sometimes forgot that not everyone enjoyed the same access to them that she did. Kimo probably *was* grateful she'd opened a door for him.

I guess there's a certain kind of wisdom that comes from being a mother. Mothers were present from the moment of birth—and before. The bond felt suffocating at times, but it was irreplaceable. Especially when she believed in you.

Caitlin cracked open the fortune cookie and removed the slip of paper hidden inside. "Travel brings good fortune," it read. Caitlin snorted. *In my dreams.*

She tossed aside the cookie and wrapper and wheeled her chair into the dining room for Martha's special Easter dinner. Her mother was a good cook, and Caitlin appreciated the wholesome foods she prepared. With mixed emotions, she remembered the many family dinners the four Roses had shared together.

∽ 43 ∽

Sam sat in the rented car across the street from Caitlin's town-house. He watched as a man with a ponytail helped Caitlin up the steps; the guy left soon after. Sam still hadn't gotten a good look at Caitlin, and from a distance he couldn't make out details. It had to be her, though; the address matched the one he'd found online months before, and clearly this woman was disabled. To Sam's relief, she was alive.

He hadn't meant to cause an accident; he'd taken the turn too fast and lost control of the SUV. He shouldn't have been drinking, but the liquor helped calm his nerves. He had wanted to impress everyone and instead he'd fucked up big time. He would never forget the sight—and sound—of the crushed BMW and its injured driver, her body slumped against the steering wheel. The horn blared continuously. Sam's self-preservation instincts won out over his physician's impulse to provide aid. The vehicle he was driving wasn't his; other people's interests were at stake. Even if he had wanted to turn himself in, he couldn't betray Neil and the others.

He'd driven the damaged GMC, with its tailpipe dragging, off the main roads to a discrete location and called Carter Simms. Simms was irate. He told Sam to thoroughly clean and vacuum the SUV—to eliminate any evidence that could lead detectives back to any of them—and then abandon the vehicle by the waterfront. The VIN number had already been removed as a precautionary measure, and the SUV had never been registered; Sam's involvement would only be suspected if eyewitnesses provided a detailed description of him and his movements or if he left traces of hair, blood, finger-prints, or any other incriminating evidence in or on the vehicle.

The waterfront was a long five-and-a-half miles away and the damned tailpipe scraped against the pavement the whole way. Fortunately, the heavy rain provided some cover, and city streets were practically deserted. Sam found a run-down self-service car wash that was empty. He purchased spot remover, towels, and wipes from the vending machine and vacuumed the car as best he could with one working arm. His left forearm had been broken in the crash. The shock of the accident helped numb the pain for a while, but the arm was useless. Sam searched the car for personal items and wiped down surfaces to clear away fingerprints, then he grabbed the manila envelope he'd picked up from the ground at the accident scene and made his way back to his safe house, the Embassy Suites Hotel near the airport.

After showering, he dressed his wounds and created a makeshift splint; next, he tied a t-shirt into a sling. He figured he would arouse fewer suspicions by seeking treatment once he got back to the base hospital. He'd claim he was clumsy and tripped over his luggage at the airport. That would also explain the bruise on the left side of his face.

He paced the floor until after midnight, wondering if she was dead or alive. Unable to stand not knowing, he called several hospitals until he found out where she'd been admitted. When the rain let up, he threw his blood-stained clothes into a trash can in the men's room on the first floor of the hotel, called a taxi, and went to the hospital. He felt compelled to see her—maybe her condition wasn't as serious as it had looked at the scene. He asked the driver to wait.

That was probably a stupid move.

He pilfered a long-stemmed white rose from a bouquet on a table by the elevator and hid it inside his jacket, flashing his medical credentials to gain admittance to the ICU, a restricted area. The inattentive staff didn't bother with questions at one a.m.

Sam left the rose outside Caitlin's door as a sort of peace offering—he didn't dare enter the room. He had no right to even be there. It was a simple gesture, meant to alleviate his guilt. He didn't wish her any harm; she'd gotten in the way of his plans. Yes, he'd been careless, driving so fast in the rain. But if she'd gotten through that light, if she'd talked to that reporter . . . No, he couldn't have allowed that to happen. Too much was at stake.

He returned to his room and crashed. Sunlight was streaming through the window when he awoke. He packed quickly and grabbed a donut and a cup of coffee from the breakfast bar. A taxi was just pulling up to the front entrance of the hotel when he walked outside. Sam climbed in after the previous passenger got out.

"Airport. ASAP," he told the driver.

Even if he could be exonerated for causing the accident, leaving the scene was a felony. Neil said the police had already impounded the SUV when Simms arrived at the waterfront at dawn, so they all hoped Sam's once-over had been sufficient. When Carty learned that Sam had made several calls from the phone in his room, he grilled him about all his movements after the crash. He was furious when he found out that Sam had dumped his clothes in the hotel restroom.

"I didn't leave them in my room," Sam said in his defense.

Simms's face turned red with rage. "This guy's an idiot!" he told Neil.

Neil Morton remained calm through it all, telling Simms he'd take care of it and reminding him that Sam was untrained.

Sam didn't want to confirm their assessment by telling them he'd gone to the hospital. The move was impulsive and risky, and Sam had been berating himself ever since. At the time, though, he felt an overwhelming need to take action. He was still in shock, he concluded later; he wasn't thinking clearly. Maybe it was the painkillers. He always carried a supply of medical essentials in his Dopp kit.

During the flight home to California, he opened the manila envelope he'd found on the ground near the BMW, covered with some slimy food purée. The contents were disappointing—a few journal articles about thimerosal and some notes Ms. Rose had typed up about legal precedents. Sam doubted the papers added anything of value to the notes and files in Caitlin's office, and Neil had already gone through those.

Sam hadn't disclosed the existence of the documents to Neil; he was waiting to see how this trip turned out before laying all his cards on the table. In spite of Sam's blunder, Neil had followed through on his promise to recommend Sam to fill a sudden vacancy on the ACCV, the Advisory Commission on Childhood Vaccines that oversaw the NVICP, the National Vaccine Injury Compensation Program. Sam had attended his first meeting two weeks earlier. The agenda included an overview of the NVICP and discussions about whether the statute of limitations for filing a claim ought to be extended. Sam had also met with Neil and his associates; they prepped him for his upcoming testimony before the Senate committee. Even with Neil's connections, the matter kept getting delayed.

Neil had mentioned that Caitlin had been released from the hospital. Sam decided to find out to find out for himself how she was doing. Now that he'd seen her, he needed to get to the airport and head home. Jacqueline and Yvonne were spending Easter with his mother and his sister, and he was scheduled to pick Jacqueline up at the end of the day. Now that she was a little older, Sam was allowed overnight visits. His mother often served as intermediary so that he and Yvonne didn't cause a scene and upset Jacqueline.

Caitlin Rose was still on Sam's mind as he drove toward the George Washington Memorial Parkway. He pushed away fears that his role might be discovered, but his conscience plagued him. *She wasn't exactly an innocent bystander,* he reminded himself. *She should have minded her own business, and stayed out of Neil's affairs.*

Sam dismissed his negligence as an unfortunate occurrence. *Far worse crimes have been committed in the name of "the mission."* Some people seemed to consider bombing an abortion clinic a justifiable form of protest, though, being a doctor himself, Sam didn't understand the logic that said killing a medical professional was somehow acceptable while removing unwanted fetuses was not.

And how many crusades had been waged in the name of religion? The Jesuits, Sam had read, had infiltrated societies throughout the world at times in their dark history, using whatever means necessary to advance the interests of the One Holy Catholic and Apostolic Church. Countries had expelled them, and popes had banned their order. They justified their sometimes-heinous acts as being in service of their leader, the Supreme Pontiff of the Universal Church.

Sam wished he felt that kind of devotion. He was still looking for something to serve wholeheartedly. It hadn't been religion or medicine; it hadn't been his country or his family. But maybe he'd finally found his way out of the desert.

∽ 44 ∽

A week after Easter, Caitlin woke early from a vivid dream about skating on ice. Leaping and twirling with joyful exuberance, the dream skater moved gracefully and freely, with no fear of falling. Though Caitlin had never been quite so accomplished, she'd loved skating on the frozen pond at her grandparents' farm near Olathe.

It was the same land that her great-grandparents had farmed. Jesse Clayton bought the property from his parents before they died. For years, he rented the land to a neighboring farmer and used the house as a weekend retreat. He and Elizabeth worked in the garden and enjoyed the quiet of the prairie. Caitlin thought her grandmother seemed happiest when she was at the farm. Elizabeth sang as she did her chores and proudly displayed the vegetables she'd harvested from the garden before finding some creative use for them in a salad, soup, casserole, or side dish.

When Jesse retired from the bench, he and Elizabeth sold their house in town and moved to the farm full time, ending their days in the same house they'd shared with Jesse's parents many years before, when Caitlin's mother and Aunt Susan were small. Caitlin's Uncle Jimmy was born later, after the Claytons moved to town.

After the Judge suffered a stroke, Elizabeth lost interest in the garden and it was soon overrun with weeds. The Judge was buried on the property, alongside his parents. Since Elizabeth's death, the house had sat empty and in need of repair. Susan had always been the decisive one; she'd died of breast cancer, and Martha and Jimmy couldn't agree on what to do with the property. Caitlin wondered if she and Bobby might inherit it someday. They probably wouldn't agree on what to do with it either.

A new family tradition. What a waste.

When she'd left Kansas, Caitlin had been ready for a new life, free from the past, and she hadn't looked back. Only now was she discovering how much the past was still with her.

Inspired by the dream, she got out of bed and moved first the wheelchair and then the walker to the garage. Then she chose a spot in the living room and began to practice the taijiquan movements Kimo had shown her. Perhaps she would never skate again, but she could learn to move with ease and grace. Maybe she could even learn to relax.

After several weeks of daily practice, Caitlin noticed that her body felt lighter, and her mood improved. She and Martha started taking day trips to local attractions. Martha was only willing to drive into Washington on Sundays. On other days, they left the car at the King Street Metrorail station in Old Town Alexandria and rode the train into the city. They visited the Smithsonian Institution, the National Arboretum, the White House, and the Capitol.

Caitlin still tired easily and by evening had little energy for thought or conversation. Her speech had improved as much as her speech therapist believed it was going to, and she felt embarrassed by the remaining impediment. Now, every word she spoke required careful consideration.

Intention—maybe that's not such a bad thing.

Kimo came by on Saturdays and showed her more taiji positions. There were twenty-four, he said, in the simplified form he was teaching her. He introduced three new positions each week and told Caitlin that after she learned them all, he would take her out to the park and they could practice the entire routine together.

Caitlin looked forward to Kimo's visits. She tuned out when Martha asked him about organic foods and nutrition but perked up when he discussed religion and philosophy with her. Their conversations stimulated interest in topics Caitlin hadn't thought about in years. She'd first discovered the wonders of ancient Greece and the classical world in a college course on the history of theater. Captivated by the period, she later studied Greek philosophy, myth, and ethics.

She was impressed by Kimo's knowledge of the world's religions. He was well versed in the Bible as well as other spiritual teachings, but his own views seemed to be an eclectic blend. His grandparents were Christian, but his parents had always encouraged him to think for himself, and he was free to accept the kernels of wisdom he garnered from various traditions without guilt or fear of retribution if he didn't buy the whole package. He once told Caitlin he listened to the wind for answers to the questions his heart propounded. She heard his words but didn't fully comprehend his meaning.

Dissatisfied with the interpretations inculcated in childhood Sunday school classes, Caitlin had put aside the God question long ago and turned her attention to more practical endeavors. She'd studied the laws that humans had devised to manage their affairs. Now she yearned to understand the higher laws that governed the cosmos, to discover the truths alluded to by ancient teachings.

She wasn't looking to substitute one belief system for another, though, and stories about miraculous events didn't interest her much. She wanted to witness miracles and experience Spirit at work in her life. She wondered who, among her contemporaries, exemplified the highest expression of human potential.

She was eager to learn—even from Kimo. Previously, she had ignored his rambling explanations, but now she listened closely to what he had to say, grateful he was willing to share the wealth of knowledge and insight he had accumulated.

✐ 45 ✐

With the help of her mother and an occupational therapist, Caitlin gradually regained her independence. She relearned how to change the sheets on her bed, do her own laundry, load and unload the dishwasher. When her mother went grocery shopping, Caitlin went along. Martha helped her file her tax return, shop for a new car, and find a lawyer to pursue her claim for compensatory damages from the crash. Whether she was learning to drive again or walking through the woods, her mother's presence was comforting.

Without the words being spoken, Caitlin knew that her mother was preparing to leave, and she wanted their remaining time together to be as enjoyable as possible. They had learned to respect each other's sensitivities and tread lightly to protect the fragile bond they were forming. In the evenings, they sometimes played Scrabble at the kitchen table; other times, Martha worked on a crossword puzzle in the living room while Caitlin painted.

As Mother's Day approached, Caitlin wondered what gift she could give her mother that would last longer than a bouquet of flowers. Remembering the pansies outside their house in Olathe, she sketched an outline to paint on a canvas. For two weeks, she painted in her room. She stored the finished work in her closet.

Mother's Day arrived and Bobby phoned early. Caitlin said her obligatory "how are you"s to him and Sarah. She and Bobby hadn't had much to say to each other since their argument about what to do with their father's ashes. Caitlin wanted to take the ashes with her to Ireland, but Bobby was adamant that Charlie's remains be buried on family property, at the lake house. Caitlin realized her suggestion seemed unusual to everyone else; her father hadn't shared his dream of going to Ireland with anyone but her. The family's refusal to see her viewpoint and honor what she believed her father would have wanted was the final insult that drove Caitlin away—and made her all the more determined to go to Ireland, with or without the ashes.

While Martha gushed over her grandson, Caitlin stared out the window at the steadily falling rain. She was nervous about driving in the rain, but she also felt anxious about returning to Potowmac Landing, the restaurant that had once been a favorite spot for her and Jayson. They had often lingered in bed on Sunday mornings, making love or reading the newspaper while listening to classical music. Later, they would go out for a sumptuous meal.

After the breakup, painful reminders of Jayson seemed to be everywhere. They had eaten dinner at many of the restaurants in Old Town and often attended musical and cultural events. On weekends, they had enjoyed exploring historical sites in the area. For a long time, Caitlin avoided the places they'd frequented and even the friends they had in common in an effort to put the past behind her. Her life became narrower, but less tormented.

She might not feel ready to drive in the rain or face the ghosts from her past, but she knew she must. Potowmac Landing was the best choice around for both food and atmosphere. It wasn't far, and traffic would be light on a Sunday morning. Martha was dressed and ready to go. Caitlin had reserved a table weeks earlier and disliked the idea of canceling on short notice. She took a deep breath and picked up her car keys.

After Martha had finished talking to Bobby and his family, Caitlin drove her new car—a practical and sturdy wagon—to Daingerfield Island, a strip of land just off the GW Parkway, about a mile south of the airport. Once inside the restaurant, she and Martha were seated at a table overlooking the water.

As she had expected, she was engulfed by memories of happier times. Surrounded by families, she wondered if she would ever be blessed with children of her own. One young family in particular looked like they were living the kind of life that Caitlin had envisioned for herself and Jayson. After ordering two mimosas, she excused herself from the table. She couldn't repress her feelings, but she didn't need to put them on public display. Alone in the restroom, she cried.

When she felt calmer, she returned to the table and led Martha to the buffet line. While Martha ordered a custom omelet, Caitlin piled eggs Benedict, fresh fruit, and pancakes onto her plate and went back to the table. She watched as Martha chatted with the staff at the carving table. The years of separation had helped Caitlin look beyond her mother's values rather than see life through them. She stifled a laugh, wondering if moving to another continent had been Bobby's way of creating distance.

Caitlin was already eating when Martha joined her. Forced to chew her food thoroughly before she could swallow it, she had learned to take the time to really taste the food and appreciate its texture and the subtle nuances of flavor. Never again would she be able to wolf down a sandwich at her desk while simultaneously checking the messages on her voicemail and computer. The days of driving to work, late, while balancing a cup of coffee and eating a breakfast burrito from the drive-through window at a fast-food restaurant were over. Nobody could have convinced her that anything was wrong with that kind of harried lifestyle at the time, but now she had adapted to a slower pace and had no desire to return to the hustle and bustle that had seemed normal in her previous existence.

Caitlin asked Martha about the news from Down Under. In recent weeks, she had begun inquiring about Martha's life—her hopes and interests as a young woman, her life with Ray. She'd found high school boring, Martha had said, and admired Caitlin's discipline and achievement. Years before, she'd hoped to spend her golden years with Charlie, but it was Ray who took her on cruises and introduced her to new friends. He'd even taught her to play golf. She talked about the bridge group that met weekly and her regular activities at church. She seemed eager to share with Caitlin and grateful for her interest.

Perhaps none of us ever really listened to her before, Caitlin thought as she raised her glass in a toast. Only rarely had Caitlin caught a glimpse of the spirited young woman she imagined her mother might once have been. *It must have taken a lot of courage for her to defy her family's expectations.*

What could have been more scandalous for a small-town Kansas girl in the 1950s than conceiving a child before marriage? Was she sorry she'd married so young? How did the Claytons react? Did Charlie ask the Judge for Martha's hand? Maybe someday she would inquire further, Caitlin thought—when their relationship was more stable.

Misunderstandings, resentments, hurt feelings—why is it so hard to get along with loved ones? Acceptance and forgiveness— these are the keys to moving forward in a new way.

And what did Caitlin have to forgive her mother for—mistakes in judgment? Caitlin regretted her part in their estrangement; she knew she was the one who needed to open her heart. Her mother had never stopped loving her, even when she behaved badly.

After brunch, they returned to the townhouse. Forgiveness was still on Caitlin's mind. She consulted Martha's Bible. According to Matthew's Gospel, Jesus taught his followers to confront those who offended them. If the sinner repented, the Christian was told to forgive—not seven times, but seventy.

Caitlin closed the book. She could only imagine how many times her mother must have forgiven her for her failings. She was grateful for her mother's unconditional love. Sure, there were still problems in their relationship that needed to be addressed— changes to be made, lessons to be learned. But loving meant continuing to forgive, again and again. It meant accepting each other even while disagreeing, loving each other in spite of imperfections and failings.

Trying to change another person to match her idea of the perfect lover, parent, boss, or friend would be futile, Caitlin realized.

Why try to change a pansy into a rose? she thought as she retrieved the painting from her closet. *Pansies are beautiful, too—and variety is a desirable feature in a garden.*

ᨔ **46** ᨔ

Martha was overcome with emotion when Caitlin handed her the painting. She laughed, she cried, she breathed a heavy sigh and smiled broadly at Caitlin. She felt so much gratitude she thought her heart would burst. How far Caitlin had come from the stick figures she was drawing in the hospital! The painting was beautiful. Her daughter was recovering. They were learning more about each other, and their relationship was progressing. Martha felt truly blessed. She couldn't be happier. Except . . . if Ray were part of the celebration; if Caitlin would allow him into her life. Martha had faith. They would get there, in time. Her work here was nearly done. Soon, she could go home.

Ray was planning a dinner party to celebrate her return, and Martha was eager to get back. She could scarcely contain her excitement. This reunion would be almost as special as the one that had brought Ray into her life again.

She giggled as she peeled potatoes for the evening meal. *I feel as giddy as a schoolgirl!*

What a crush she'd had on Ray in high school! But he was two years older and captain of the debate team as well as a star of track and field; he never noticed Martha, despite her attempts to attract his attention, and her hopes were dashed when he joined the Army after he graduated.

The Korean War had ended, and Ray's older brother had returned home to a hero's welcome. Ray was determined to prove himself, too. After he left for basic training, Martha gradually forgot about him. He'd been a fantasy anyway. Years later, she heard he was newly married and back in the area. By then, her two young children kept her too busy to wonder "what if."

After Caitlin finished high school and went off to college, Martha's dissatisfaction with her marriage intensified. To occupy her time, she started playing piano for the church choir, took a part-time bookkeeping job with a small company, and reconnected with some old friends from high school. Every October, they attended the high school homecoming game. One year, Ray Johnson showed up. He was a successful entrepreneur, Martha learned from Laura Brennan. His wife had passed away a few years earlier, Laura told Martha as they stood in line for the ladies' room.

The gang went for drinks and snacks at their favorite bar and grill after the game ended. Ray sat next to Martha. At the end of the evening, he walked her to her car and told her how good it was to see her. He remembered her as Susan's younger sister and expressed his sympathy that Susan had died so young.

"She was so full of life," he said, reminiscing.

"Yes, she was a lively one," Martha agreed. Martha had felt like a wallflower compared to her flamboyant sister. Susan had wanted to study fashion design. Even in high school, she was known for her flair and style. When Susan entered a room, people noticed. *Men* noticed. She moved to New York City after receiving her diploma, and though she never achieved her dream of designing a line of clothing, she did carve out a career in the fashion industry, surrounding herself with glamorous friends and associates. "She lived hard," Martha said.

Ray wanted see Martha again; she said she'd have to think about it. She was a married woman, after all. And despite what Caitlin may have assumed, she was never unfaithful to Charlie.

She didn't have to think too hard to figure out that she was still attracted to Ray, however. They started meeting for lunch, and their friendship seemed innocent enough at first. Before long, Martha knew she had to leave Charlie—regardless of what happened with Ray. By the time Caitlin finished law school, Martha had filed for divorce. She didn't bring Ray to the graduation ceremony, but Caitlin was cool toward her. A few months later, she and Ray were married in a small ceremony in Overland Park, where they made their home. Martha sent Caitlin an invitation, but Caitlin didn't respond. Martha thought she would see her at Charlie's funeral, but Caitlin didn't attend that, either. Martha grieved her losses, comforted by her newfound joy in her life with Ray. After being away for so long, going home would seem like a second honeymoon.

Martha missed morning talks with Ray over breakfast and their evening strolls through the park; she looked forward to dining and dancing at the country club. She and Ray still had so much to share together. She was fortunate to have found a good man. She hoped Caitlin would find happiness, and love. And though she was willing to stay as long as Caitlin needed her, she was getting restless. Phone calls were a poor substitute for Ray's warm embrace.

Martha set the table. If only Ray could come for a visit, then her contentment would be complete. She called Caitlin to supper. *Someday,* she thought, *we'll all sit down together for a meal.*

⁓ 47 ⁓

By the middle of May, Caitlin had learned all the taiji forms that Kimo had taught her. As promised, he took her to Rock Creek Park, where they practiced the complete sequence together. Afterward, he took her to lunch at his favorite Ethiopian restaurant in Adams Morgan.

Caitlin listened attentively as Kimo talked about karma and chakras and told tales of enlightened masters from the East who communicated with their disciples through telepathic impressions. She was familiar with Carl Jung's idea of a collective unconscious—a sort of "group mind" we all are part of and influenced by—but the concept of "national karma" was new to her.

"The ethos of a nation—or a town or corporation or any organized group—is expressed through its culture and myths and policies," Kimo explained as they walked along a paved path in the park after lunch. "What values are expressed in guiding documents? How are leaders chosen? How are resources distributed? How is patriotism demonstrated? Nations have destinies; they rise and fall depending on their actions, just like people. Leaders make choices that have consequences for the whole. Life in a country that promotes education and freedom is very different from a place where people are exploited and terrorized."

"I guess the mem-bers of any group share in per—pros-pe-rous times and suf-fer through hard-ships to-ge-ther," Caitlin said.

"Whole groups of people go through recessions and wars as well as golden eras. They shape the times as much as they are shaped by them. The idea of naming generations acknowledges that."

"Like Baby Boomers. Or Ja—Gen X."

"Right. And each of us is part of a soul group, just as we're part of a family, a tribe, a race, and a nation. The differences between groups sometimes cause conflicts—people can always find something to disagree about as long as they feel a need to create separation. We reject in others what we're unable or unwilling to accept in ourselves, the things we prefer to keep in the dark. But at a micro-cosmic level, we're all made of hydrogen, oxygen, nitrogen, and carbon. And from the perspective of other planetary systems, we're all Earthlings."

"Maybe we need an ail—a-l-ien . . . in-vasion to u-nite us all so we stop getting ha—hung up on our dif-ferences!"

"That may not be as far-fetched as you think," Kimo said. "Cave paintings and other artifacts seem to suggest that ancient peoples may have been assisted by more advanced civilizations. Look at Ezekiel's description of the fiery chariot in the sky."

"Oh, come on. Those were just vish—vi-sions."

Sometimes Kimo's ideas zoomed a little too far out of Caitlin's comfort zone. Was he suggesting that centaurs and the pantheon of Mount Olympus had some basis in fact? Still, much in life was utterly amazing.

Who would believe that dinosaurs existed if we didn't have their skeletons?

"Legends tell of ancient civilizations with great technologies to rival our own," Kimo said.

"Like At-lantis?" Caitlin asked. *A well-known myth*, she thought. *Even in Plato's time, people wondered whether the account was true.*

"Maybe those stories persist for a reason."

"Or maybe we cre-ate gods in our own i-mage 'cause that's all we can ima-gine."

"Maybe what happens here is a microcosm of larger forces at work. As above, so below—a basic hermetic principle reflected in the Lord's Prayer: 'on earth as it is in heaven.'"

"Her—her-met-ic, like the Greek god . . . Hermes?"

"Greek name, Egyptian influence. He was often depicted as a shepherd with a lamb. As was Orpheus."

"In other words, Jesus wasn't the first shep-herd to the faith-ful flock."

"He wasn't the first to be betrayed for thirty pieces of silver either. A lot of those stories were teaching tools, like the parables."

"Or the . . . alle-gor-y of the cave."

"Exactly. They persist because they reflect universal principles that operate deep within the human psyche."

"You mean, like Paul—no, Pla-to's belief that everything in cre-a-tion first egg . . . ex-isted as an un-mani-fest idea—or Carl Ya—Jung's theories about ark . . . arche-types?" Caitlin asked. She was excited that she understood something Kimo was talking about; so many of his ideas were foreign to her. But carrying on a conversation still took tremendous effort and focus.

"Or just common human experiences. Modern agricultural practices don't lend themselves to religious symbolism, but even the word 'pastor' shows the connection between religion and the pastoral lifestyle that once was prevalent. The idea of living in harmony with nature is being rediscovered, but it's hardly new. The most common depiction found in early Christian art from Roman catacombs and villas is the Orpheus-like figure of a shepherd holding a lyre and surrounded by animals."

"Bible stories did include a lot of ob . . . obser-va-tions of nature—mist . . . must-ard seeds and lilies and lost sheep. Twist—sorry, trust-ing God to pro-vide for our needs."

"And looking within to find the kingdom of heaven. Do you know what the word 'heathen' means?"

"Umm . . . people who don't know God?"

"People who don't follow the Jewish, Christian, or Muslim version of God," Kimo said. "The Abrahamic faiths all stem from a common source. *Heath* is an open area of uncultivated land, usually because the soil is poor. The *heathen* who lived there were probably poor and uneducated."

"And more likely to be-lieve in super-sti-tions."

"And to live in accordance with natural laws. Shamans and healers tend to follow their own wisdom and intuition. Their seemingly irrational methods and practices fail to satisfy the bureaucrats who are in positions of authority—*they* like rules and order and predictability, and abhor chaos. People feel threatened by what they don't understand. And when they feel threatened, they attack."

Caitlin thought about her Irish great-grandmother. Was Katie Moran suspect because she dispensed natural remedies? Did she pray to saints or invoke deities to assist in her healing work?

Caitlin's lifestyle was very different from that of her ancestors, but the past was a part of her heritage. Her mother's kin included prospectors and pioneers—hardy souls who didn't shun physical labor. In her younger years, Caitlin passed many hours helping out on the Clayton farm or in Martha's garden. Summer at the lake house was a time for outdoor activities and recreation. Fashion trends came and went without notice. Martha kept regular appointments with her hairdresser, dressed respectably, and maintained a comfortable home, but she was neither trendy nor ostentatious.

When she became a professional woman, Caitlin adopted a cosmopolitan lifestyle—living and looking the part was expected. Now that her career as an attorney was over, she could admit to herself how much she disliked being cooped up in an office. Since the accident, she'd stopped wearing makeup and nail polish. She wanted to look her best; she wanted to be attractive. But mostly, she wanted to *be* her best.

When did natural beauty stop being good enough?

Advertisers spent a lot of money telling consumers how to be sexy and attractive by using the right products. Photo retouching created artificial standards that top models could not satisfy.

Allowing media images to set the standard for beauty was a dangerous trend, Caitlin thought. The resulting expectation of perfection was, she concluded, inhuman.

"Things in the real world . . . don't ever line up with the images in our minds, do they?" she asked, ever aware of her own imperfect speech.

"The world is always changing—becoming, evolving. But it's possible to find perfection in imperfection. The Japanese term *wabi-sabi* acknowledges this idea. Think of handmade pottery. No two pieces are ever alike, even when made by the same artist. The differences give them character and uniqueness. Some Native American artisans intentionally include a flaw in their work. If something is done perfectly, they think, they have nothing to look forward to, nothing more to create."

"Maybe I should join a band of In-di-ans."

"It would probably be good for you," Kimo said, laughing. "I've often thought of joining the Amish myself. But then dancing would be a sin." He winked. "Did you know the original word for 'sin' simply meant 'missing the mark.' It was an archery term."

"Enough!" Caitlin said. She spotted a line of kids by an ice cream truck. Slipping her arm through Kimo's, she said, "Let's go get some ice cream. My tweet—*grrrr! Treat.*"

✍ 48 ✍

Caitlin's outpatient program continued for another month and then she was discharged. Her ability to perform activities of daily living had progressed enough that she could function independently. Home visits by the occupational therapist stopped. Caitlin's physical therapist said her mobility was good; she needed to develop stamina, and that would take time. She could safely continue the exercises on her own; if she ever needed help, she knew where to go. Her doctors and therapists had taken her as far as they could, and she was ready for a break from appointments and therapies.

Her newfound passion was painting roses. She'd read that the scent or appearance of roses was often associated with saints and miracles. For Caitlin, the attempt to capture the essence of a rose was a meditative exercise. When the weather was good, her mother accompanied her to area parks and the U.S. Botanic Garden so she could paint in natural light. She experimented with color and began noticing the subtle shifts that occurred as the light changed.

Light was one of those everyday miracles that Caitlin usually took for granted, but she started thinking about its properties after listening to Kimo talk about frequencies and electromagnetic radiation. The full spectrum, Kimo said, includes not only the visible spectrum and colors of the rainbow that human eyes can see, but also x-rays, radio waves, and other kinds of waves. Caitlin knew that animals could detect sounds outside the range of human hearing and wondered what invisible dimensions might be present around her that she couldn't see or hear—but maybe some souls gifted with extrasensory perception could.

In the middle of June, Kimo invited Caitlin to a summer solstice celebration in the Pennsylvania countryside. The gathering was going to be a huge affair, with participants from around the Mid-Atlantic region. They would feast, dance, sing, and play music for three days, camping on land owned by an organic farmer.

"A change of scenery might be good for you," Kimo said.

Caitlin declined. She still felt vulnerable and never ventured far. She who had traveled the country confronting white-collar criminal enterprises and corrupt financial dealings now feared leaving her secure base. Having opened the door to her closet of nightmares, she had no choice but to see the process through, whatever that might require of her.

She was slowly learning to trust Kimo but hesitant about depending on him for her welfare. He didn't seem to be advocating a revolutionary uprising or terrorist acts, but his ideas were unsettling. This "solstice ritual" sounded like an excuse for a bunch of tattooed hippies to gather in a field and get drunk and high and run around half-naked; all Caitlin could picture was a mini version of Woodstock. Still, she was curious about Kimo's lifestyle and thirsty for new ideas. Like a virgin wondering about the mystery of coitus, she felt a mixture of fascination and apprehension when Kimo spoke about secret rituals and traditions. Like most people, she was frightened of the unknown—and wondered what all the fuss was about.

"Is this a pa—pa-gan thing you're going to?" she asked Kimo when he stopped to see her before leaving for Pennsylvania. They sat in the living room sans chaperone; Martha was out shopping.

Kimo laughed. "I'm sure it would seem that way to some. Originally, *pagans* were simply people who lived in the country."

"Stop!" Caitlin grabbed a pillow from a chair and threw it at him. "You sound like a—uh . . . ency-clo-pe-dia!"

Kimo caught the pillow and used it as a cushion for his back. "Just setting the record straight," he said, leaning back against the pillow.

"Mean-ings change. What's the big deal?"

"Sometimes the distortions are intentional—propaganda. People take what's held sacred by others and turn it into something vile and despicable, either because it's foreign and they lack understanding, or because they have an agenda. They demonize it."

"Like Hitler did with the Jews."

"And the Chinese government still does with the Dalai Lama, accusing him of fomenting separatist violence because he seeks autonomy for Tibet. The government suppresses information it doesn't want the Chinese people to know, and slants the information it does permit. People can't determine what's true if they only ever hear one side."

"Didn't President Lick—Lincoln order newspapers shut down during the Civil War?"

"I don't doubt it. Attempts to control the flow of information are nothing new. Unauthorized translations of the Christian Bible were banned in the Middle Ages," Kimo said. "Only clergymen were permitted to read the scriptures. A Protestant reformer named William Tyndale wanted to make the Bible more accessible to common folk. He fled England after his request to translate Hebrew and Greek texts into English was denied. Printed copies of his work that were smuggled into England and Scotland were burned—as Tyndale later was after he was apprehended. The irony is, a few years later, English translations of the Bible were commissioned and printed. The scholars who produced the authorized King James Version drew heavily on Tyndale's work."

"So he g-got it right but was . . . silenced for it."

"The Catholic Church didn't approve of some of his characterizations, which could be read to cast doubt on the claim that papal authority issued directly from Jesus, through the apostles. The Church maintained that priests were essential to the correct interpretation of scripture," Kimo said. "Look how influential the Bible has been, for centuries. Changing one word—or even one *iota*—can alter the meaning of a passage. It's been done, of course—both intentionally and inadvertently."

Caitlin knew that the inclusion or omission of information sometimes meant the difference between winning and losing a case. During trials, she'd been quick to object to misrepresentations by opposing counsel and sought to discredit witnesses who gave inaccurate or misleading testimony. Attorneys were trained to slant information in their clients' favor without suppressing or fabricating critical facts or legal precedent, but the line separating good practice from ethical violations was a blurry one for some lawyers. And despite a judge's instructions, jurors sometimes formed opinions about a case during opening statements—before they even heard the evidence. If Caitlin didn't dazzle the jury from the start, she had a harder time winning them over later. People tended to look for evidence that supported their beliefs, and discounted anything contrary.

"Hmm. It is hard to undo a false im-press-ion," Caitlin said, thinking about political campaigns and the ability of strategists to create an image—or destroy one. "Now, with mass me-dia, everything happens fas-ter."

"Even aside from outright forgeries and mistranslations, many words used in ancient manuscripts have taken on a different meaning from when they were written," Kimo said. "Word play and symbolism often get lost in translation. And people say a lot of things that aren't meant to be taken literally."

"That really 'takes the cake.'"

"Going 'the whole nine yards,'" Kimo said. "At one time, those phrases probably had specific meaning, but now they get used as a kind of shorthand way of conveying an image or idea. Our modern conception of who Jesus was is very different from how he was viewed by the people of his time. When his story spread to different lands, it got embellished."

"Like the game of tele-phone."

"Or the fish that starts as ten inches and gets larger with each retelling of the tale. If you want to know the truth, sometimes you have to peel off the layers and go back to the beginning."

"In the be-ginning was the Word," Caitlin said.

"An overly simplistic translation, perhaps, of what the Greeks meant by *Logos*," Kimo said. "It's not 'word' as in 'command' but more the principle of order or reason underlying all things, like natural law. The Creator breathed life into the created world, but it all originated as thought. We, in turn, know Divine Will first as an impression or thought. We often communicate the thought through speech, which uses the breath. Sound carries vibration. Syllables are like seeds; the seed contains the essence and potential—the blueprint or design of what a thing will become if it matures. A pine tree doesn't grow out of an acorn, an oak tree does. Of course, other factors affect development—favorable climate, healthy soil."

"Yeah, but what some-thing is called doesn't change the . . . qual-i-ty of the thing. 'A rose by any other name,' right?"

"Yes and no," Kimo said. "Some people believe that knowing the true name of a thing gives one power over it. A magician has to know the names of the gods to call upon their powers. By aligning themselves with a particular god, magicians perform wonders in the name of the god. Catholic priests perform exorcisms and other rites, yet the Church opposes 'magic.' What we call 'spells' are just prayers of invocation; the intention is what determines whether someone is practicing black magic or white magic."

"I see what you mean about par . . . propaganda. Make people believe all witches are dangerous and evil."

"People who lack power and knowledge fear that others will try to control them, and sometimes that's what happens. But domination of another's free will is a misuse of power. Power in itself is not a bad thing—one who has attained mastery can do a lot of good in the world."

"Like Jesus. 'By their foo—fruits shall you know them.'"

"In his time, Jesus was accused of 'having a demon' and being a sorcerer. Some feared that he controlled the spirit of John, the Baptizer, and that's how he worked his miracles."

"Weird!"

"In the early part of the first millennium, being called a magician—a *magos* or *goēs*—was a pejorative term, but in the Græco-Roman world, divine men held a higher status and were presumed to use their powers wisely, in accordance with moral principles for the greater good. Philostratus, the Greek sophist who wrote *The Life of Apollonius of Tyana* in the third century, believed wizards relied on lost spirits or barbaric sacrifices to work their magic—an unethical use of natural powers."

"Appa— Who?"

"Apollonius. The Arabs called him Balinas. He was a Greek philosopher and reformer who was born in Asia Minor around the same time as Jesus. He followed the teachings of Pythagoras, abstained from meat and wine, and believed in reincarnation. An empress who admired him commissioned Philostratus to write his biography; I recently tracked down a translation. Apollonius wrote several books and many letters, like the Apostle Paul. In fact, he visited many of the same cities—Ephesus, Corinth, Antioch—and was educated at Tarsus—Paul's hometown—and at the temple of Æsculapius at Ægæ, which wasn't far from Tyana."

"So Paul might have known him?"

"About him, anyway. Apollonius was well-known in the region, and statues and temples were erected in his honor. The language Paul used indicates he was an initiate in some mystery religion; he may have sought to combine Jewish and Pagan traditions. Syncretic practices were common in the ancient world, blending together names and elements of separate traditions. Ancient artifacts have been found of charms and spells that include Jesus's name along with other gods of the time."

"Really?"

"Both Jesus and Apollonius were believed godly by their followers and treacherous by their opponents because of their displays of power. Critics of wonder-workers didn't necessarily allege that the cures weren't real—as in a mere show and trickery. Early Christian apologists couldn't deny Apollonius's existence or his deeds—some even admired him as a virtuous man."

"Virtuous—but not divine like Jesus?"

"Philostratus lived at a time when Origen was defending Christianity against attacks by Pagan writers like Celsus. Christians were still subject to persecution at the whims of different rulers. The defenders of Christianity were trying to make a case for its acceptance—not even its superiority, just a claim that Christians' beliefs about Jesus were as legitimate as those held by the followers of Pagan cults. Apollonius was a revered figured who had already been written about; Philostratus relied on an early account by an Assyrian disciple named Damis, who had traveled with Apollonius and kept a 'scrapbook' of his teachings and prophecies and wondrous deeds. It was called *Scraps from the Manger*—"

"Man-ger, like what Jesus was born in?"

"The parallels between Jesus and Apollonius are striking—which was why the early Church fathers were hell-bent on destroying information about him. Apollonius was honored as a prophet and traveled as an itinerant wanderer, studying with sages and wise teachers of different lands, advising citizens about ethical behavior, reforming cultic practices at various temples, performing cures and miracles. There's even a raising-from-the-dead story—a young woman from a prominent family."

"Like Ja—Jairus's daughter—"

"Yep. Apollonius expelled demons and cured a man of rabies. He also opposed blood sacrifices in the temples, which the temple priests probably viewed as an attack on a profitable enterprise."

"Like Jesus and the money changers," Caitlin said.

"You get a gold star! Other people called Apollonius 'divine,' a son of Zeus or Proteus—his mother supposedly had a visitation announcing his divine birth—but he didn't claim to be a god, any more than Jesus did. The founders of Christianity were the ones who tried to win followers by making Jesus into the One and Only Son of God."

"Wow."

"Religion is no different from any other club—in order to survive, it needs members, and the mystery cults were very popular in the Roman Empire. The strict discipline required of a master— vows, selfless service, strict dietary practices, silent prayer and meditation—wouldn't appeal to the uneducated multitudes. They prefer charms, spells, pursuit of wealth and amusements—and a glorified savior who requires only their devotion."

"Yeah, I can see that. But even if other saintly figures could work mir-a-cles, the rez—res-ur-rec-tion theme does make Jesus stand out as . . . unique."

"Not really," Kimo said. "Apollonius was an outspoken critic of tyrants like Nero and Domitian. He willingly sailed to Rome, even though philosophers had been banned from the Eternal City, and he was incarcerated. He defended himself at his trial and was acquitted; then he quietly slipped away and returned to Greece, where he supposedly wrote about Pythagoras's teachings. At the end of his life, he was said to have ascended from a temple on Crete—and then appeared to a young man in a dream, to affirm the soul's eternal life."

"So . . . do you think one story was copied from the other?"

"You can bet the Christians claimed that! On the other hand, some commentators have suggested that traditional depictions of Jesus are based on an image of Apollonius. And Irenæus, the bishop who wrote volumes refuting the heretics' wrong views, believed that Jesus lived to be an old man. Of course, stories about both Jesus and Apollonius may have been embellished with the divine attributes that were typically applied to revered men of their time."

"Hmm. How come I've never heard of Apa—"

"Apollonius. Probably because once the Christians were in control, they destroyed all the writings of the Pagans that they could get their hands on. They burned the renowned library in Alexandria, shut down the mystery schools, destroyed the Pagan temples and plunged the world into the Dark Ages. So much understanding was lost. . . . These Pagans weren't primitive cannibals who were performing sadistic rituals; these were pure men—and women—who were practicing what Christianity preached: tolerance, philanthropy, service. Philosophers—lovers of wisdom—and Gnostics who sought *gnosis*—knowledge."

Kimo shook his head slightly, his eyes downcast. Caitlin noticed his jaw was clenched; she didn't dare interrupt. After a few moments of silence, he continued.

"When Christianity became allied with Rome's imperial expansion-and-unification campaign, religion became compulsory, and those who sought to learn the truth were driven underground. Like any other authority intent on staying in power, the Church wanted to maintain control. As a result, a lot of blood was shed. You can't let the masses get too powerful. No pun intended! Fortunately, some of the lost writings were preserved in the East. In many cases, it was Irish monks who copied the classical manuscripts from antiquity and reintroduced them into the Western world after Rome was overrun by barbarians."

"Oh, yeah! I remember when we went to see the Book of Kells," Caitlin said, pleased that at least some memories of her travels remained intact.

Kimo gave her a weak smile and then reverted to his serious tone.

"Apollonius was involved with mystery cults, which by their nature are private. He was an ascetic—he spent five years in silence. Philostratus said that he studied with the Magi in Babylon and the Brahmans in India, and then taught throughout the Roman Empire."

"People still go to India to seek wisdom and . . . enlightenment."

"In the East, there are tales of yogis who can bilocate—be seen in two places at the same time—and accomplish all kinds of other feats we would consider miraculous or impossible. Some of them are said to materialize objects at will."

"Jesus said, 'Ger—greater things than I have done ye will do.'"

"*If* you believe," Kimo added. "The mind is a very powerful instrument. When will is coupled with faith, intention, and knowledge—who knows what's possible? I'd like to believe there are advanced beings who show us all the way into the future. But power must be handled with care; it's easy for people to abuse it, or take on more than they really know how to handle. That's why the inner mysteries were so secret. Initiates had to be properly trained and prepared—and worthy. Abuse of power can result in a lot of destruction."

"So you don't think Je-sus was the long-awaited Mas—Messiah?"

"Again, that's a word that means different things to different people. Two thousand years ago, Palestine was an occupied land. The Jews wanted their sovereignty back. They were waiting for a leader to reclaim their nation from Roman rule. They expected the *mashiah* to come from the line of Davidic descent. David and Solomon were military and secular leaders. They were anointed when they were coronated—hence, 'anointed of the Lord.' That's what the Greek term *christos* means—anointed."

"Like when a baby is kar—*christened*," Caitlin said. "Do you think Jesus was a . . . pol-iti-cal leader?"

"One of Jesus's disciples was Simon the Zealot—he may have even been his brother. Galilee was a radical area and, as you probably know, crucifixion was the punishment for insurrection and other crimes against the *Pax Romana*. Roman citizens couldn't be crucified—only slaves and insurgents and the like. Crucifixion was a public event—like public hangings in the square in this country. A warning that troublemakers would not be tolerated."

"And Jesus was a . . . se-cur-ity risk."

"By then, Rome was appointing the High Priest of the Temple—much as China is plotting to control the selection of the next Dalai Lama in Tibet. The High Priest acted as a mediator between the Jews and the Romans. When crowds descended on Jerusalem for Passover, there was always concern about unrest; the Romans were on high alert. Passover was a celebration of liberation from oppression in

Egypt. Anyone talking about a new kingdom would be closely watched, and Jesus was causing a stir."

"But the Romans allowed the Jews to prax—no . . . prac-tice their faith?"

"It depends on when you're talking about in the span of the Empire," Kimo said. "Prior to Constantine, most Romans were Pagans and tolerated a certain amount of diversity. When the Emperor Caligula declared himself divine and ordered that his statue be placed in all temples in the Empire, the Jews refused to allow their Temple to be defiled—much as the early Christians in Rome refused to sacrifice to the Pagan gods and were martyred as a result. Anyway—tensions increased, and the Jews revolted in the year 66 and again sixty years later, with the Bar Kochba revolt. He was a rebel leader whose aim was to deliver the Jews and establish a new kingdom. His name meant 'son of the star.'"

"And Jesus's name?"

"*Yeshua* was the Hebrew name," Kimo said. "It was short for *Yehoshua*—like Joshua, who led the Israelites into 'the promised land' after Moses's death. *Moses* was an Egyptian name, and he was raised in Egypt. The Gnostics read the Exodus story as a metaphor for the secret initiation rites that led to gnosis—the promised land. Remember, Moses was saved from a 'massacre of the infants'—just like Jesus. Matthew's Gospel drew all kinds of parallels between Jesus and the Hebrew scriptures that Christians call the Old Testament."

"Because Jesus was the fa—ful-fill-ment of the pro-phe-cies," Caitlin said. She yawned as she stretched her legs out and shifted into a reclining position. As interesting as she found the conversation, it was beginning to tire her. She looked over at the clock on the mantle, wondering when Martha would return. Perhaps she'd take a nap before dinner. She looked back at Kimo and noticed he wasn't wearing a watch. He still had a long drive ahead of him, and Caitlin knew from experience that he sometimes lost track of time. Should she point out the time, or would he think she was trying to get rid of him? Was she?

"The Jews weren't expecting God to come down from heaven and take the form of a man," Kimo said. "The ineffable Hebrew God *inspired* Moses and Abraham—spoke to them, commanded them, worked through them, but the prophets were mortal. The dying-and-rising tradition came from the Pagan religions and mystery cults."

"And today—where do people go to learn these . . . 'eso-teric' se-crets?"

"Knock and the door shall be opened," Kimo said. "True teachers don't wear a sign declaring, 'Enlightened Master'! The most advanced souls quietly perform their tasks. They don't seek acclaim; they shun it. They often live in remote locations like deserts and mountain tops, except when their mission requires them to teach among the people. It's usually their followers who write their biographies and sometimes distort the facts, so it's hard to know what really happened."

Caitlin reached for a lightweight blanket that was lying on a nearby ottoman; Kimo helped her spread it over her legs.

"And this thing you're goin' to in Pencil—Penn-syl-vania—is it a se-cret ga-thering?" she asked, almost wishing she had agreed to go along.

Kimo shrugged. "It'll just be a good time."

✐ 49 ✐

Caitlin grew restless as her strength returned, but liberation required planning. She wasn't sure where she would go after Martha left; she only knew she could no longer stay in the townhouse that had been the site of so much misery. A year had passed since the accident, and the time had come for her to take another step toward independence: using the telephone. She needed to inquire about moving vans and travel options. She also needed to call OSP about the official termination of her employment.

Until now, she hadn't felt strong enough to approach Neil or the office. She could no longer delay the inevitable. She walked to the kitchen, poured a glass of orange juice, and then dialed the familiar number for Neil's office.

Of all the useless things to remember . . .

"I don't believe Mr. Morton has signed off on that," Betty said.

"Why not? It's been a year since . . . I left."

"You'll have to speak to him about it."

Caitlin sighed. "Is he there?"

"He's in a meeting."

"All right. Just . . . tell him I called," Caitlin said. Nothing was likely to get done so close to the holiday weekend anyway.

On the Fourth of July, Kimo phoned and invited Caitlin to a picnic with a group of his friends to celebrate Independence Day. For Americans, the holiday commemorated a birth. For Caitlin, the anniversary felt more like a death. She wasn't in the mood for a party. Kimo stopped by on his way to the picnic and joined her on the back patio. Martha served them fresh lemonade.

Caitlin had been reading about the signing of the Declaration of Independence, the fateful act that severed ties to the British crown and established the United States of America as a sovereign nation. Britain would not be deprived of its colonies without a fight, and so the outcome was determined by the American Revolution.

"Do you sup-pose birth al-ways has to be bloody and pain-ful?" Caitlin asked.

"A birth is a death too," Kimo said. "A baby leaves behind the protection of the womb and has to survive on its own. A lot of addictions are futile attempts to escape from pain by returning to a state of unconsciousness."

"I guess the trip down the birth canal is nothing short of . . . he-roic."

Kimo nodded. "Babies born by Caesarean section are at a disad-vantage. They have a greater likelihood of developing allergies and respiratory problems, and of becoming obese."

"And the natural timing of the birth is upset."

"Yeah, who knows how babies of the future will be conceived, incubated, and birthed." Kimo sighed. "Someone will find a way to subvert nature on that too, and eliminate the messy business entirely."

"Nature can be pretty vy—vi-o-lent."

"It's hard to know how nature would respond if humans lived in harmony with the earth rather than trashing it. But, dark and light are inseparable. The light is born out of the darkness of the Void. People fear the dark but there's nothing bad about it. It's the unformed. That not yet birthed."

"You don't think there's such a thing as evil?"

"That's a different matter entirely," Kimo said, inhaling deeply. "There's a difference between a natural, timely death and a murder."

"Absolutely."

"Evil intentionally directs power against creation. Whether it's an army or a disease, it invades and destroys that which life has built. It reverses the natural flow of the creative cycle."

"Like the Nots—Nazis turning the swas-ti-ka backwards," Caitlin said.

"Exactly. Clockwise, the Hindus considered the swastika a sign of good luck, an evolutionary principle. Reversed, it's a symbol of involution. The same goes for the five-pointed star," Kimo added. "With the head pointing upward toward the heavens it was a symbol of the human being."

"Like . . . Da Vinci's famous sketch of a naked man?"

"*Vitruvian Man.* When you invert a star—turn it on its head— it becomes the Satanic pentagram. The flow is then downward into the materialistic realms. Start messing around with the rightful order of creation and you're getting into black magic." Kimo drank some lemonade and chewed on an ice cube. "You can tell a lot about a person or a country or a group by the symbols it adopts. Trademarks, logos. You know, the NBC peacock used to face left. When GE took over, they flipped it. Now it faces right."

"Really?" Caitlin made a mental note to take notice the next time she saw the familiar bird. Earlier, she'd watched her mother hang an American flag outside the front door, as Martha had done on Independence Day for many years. "Here's to freedom and in-de-pen-dence," Caitlin said, raising her glass of lemonade.

Kimo touched his glass to hers. "E pluribus unum."

Caitlin giggled. "Fif-ty states, united in one nation."

The country had come a long way since early settlers traveled to the New World in search of freedom from tyranny and religious oppression, Caitlin thought. Now a dominant force globally, the American Superpower protected its interests internationally with military installations in dozens of countries.

Are we the new imperialists—the new Rome?

As part of her legal training, Caitlin had studied the Constitution and the Supreme Court decisions that had helped define the scope of the federal government's powers. The founding fathers had created three branches—similar to the model used in the Roman republic after the defeat of kings and before the reign of emperors. In the United States of America, some matters were reserved for states to make their own laws, free from federal inter-ference, but state laws could not violate rights granted to all U.S. citizens.

Thomas Jefferson, drafter of the Declaration of Independence, considered it "self-evident" that all men were created "equal" and endowed by their "Creator" with certain rights that could not law-fully be taken away. Yet, in Jefferson's time, only *free men* were assumed to have rights, and Old World practices—such as slavery—were not surrendered easily.

And what of the founding *mothers*? How could anything be birthed without a feminine presence? For that matter, how "equal" were women in a country that had failed to pass an Equal Rights Amendment to the Constitution?

The Declaration of Independence referred not only to the Creator but also to the "Laws of Nature" and "Nature's God" in a time before Charles Darwin's book, *The Origin of Species,* intro-duced the controversial view that humans and apes share a common ancestor.

Maybe some barbarians are simply reverting to type, Caitlin thought.

"I wonder what *vert* means," she said.

"Huh?"

"*Re*vert, *sub*vert, *in*vert, *di*vert, *con*vert . . . What's the woot—*root*?" Getting her mouth to form so many *r*'s took concentrated effort.

Kimo stroked his chin, a habit that annoyed Caitlin. She didn't like his new goatee look, and watching him fondle his facial hair only increased her distaste.

"In Latin, *vertere* is 'to turn.' *Vertical* is upright. And don't forget *per*vert," Kimo said, grinning.

Caitlin was astonished. "How do you know these things?"

Kimo shrugged. "I haven't spent my life chasing after money and possessions like a lot of people," he replied calmly.

She must have looked shocked by his reply, Caitlin thought, because he quickly added, "I didn't mean you."

"No, it's all right. It's true . . . I spent a lotta years pursu-ing outer goals."

Kimo glanced at his sporty new watch. "Maybe we're switching roles."

"Maybe."

"To everything there is a season," Kimo said. "Ecclesiastes." He hummed the tune of "Turn! Turn! Turn!," the song made popular by the Byrds.

They both laughed.

"Seriously, though, the trick is to find out what season you're in and live it to the fullest. Despite the best intentions, an action that's not in harmony with the times is not likely to turn out well."

"Like Mary Lin-coln lav-ishly re-fur-bishing the White House in the middle of the Civil War?"

"She was likely to get criticized no matter what she did. Even then, the Washington establishment didn't take kindly to outsiders."

"Yet it does seem like . . . like some people's lives are bound up with a country's, for better or war—worse."

"We all have a destiny. We're all here for a reason."

Caitlin thought about Abraham Lincoln, who sacrificed so much to preserve the Union when it was being torn apart by divi-sions between North and South. Now revered as a hero, in his own time his enemies hated him with murderous rage. Whether or not people were destined to play certain roles, some people rose to the occasion with the right combination of qualities appropriate to the moment.

"Why is it," Caitlin asked, "that peop-le who ad-vo-cate peace are the ones who rou-tinely get shot down? And not just pro-phets and poli-ti-cians. Even John Lennon."

"Those who catalyze great changes are bound to meet with resistance. When people feel vulnerable and powerless, they look for a scapegoat. That's easier than examining their own lives."

"Are you study-ing psy-chol-o-gy too?" Caitlin teased.

"A bit. It all fits together. All grist for the mill. Even sex isn't separate from spirituality, though some choose celibacy for a time."

When Kimo looked away, Caitlin realized that her short summer attire exposed her legs down to her bare feet. Self-conscious, she crossed her legs.

The first fireworks of the evening started popping in the distance. Kimo stood up to leave. "Last chance for a front row seat."

Caitlin shook her head. "No; thanks, though."

Kimo took his glass to the kitchen and said goodbye to Martha.

Caitlin lingered outside, watching the darkening sky and awaiting the first glimmer of starlight.

The night sky is full of stars, but in the light of day there is only one sun.

At least, in this solar system. Other suns might exist in other systems, and in other galaxies. Perhaps they all revolved around one central sun . . . or perhaps the observer became the center of the universe.

✑ 50 ✑

For Caitlin's birthday, her mother took her to dinner at an elegant French restaurant in Great Falls; she said she'd discovered it when Ray was in town, while Caitlin was in the hospital. Caitlin was gradually accepting Ray's importance in her mother's life. She still had no use for a stepfather, but she no longer scowled when she heard Ray's name.

Caitlin enjoyed the prix fixe meal, but she couldn't stop thinking about Kimo. When was his birthday? Was he an only child? Where did his parents live? And why hadn't she seen him in weeks? She missed his company.

Several more weeks passed before she heard from him. When he showed up in the middle of August, he said he'd been busy preparing for exams, and summer courses were especially intense because a full semester was crammed into a short session.

He took her to a park in Arlington where they went through all twenty-four taiji positions together. Caitlin moved gracefully but carefully through the sequence. When they had finished, they bowed to each other and then sat on the grass under a large oak tree.

"When does your mom leave?" Kimo asked.

"Tues-day." After a pause, Caitlin added, "I sold the town-house. I need the money to pay all the bills."

"Won't your settlement cover that?"

"It's . . . com-pli-cated. No driver was found, and there don't seem to have been any wit-nesses. The ve-hicle they think hit me wasn't even . . . regis-tered. I basically have to sue my own insur-ance company . . . and they'll defend against it as vig-orous-ly as any other lawsuit. I can't even say much because I . . . I don't remem-ber any-thing. I found a good lawyer, I think. His office is in Alexan-dria. I can't really move away until all that's done."

Kimo was quiet for a moment. "Why don't you come and stay at my place for a while?"

Caitlin shook her head and laughed. "Me, at 'the com-mune'? I don't think so."

"Group house," Kimo said calmly. "We're having a potluck dinner Sunday night, before fall term starts up and I get really busy. Come and meet some new friends."

Caitlin tensed at the idea of conversing with strangers. "I dunno if I'm ready to . . . socialize." Her thoughts were occupied with long-range concerns. Her mother was leaving; she was giving up her home. What *was* she going to do next? How was she supposed to decide?

"It's a supportive group," Kimo said. "Lots of healers. Of course, it's up to you."

Kimo leaned back and nibbled on sunflower seeds, and then tossed a handful to the birds. He seemed at peace with himself and his life. His acceptance, Caitlin was beginning to realize, made her feel safe. But what did he want? What did he value? In this last year she had put all her energies into her own healing. She hadn't felt like she had anything to offer a man, but someday, she hoped, she would again be ready for an intimate relationship.

"Kimo," she said after a long, reflective pause, "What's your dream? What do you wanna cre-ate in your life?"

He grinned. "What do I want to be when I grow up? I'm a simple guy. I'd like a piece of land. Big house with a garden. Good friends around. A few kids. Maybe I'll have my own clinic someday. See patients, teach."

"That's a nice dream," Caitlin said.

She liked listening to him. Having glimpsed the depths that lay hidden beneath his cavalier attitude, she knew he wasn't as carefree as he pretended to be. Sure, he'd had his wild times, had taken a different road from hers. Despite a rebellious streak, she had readily believed what her teachers, parents, government, and religion had told her to believe. She wanted to do the right thing. She was learning that wasn't as simple as she'd once thought.

"How about you?" Kimo asked.

"I'm still try-ing to ima-gine how a different kind of life might look."

"Well, don't spend too much time trying to figure it out. Just get out there and do something. Use the feedback to modify your course, if you need to. Sometimes, if you let go of all your preconceived ideas about how life should be, you can discover something truly original."

Caitlin was getting tired of Kimo's pontificating. She needed connection, not advice. Kimo seemed to have an opinion about absolutely everything. Still, he was a good listener, and his ideas were usually entertaining—sometimes even enlightening.

"It's a process more than a destination," he added. "What do you love? Love can take many forms."

"You're right," Caitlin said, standing up. "I can't let my . . . f-fears hold me back." She continued talking as she tugged on a low-hanging branch of the oak tree, testing its sturdiness. Climbing onto the branch, she said, "I al-ways loved mu-sic. In high school I used to dance in front of the mir-ror, pre-tending to be a sing-er. I guess that's not very . . . orig-i-nal." She crooked her legs over the thick branch and hung upside down. "Look," she said, laughing, "I'm inverted!"

Kimo turned to look. "Being too ordinary is not something you need to worry about," he assured her.

Caitlin grew tired more quickly than she'd anticipated and didn't have the strength to pull herself back up. She knew her legs would not hold out much longer, and the ground was too far away to reach with outstretched arms.

"Uh . . . y-ya think you could help me da—down?" she asked, trying not to panic.

Kimo glanced up at her and nonchalantly said, "Yes, I think I could," but he didn't budge.

"*Would* you h-help me? Now. *P-pleease!*"

"Of course," Kimo said, rising to help her.

Safely on the ground, Caitlin felt shaken and wanted to leave. She and Kimo collected their things and walked to the parking lot.

"Ya know, it's funny," she said. "It's been years since I played the pea—pi-a-no but I was teaching an au-tis-tic boy I know. Music seems to get through to some people in a way that—" She lit up with the sudden realization that music might help her as well. "Because the whole brain re-sponds!"

Of course! Why hadn't she thought of it before? *Music* had been missing from her life all these months!

"You should talk to Melody, my housemate," Kimo said. "She knows a lot about the healing effects of music."

Caitlin was intrigued. "Hmm. Maybe I do need to come to that party!"

"Bring your mom," Kimo said as they walked toward his convertible.

"My mother at 'the com-mune'—that'll be somethin' to see."

≪ 51 ≫

Caitlin noticed that index cards had been placed in front of many of the casseroles and salads that were spread out on a long table, buffet style. She leaned closer and read the ingredients for each dish; in some cases, even spices were listed.

"These people are very careful about what they eat," Kimo explained. "Some are macrobiotic; others only eat raw foods. Most won't eat animals."

Many of Caitlin's friends had tried weight-loss diets over the years, but nothing like this. She couldn't remember whether Kimo was vegetarian.

"I eat some meat," he said when she asked, "but only from animals that have been treated humanely and aren't fed hormones and antibiotics."

Caitlin held up a cake box from a local bakery. "I ber—brought a . . . cheese-cake," she said. "I wish I'd known—"

Kimo put one hand on her shoulder and took the box with the other. "Don't worry," he assured her, "it will get eaten."

He led her to the kitchen and set her to work cutting the cake while he retrieved trays of ice from the freezer for iced tea. Guests filled their plates with food and found places to sit and eat. Martha sat on the sofa and set her glass on the coffee table in front of her. Caitlin chose a spot on the loveseat nearby.

She felt out of her element as she listened to people talking about topics that seemed familiar to everyone else: popular retreat leaders for personal growth seminars; political issues, such as genetic alteration of food products and the voting history of congressional representatives; astrological horoscopes and planetary transits. When she had finished eating, she looked over at Martha, who seemed utterly bewildered as a man read her palm. Caitlin smiled.

She gathered up some plates and took them to the kitchen, where worker bees were already busy preparing a load for the dishwasher.

Kimo took Caitlin by the hand and introduced her to Lisa, one of his housemates. Lisa's background was in education; Kimo told her that Caitlin had been researching hazards associated with vaccines and the potential link between thimerosal and autism. He left so they could talk. Lisa knew little about autism, so the conversation was short-lived. Vaccines were far from Caitlin's thoughts, and she happily returned to the loveseat. Soon, Melody joined her.

Melody spoke enthusiastically about her interest in sound healing modalities. "People don't realize what a powerful instrument the voice is. A lot of creation legends talk about the world being sung into being. I sometimes wonder if the first humans sang before they spoke. Chanting is such an ancient practice."

She had visited the monastery in France where Gregorian chant had been revived after centuries of silence, Melody told Caitlin. She had traveled to India and learned to play the harmonium, and she could lead some Hindu chants. She had gone to Colorado to study with Western practitioners of sound healing who used vocal tones and singing bowls. But it was in Santa Fe that she developed a passion for yoga. At a teachers training, she gave up drugs and alcohol as well as caffeine, sugar, and artificial stimulants. Now, her classes reflected her interests, and she incorporated music and sound with yoga and meditation.

"I was fine 'til I had a head in-jury," Caitlin said.

"Trauma, sure, that can cause all kinds of problems."

"You think sing-ing could help me speak better?"

"No question. A lot of women have a blocked throat chakra. I'd start with toning and chanting if I were you."

Melody was a vibrant redhead with long hair that she wore in a ponytail. She seemed so upbeat and confident, Caitlin wondered if she ever had a down day.

"I have a couple of classes here at the house, if you're interested."

"I might be," Caitlin said. Despite her worries, Melody and Lisa didn't seem strange at all. Maybe staying in Kimo's guest room wasn't such a bad idea. "Kimo invited me to move in for awhile. But first I'm goin' to Hawai'i—kind of a birth-day gift to myself."

Caitlin had not yet mentioned her plans to Kimo, but she would be leaving as soon as the packing was done and the sale of the townhouse settled.

"Great! I'll be here a few more months."

"Then what?" Caitlin asked.

"I'm moving to Santa Fe. I love it there. The remoteness, the energy. There are a lot of conscious people there."

"Con . . . con-scious of what?"

Melody seemed surprised by the question. "I guess I'd call it unity consciousness," she said after thinking for a moment. "An awareness that everything is interconnected. That what I think and feel affects my body. That my choices affect the environment. That we're all in this together—it's not about getting what I can at someone else's expense. Does that make sense?"

"It makes a lotta sense. I think I need more friends like you."

Kimo appeared and offered to give Caitlin a tour of the house. She glanced at Martha, who was yawning. "It's late," she said. "Neck—Next time." She smiled at him. "I've de-cided to ac-cept your in-vi—*offer* to stay awhile. I'll call tomorrow and we can make a plan."

Kimo accompanied Martha and Caitlin to the door. "You've got great friends, Kimo," Caitlin said. "I'm glad I came."

"So am I," Martha chimed in. "Nice to have met you, Kimo," she said, shaking his hand. "Good luck with your studies. I'm sure you'll make a fine doctor."

"Thank you, Mrs. Johnson," he said. "Have a safe trip home." He looked at Caitlin and smiled. "Until tomorrow, then."

∽ 52 ∽

Caitlin spent the next several days packing up the small personal items that she intended to keep; the movers would handle the larger pieces. Things that once were meaningful to her no longer mattered, and she was determined to adopt a new attitude toward the comforts she'd once considered essential. *Can't let my possessions possess me.* She wished she could burn the clothes she'd been lounging around the house in all these months. Those she would donate to one of the local charities that called periodically, looking for used items.

When Tuesday arrived, she sat on the floor amidst a mess of belongings. Martha stood watching; she was packed and ready to go pick Ray up at the airport. From there, they would drive to Kansas at a leisurely pace.

"What will you do with all this stuff?" Martha asked.

Caitlin sighed. She'd spent so much of her life justifying her choices and actions to somebody. But, it was a simple enough question. *Why stir up trouble now?*

"I'll put some in straw—sto-rage," she replied. "And give a lot away."

Caitlin removed a crystal vase from a box that she was about to wrap. "This was an engage-ment present from Bobby and Sarah. It's beauti-ful and I love it, but I don't want to be sur-rounded by reminders of my old life." Caitlin carefully replaced the vase. "I thought I'd send it to John and Patrice as a bee—be-lated . . . wed-ding present."

"Oh, Caitlin, really—you can't give a used gift as a wedding present!"

Caitlin bit her lip. "I haven't been shop-ping in over a year. Someone else might enjoy it even if I can't. It's not as if it *looks* used."

Martha threw up her hands in surrender. "I'm sure your friends will appreciate it."

"Just cuz it's not what . . . Miss Manners would say . . ."

"I just think you should be careful what you throw away. Some things are irreplaceable."

"Is there some-thing here you'd like, Mother?" Caitlin asked with a sweeping gesture.

"I only want what's best for you."

"Then . . . let me find my own way."

They stared at each other for a moment, and then Martha glanced at her watch and picked up her handbag.

"Whatever that looks like, you have my support," she said, with a weak smile. "Now, it's time for me to leave."

Caitlin rose and walked with her mother to the front door. They shared an awkward embrace. "Thanks for all your help," Caitlin murmured.

"I'd never have forgiven myself if—well, I'm glad you're all right. And that we had this time," Martha said. She touched Caitlin's cheek. "Take care, Catie. I love you."

"Tell Ray thanks . . . for let-ting you go for so long." Caitlin doubted her father would have been very understanding about his wife attending another man's daughter.

"He's a good man," Martha said as she opened the door. "Come and see us sometime."

Caitlin wasn't one to promise anything unless she believed she would follow through. She waved as her mother drove away and then closed the door.

Staring at the open boxes, she started to feel excited about her upcoming trip. She glanced at her to-do list; she needed to call Neil Morton. She still had not received any notification of termination and wanted the matter taken care of before she left for Hawai'i. Betty told her he was out for the rest of the day.

"I still have to pick up my things," Caitlin said. "I'll come by . . . after Labor Day."

Kimo had offered to drive Caitlin to the airport and agreed to stop at OSP on the way. He waited in the car. Knowing he was there gave Caitlin the strength she needed to face Neil.

The halls of OSP looked familiar, but being back at the Justice Center felt strange. No longer rushing around, stressed, trying to do the impossible, Caitlin walked at a relaxed pace. She thought of visiting some former colleagues, but she was on a schedule—and had planned it that way. She left the gift for Patrice at the front desk, retrieved the box of belongings Patrice had packed for her, and headed for Neil's office.

As she neared Betty's desk, she was gripped by fear. She looked around, wondering what had caused her sudden dread. Feeling weak and unsteady on her feet, she placed the box on a chair.

Betty hung up the phone. "He'll see you now."

Neil moved from behind his desk and greeted Caitlin with a

friendly smile as she entered his office. "Caitlin! You're looking well." He placed his hand on her back and guided her inside as he closed the door behind them. "Won't you have a seat?"

"No, I'm not stay-ing," Caitlin said. "You realize you have no le-gal basis to with-hold signing my term-i-nation papers." She'd been rehearsing that line all morning and was glad she was able to muster some of her old determination in reciting it.

Neil laughed. "Now who's skipping the polite banter?"

Caitlin wanted the meeting to be over as quickly as possible and declined comment.

"I wanted to see you again and I knew you wouldn't agree to a social call."

Indeed. Perhaps she should have felt flattered; she felt only annoyance that Neil used manipulative tactics to get what he wanted. "So you set the bait. The way you play with people's lives," she said, slowly shaking her head.

"I hoped we might continue to play together. We had some good years. It doesn't have to end. Your disabilities aren't anything we couldn't manage. I'd give you a desk job; you probably couldn't hold up in a courtroom. You've lost your edge."

He walked slowly toward her, as if he expected her to bolt at any moment. When she was within his reach, he handed her a long-stemmed red rose.

Confused, Caitlin took the rose. She vaguely recalled her mother saying something about roses left outside her room at the hospital when she was in a coma. She quickly regained her composure.

"You don't give up, do you?"

"Not when I want something."

"I'm not prepared to—"

"Of course," he said loudly, interrupting her, "a cynic might say you're malingering to get a more sizable settlement."

Caitlin's face flushed. What was it she used to do to keep herself from saying something that she might later regret? Whatever it was, she no longer needed it. The verbal barbs didn't fly out of her mouth as swiftly as they once did. She turned to leave.

"What's the matter? Cat got your tongue?"

Martha irritated her, Caitlin thought as she opened the door, but Neil knew right where to plunge the knife in and how to twist it for maximum effect.

She left the rose on Betty's desk and picked up the box. "You can s-send the final papers to my home add-ress," she told Betty. "My mail will be forwa—sent on to me."

✌ 53 ✌

Watching from the window, Neil saw Caitlin exit the building and walk toward a parked car. She was carrying a box; a man took it from her and placed it in the trunk of the car. Neil recalled the description he'd been given of the guy Caitlin was with in Ireland; this one fit the bill.

Caitlin took her place in the passenger seat. Seeing her with another man made Neil's heart race. He couldn't explain his reaction, even to himself. Why couldn't he let her go? He didn't know why; he just knew that he couldn't.

"Damn!" he yelled. He slammed his fist on the desk and rubbed his hand absentmindedly before picking up the phone to make a call.

✌ 54 ✌

Kimo dropped Caitlin at the airport and then drove her car back to his house. His convertible was too small for her and her luggage. He chuckled, remembering her worries about the size of the rental car in Ireland, when she wanted an upgrade. He should have agreed—given her what she wanted, made her happy. He was learning.

He put her keys on a hook by the back door. In two weeks, she'd be staying in his house, and he was thrilled. She didn't say how long she'd stay; she probably didn't know. If things worked out in his favor, she'd never leave.

They'd moved some of her things into the spare bedroom before leaving for her old office building. She parked the car in a no-parking zone near the front of the building and asked him to wait there. He did as she asked, but he had a bad feeling about the whole thing. He'd never say it, but he was glad she was no longer working for the feds. Maybe his own issues with authority played a role; maybe he knew too much about abuses of power. But he had a bad feeling . . .

He burned some incense and chanted *Om mani padme hum* before returning to his room to study. On his way, he glanced down the hall. The door to what would soon be Caitlin's room was open; dappled sunlight danced across the floor. Kimo smiled. Maybe they would soon be dancing, too.

PART FIVE

ROMANCE

✏ 55 ✏

Sam Burn scanned the scene from behind dark glasses. He ordered a vodka tonic and sat at a table by the pool. After tossing aside the silly paper umbrella that came with the drink, he took a gulp.

His participation in clandestine information-gathering activities would begin and end with Caitlin Rose, it seemed. Carty didn't think Sam was cut out for surveillance operations and had advised Neil against sending him to Hawai'i, but Neil said he knew Caitlin's pattern and the type of man she found attractive. Alone on an island in the Pacific, she'd be more vulnerable and unsuspecting than at home in familiar territory, Neil reasoned. Neil wanted Sam to win Caitlin's trust and find out her plans—and what she remembered.

Tracking Caitlin Rose was part of Neil's personal agenda, so no one could really argue with him, and Sam wasn't complaining about an all-expense-paid trip to Hawai'i. Still, he wished he shared Neil's confidence in his ability to pull it off. He'd never had much success when it came to women. Caitlin was no longer a threat to the Club's interests, so he couldn't botch things too much, he convinced himself. He slugged the last of his drink, slung his beach towel over his shoulder, and walked along the shore toward the spot where he'd seen Ms. Rose park herself at this hour in recent days.

In a few months, his military tour of duty would be over and he'd be in command of his life again. Maybe working in a busy emergency room somewhere would provide the stimulation he craved. Maybe by helping others he could atone for his sins.

He kicked over a deserted sand castle and picked up a broken shell that a wave deposited by his feet. His antipathy toward religion didn't mean he wasn't grateful for a second chance. Before flying to Hawai'i, he'd attended another meeting of the ACCV in Rockville, Maryland. This one covered the adjudication process under the National Vaccine Injury Compensation Program—great preparation for meeting Ms. Rose; if she wanted to talk about her work, he could carry on an intelligent conversation.

But would she? Her career was over, thanks to him. She'd occupied his thoughts for over a year, but as he prepared to meet her, Sam's worries intensified. What if she did remember something?

When he saw her, his knees went weak. He removed his sunglasses and stopped for a moment to reassure himself: he could act charming; he could be witty. She didn't know him. For a few days, he could be anyone he wanted to be.

☙ 56 ❧

Caitlin walked toward her favorite spot on the beach after a refreshing swim in the lagoon. The swank resort hotel nearby was situated on prime real estate, but she preferred a secluded area by the cliffs.

She had developed a routine during her stay. After eating a light breakfast of granola, fruit, and yogurt, she headed for the beach. Mornings were especially nice for a stroll by the water. She'd picked up a paperback at a newsstand and enjoyed losing herself in a romance novel for the first time in years. Later in the morning, she swam and then baked in the warm sun. After a shower at her motel, she walked to one of the nearby restaurants for lunch. Sometimes in the afternoon she took a nap; if she felt ambitious, she explored the area on foot. For dinner, she ate a large salad.

She'd wanted a room with a kitchenette so she could prepare some of her own meals and had chosen a motel that was several blocks from the water. Eating dinner alone was less depressing in her room than at a fancy restaurant. When she finished, she returned to the beach to watch the sunset. The beauty of the surroundings and the relaxing rhythm of the waves banished most of her cares.

Three days left, she thought as she picked up a towel to dry her face. When she looked up, she was startled to find herself gazing into the eyes of a trim, dark-haired man.

"Hi," he said with a wide smile that displayed sparkling white teeth. "Mind if I join you?"

Caitlin hesitated. She had not come to the island to meet men and had enjoyed her solitude for over a week. The sun, sand, and surf soothed her soul as well as her body. But she was beginning to fidget and fret with no one to talk to.

What would be the harm in that?

"Uh . . . No . . . I don't mind," she said. "I'm leaving soon, though."

She felt safer having an exit strategy. *Always good to be thinking ahead—like in chess.* Her father had taught her the basic moves when she was ten, and the early discipline had helped her learn to think strategically.

"Leaving Hawai'i or leaving for the day?" the man asked, spreading his towel near hers.

"For the day," Caitlin replied.

She watched as he removed his shirt. He was about her height, with thick, wavy hair. She suspected his tan was only a shade darker than his natural coloring and wondered about his ethnicity. Caitlin put on a long t-shirt over her wet swimsuit and sat on the towel with her legs outstretched.

He sat down and put on sunglasses. "I've seen you here the last couple of days."

Caitlin raised an eyebrow.

Responding quickly, he said, "My room's just up there." He

pointed to a balcony at the hotel, as if that would be enough to reassure her. "You're here alone?"

"Yes," she said, thinking, *He obviously already knew that.*

When his eyes traveled to the scar on her leg, Caitlin shifted to a cross-legged position. "I came here 'cause I needed a break from dop—doctors," she said tersely. Her speech always worsened when she was nervous.

He laughed heartily. "That makes two of us!"

Caitlin looked at him curiously. He held out his hand.

"Doctor Sam Burns. I flew over here for a few days after attending a seminar in Honolulu."

Caitlin smiled and shook his hand. "Caitlin," she said, relaxing. *A doctor. He understands about healing and recovery.*

For the next half hour, Sam entertained Caitlin with humorous anecdotes. She told him she'd been injured in an auto accident. He showed her the scar on his arm and told her he too had suffered injuries in a recent collision. He listened attentively when she spoke; he nodded, he smiled, he radiated warmth and enthusiasm.

"Where do you live?" Caitlin asked.

"I work at a federal facility near L.A., but I'll be retiring soon."

"We seem to have a lot in common. I'm retired from the federal gov—govern-ment." Caitlin's rumbling stomach reminded her that lunchtime was approaching. "I think that's as much sun as I can han-dle . . . for today." She stood up and shook the sand from her towel.

Sam jumped to his feet. "If you'll have dinner with me, I promise not to tell any cripple jokes."

"Ac-tually," Caitlin confided, "it's speaking that's hard for me."

Sam leaned closer. "Then we'll just have to practice our non-verbal communication."

With his face close to hers, Caitlin noticed a small scar on his chin. She smiled shyly and picked up her handbag.

Sam persisted. "Tonight, then? I'll meet you in the lobby at 6:30. In time to watch the sunset."

That's safe enough. He doesn't even need to know where I'm staying.

"All right."

Sam picked up his shirt and towel. "Great! I'll see you tonight. I'm going for a swim in the pool."

He grinned and walked away. Caitlin gazed out at the glistening turquoise waters of the lagoon. The scene was so beautiful, it nearly made her cry.

Why would anyone choose a chlorinated pool over this?

Walking back to the motel, Caitlin realized she had no clothes to wear for a dinner date. When she arrived at her room, she quickly ate a ripe banana and a handful of cashews, then showered and dressed in shorts and a sleeveless top. After admiring her tan, she smoothed sunscreen on her face, grabbed a straw hat, and walked the short distance to a small shopping plaza.

She browsed through several boutiques until she found what she was looking for: a colorful sarong-style dress. Full-length with a slit up the side, it was at once comfortable and elegant—perfect for evening wear at an island resort. Caitlin added a pair of shell earrings to her purchase and returned to her motel room. After rinsing the dress in the sink, she hung it in the breeze to dry while she napped.

Caitlin awoke in a cold sweat. She'd been dreaming about a large cat. It lashed out at her, drawing blood when it scratched her face. She remembered Neil's taunt: *"What's the matter—cat got your tongue?"*

She splashed cold water on her face, and then put on lipstick, mascara, and the new dress. She was glad she'd agreed to meet Sam; the distraction would help her shake off thoughts of Neil and the disturbing dream.

Sam was waiting in the hotel lobby, dressed in khaki pants and a short-sleeved aloha shirt. He kissed Caitlin's cheek and placed a lei of orchids around her neck.

"How boo—beau-ti-ful," she said, gently touching the delicate flowers.

They entered the restaurant and were seated at a table with a view of the setting sun. The hostess lit a candle and told them about the dinner specials that were available that evening. Hawaiian music played softly in the background.

Caitlin looked out at the horizon. Being in a foreign environment helped her feel far removed from the pain of the past. "I can see why it's called pear—par-adise," she murmured.

"Ever seen the green flash?" Sam asked.

Caitlin shook her head and gave him a quizzical look.

"At the moment the sun sinks below the horizon you can sometimes see a bright green spark. Something to do with the refraction of light waves. For some people, the experience is almost mystical."

"Really?"

"Would I lie?"

They watched for the effect as the sun disappeared.

"Binoculars help," Sam added. "It only lasts an instant."

Neither of them saw anything unusual.

"I guess atmospheric conditions have to be just right," Sam said.

Caitlin felt disappointed, but the idea of witnessing the occurrence of a rare phenomenon sparked her imagination. What an omen of good fortune that would be if a first date were marked by such an event!

She had difficulty choosing from the many selections on the menu and finally decided upon lobster bisque to start and opakapaka, a local fish caught that morning, as an entrée. For side dishes, she chose Moloka'i sweet potatoes and caramelized Maui onions. To her delight, the Hawaiian language rolled easily off her tongue.

She shared a crab cake appetizer with Sam and listened as he talked about his hobbies: building furniture in the shop he'd set up in his garage and riding trails near his house on his dirt bike. He asked about her accident. Caitlin told him what she knew. She'd lost all memory of the day it happened, she said, and focused on getting well and finding a new direction.

"I've spent so much time being an-gry, fighting . . . injus-tice or crime or the boy—burea-cra-cy. I don't have the energy for that anymore," she said. "But letting go hasn't been easy. Anger was my strength, in a way. Now I feel so . . . so . . . vul-ner-able."

She took another bite of crab cake. She was beginning to sense that power was something more than a show of force. True strength was something different—simple and quiet, yet more effective than dramatic displays.

"Your sensitivity is what I find attractive," Sam said. "You have an openness I don't find often. Most people are trying to prove something rather than trying to understand."

"I've learned a lot through all this," Caitlin said. "I feel more . . . compassionate. I wanna live more from my heart."

Sam nodded and ordered a drink with an exotic name. Caitlin sipped white wine.

"What's your spesh—spe-cial-ty?"

"Cardiac. Speaking of heart!"

Caitlin laughed and Sam laughed along with her. "You like your job?" she asked as she sampled the bisque.

"I don't think about it in those terms. It's what I do."

"Why'd ya go into medicine?"

Sam reached for a dinner roll. "My father died of a heart attack when I was fifteen. We were out on the golf course. One of the few things we had in common," he said, pausing while the waiter served their meals. "I think part of the reason I chose medicine was to relieve my own guilt," he confided as he buttered the roll. "To convince myself there wasn't anything more I could have done to save him."

Caitlin was moved. Her fork was poised midair as she listened, completely absorbed. "I thought my f-fa-ther died of a heart attack," she said. "I only recently learned—it was really a sue—su-i-cide."

She stared at her plate, breathless. Saying the words out loud made it feel more real.

"I've been asking myself a lot of the same kwa—ques-tions," she continued. "Was there something I should have done dif-ferently?" She looked up when Sam spoke.

"At some point I learned to just accept that he was gone," he said quietly. "And to forgive myself."

Caitlin tasted her entrée. "I don't think I'm there yet."

"So how about you. What kind of law do you practice?"

"As I said, I worked for the govern-ment in War—Wash-ing-ton. No silk stockings for me."

She wondered if Sam knew the reference to high-paid boutique law firms. He didn't look confused, so she didn't explain. What a relief not to have to explain herself!

"You don't strike me as the unshaven, granola, protest-marcher type either."

Caitlin laughed. "No! More like the naked truth. Though I did start eating granola recently."

"I like the naked part," Sam said, leaning forward to gaze into Caitlin's eyes.

"Yeah, the tooth . . . *truth* doesn't make me very popular."

"From your lips it would sound all the sweeter." Sam pushed his plate to the side and reached across the table for Caitlin's left hand.

Caitlin smiled nervously and continued eating her dinner. When she was finished, their waiter cleared their plates. Caitlin withdrew her hand.

She and Sam both claimed they rarely ate sweets, but after looking over the dessert menu they decided to indulge. They waited in awkward silence for their waiter to return.

"This coconut crème pie is fantastic," Sam raved after tasting it. "Try a bite," he said, extending his fork.

Coconut wasn't one of Caitlin's favorite foods, but she humored him and opened her mouth. "Mmm," she murmured politely and nodded. She offered Sam the last spoonful of her macadamia nut ice cream.

"No thanks," he said. "I'm allergic to nuts."

For a moment Caitlin felt disappointed, as if Sam's refusal validated her fear that she had nothing to offer him.

"Sounds like you haven't seen much of the islands," he said as he glanced at the bill and removed his credit card from his wallet. "Why don't you join me for some sightseeing? We could start with sunrise at Haleakalā."

"Okay. Sounds fun."

Caitlin felt uneasy about Sam, but she couldn't pinpoint why. Something about him seemed familiar, though she couldn't imagine where she would have seen him, unless they had crossed paths on the beach or around the hotel in the days before he introduced himself. Caitlin had eaten lunch at the hotel's other, less expensive restaurant and had gone to the hotel spa for a facial and a massage.

That must be it, she decided. In any case, life had brought him to her, and she was learning to trust that life was good.

❧ 57 ❧

Caitlin snuggled close to Sam, grateful he'd brought a blanket with him to the summit of the dormant volcano. They stood amidst a row of onlookers lined up along the guardrail at the rim of Haleakalā Crater waiting for the first rays of light. The temperature was cold at that altitude, but the breathtaking display that streaked across the sky like a watercolor painting was well worth the trek in the dark of night.

"Morning has broken," Caitlin said. "Wasn't that a song?"

She knew it was a hymn—she used to sing it in church in Olathe—but it bothered her that she couldn't remember which musician had recorded a popular version. She knew she should know—no; she knew she *did* know. Why couldn't she access her own storehouse of information?

Sam shrugged. He'd never been a fan of pop music, he said.

Hungry and cold, they descended the long and winding road to sea level to find breakfast and then drove around the island admiring the landscape. By midafternoon, Caitlin was ready for a nap. Sam drove to the motel where she was staying and walked with Caitlin to her room, kissing her lightly on the lips before departing.

Sam played tour guide for the next several days, introducing Caitlin to the island's delicacies and delights. They played together in the waves, kayaked alongside dolphins, and explored the shallow waters with snorkeling gear. In the evenings, they took long walks on the beach, hand in hand and barefoot, gazing at the stars and planning the next day's adventure. Pampered and indulged, Caitlin basked in the attention Sam showered upon her.

Now this is a vacation! she thought as she inhaled the sweet fragrance of plumeria. Her eyes feasted upon the rich, vibrant colors of the surroundings. She sampled succulent fruits and fresh-caught fish, and the joyful sounds of island music lifted her spirits as much as Sam's touch warmed her heart.

For their last day on the island, Sam drove to a site recommended by a clerk at the hotel. He parked his rented car on the gravel strip along the side of the road, near several other vehicles. From there, he'd been told, they would find a trail that led to a secluded water-fall and swimming hole that locals used.

"Sounds egg—ex-otic!" Caitlin said when Sam told her where he was taking her. She vaguely recalled following a trail in Ireland with Kimo to find a secluded pool of water, but that seemed like a lifetime ago.

Sam opened the trunk of the car and removed their backpacks. "Water, snacks, towels—I think we've got everything," he said, taking inventory. "Oh, shit!"

"What's ra-wrong? Did you forget something?"

Sam looked down at his sandal. "Shit!" he said again. "I stepped in dog shit!"

Caitlin thought he was overreacting; as a doctor, he must deal with bodily discharges all the time. As he lifted his leg to inspect the offended shoe, a dog came along, out of his owner's sight, and lifted his leg, too—urinating on the leg Sam stood on.

"What the hell is going on here?" he bellowed.

Caitlin watched in horrified amusement and couldn't contain her laughter, which erupted in equal measure to Sam's fury. "I'm sorry," she tried to say, but only laughed harder every time she looked at him.

"It's not funny!" he snapped. He caught himself and softened. "All right, I suppose it is funny. For you." He slammed the trunk closed, leaving the keys in the lock.

Caitlin was in good humor. The islands enchanted her. The pri-mal lushness, teeming with life, made her feel closer to nature in its many manifestations. "Come on," she said, tugging on Sam's arm. "Let's go find that waterfall . . . and get you ca—cleaned up!"

Sam stiffened, but he didn't push her away. When they reached the pool, he undressed and dived in; Caitlin did the same. They floated and swam and giggled and kissed. Caitlin felt self-conscious about her thin shape but the look in Sam's eyes, the hunger in his kiss, and the clutch of his embrace told her he was not disappointed.

When they returned to the car, Sam suggested they go to Lahaina and find something to eat. Caitlin was about to respond when Sam's angry tone returned.

"I can't believe it!" he said, snapping up a note on the windshield. "This isn't my day."

Caitlin looked over Sam's shoulder and read the beginning of the note. "Oh, my God—you left the k-keys . . . in the lock?"

He crumpled the paper. "I was a little distracted, you might recall!"

"Calm down, I—I'm not . . . blam-ing you," she said, flustered.

"The park patrol found them," Sam muttered.

"That's a blessing. Coulda been anyone."

"Yeah, but they took the keys back to headquarters. That could be miles from here. How are we supposed to get there?"

His tone was so accusing, Caitlin almost thought he blamed her. She looked around. They were in a remote location, but not far off the main road. Other than the fellow with the dog they had encountered earlier, they hadn't seen other hikers, but cars were still parked nearby.

"Someone will come along," Caitlin said. She sat on the hood of the car, and no sooner had she spoken than a park ranger on patrol pulled up in a Jeep. "See?"

Sam flagged the ranger and approached the Jeep. When he returned to the car, he informed Caitlin that the woman had just come on duty and didn't know anything about car keys. "She's calling in," he said. "This has been a very strange day."

"More and more, I feel like there's some force or . . . Intelli-gence in the universe . . . looking out for me," Caitlin said. "Like a . . . a guardian angel, maybe."

Caitlin had found the idea of angels comforting as a child, when she'd learned to say prayers for guidance and protection. As she grew older, she didn't have time for such childish notions. She never lost prayer completely, though, and turned to God in moments of crisis. In recent months, she'd been learning to not only unload her burdens but also to be grateful for her blessings.

Sam leaned back against the car, arms folded across his chest. "I don't believe in those things," he said. "I've seen too much suffering."

"Too many things feel beyond my con-trol for me to thick— *think* that way," Caitlin said. "How do you explain sink . . . synchroni-city, for example?"

"Statistics and probabilities," Sam said.

"And destiny?"

"It's up to each of us to make the most of what we have to work with."

"That's true, but . . . we can also ask for help. Don't you ever pray?"

Sam stared straight ahead. "No."

"Wow. I talk to God all the time."

Maybe she was just communicating with herself, but Caitlin didn't feel so alone since she'd started sharing all her experiences with Whoever was listening. "My life would feel pretty . . . empty without that feeling of . . . connection to something greater."

"It does sometimes."

The park ranger approached them. "You're in luck. The ranger on the last shift found your keys. He was supposed to turn them in." She held the keys out to Sam. "They were under the seat."

Sam was visibly relieved. "Oh, thank you!" he said, taking the keys.

With Sam's back to her, Caitlin looked skyward and mouthed a "thank you" of her own. She wanted to enjoy the rest of the day and hoped Sam's mood would lighten.

He opened the car door for her. "Now—let's go get something to eat!"

Sam drove around Old Lahaina Town looking for parking, finally opting for a paid lot on Front Street. Ambling along the main street lined with boutiques, art galleries, and trendy eateries, Caitlin noticed a sign for a place called "Kimo's."

"Oh, look! Let's go there." She quickened her pace; Sam lagged behind. Caitlin was buying a t-shirt bearing the "Kimo's" logo when Sam entered the restaurant.

"What's the big deal?" he asked.

"I have a friend whose nickname is Kimo. He'll love this!"

The hostess led them to a table and informed them that the nightly sunset ritual was about to begin. They quickly placed their orders and then watched as a native islander blew into a conch shell and other performers lit torches around the perimeter. Caitlin was entranced but uneasy. The scene seemed surreal. She felt as if she had entered some timeless dimension. After the ceremony ended, she looked over at Sam. His brow was furrowed and he looked glum and distracted. Caitlin strained to catch a glimpse of the sun, still hoping to experience the elusive green flash, but clouds got in the way.

"Is he in Washington?" Sam asked.

"Who?"

"This 'Kimo.' How good a friend is he?"

"I guess he's my best friend," Caitlin said. "I never really thought about it before, but, yeah . . . We've been there for each other . . . in tough times." *But we've never been more than friends,* she thought wistfully as the waitress set a plate down in front of her.

"You're lucky to have people in your life who care about you," Sam said sullenly, his eyes downcast.

"Don't you?"

"Not so many." He bit into his Black Angus cheeseburger. "I'm divorced. I have a young daughter, Jacqueline. She's four. Her mother and I are not on the best of terms."

Caitlin was surprised by Sam's disclosure but had learned from his reactions throughout the day to leave the matter alone. He seemed in a hurry to leave, so she quickly finished her salad and fish sandwich.

They stood on the wharf and enjoyed the view. Caitlin closed her eyes; a gentle breeze caressed her skin. Sam put his hand on her back and started softly kissing her neck.

"This is our last night together. I want it to be special. Why don't you stay with me? I'd like to hold you in my arms all night long," he said, enfolding her in his arms.

Caitlin giggled as Sam nibbled on her ear, her uneasiness forgotten. "How can I refuse an invi-ta-tion like that?"

Sam waited in the car while Caitlin packed her things and checked out of the motel. He drove to his hotel and carried her suitcase up to his room. After opening the sliding door to the balcony, he called room service and ordered a bottle of wine and a tray of desserts. Caitlin stepped outside and looked down at the beach. She saw the spot by the cliffs where she and Sam had met. He joined her on the balcony.

"I didn't know what to think when you came up to me on the beach. You said you'd been watching me. I thought you might be some crazed . . . stalker."

"I said I'd *seen* you," Sam said. "There's a difference. But now," he said, kissing her neck, "now I'm stalking you."

"Maybe I should have asked to see your crew—creden-tials!"

"Hello, I'm Dr. No," Sam joked before moving inside. "That was the first Bond film, you know. I read a lot of spy novels when I was a teenager. Always seemed like an exciting life—fast cars and cunning villains." He picked up the newspaper that was lying on the table and opened the sports section.

Caitlin came inside and looked around. The suite came with a small kitchen and a living room area that was separate from the bedroom. "Nice room."

Sam folded the newspaper. "Mind if I watch the news?" he asked as he picked up the remote control for the television.

"No, go ahead. I was thinking of taking a shower."

With Sam's attention glued to the tube, Caitlin unpacked a few things and headed to the bathroom.

While she showered, she thought about how far she wanted to take their relationship. She had not been physically intimate with a man since Dru. Could she risk her heart again with a man she'd known for such a short time? With Dru, she'd felt confident and uninhibited. Now, she felt cautious.

Stepping out of the shower, Caitlin caught a glimpse of her bony figure in the mirror and winced. She had lost so much weight. Sam had seen her naked already and still invited her to stay. Being a doctor, he'd seen all kinds of naked bodies. Maybe he found her attractive in spite of her thin shape.

In spite of his moodiness earlier in the day, he seemed like a decent man, she thought as she slipped into a silk nightgown. She was tempestuous herself—how could she judge him for that? At least he lived in the United States. Dru had shown her a good time and Kimo led her into strange territory, but perhaps true partnership required a man who was her professional equal, Caitlin thought as she wrapped herself in a plush hotel robe.

Sam was opening a bottle of wine when she emerged from the bathroom. Caitlin bit into a small confection and offered him the rest. He kissed her hand and spread kisses up the length of her arm until he reached her neck; then he pulled her close to him. Caitlin melted into his arms, intoxicated by imaginings of the intimacies they would share. They swayed to the slow rhythm of soft island music until Sam danced her into the bedroom.

≈ 58 ≈

In the morning, Caitlin lazed in bed. She stirred when she heard the bathroom door open. Her vacation had come to an end.

"Shower's all yours," Sam said. Wearing only boxer shorts, he quickly dressed in long pants and a polo shirt, then pulled a suitcase from the closet and started packing.

Caitlin rose and opened the curtains. Clouds.

Cat Stevens—that's who sang that song.

She picked the bedspread up off the floor, put the room service tray outside the door, and brought the complimentary newspaper inside.

First encounters are often awkward, she thought as she headed for the shower. She sought more than physical pleasure and satisfaction; she wanted a communion of souls. *I guess everyone is looking for a soul mate.*

Sam read the newspaper while Caitlin dressed, and then they wordlessly made their way downstairs to the breakfast buffet. Sam broke the silence.

"I know it's sudden," he said as he poured maple syrup over a stack of pancakes, "but I'd like you to consider coming to California."

"Wha— With you? Today?" Caitlin asked, stunned.

"Yes," Sam said, unwavering. "I'll be working, but you can relax. We can be together in my time off."

Caitlin had pondered the notion that she and Sam might meet again sometime, but the idea of going home with him had not crossed her mind. Could she be that spontaneous, as she'd been with Dru?

She looked at Sam for a long time. What was waiting for her in Virginia? She had no rent, no mortgage, no obligations. She'd need to return for a trial—if her lawsuit went that far—but she couldn't be of much more help to her attorney. The extent of her damages and her lack of culpability would be shown through expert testimony. Winning a judgment against her insurance company for recovery under the uninsured motorist provision of her policy required proof that the driver of the other vehicle was unknown; the police officers who had arrived at the scene would testify that another vehicle had crashed into her BMW and shoved it into the cement barrier—and then disappeared.

Bastard, she thought. What kind of coward would leave her for dead and run away?

Imagining the case going to trial filled Caitlin with dread. The thought of listening to experts reconstruct the accident scene and describe the nature of her injuries in detail was too upsetting to dwell upon. She'd never spent much time in California, but if things went well between her and Sam, the idea of passing the winter in a sunnier clime seemed appealing.

"Umm . . . I guess . . . there's nothing I need to be back for im-med—right away."

"Is that a yes?"

Caitlin nodded. "I have a layover in Los Ang—L.A. I'll just get off there and get another ticket to Washington . . . later."

When I know whether to make it round trip or one way.

She called Kimo from a pay phone at the airport; he was expecting her to return that night. She listened to the latest message on his answering machine.

"Silence is golden, but I wouldn't recommend it if you want a call back. Here's your cue."

Caitlin smiled and waited for the familiar beep. "Aloha, Kimo! The last few days here have been ink—in-cre-di—oh, you know what I mean! I met someone and I'm gonna stay in . . . California awhile."

A gate attendant announced that the flight was boarding. "I gotta run," Caitlin said. "I'll call when I know more." She hung up the phone and joined Sam in line.

They didn't talk much on the long flight. Caitlin looked out the window dreamily, wondering if Sam thought they might have a future together and imagining all the amusements she could find in a city like Los Angeles.

Sam put away the spy novel he was reading when the plane encountered turbulence and the "fasten seat belt" sign came on. "There is something I should tell you, in all fairness, if you're going to be staying with me," he said.

Caitlin gripped the armrest and looked warily at Sam.

"Part of the reason my wife—sorry, former wife," he said, clearing his throat, "and I are not on good terms is because I, uh—I broke her nose." He paused, waiting for some reaction.

Caitlin felt a cold chill pass through her but said nothing. Her eyebrow twitched.

"I used to have a problem controlling my anger," Sam explained, "but that's all in the past. I've been in therapy since the incident, and I know myself much better now—what the triggers are, and what I need to do; how to de-escalate conflicts. I'm very safe, but I did think you should know."

Caitlin looked out the window and cringed. *"The incident"?*

What was she supposed to say? Should she reconsider and find her connecting flight to Washington after all? She had to decide quickly, and strong emotions fogged her thinking. Maybe life with Sam would be a nightmare rather than a dream.

Her mood deflated, Caitlin closed the shade on the window by her seat as the plane lowered its landing gear. She didn't want to see what was coming. But she wouldn't run because of fear. If Sam's intentions were sinister, he wouldn't have warned her. She felt grateful for a chance to do things differently; didn't others also deserve an opportunity for a second chance—"turn the other cheek" and all that?

"Thanks for telling me," was all she said.

✑ 59 ✑

Sam looked at the familiar H-O-L-L-Y-W-O-O-D sign through the windshield of his pickup truck and remembered the night he and Yvonne had driven up into the hills so they could enjoy the views of the stars above and the city lights below. With the top down, they sat talking into the night.

As newlyweds, they'd enjoyed exploring the area together. Sam sighed. They'd had so much promise then, before Jacqueline was born. Yvonne lived in Santa Monica now, and Sam's old two-seater convertible sat in his garage, waiting for him to get it fixed up and running.

An apt symbol for my life: badly in need of repair.

Maybe inviting Caitlin to come back with him had been a mistake. Any further expenses would be on his tab, not Neil's. Sam still resented paying alimony and child support. Did he really want a dependent guest to entertain? Already he felt trapped, and he knew what happened when he felt cornered.

Once they were through the worst of the traffic, he breathed easier. What had he learned about Caitlin that he could report back to Neil Morton? She didn't seem to remember much about the accident; obviously, she didn't suspect Sam's involvement. She wouldn't say much about the vaccine case or her former duties with OSP. That was all part of her old life, she said, and Washington was the last thing she wanted to think about. Perhaps with more time he could probe more deeply.

He looked over at her. He'd been surprised by how easy it was to be with her. Women usually brought out the worst in him. Her eyes were closed but he wasn't sure if she was asleep. When they entered San Bernardino County, she finally spoke.

"You said you lived near L.A."

A relative determination, Sam thought.

With over four hundred and sixty square miles, the City of Los Angeles pretty well set the standard for urban sprawl; the county extended even farther. Besides, when he said that, he had no expectation that Caitlin would be visiting.

"It's a little farther," he told her.

She sighed and closed her eyes again. When Sam turned off Interstate 10 and headed north into the Mojave Desert, Caitlin sat up and looked around.

"What the— Where . . . where exac-tly are you t-taking me?"

"I live by a national park."

They passed a road sign for upcoming destinations.

"Josh—Joshua Tree!"

"That's right."

"Oh God," Caitlin said, putting her hand to her head. "This was a mistake," she muttered. "I knew it was a mistake. Why don't I . . . listen to myself?"

Sam's fingers gripped the steering wheel. Back on his own turf, his confidence was growing. He glanced at Caitlin. She looked sour.

Spoiled princess. Happy as long as she's treated like royalty. This ain't Disneyland, honey.

Nothing about his life here was impressive. The most he could say was that sunshine and fresh fruit were plentiful. He had adapted.

Yvonne never did; she hated the desert. Sam hated her bad attitude and her whining. *Sour.*

After passing through the town of Joshua Tree, he pulled into the parking lot of the Las Palmas Restaurant and Bar and turned off the motor. "You like Mexican food?"

Caitlin mumbled some vague reply and followed him inside. Sam nodded to a few locals and sat at a small table covered with a plastic tablecloth and decorated with a plastic daisy in a plastic vase. Caitlin studied the menu.

"The burritos here are really good," Sam said. "I get the fajitas a lot, too."

"You have anything with . . . veg-etables?" Caitlin asked the plump, dark-skinned waitress when she brought two tumblers of water to the table.

"Salad," the waitress replied. "And the vegetable soup," she added. "It has pork."

"I'll have the sal—salad," Caitlin said, closing the menu. "And iced tea."

"That's it?" Sam asked, glancing at Caitlin. "I'll have Combo Platter Number Five," he told the waitress. "And a Dos Equis."

Caitlin left to use the restroom; Sam read a local newspaper. They ate quickly and soon were back on the road.

Sam thought about the first time he had driven down this road. Yvonne had endured three years at an even smaller base, at China Lake, without complaint. She was happy to have him home from the Persian Gulf, she'd said, and seemed to adjust easily to marriage and motherhood. But she'd thought his next tour of duty would be in a more desirable locale. When he was assigned to Twentynine Palms, the prospect of another three years in the desert turned her into a shrew. She started harping about his inability to get a better assignment, and before he knew what had happened, her nose was bloody and she was crying. Then the baby started screaming.

What a nightmare that had been, Sam recalled as he drove toward the base hospital. He'd driven Yvonne there that day—and threatened to break her jaw too if she told anyone he'd hit her. After she was treated, he felt guilty and promised her they could buy a home of their own, away from the base. He thought that would make her happy. But she piled complaint upon complaint. Then Jacqueline was diagnosed with developmental disabilities, and Yvonne moved out. Soon after, she filed for divorce.

Caitlin would be the first woman to enter the house since Yvonne left, and she had no firm date of departure. What if she wanted to stay the entire six weeks until her trial? Sam jealously guarded his time with Jacqueline; he wasn't ready for an outsider intruding into the most private parts of his life. Already, he felt a gnawing tension in his gut.

∽ 60 ∾

Caitlin's agitation increased when Sam turned off the main high-way and onto Adobe Road, which led straight into the Marine Corps Air Ground Combat Center. A guard waved them through the front gate.

Caitlin gasped. "You work for the . . . m-mili-tary?" She felt an overwhelming desire to get out of the truck—immediately, before they drove any deeper into the heart of the base. But where could she go for help? How would she get back to civilization?

Sam nodded toward the Robert E. Bush Naval Hospital. "I work in there." He parked near the entrance and turned off the engine. "I'll just be a minute."

Caitlin watched him walk toward the Family Medicine Clinic. He'd taken the keys with him, she noticed. She wanted to cry but refused to allow Sam to see how upset she was. She thought of Kimo and Melody and their house in Arlington; she would be sleeping there tonight if she'd stuck to her original plan.

Her fears were irrational, she told herself. Just because Sam had hit his wife didn't mean he would harm her. *People can change.* She wanted to believe that. She *had* to believe that.

Sam was hardly the beguiling bachelor doctor he had seemed in Hawai'i and, out here, she would be completely dependent upon him. Had that been his plan when he invited her?

He returned with his mail and handed her a flyer advertising a meditation class at a nearby metaphysical bookstore.

"I've been thinking of learning to . . . meditate," Caitlin said as she looked over the flyer. On the plane, she'd read a magazine article with tips for reducing stress. A meditation practice might help her better manage challenging situations, she thought. *Like now . . .*

"You'll have to meet my mother," Sam said as he drove off the base.

"Yeah?" He planned to introduce her to his mother? Was he that serious about her?

"She lives in an ashram a couple of hours from here. We'll go for dinner some night."

They returned to the main highway, continuing beyond the town of Twentynine Palms.

Caitlin brightened at the idea of seeing other parts of California. Maybe her stay with Sam would turn out all right after all. She was tired. She'd rest for a few days and soon it would be the weekend. Sam could take her sightseeing, as he had in Hawai'i. She wasn't entirely sure what an ashram was, but she knew it was connected to Eastern religions. Didn't practitioners chant mantras and hold their fingers in different positions while they meditated?

The sun was setting when Sam turned onto the road that led to Joshua Tree National Park. When they reached his property, Caitlin asked, "Did your wife work when she lived here?" She wondered how anyone managed to stay sane, alone all day in such a secluded place.

"Nah. She was a full-time mom," Sam said. "We weren't here that long before she left. Couldn't wait for an excuse to move to town." He parked the truck inside a large garage that housed a small car, his dirt bike, and his workshop.

Caitlin wondered which "town" he meant, but she knew from his tone that asking further questions about his former wife would be ill-advised. Most parents liked talking about their kids, and

Caitlin thought she might meet Jacqueline during her stay. "How often do you see your daughter?" she asked.

Sam turned off the motor. "Usually every week but they're in France for another couple of weeks. Anything else you want to interrogate me about?"

"S-sor-ry!" Caitlin said, looking away. "I'm just . . . trying to get to know you."

"Right." Sam got out of the truck and grabbed the heavier pieces of luggage.

Caitlin carried what she could and walked slowly behind him, disheartened. What had caused the change? Had she said or done something to alienate him?

Caitlin moved toward the edge of the bed. Sam's snoring seemed to start up every time she was on the verge of sleep. Had he snored the night before, in the hotel room? He had fallen asleep shortly after ejaculating, she recalled. He held her for a short while, but then he turned away. He hadn't touched her since.

Sam shifted his position and his breathing pattern changed. Caitlin fell asleep listening to the far-off calls of coyotes. With the first glimmer of dawn, Sam moved toward her.

"Sun's coming up," he whispered. "The flag is raised."

Caitlin murmured a groggy "Already?" It seemed like she had only just fallen asleep.

"How about some revelry? Wanna blow my bugle?" Sam laughed and tickled her.

Military humor?

Caitlin winced and resisted opening her eyes. She'd gotten caught again, hadn't she? Ensnared by dreams of the fairy tale romance. How many young girls had been brainwashed into looking for Prince Charming in the guise of doctor or lawyer?

When Caitlin and Jayson met, they were still students. After the move to Virginia, Jayson acquired an arrogance Caitlin had not seen back in Kansas City. Being a lawyer herself, she was unimpressed by his new status. His paralegal was impressed, and made no secret of her adoration. That, it turned out, was why he'd worked late on Valentine's Day. He'd betrayed Caitlin, and she'd sought comfort with Neil. Like the chocolate she once relied upon to perk her up on a gloomy day, her dalliance with Neil was a temporary fix for complex problems. Dessert was best served as the complement to a good meal; it couldn't make up for a bad one, and it provided no sustenance.

Had she been enamored of Sam? Maybe, a bit. Much of their time together in Hawai'i had been idyllic. He had courted her and she had fallen for the performance. She'd bought into the image he had invented about himself and his life. They were playing a different game now, and he expected her to accommodate him.

Wasn't that the unwritten rule? He paid the bills and she took care of the house—and him. No love play, no sweet words, no tender caresses or affectionate kisses. The mating dance was over; what they had now was an arrangement. He sought raw physical release, like a workout at the gym. Caitlin was tired and preferred sleep, but she made an effort to respond. Relationship was compromise, right? She had chosen to be there, and for however long she remained, she would make the best of it.

"Ooh, it's Doc-tor Feel-good!" She smiled and snuggled closer to Sam. "Or is it Doctor Strange-love?" she asked, more awake now. She chuckled at her attempt to be funny, and gazed at Sam, hoping to find a connection in his eyes.

His face turned stony and he pulled away. "What's that supposed to mean?" he asked coldly. He sat on the edge of the bed for a moment, then stood up and quickly got dressed.

"It . . . it doesn't mean anything," Caitlin said, confused by his sudden rejection. "It's a movie . . . from the six-ties. You know— Peter Sellers? The bomb?"

Sam fastened his belt. "No, I don't know," he said. "I don't have time to discuss your taste in film. I've got a big day ahead." He grabbed a cap and headed out the door. "See ya."

Caitlin was stunned. *That was a bomb.*

She felt like she was trying to communicate with an alien species. So far, it wasn't working.

This isn't how a man treats a woman he cares about.

She understood now why Sam was divorced. She cried herself back to sleep, wondering if Sam cared about anyone—even himself.

Later in the morning, Caitlin explored the property, inside and out. Sam's house, an old adobe, was spacious but dark. Only the remodeled kitchen was bright and cheery; the rest of the house was poorly lit and felt cold, like a dungeon. The atmosphere reminded Caitlin of the old castle she and Dru had toured in Scotland.

She walked out to the garage. Sam had taken the truck to work. Did he ever drive the car? Did it even run?

Caitlin went for a walk, hoping to pick wildflowers, but it was the wrong season. The sandy soil was hospitable terrain for snakes, lizards, wood rats, and cacti. A lone Joshua tree marked the edge of Sam's property. Caitlin stared at it curiously and then walked along the road. Waves of heat streamed up from the pavement; even with sunglasses, the intense glare of the midday sun was blinding. A van carrying Japanese tourists passed by; its occupants smiled and waved. Caitlin waved back. The road led to one of three entrances to the national park. People drove for hours to come here, Caitlin knew, but all she saw was a parched and dusty landscape. She preferred the mild temperatures and tropical foliage in Hawai'i.

She returned to the house and cleaned up Sam's kitchen, discarding an outdated milk carton and rotten oranges she found in the fridge. The freezer contained a stack of pizzas and one package of peas. Caitlin had never learned to cook, a failing her mother considered a personal affront.

"Don't let her get you down," her father had whispered during an after-dinner game of gin rummy. "There's an answer for every question the mind can conceive." He confidently surveyed the cards in his hand and winked at her. "You just find yourself a man who likes to cook," he said before playing his cards and winning the game.

That man clearly isn't Sam, Caitlin thought as she checked the date on a carton of eggs.

Nor had it been Jayson, whose sentiments echoed Martha's after they were living together. For Caitlin, dining out was an adventure, and she savored the new delights she found in the Capital's multiethnic fare. For Jayson, eating out was an unnecessary extravagance. He wanted the simple foods he was accustomed to—and he wanted Caitlin to cook them, the way his mother had. What would their children learn from her example? he asked. That they have choices, Caitlin answered. Why did he assume that *she* would be the cook and nanny and maid and chauffeur? Her career was as important as his. To her, anyway. She accused him of being selfish and refused to be a domestic slave. He claimed he was considering the needs of his future children. The topic became an issue they could not discuss dispassionately; they defended their positions as tenaciously as if they were fighting for the rights of their respective genders.

Caitlin looked around the kitchen helplessly. She wished she had paid attention to Kimo's discussions with Martha about recipes. Now that she had free time and an interest in eating nutritious food, she was ready to learn how to cook.

She picked up a booklet about shrubs and trees of the Mojave Desert and sat on a couch in the living room to read about the Joshua tree. She learned that the *yucca brevifolia* is a member of the lily family. Native Americans wove its tough leaves into baskets. Tradition held that Mormon pioneers had named the tree for Moses's successor, Joshua, who led the Israelites into the Promised Land and vanquished the previous occupants.

The Israelites wandered in the desert for forty years before reaching the Promised Land, Caitlin thought as she closed the book. According to the New Testament, Jesus faced off with Satan in the wilderness. Kimo said Siddhartha conquered temptations under a Bodhi tree as part of his journey to enlightenment.

Caitlin had been tested by many challenges in recent years. Was her soul being purified through suffering?

She set the book on the end table by the couch. Sam walked in, carrying bags of groceries. "I see you've had a rough day," he said.

I see your mood has not improved, Caitlin thought. "I have had a rough day," she said. "It didn't begin well." She went to assist him and noticed a bandage on his hand. "What hap-pened?"

"Oh, it's nothing," he said. "Occupational hazard."

Caitlin helped Sam unload the groceries and watched where he stored different items. Canned goods in the pantry. Cereals in the cupboard. Cooking supplies went with the little-used small appliances in the cabinet above the stove. She was learning that Sam had very specific ideas about how things should be.

While he took his toiletries to the bathroom, she placed the fresh produce into the refrigerator bins, remembering the time Kimo brought her to the farmers market in Clarendon. He showed her how to select fruits and vegetables at their peak of freshness and ripeness. During one of their later outings, they stopped at a natural foods supermarket to shop. Kimo explained that concerns about the way foods are grown, caught, raised, and processed go beyond the synthetic fertilizers, chemicals, antibiotics and growth hormones that are typically associated with conventional farming and the meat and poultry industries. He told her about dolphin-safe tuna and free-range chicken, about fair-trade cocoa and the emulsifiers and hydrogenated fats that are added to many packaged products, about irradiation and genetically modified organisms. For Kimo, supporting organic farmers and socially conscious companies was a political statement. Avoiding pesticides and additives made sense to Caitlin; she paid attention now to labels and ingredients and had grown accustomed to using brands not carried by most grocery stores.

"I'll take you to get groceries sometime," Sam said when he returned to the kitchen. "Then you can buy what you want."

"I don't suppose there's a . . . health food store nearby," Caitlin said.

"I don't know. You could ask around."

"Who would I ask?"

"I'll introduce you to some of the neighbors. If you stick around long enough."

Caitlin wondered who the neighbors were. She hadn't seen any signs of human activity—no kids playing in the street, no one out for a walk or tending a garden. On the outskirts of town, large tracts of land separated homes.

Sam filled a large glass with tap water and gulped it down. "I think I'll go to the gym," he said. "Don't wait up." And he was gone again.

Caitlin wasn't sure whether to feel relieved or annoyed about being left alone. She dismissed her concerns as unwarranted. Sam probably wanted to get back into his normal routine after being away. Surely they would have time together over the weekend.

∽ 61 ∽

For the next few days, Caitlin prepared simple meals from the foods that were available in Sam's kitchen. For breakfast, she boiled an egg and chopped it up on top of a bagel, added boiling water to instant oatmeal, or spread peanut butter and jelly on a slice of bread. Lunch was a salad with a grilled cheese or tuna sandwich. Dinner was more challenging, especially if she wanted to serve something that would please Sam. She followed the instructions on packages of rice and macaroni and cheese, heated frozen pizza in the oven, and cooked canned and frozen vegetables in the microwave. She guessed that must be how Sam normally ate, along with the burgers he sometimes grilled in the backyard.

After being alone all day, she eagerly greeted him when he came home from work, but he remained distant. He ate dinner quickly and then vanished into the hills on his dirt bike or holed up in his study. One night he stayed in the garage, tinkering with the car, until after midnight. The clatter of metal tools landing on concrete was accompanied by Sam's swearing. Caitlin went to bed without him and fell asleep quickly.

When the weekend arrived, Sam said he needed to catch up on yard work and errands. He took Caitlin with him to the base commissary on Saturday so she could choose the groceries for the coming week.

She added a box of cold cereal, a carton of orange juice, and a container of yogurt to the shopping cart and then gathered ingredients for a special dinner she was planning. She'd found a cookbook stashed behind a blender; it included a recipe for lasagna with a vegetarian variation. As she shopped, Caitlin checked off each item on her list: noodles, tomato sauce, cheeses, vegetables and salad, red wine, and rolls. In the frozen food aisle, she found a cheesecake for dessert.

Sam seemed more relaxed after eating lunch, but a drive through the national park later in the day was the extent of their sightseeing. Caitlin was surprised by the jumbo rock formations that covered the landscape. They watched rock climbers at Barker Dam, and then Sam drove to a remote spot to catch the sunset. His pickup truck handled the unpaved roads with ease. Reminded of their romantic evenings in Hawai'i, Caitlin reached for his hand.

When they returned to the house, Sam grilled steaks; later, they had sex. Caitlin couldn't call it making love. Once she accepted that the situation wasn't going to improve, she knew she needed to make plans to leave. She would call the airlines on Monday for a plane ticket to Washington, she decided as she lay awake listening to Sam's snoring.

One way.

On Sunday morning, Sam suggested they make breakfast together. He playfully licked Caitlin's fingers, wet and sticky with freshly squeezed orange juice. She giggled. He overcooked the omelet; her French toast was a little soggy. They laughed about their flawed creations. After they finished eating, he washed the dishes; she dried them. For an unguarded moment, they looked at each other tenderly and shared a heartfelt kiss.

Caitlin was content for the rest of the day. While Sam worked on his car, she sat outside drawing a picture with the colored pencils she'd found in Jacqueline's room. In the evening, she wrote a letter to her mother.

Before turning out the light, Sam told her that his mother had invited them to dinner on Wednesday. Caitlin smiled and kissed his cheek. This was the kind of relating she'd hoped for. Maybe they'd needed some time to understand each other and adapt to new rhythms.

❧

Before he left for work on Monday, Sam gave Caitlin a list of household chores he wanted her to complete. Later in the morning, she removed a load of towels and Sam's socks and underwear from the dryer and moved the next load, including Sam's uniforms, from the washer to the dryer.

After folding the clean laundry, Caitlin restocked the drawer in the kitchen and the shelf in the bathroom where Sam kept towels. When she opened a drawer in the bedroom to put away his underwear, she found a videotape and literature on bondage practices. Behind his socks, handcuffs. Caitlin held her breath as she dangled them. She put the cuffs back in the drawer and stood staring blankly at the dresser, wide-eyed. Her mind was numb but her body instinctively moved toward the closet in Jacqueline's room, where she had stored her luggage.

If not for the small canopy bed and matching bedroom furniture, Caitlin might have questioned whether Sam really had a daughter. He never spoke of her and discouraged all questions about his life. Caitlin retrieved her luggage from the closet and pulled out her airline ticket from the trip to Hawai'i. She used the phone in the kitchen to call the toll-free number printed on the envelope. Busy signal. Feeling like a caged tiger, she paced the kitchen and then went to talk to the Joshua tree she had adopted as her confidant.

"Look at me," she yelled, "I'm talk-ing to a tree!" She looked around at the desolate landscape. "How did I get here?"

Away from the dark house, out in the bright light of day, she could think more clearly. A disconcerting awareness was emerging that the conclusions her brain had been generating all her life were less original thoughts and more predictable responses to messages gleaned from a culture in which the same ideas were circulated and repackaged in different forms, reinforcing each other in a web of shared values and beliefs. Prescriptions about clothing, friends, and activities that made one acceptable and desirable. Ideas about suitable marriage partners. The nature of life, the universe, and everything in it. Deviants were expelled from the group or targeted for reform, either overtly, in extreme cases, or more subtly, through disapproving looks and deprecating remarks or criticism designed to induce guilt.

A cacophony of voices filled Caitlin's head.

"You can't have everything, they say," she told the tree.

"We don't asso-ci-ate with those kinds of people."

She sang the familiar jingle of an old television commercial that popped into her mind: "'Sweeter than honey, fresher than spring; flavorful Zingers will make your mouth sing!'"

And if she was ever in danger of having too much fun, she needed only to remember Grandmother Clayton scolding, "There's more to life than fun and games, young lady."

Conventional wisdom. Advertising. Someone else's truth. No wonder spiritual teachings emphasized the importance of an empty mind. Were her desires even her own, or had she been taught to want particular things—been trained to be a good consumer, a good employee, a good daughter, a good citizen? All cultures socialized newcomers into the rules of the group, but didn't self-actualization require separating from the pack, being true to one's self?

Caitlin's life had slowed down enough for her to regard her own mental activity with detachment. She was better able to notice the habits of thought and the stories she told herself—about herself and other people, about life. She saw that self-defeating loops became self-fulfilling prophecies. What basic beliefs informed her choices about men, work, sex, money, friends? What would it be like to take some time out—away from books and television and other people and their ideas and opinions—and listen to her heart? What would it tell her?

Joshua was a good listener but not a very good conversational-ist. When she felt calmer, Caitlin headed back to Sam's house, deter-mined to find her way home. On the way, she realized that when she sang the jingle, her speech was fine. That had happened before, when she was packing up the townhouse after Martha left. With all the last-minute details of moving out and then leaving for Hawai'i, Caitlin hadn't thought much about it at the time. She'd played the cast album from *A Chorus Line* and sang along with "What I Did for Love." She sang the song again as she walked.

She needed to sing more often.

Therein lies the cure.

✑ 62 ✑

Caitlin was distant toward Sam all evening. He asked if anything was wrong. She said she wasn't feeling well. That wasn't far from the truth; she felt ill at ease, worrying about the cuffs. Had he ever used them? Was he planning on using them—on her? Maybe she was getting paranoid after too much time alone. Her fears took hold, and she obsessed about the handcuffs all night.

She was sleeping soundly when Sam left for work on Tuesday morning. When she awoke, she felt refreshed and energetic. She went for a brisk walk and returned to the house to shower. With no one to talk to, she wanted to write about her feelings and concerns, but she worried that Sam might find her private papers if she did. She thought about writing a letter to herself, but she had no address of her own to send it to. The realization was unsettling. How long could she live the transient life? she wondered.

After lunch, Caitlin started preparing the lasagna. She overcooked the noodles and forgot to rinse them, so the long strips stuck together and ripped. She laid them in a mosaic in the pan, saving the more intact pieces for the top layer. Excited about creating a complete meal, she enthusiastically grated cheese, rinsed spinach, and chopped red peppers and zucchini.

Sam was usually home by five thirty and hadn't mentioned any plans for the evening. At five o'clock, Caitlin set the table. At five thirty, she lit candles she found in a drawer. At six, she ate the last of her dinner. She wondered if there was an airport closer than Los Angeles. She still didn't have a reservation. Why was she unable to muster the energy to leave? Was she worried about causing a scene, afraid of Sam's reaction?

She didn't want to disappear and leave a note—Sam Burns was the type who would track her down and make her pay for abandoning him. But something else contributed to her inaction. Sam sent mixed messages. He sensed when she was slipping away, when she'd had enough and was about to flee. Then he did something nice, something that gave her hope that if she just hung on a little longer . . .

The phone rang. It stopped ringing and then started again— their signal that Sam was calling and Caitlin should answer. He said he was going out for a beer with some buddies. She hadn't told him she was planning a special dinner; she'd wanted to surprise him. But he seemed to find a way to ruin every effort she made. She blew out the candles and dumped his serving into the garbage.

Sam woke Caitlin when he turned on the overhead light in the bedroom. She opened her eyes and saw him looming over her.

"What?" She squinted and rubbed her eyes. "What . . . time is it?"

"Time for you to learn how to follow orders," he said. "You left my shirts in the dryer." He removed his belt and unbuttoned his shirt.

Caitlin slowly sat up. "Wha— Oh, I guess I . . . I forgot to take 'em out. I fell asleep," she said, yawning. "I was really tired. I went for a long walk and then made a nice dinner. There's left-overs."

Sam leaned closer. He reeked of cigarette smoke and alcohol. "Didn't I give you explicit instructions?"

"Y-yes, you did. I'm sorry, I'll . . . I'll redo them in the morn-ing." Caitlin could see that Sam was unhappy with her answer. "Look, I'm exhausted. I don't wanna fight."

"So don't fight!" he yelled. "Do what you're told!" He kicked the wastebasket over, scattering the few items inside. "What am I supposed to wear tomorrow? You want me to look like a rumpled bum?"

Caitlin gasped as she suddenly recalled a moment at work, when Neil grabbed her arm. "N-no, of course not."

"You've been living in my house for, what, a week, ten days now? Eating my food. I ask you to do one simple thing for me—"

He looked around as if to find a target for his frustration.

Seeing the wild look in Sam's eyes—and the belt in his hand— Caitlin glanced toward the door, desperate for a plan, aware of her isolation. She knew better than to provoke Sam and give him a reason to react impulsively. Drawing the blanket around her, she slowly stood.

"Why don't I go steep—sleep in the other womb—*room* tonight and you can get a good night's sleep here?"

"Don't you dare leave now!" He pushed her onto the bed. "You know how that pushes my buttons!"

"Ha-how can I know that?" she whimpered, on the verge of tears. "I hardly know you—"

"Are you stupid or are you trying to piss me off?"

"I-I don't think I'm stupid but I sa—cer-tainly don't want to make you ang—mad." She was the deer on the highway, staring into the headlights of a speeding vehicle, about to be creamed, and she couldn't move.

Sam sneered. "Everything's about you. What about my needs?"

"Ya—you're abs— You're ab-so-lutely right," Caitlin said, slowly nodding her head. "I'm not what you need. I should probably make plans to leave soon."

Sam looked stricken. "But . . . we can talk about that some other time," Caitlin said. "Why don't you just . . . tell me what you want and I . . . I'll be happy to do it." She thought of the handcuffs and wondered how far she was willing to go to appease him.

"I want you to go iron my shirts."

"Fine," Caitlin said, rising. She took the blanket with her.

Sam let her pass. "And don't forget the starch."

The slate floor in the laundry room felt cold beneath Caitlin's bare feet. She latched the door. It wouldn't stop a raging bull but it was a symbolic gesture, if nothing else. Her knees were weak, her hands shaking as she removed Sam's damp shirts from the dryer.

How do I get myself out of this one?

ᐁ 63 ᐁ

Caitlin was curled up in a chair in the living room, asleep, when Sam touched her shoulder, startling her. He was dressed and ready to leave.

"Hey. Sorry about last night," he said matter-of-factly. "I guess the stress from the job gets to me sometimes."

Caitlin held her breath and stared at him.

"Thanks for the shirt," he said. "I'll leave work a little early and pick you up about four."

Caitlin nodded and forced a smile. She'd forgotten about dinner with Sam's mother. She was exhausted, emotionally and physically. Maybe she could get some rest after Sam left.

He squeezed her knee and gave her an uneasy smile; he seemed reluctant to leave. Before walking out the door, he turned and said, "My mother complains I'm always late. Please be ready."

Caitlin frowned. *Was that a request or a command?*

She was angry. With Sam—for treating her like an unwelcome guest. With herself—for staying. And now, she was angry enough to take action.

She cooked an egg for breakfast and then phoned the airline again. Another busy signal. She called the travel agent who had arranged her Hawai'i trip. *Don't know why I didn't think of that sooner.* The agent was on another call; she said she'd look into flights and call back.

"No, I'll call you," Caitlin said. She didn't know how she'd get to the airport, but she was determined to find a way. She wished she had never come to California with Sam. *Seemed like a good idea at the time . . .*

She entered Kimo's number on the keypad of the touch-tone telephone. *Oh, please be there!* After several rings, Melody answered.

"Oh—Melody. Hi . . . it's Caitlin."

"Hi Caitlin."

Caitlin didn't know Melody well enough to ask why she was answering Kimo's phone; what went on in his house was none of her business.

"I'll be coming back in a few days. I'll let Kimo know the . . . details."

"Okay, I'll tell him. We were wondering how it's going. You're in California, right?"

"Yeah, and I'm more than ready to leave. This man I'm stay-ing with—I dunno, he scares me."

"Mmm. It's easy to mistake drama for passion. But some women like drama."

Caitlin grew quiet. Her relationship with Jayson had been good for a long time. Sam was an aberration, she told herself.

"Mmm . . . you okay?" Melody asked.

"I'll be fine. I just wish I could come back sooner. He's . . . vol-a-tile."

"Is there somewhere else you could go?"

"Not really. Unless . . . We're going to dinner at his mother's place tonight. She lives in some osh—ash-ram," Caitlin said. "I hope they're not part of a cult or something!"

"I wonder if it's the Ananda Center," Melody said. "I've been wanting to visit there."

"I don't know," Caitlin said slowly. She felt stupid for being in such a predicament. "I'll call Kimo another time. I'd rather he didn't know . . . about this."

"No worries."

Caitlin hung up the phone and walked out to the garage. Could she put her luggage in the car without Sam knowing? Would he even take the car? Too risky. She packed her bags and put them back in the closet. Knowing she was a step closer to leaving would help her make it through another day.

Sam smiled when he saw Caitlin in the dress she'd worn for their first date in Hawai'i. He kissed her cheek and held open the car door for her. He was grumpy through the stop-and-go traffic on the free-way, but driving into the hills he reached for Caitlin's hand. Reluctantly, she played along. She had no wish to aggravate him while he was behind the wheel.

She breathed a sigh of relief when she read the large sign at the front gate of the ashram: "Welcome to the Ananda Center." Nestled in the foothills, with buildings and residences clustered around a dining hall and a small chapel, the setting reminded Caitlin of a college campus. The grounds were beautifully landscaped with flowers and fountains and included a community vegetable garden as well as a rose garden with a gazebo.

Caitlin smiled and said a prayer of thanks. She would be safe here. Divine Order was in charge.

✑ 64 ✑

Caitlin followed Sam up the stairs to the second floor of an apartment building. His mother greeted them at the door. Slim and elegant, she wore her gray hair in a tight bun. She was dressed in casual slacks and a simple blouse. Caitlin noticed colored gemstones in her ring, necklace, and earrings.

She doesn't look unusual, she thought.

For dinner, Sam's mother served a simple meal of red beans and basmati rice with salad and steamed vegetables.

I could cook this—but would Sam eat it? Caitlin looked over and saw Sam shoveling food into his mouth. *Guess so.*

"Adzuki beans are good for strengthening the kidneys," his mother told her.

Sam's mother spoke to him about people they knew. A postcard from Yvonne. A visit from Suzanne. A call from Uncle Ed. Sam grunted and nodded but said little. His mother turned her attention to Caitlin.

"Sam tells me you live in Washington," she said, looking Caitlin over. "Is that where you two met?"

"N-no," Caitlin said hesitantly. How much had Sam told his mother? Should she say more?

His mother shrugged. "Sam goes there often, so I thought . . ."

Caitlin glanced at Sam. He had never mentioned a connection to Washington. But, then, he kept a lot hidden.

"What's that committee you're on, dear?" his mother asked him. "Vaccine safety, isn't it?"

Sam's mouth froze, mid-bite, but he did not look up.

"Yes, that's it," his mother said.

Sam slowly chewed the food in his mouth and calmly put down his fork.

Caitlin felt dazed. Something was amiss, but she couldn't quite fit the puzzle pieces together.

"It was their arguments over whether to have Jacqueline vaccinated that finally ended the marriage," his mother confided, as if Sam wasn't sitting right next to Caitlin.

"I have a professional duty to serve the public health!" Sam snarled. "Vaccines have saved countless lives—they're the first line of defense against epidemics."

The women looked blankly at him.

"Oh, it's no use!" he said, throwing his cloth napkin on the table.

Caitlin's throat tightened and she felt the blood drain from her face. She could hardly breathe and worried she might faint. She reached for a glass of water and took a sip. She was afraid to look directly at Sam, yet felt that she must see his expression. She stole a sideways glance; his face was turning red.

He's gonna blow, she thought, and inched away.

"Caitlin isn't interested in the sordid details of my divorce, Mother!"

Caitlin heard Sam and his mother arguing, but the words seemed muffled and distorted. Her thoughts flashed to the moment just prior to the collision, when she'd glanced in the rearview mirror. She remembered seeing two specks of light approaching rapidly. After that, everything was darkness.

This was the first recollection she'd had about the day of the accident. Unable to grasp more details, she shook off the memory and returned her attention to the present.

". . . Especially after Yvonne learned he holds stock in pharmaceuticals!" Sam's mother was saying to her.

Yvonne? Caitlin didn't understand what Sam and his mother were so lathered up about. *Must be his ex-wife.*

"I've already told Caitlin about breaking Yvonne's nose, if that's what you're getting at!" Sam shouted. "Your meddling is pointless."

He pushed his chair away from the table. "It's time we got back," he said to Caitlin.

She didn't respond.

Sam's mother rose to clear the dishes from the table. "Nonsense. I baked shortcake," she declared, as if shortcake was the answer to their differences. "You can't leave without dessert. I insist."

Caitlin watched to see how Sam responded to this approach. He grimaced but seemed docile. Caitlin got up from the table, chattering nervously, and kept a safe distance from Sam.

"Tha—that was a lovely meal, Mrs. Burns," she said. She carried a few plates to the tiny kitchen. "Are most people here vege-tar-ian?"

Sam snickered. "Most people here have an alias," he said with disdain. "Mom's is Satchidananda."

Mother and son clearly embraced different values. Caitlin was curious to learn about Satchidananda's lifestyle, but more immediate concerns were at the forefront of her mind. "Is that Sand . . . Sanskrit?" she asked, grateful for a diversion.

Satchidananda nodded. "Yes, devotees are given Sanskrit names when we agree to follow the teachings of the Indian saint who founded this community. And, yes, those who live here eat a vegetarian diet."

"Does the whole . . . com-mun-ity eat together sometimes?" Caitlin asked. Ignoring the sound of Sam's fingers drumming on the table, she cleared the last of the dishes from the dining room.

Satchidananda started a fire under the kettle. "Yes, but the Center gets so many visitors, most residents keep to themselves. Except on special occasions. Next month, our guru will be here. People will come from all over for that. It's quite a sight," she said, visibly excited. "Tents everywhere, RVs. We always find room somehow."

"Are we having dessert or aren't we?" Sam yelled.

"Yes, yes," his mother answered. She handed Caitlin dessert plates to take to the dining room. "Perhaps we can go for a walk later and I'll show you around."

"I've got an early day," Sam said loudly.

"Oh, Sam dear," his mother said sweetly as she scanned the shelves inside her refrigerator. "I forgot the whipped cream. Would you run out?"

Sam groaned. "We can eat it without whipped cream."

Caitlin set the plates on the table and returned to the kitchen as Satchidananda exited. She heard the harsh whisper: "Come now, we have a guest."

"Oh, all right," Sam said. He picked up his jacket and headed toward the door. "She's an awful lot of trouble for little reward," he mumbled.

"Would you like some money, dear?" his mother called after him.

"My treat!" he replied with mock courtesy.

Caitlin jumped when the door banged shut. Satchidananda returned to the kitchen.

"His blood has a low boiling point," she said with a chuckle. "He's like his father that way!"

Incredulous, Caitlin followed her into the living room. *She sounds like she's talking about a dimple in his chin!*

"Sam hasn't told me a lot about his father—or much of anything, really," Caitlin said with a sigh. "Have you lived here since he died?"

"Practically. I came for retreats and gradually made peace with his passing. Once Sam and his sister were grown and out of the house, I moved here full time."

"I didn't even know Sam had a sister!"

"I'm not surprised. She's close to Yvonne and takes her side. They believe Jacqueline's learning disability was caused by the vaccinations, which we all opposed," she said as she poured chai from a pot. "But Sam insisted, and he's the doctor."

Satchidananda handed Caitlin a cup and saucer. "Oh, I forgot the milk," she said. "Would you mind, dear? There's a little white pitcher in the fridge."

"Yes, of course."

Caitlin went to the kitchen. When she opened the door of the refrigerator she saw, plainly visible, a half-pint of whipping cream.

Her mind was spinning; she didn't know how to absorb all this new information, or what it meant. Had Sam's daughter had an adverse reaction to a vaccine? Was that why he avoided talking about her? Did he feel guilty? The women clearly blamed him—and let him know about it, still. Caitlin returned to the living room with the milk.

"Sam does have his challenges with women," Satchidananda said. "Including me."

Sam's mother was a gracious hostess, but Caitlin saw the sadness in her eyes. "Then perhaps . . . you'll under-stand why—"

She paused. She didn't know how to ask Satchidananda for help and could find no tactful way to say she was afraid of Sam. Aware that this might be her only opportunity for escape, she blurted out, "I—I don't wanna go back there!"

"Back where, child?" Satchidananda asked, setting down her teacup.

"To . . . to Sam's house," Caitlin said before looking away.

It can't be easy having a jerk for a son.

"I see," Satchidananda said. She was silent for a few moments. "I'll find you a room for the night," she said quietly. "You can stay as my guest, if you'd like."

Caitlin responded immediately with a heartfelt "Thank you!" She wished she had some way to show her gratitude.

After a good night's rest—when she was thinking more clearly—she would be better able to plan her travel. Maybe she could stay at the Center for a couple of days. She would leave her luggage at Sam's house if she had to—she just wanted to go home. On second thought, she didn't want him holding on to any part of her.

⤳ 65 ⤳

While she waited for Sam to return, Caitlin glanced at the titles of the books on Satchidananda's coffee table: *The Bhagavad Gita, Autobiography of a Yogi, The Yoga Sutras of Patanjali.* Kimo had told her a little about Buddhism; Caitlin knew even less about Hinduism.

In childhood, she'd been taught that the souls of heathen worshippers were in danger of suffering eternal torment if they didn't receive the Christian sacraments and obey the revealed Word of God. Did Jesus say that? Or was it one of the religious doctrines that had arisen over two thousand—or more—years? Would a merciful God damn non-Christians for all eternity—or was the idea of a vengeful God a convenient way to ensure obedience?

Do teachings that emphasize sin and suffering add more love to the world? Doubt it. You don't teach a child tolerance and compassion by beating him.

Caitlin chewed on a fingernail. Surely Sam wouldn't create a scene with his mother in the next room. She smoothed her hair when she heard the front door open and close.

"Where's my mother?" Sam asked, looking around.

Caitlin shrugged. "Not sure."

Sam removed a small carton of whipping cream from the brown bag he was carrying and set it on the table in the dining room. "We should go. I got a box of doughnuts. We can eat those for dessert. In the car."

Caitlin stared at the floor. She took a deep breath and said, "I . . . uh—I'm not c-coming with you."

"What do you mean?"

"I'm staying here tonight . . . at the Center. Then I'm going back—to Washing-ton."

She looked up in time to see Sam's face change as he registered the news. At first, he looked shocked and raised his eyebrows in disbelief. Then, he understood. His nostrils flared; his eyes narrowed.

"I should have known," he said as he walked past her. "You're all alike."

Caitlin watched closely for any sign of aggression. She was prepared to scream or defend herself if Sam came near her. He stopped and slowly turned around. He looked contrite, but Caitlin kept her guard up.

"Look, I know I haven't been very good company lately. We had such a great time in Hawai'i—I know we can recapture that. Why don't you come with me and give it another chance?" he asked, his eyes pleading.

"No, Sam," Caitlin said. "We did have a great time in Hawai'i. It should have ended there. I'm not cut out for . . . the desert."

"I'll be done with the Navy soon—"

Caitlin shook her head. "I don't wanna hear it. You've hardly spoken to me for the last week, ex-cept to com-plain. It's too late. I've already packed."

Sam's bitterness returned. "I see. Very well." His head bobbed rapidly. "Goodbye, then." He turned away.

"I'll stop for my bags . . . on my way to the air-port," Caitlin said.

Sam ignored her and opened the front door. "Goodbye Mother," he yelled.

Satchidananda emerged from her bedroom with a cheerful countenance. "Are you leaving? When am I going to see my darling granddaughter?"

"Sometime next week," Sam said. He kissed her cheek. "I'll call you."

"Goodbye, dear."

Satchidananda closed the door and invited Caitlin to sit at the dining room table.

"I'll just be a minute," she said, picking up the carton Sam had left on the table. She retreated into the kitchen to finish her dessert preparation. She returned with two plates and joined Caitlin at the table.

The round mound of cake was covered with ripe strawberries and topped with a cloud of freshly whipped cream; it looked delicious. Caitlin ate a bite but hardly tasted it.

"I don't understand," she said, shaking her head, "why this hap—hap-pened to me now . . . after all I've been through. Sometimes I feel like . . . like I'm being punished—or I keep . . . making the same mis-takes."

First Dru, now Sam. She'd need to be more careful about going home with men she hardly knew and stop acting like a stray dog looking for a home. Maybe her mother was right—she wasn't very smart when it came to love and romance.

And no wonder.

What models did she have of healthy relationships? Bobby had teased and tormented her; Martha had tried to reform her; Charlie had ignored her much of the time. They'd had the essentials, but they lacked solidarity. Caitlin didn't blame her parents; they couldn't give her what they didn't have. Martha's kin were stern and undemonstrative. Charlie's parents were poor and uneducated. Caitlin longed to feel that she belonged somewhere, to be at home among her own kind.

"Don't be too hard on yourself," Satchidananda said. "The path of awakening is like a spiral. We all have issues we work on—for our whole lives sometimes. We keep meeting them again and again, and if we're doing the work, we make a little progress each time, so that the next time perhaps we catch ourselves sooner and choose to do something differently."

Caitlin wished she could speak so candidly with her own mother. She was sure she tested Martha's patience, and Caitlin derived little satisfaction from their interactions. Of course, Sam and his mother also clashed. Maybe blood ties bound people together in ways that ensured lessons would be learned and scales balanced, Caitlin thought. If nothing else, childhood experiences laid the foundations of character and established patterns that would influence the course of a lifetime.

"How do you ex-plain your son's be-hav-ior?"

A shadow came over Satchidananda's face. "I don't," she said.

"I accept him where he is in his own journey of understanding. It's dangerous to think we know what's best for another. We can only be responsible for the weeds in our own garden."

Caitlin recalled a quote from the Gospel of Matthew: *"For with what judgment ye judge, ye shall be judged; and with what measure ye mete, it shall be measured to you again."*

In the past, she'd been forced to memorize passages from the Bible. Could she find wisdom in the words now?

"Sam's suffering will lead him to the experiences he needs, in his own time." Satchidananda ate the last strawberry on her plate and put down her fork.

"As ye sow, so shall ye reap" was accepted Christian theology, Caitlin thought. Did the Eastern idea of karma express a similar concept of cause and effect?

"He's still bitter about the divorce," Satchidananda added.

"Why's he . . . tak-ing it out on me?"

"Why do you allow it?"

"I—I didn't know what else to do, in a strange place . . . no car even. I'm still not sure where I am!" As she spoke, Caitlin realized she sounded like a victim. She could have left sooner, if she had mustered the initiative. What spell had she been under?

"Are you saying you had no choice? Were you held against your will?"

"No," Caitlin admitted, embarrassed by her inaction.

"Did you ever tell Sam you wanted to leave?"

"Yes—last night."

Why not sooner?

Where was her pride? She'd never tolerated mistreatment by a man before. She'd never had to—the men she dated didn't exhibit such crude behavior. Even Neil, arguably more dangerous in his power plays, knew how to finesse a situation.

Sam had never physically harmed her, but Caitlin had feared that he would lose control. She'd felt paralyzed. Whether the trauma she'd suffered in the accident contributed to her feeling of powerlessness or simply revealed flaws in her character, she couldn't say, but she was profoundly aware of her inadequacies.

Awareness is the first step toward change, she reminded herself, and then a realization hit her like a slap in the face.

"Oh my God—my mother! She was . . . afraid of my father. This must be how *she* felt!"

Had she been drawn into a situation that paralleled her mother's experience—and if so, was it because she had judged and blamed her? How did that happen? What devices of fate or psychology arranged such an occurrence?

"My mother told me that my father was . . . a-bu-sive. I guess I didn't believe her. Now I have some sense of what she must have put up with," Caitlin said quietly. "And why . . . she had to go."

"Understanding paves the way for compassion and forgiveness."

Caitlin smiled. She felt lighter, amazed by the mystery of life.

"Are you ready to go to your room?" Satchidananda asked.

Caitlin nodded.

The moon was full overhead as Satchidananda led Caitlin past a shrine and down stone steps. They passed a building with a sign that read "Meditation Hall."

"If you're up early," Satchidananda said, "chanting begins at four thirty, followed by a period of silent meditation."

"Okay."

They walked along a paved path. Satchidananda paused in front of the dining hall. "Breakfast is at seven thirty. You can ask about transportation at the front desk. Someone should be there by nine. I'll leave word to expect you."

"Sounds like I might not see you again," Caitlin said as they walked toward the dormitory-like building that housed short-term residents and guests. She would always be grateful to Satchidananda for providing refuge in her time of need.

"Probably not. I read stories to the children on Thursday mornings. And I fast when the moon is full, so I won't be attending any community meals."

"Thank you again, Sa-shi—"

"Satchidananda. It translates as 'bliss consciousness.'"

"You've given me a lot to . . . consider."

"There is a saying, 'When the student is ready, a teacher appears.' We're all students and teachers to each other." Satchidananda paused, as if listening. "Life brings you all you need, if your heart is open to receive it. Trust in life and where it leads you."

"I don't even know who I am anymore," Caitlin confessed. "Everything's . . . chang-ing so fast."

"Be gentle with yourself. Truth is simple; our minds make it complicated. That which is true remains when the illusions are stripped away."

"You sound like my friend Kimo," Caitlin said, chuckling.

"Perhaps he is a true friend," Satchidananda said. She bowed slightly, her hands in the prayer position at her heart. "Sat nam."

Caitlin bowed her head respectfully. "'night."

∽ 66 ∽

Sam stopped at a liquor store near the highway and bought a six-pack of beer. He tossed each can out of the window after he'd emptied it. He didn't care. About littering, about drinking and driving—about anything. The future looked as black and uninviting as the present. All he wanted was a way out.

He returned to the house and unlocked the cabinet off the dining room where he kept liquor and a handgun. He finished off what remained of a bottle of vodka; next, he opened a quart of tequila. When he'd had enough, he smashed the bottles against the wall of the laundry room. Shattered glass covered the slate floor.

Anger mingled with grief, shame, disgust. He felt like a complete failure. How much lower could he sink? He railed against everyone who had ever hurt him. Brandon and Yvonne topped the list, but he also shouted obscenities at Caitlin. He was angry with his mother but incapable of swearing at her.

In a lucid moment, he might have realized how well sound travels in the crystal clear stillness of the desert. In his stupor, he didn't care.

He was awakened by a man in uniform shining a flashlight into his eyes. A neighbor had reported a disturbance, the officer said. Sam sat up and rubbed his eyes. He saw two sheriff's deputies in his bedroom and assured them that no one else had been there; he was just blowing off steam after some disappointing news. Satisfied, the men left, and Sam passed out again.

When he woke at noon, he called the hospital and requested permission to go on terminal leave. He had accumulated more than enough leave to finish out the three weeks until his date of separation, he told his commanding officer.

Sorry for the short notice, but I'm not in any condition . . .

Sam grabbed the gun and clambered into his truck. He stopped at the base to sign the necessary papers and then headed east, deeper into the desert. He wanted to go far away. Away from the pulse of urban growth that was creeping inland. Away from his mother and sister; away from everything he'd ever known. Away from Yvonne, and yes, even Jacqueline. He was no use to her now.

⋘ 67 ⋙

Caitlin reached for her watch after the sound of a bell tinkling in the hallway outside her door woke her.

Four o'clock.

She lay awake for a while as people shuffled past her room going to and from the washroom. On another day, she might have been interested in attending the meditation gathering. Now, she needed sleep. She shifted around in the twin bed, trying to find a comfortable position. She felt peaceful and serene simply being there—away from Sam.

She couldn't undo the past, but maybe she could find meaning in it. If she understood herself better—recognized her blind spots—perhaps she would make better choices in the future. She'd gained a new understanding of her mother that helped her see from a broader perspective. Could she move beyond her need to understand everything and learn to trust that all is well, even when it doesn't appear to be so?

Kimo once said that the patterns of our lives take shape over time; only when we honestly examine choices and outcomes do we begin to see the patterns. Satchidananda said that trusting in life, rather than individuals, was the key to accepting disappointments. People are fallible and corruptible, but life is abundant. Blessings can appear unexpectedly, even when specific people fail us.

Caitlin heard the faint sound of music and chanting every time someone opened the door to the meditation hall. Unable to sleep, she got up and dressed in the clothing she'd worn the day before. At seven thirty, she walked to the dining hall.

She selected fruit, oatmeal, nuts, and yogurt from the breakfast buffet and sat on a bench at a wooden table where she could observe the people and the protocol. The room was quiet and people ate silently. What kinds of people were drawn to live in a community like this? she wondered. Was talking even allowed?

Soon, a group of lively, chattering twenty-somethings entered the dining room. Caitlin hid her smile with a napkin, amused by her own misconceptions.

Years before, she had seen devotees of some guru handing out literature at airports. Scandals about cults occasionally made the news, but the choice to follow an unusual lifestyle didn't mean a group was diabolical or dangerous, and commitment to a group's ideals didn't mean members were required to give over all their possessions and sever ties with the outside world. Caitlin saw no evidence of forced cooperation; on the contrary, people seemed happy to be there. The lifestyle didn't appeal to her, but she thought a short stay might be rejuvenating.

After breakfast, she browsed through the books in a small reading room while she waited for the office to open. A multi-volume set bearing the title *The Sacred Books of the East* caught her eye. She selected volume XXV and opened the tattered old book to read the table of contents. This volume, *The Laws of Manu,* was divided into twelve chapters. Topics ranged from civil and criminal law and the duties of kings to transmigration and "supreme bliss." Fascinated, Caitlin sat down and read the story of creation.

The verses were numbered, much like the Christian Bible. The first chapter said the universe existed in darkness until the Self-existent one—"He who can be perceived by the internal organ"—dispelled it. "With a thought" the eternal "first cause" created the waters and placed there his seed, which became a golden egg and was born as Brahman, the Lord.

Caitlin chuckled. *Does this mean the egg came before the chicken?*

She turned to the introduction, wondering if the Hindu author had been influenced by ancient Hebrew texts—such as the account in Genesis of the world being created in six days and God resting on the seventh.

The Laws of Manu, Caitlin learned, was the first Sanskrit text that had been translated into English. Originally translated in 1794 by Sir William Jones, the book in her hands, dated 1886, was translated by G. Bühler and published by the Oxford University Press. Manu was a legendary son of Brahman whose teachings were recorded by his disciple, Bhrigu, one of ten great sages that Manu called into existence—the "lords of created beings."

Chapter One explained that a "day" of the gods who created the manifest universe was equal to one-half of one of our solar years; a "night" was the same length and followed a day. One "age" of the gods was said to be twelve thousand years, but it took one thousand ages of the gods to equal just one day of Brahman, who slept during the following night.

Caitlin turned to Chapter Two. He who followed the prescribed duties—for only men were permitted to study sacred texts—could reach "the deathless state," even in this lifetime, said verse 5.

The deathless state—is that like eternal life?

She turned the page. Verse 26 referred to "holy rites" and "sacraments" that purify "twice-born" men.

Who were the 'twice-born'?

Jesus said people needed to be born of water and of spirit before they could see the kingdom of God. Were Hindu sacraments similar to those of the Christians?

Kimo said the early Christians borrowed traditions and ideas from more ancient cultures, Caitlin recalled. She turned to another page. Verse 112 said good seed must not be thrown on barren land.

That sounds a lot like Jesus's admonition not to throw pearls before swine.

Verse 113 explained further: "Even in times of dire distress a teacher of the Veda should rather die with his knowledge than sow it in barren soil."

Caitlin remembered the Indian parable about the blind men and the elephant—the one holding the tail and the one holding the trunk drew different conclusions about the elephant; each had only glimpsed a part of the whole. *A little knowledge can be a dangerous thing when people think they know the truth but only know a portion.*

"The teacher, the father, the mother, and an elder brother" all must be treated with respect—even if they caused grievous offense—said verse 225. Caitlin thought of the Book of Exodus and the commandment given Moses on Mount Sinai to "honor thy father and thy mother."

This Hindu "commandment" goes even further.

Skimming through the book, Caitlin saw rules about what to wear, how to address elders, the performance of rituals, and numerous other requirements.

Priests—and priestesses—in many cultures were bound by expectations and vows that were more stringent than the standards that applied to other people, but for the members of some societies, roles were imposed, not chosen. People knew their place. They were born into families of priests or rulers or craftsmen, and they carried on the traditions of their ancestors.

The modern Western world imposed no rigid rules comparable to India's ancient caste system, but social stratification was evident,

Caitlin thought; marked differences in education, income, and living standards distinguished members of the upper and lower classes. The rich and powerful were treated like royalty. Breaking out of poverty was especially difficult when barriers became institutionalized. In the U.S., resistance to desegregation had been widespread. Long-standing prejudices were slow to disappear.

Caitlin put the book down when the staff arrived. She asked about the nearest airport and learned that the Center could provide transportation with twenty-four hours' notice. A weekend silent retreat was the only option available to her if she wanted to extend her stay. The last thing she thought she needed was more silence, but she needed more time. Feeling safe with Satchidananda nearby, she registered for the program. It would begin Friday evening, leaving her a day to herself. Because she'd stayed the night as Satchi's guest, she was permitted to stay another night.

Caitlin smiled as she signed her name. She had teased Kimo about living in a commune and now here she was, staying in an ashram!

The staff arranged for a driver to take her to Sam's house. The fee was reasonable, considering the distance. Caitlin phoned Sam at work, but he wasn't available. She left a message on his home answering machine that she'd be coming by to collect her things.

"I'll leave the key under the mat."

Next, she called her travel agent.

Caitlin was not prepared for the mess she found at Sam's house. She walked through the kitchen and found dirty dishes in the sink, half-eaten pizza on the counter, cupboard doors open. Sam was nearly fanatical about order and cleanliness.

Or was that just a show too?

Her irritation turned to anxiety when she noticed the back door was open. She rushed to Sam's bedroom. The light had been left on. Clothes were strewn across the floor, and the bed covers were in disarray. Caitlin slowly moved toward Jacqueline's room, afraid of what she might find there. Her luggage lay open; her clothes had been shredded. A lightweight sweater in her carry-on bag was the only thing left untouched.

Caitlin knelt down on the floor. She sobbed as she heaped the remains of her clothing into a pile. She'd given away most of her old clothes and had only kept the ones that still fit her. Now, she'd been stripped of those too. After her talk with Satchidananda, she'd thought maybe she had been unfair to Sam by not giving him more notice of her plans. This destructive act confirmed her worst suspicions about him.

Reminded of how crazy Sam could get, Caitlin said a prayer of thanks for her safe exodus. Holding the sweater close to her, she carried her suitcase outside and climbed into the waiting van. She had no home to go back to. No job. No mate or children. Perhaps she'd been hoping Sam would rescue her from the need to recreate her life by including her in his. Now that she'd seen what his life was like, she knew she wasn't missing anything, but the terrible ending of their romance left her feeling forlorn and adrift.

The lunch line was closed when Caitlin returned to the Center, but someone had saved a plate of food for her. Kindnesses she might once have overlooked were now valued gifts.

Adversity is humbling, she thought as she poured a glass of iced tea.

She ate alone in the dining room while a group of residents discussed preparations for an upcoming event.

The agenda sounded typical of a meeting at any resort or conference center, with team leaders reporting on arrangements for food, lodging, transportation and the like. The meals needed to be cooked, the dishes washed, and the rooms cleaned when guests departed. Whereas most businesses were driven by a profit motive, residents of the ashram viewed their jobs as an opportunity to serve, and no task was considered too menial for anyone to undertake. People didn't seem to expect praise or rewards for fulfilling their obligations, yet they expressed appreciation and gratitude for every contribution willingly extended. Weren't these Christian precepts these devotees were practicing? The outer form was different, but the essential truths seemed similar.

Caitlin took her dishes to the kitchen and then stopped in the gift shop. The store carried books and CDs as well as candles, incense, household products, and some jewelry and clothing. Caitlin set a journal with a decorative cover by the register and continued shopping. She passed by the turbans and shawls and silk saris and selected a pair of navy yoga pants to try on. She chose several t-shirts that might go with the pants and then looked through the racks of colorful skirts and dresses until she found a red-and-gold print dress that she liked.

She took her selections to the dressing room and had fun trying on a new style of clothing. She bought a bright blue tie-dyed t-shirt, the yoga pants, and a matching sweatshirt to wear during the retreat. The dress she would wear on the plane. She added a small bottle of gentle detergent to her purchase and then returned to her dorm to wash the clothes out in the bathroom sink.

Caitlin had thought that a weekend of meditation would bore her, but the time passed quickly. Being with others and not speaking seemed odd at first, but she soon felt nurtured by the silence and preferred it to the recorded Indian music that played throughout the day in the office and the dining hall. She remembered Melody saying that toning and chanting might help her speech. She still didn't know what "toning" was, but she decided to check out the chanting in the early hours of her last morning at the ashram.

The great hall was filled with people; the air was thick with incense. Caitlin took a chant book from a table in the back of the room and sat on a meditation cushion. The language was strange to her ears and even the instruments sounded unusual, but several of the hymns were in English. One in particular touched a longing in Caitlin's soul. She closed her eyes and listened:

I've searched for you everywhere; still my soul cries in despair.

Tears streamed down her face. The depth of feeling aroused by the music caught her by surprise. Away from the chaos of the city, in the placid expanse of nature, not looking for attractions or distractions or romance, she'd had time to ponder recent events, to breathe deeply, to let go of tension, and to look ahead to her return to Washington.

Over the course of the program, she had experienced the power of silent communion. Far from being empty, the space was potent. The air seemed to sparkle with charged particles. This silence was different from the stifling, oppressive atmosphere at Sam's house, the unspoken tension with Martha, or Caitlin's solo time in Hawai'i. She recalled having glimpsed this state of being before, at Easter. Was this level of awareness one that she could learn to sustain?

Caitlin left her suitcase at the office while she stopped at the gift shop to buy a card and gift certificate for Satchidananda. She returned to the office and asked the receptionist to put the envelope in Satchi's mailbox, and then she waited outside for the van.

During the ride to the airport, Caitlin wondered why she chose men who were unavailable—emotionally, like Sam, or physically, like Dru. Was it because they allowed her to stay separate and didn't require her to risk true intimacy? Or could Melody be right—did she like excitement and drama? Was she wary because Jayson had broken her heart—or did she distrust men entirely?

While waiting in the terminal, Caitlin jotted her thoughts down in her new journal. Maybe she'd stayed so long with Sam for a reason. If she'd left sooner, she never would have visited the ashram or met Satchidananda. She might have always wondered whether she should have stayed longer and given Sam more of a chance.

She had learned to follow through on commitments. She had stayed in school until she graduated—through high school and college and then law school. She had gone to work every day, even when she might have preferred to sleep in or take a day off to go skiing or shopping. She took pride in her achievements. Responsible parents, students, employees, business owners, and leaders sometimes needed to sacrifice their personal preferences in favor of children, institutional demands and requirements, employers and clients and constituencies. But the same stick-to-itiveness that was an asset when pursuing a distant goal—the same willingness to set aside short-term happiness to achieve long-term objectives—became a liability when it hindered the ability to change course midstream.

At what point did self-sacrifice become martyrdom and delayed gratification develop into a habit of neglecting dreams and desires? Was there such a thing as being overly responsible? Caitlin wondered as she boarded the plane. She'd stayed with Jayson, even when she suspected they weren't made for happily-ever-after. She'd let Neil talk her out of leaving OSP—and he knew just how to do it. God, was it that obvious, how to play her?

She found her seat and fastened her seatbelt. Her father had sacrificed his dreams of travel and adventure so he could provide for his family—and Caitlin was grateful he'd made that choice. She saw now that her parents had been miserable for much of their marriage. Why had they stayed together for as long as they did? For the sake of their children? Following through on a promise of "till death do us part"—a vow that didn't hold up anyway?

Commitment, dedication, and dependability were admirable qualities that enabled people to follow through and complete unpleasant tasks. But Caitlin could see that adaptability was equally important, as well as willingness to walk away if she tried something and it wasn't working out. Stubbornly sticking to a plan at all costs would be as foolhardy as refusing to make any plans at all.

If she was miserable—with Sam, with Jayson, in her job—at some point she had to consider that the problem was more than a passing phase, a bad mood, an off day. Even if the job or relationship had suited her at one time, circumstances changed. *She* changed—and that was a good thing, not something to be feared and avoided. She liked variety and problem-solving; too much routine and stability and life felt stagnant. So why would she demand that other people stay stuck?

Her feelings about her parents' divorce were complex. She hadn't known they were so unhappy, so she was shocked when her mother just *left*. Sure, her parents were still her parents, even if they were no longer married, but the family was no longer a family, and Caitlin mourned its demise. Now she could see that her mother's actions had shaken her values, too. She wouldn't like herself much if she gave up too easily and walked away from something just because it was "hard." She'd stayed with Sam because she had to know that the relationship was unworkable, despite her efforts and intentions—and desires. But once she'd accepted the inevitable conclusion, staying made no sense; she wouldn't go down with a sinking ship out of a misplaced sense of duty.

Perhaps she should thank her mother for leaving a bad marriage rather than condemn her for breaking up the family. She had always wanted Martha to take more initiative—and then when she finally did, Caitlin complained because her mother's choice impacted her life as well. Martha's marriage ended the same way it started—unexpectedly—and the people close to her were forced to adjust.

Caitlin wished she could have trusted her mother more, rather than assuming she'd run off on a whim. She wished she'd understood that the choice to get a divorce must have been a difficult one. But the time apart had been important, and she needed to find her own answers, in her own way.

The best choice wasn't always clear. Knowing when to leave and when to stay required discernment, self-knowledge, life experience, and, sometimes, a leap of faith. Maybe her mother had chosen the right time to leave, balancing her own needs with those of her family. At least now Caitlin was willing to believe that Martha had done her best. *She had reasons.*

Caitlin hoped she could share a heart-to-heart talk with her mother someday, the way she had with Sam's mother. Martha accused her of being self-absorbed, but she, too, had made sacrifices for a greater good. Maybe some of her clients appreciated her hard work on their behalf—she knew that Kimo did.

Caitlin was eager to see him. She remembered only fragments of their travels in Ireland. Many of her memories were hazy, shrouded by a misty veil. Maybe, in time, the veil would part, and she would understand more about her past. For now, parts of her story remained hidden.

Maybe I'm not ready to know . . .

The plane sped down the runway and lifted into the air. Caitlin watched as the California landscape receded from view. Sam had been a hard lesson, the price paid for indulging in romantic fantasies about an enchanted evening when her prince would come and sweep her off her feet. Life wasn't a Broadway show. Her head might be in the clouds, but she intended to keep her feet firmly on the ground and move forward with open eyes, putting one foot in front of the other and following where life led.

As the jet soared higher she crafted a poem, the first she had written since high school:

> *I'm not listening anymore*
> *to what you say about who you are*
> *"I'm not like that," you insisted*
> *"I'd never do that," and I enlisted.*
> *But you are, and you did*
> *and I'm the fool who believed*
> *in the illusion you created*
> *when all along, I knew—and waited*
> *for truth to reveal*
> *what you fought hard to conceal.*
> *I'm not listening to promises and lies*
> *I'm seeing clearly through my own eyes.*

PART SIX

❦

COMMUNITY

∽ 68 ∽

Kimo waited at the gate, watching for Caitlin. Her behavior bewildered him. After all their soulful sharing, she ran off with another man. Again! Didn't she know how he felt about her?

He worried that if their friendship stayed platonic much longer, Caitlin might never see him as a potential lover or mate. Yet he felt awkward initiating greater intimacy. The timing didn't seem right. She was still sorting out her life, he told himself; she wasn't ready. Maybe he wasn't either. He needed to finish his degree and obtain a license, build a practice. Maybe then he would feel he had something to offer her.

But he couldn't pretend he didn't feel hurt, and a little resentful. It wasn't as if she'd betrayed him—they didn't have any understandings. Heck, they weren't even dating. He didn't blame her, but he was disappointed in her. Maybe he was kidding himself, believing she'd ever think of him as more than a friend.

No point worrying about it, he decided; he would hardly ever see her. His course load was heavy this term, and he had little free time.

She finally appeared, looking weary but strong. Kimo watched for her reaction when she saw him. Her smile seemed a mixture of relief and uncertainty.

He didn't offer to help with her carry-on bag and kept his hands in his pockets as they walked toward the baggage claim area. She seemed calmer, as if the usual churning and hyperactivity of her restless mind had ceased or at least diminished. From the way she kept staring at the ground, he guessed she felt embarrassed about the Hawaiian affair. He didn't need to know the details, if it was over. He didn't *want* to know the details, and from what Melody had said, it *was* over.

They arrived at the baggage carousel and waited for the parade of luggage to begin. Kimo thought about the last time he'd met Caitlin at the airport, in Dublin. He'd had such high hopes for that trip. Too high, maybe. He looked over at her. She looked softer. Vulnerable. Delicious.

"Nice tan," he said.

She glanced up at him, tentatively, and then her nervous giggle turned into a hearty laugh. Her laughter was contagious. He smiled. Their eyes met. She threw her arms around him—a welcome surprise. She was happy to see him, and that was a soothing tonic for his heart's malady.

When they arrived at the house, Kimo showed Caitlin the room down the hall from his. They would share the bathroom, he told her. He encouraged her to attend Melody's Sunday evening meditation group, which was just starting. He had assignments to complete. She thanked him for picking her up at the airport and asked where the group was meeting. He pointed her toward the living room.

He sat at the desk in his bedroom and opened a neurology textbook. He read the same paragraph several times before abandoning the effort. Caitlin stirred complex feelings in him. Keeping his mind off her would be harder now, but he had to get himself centered again so he could focus on his life and not hers.

He pulled out the special brush, ink, and paper his taiji master had given him. Several months had passed since he'd practiced his brush strokes. He looked through the book of pictographs for a symbol to focus upon and found one that represented the stillness of meditation; that seemed like a good image. He practiced painting the character, again and again, until he felt calm.

⤳ **69** ⤳

Caitlin removed her shoes and entered the candlelit room. Ten people were sitting in chairs, on the couch, and on cushions on the floor. Their eyes were closed; the meditation had already begun. Caitlin saw an open space on the floor and quietly sat down. She leaned back against the front of the couch and glanced around the circle of four men and six women.

Everyone looked serene as their attention followed the gentle movement of breath, in and out. Almost everyone. The man directly across from her looked so stiff and arrogant that Caitlin wondered if his lips remembered how to form a smile. She closed her eyes and followed Melody's direction to imagine a ball of white light suspended above her head.

"Allow the light to penetrate through the top of your head, moving along your spine," Melody said. She spoke slowly, in a soft voice. "See it moving through your legs and down into the earth through the center of your feet."

At the ashram, everyone had sat facing the shrine that was adorned with flowers and offerings and photos of the guru who'd founded the Center. The morning and evening chants were accompanied by live music. Caitlin had followed the Sanskrit words in the songbook as best she could. The meditations, though, were silent. Individual instruction was available, but Caitlin had been content to sit quietly with the others in the meditation hall, or walk alone in the woods by a stream, or peruse the literature in the reading room.

"Feel your roots going down, like a tree, deep into the earth, grounding you, completing the circuit," Melody said. "Breathe deeply, drawing in all that you need from heaven and earth."

Caitlin fidgeted. Remaining stationary for long periods of time was difficult for her, a lingering aftereffect of her injuries, and she'd already been sitting in cars and planes and airports most of the day. Melody's attempt to sound soothing was, instead, annoying. She sounded artificial, like she was reading from a program. Caitlin's stomach grumbled, and her thoughts turned to food.

At the conclusion of the meditation, Melody struck a tuning fork and turned on the lights. To Caitlin's surprise, twenty minutes had passed.

"How was that?" Melody asked. "Did anyone have any experiences they'd like to share?"

A wiry man wearing a George Mason University sweatshirt smiled and said, "I experienced waves of relaxation as I felt my connection to the planet and all of life. It was peaceful and yet energizing."

"Great," Melody said. "Susan?"

Susan said she felt the warmth of the sun and heard leaves rustling in the breeze. "The colors were spectacular. I felt very accepting of the cycles of life and embraced the quiet of the coming season."

Are these people for real? Caitlin wondered. Was she the only one having a hard time relaxing? Maybe they had all been doing this a lot longer than her. Or maybe being back in Virginia aggravated old wounds. A year earlier, she'd been cooped up with her mother for what had seemed like an eternity.

"Beautiful," Melody said, beaming at Susan. "Anyone else?"

"Yeah," Caitlin said. "I felt really un . . . un-com-fort-able, like I was trapped and couldn't move. I didn't feel rooted . . . I felt stuck."

She was pleased with herself for speaking up in a group but thought she heard a snort from the arrogant man across from her. She looked at him but he ignored her; that irritated her even more.

He certainly doesn't look peaceful or enlightened. He looked uptight and unfriendly.

"Interesting. There are no right or wrong experiences," Melody told the group. "Some people need to be more grounded and practical whereas others need more lightness and release."

Caitlin remembered being grounded as a teenager when she disobeyed her mother or refused to practice the piano.

Maybe it's the word I object to. She'd felt imprisoned for far too long. She wanted wings to fly.

"Of course, sometimes we resist the things we need most," Melody added.

What do I most need now? Caitlin asked herself. *Sleep,* she thought, yawning.

For the next exercise, Melody instructed the participants to dive into the ocean and greet the creatures they found there. Caitlin recalled the schools of fish she'd seen when Sam took her snorkeling in Hawai'i, but the beautiful memories she'd thought she would always cherish were tainted by darker images of Sam in the desert. Perhaps as she became more adept at these techniques she could banish the ghosts of the past and pacify the demons that haunted her. Maybe she could learn how to release regrets about her choices and actions and resentment about the choices and actions of others. As someone at the ashram had said, there are many paths. She just needed to find one that was right for her.

The evening ended with the group chanting *"Om"* three times. Melody explained that this Sanskrit syllable vibrates at the frequency of the brow chakra, or "third eye." Because sound is vibration and everything in creation has a frequency, some sounds have destructive qualities, she said, while others are balancing. Caitlin had seen reference to *Om* in *The Laws of Manu,* but she couldn't recall what the book had said about it.

The most sacred mantras and holy names, like the Hebrew *Tetragrammaton,* were never written down, Melody told the group.

"In ancient times, only the initiated were permitted to pronounce the Name aloud, and only to other initiates under carefully prescribed conditions. Such secrets were passed orally by a whisper at the time of initiation into the mysteries. In some traditions, only the high priest was entrusted with the highest truths, and he passed these to his successor before his death."

That much seemed accurate, based on what little Caitlin knew. Initiation into the priesthood was one of the topics addressed by *The Laws of Manu.* The Vedic teachings, too, had probably been oral long before they were put into writing. Books were sacred in ancient times; they were rare, and few people knew how to read. Priests committed the teachings to memory.

"Those who possessed the keys to the true pronunciation of the ineffable Name were said to perform great wonders," Melody said. "They guarded their secrets with their lives."

Some secrets, like the power of the *Om*, had become freely available in modern times, but others had been lost and awaited rediscovery.

"I go into this in some of my more advanced classes, but I like to introduce some of the concepts early on."

Caitlin felt like she was in kindergarten again. After years of study and practice, she'd acquired knowledge and experience, and she'd felt competent as a lawyer. Now she was entering a completely different world, about which she knew very little. An understanding of ancient traditions couldn't be acquired in an evening. Caitlin wondered how qualified Melody was to teach these things, how deep her understanding. Still, she appreciated the opportunity to participate.

The words of Jesus echoed in her mind: *Except ye become as little children, ye shall not enter into the kingdom of heaven.*

Whether Mister Stiff-Lips gained admission wasn't her concern, Caitlin thought as she walked toward her new room. She needed to keep her own heart light and not allow other people's attitudes to disturb her peace of mind.

✍ 70 ✍

Caitlin slept late the following morning. Kimo left a house key and Caitlin's car key on the kitchen table, along with a note telling her to make herself at home. "Feel free to eat anything from the right side of the refrigerator or pantry," the note said.

Caitlin looked through the communal wares. The puffed millet, amaranth flakes, and crispy brown rice cereals in the pantry looked interesting, but today she wanted something familiar. She poured raisin bran into a hand-painted ceramic bowl and added a banana from the fruit basket on the counter and soy milk from Kimo's section of the refrigerator.

Sitting at the long wooden table in the kitchen, Caitlin wrote a grocery list while she ate. She knew Kimo wouldn't accept rent money from her, but she planned to contribute to household expenses. When she had finished eating, she washed her bowl in the sink and headed out to the store.

The next few days were quiet at the house. Caitlin slept late and went to bed early. She did laundry, wrote to Martha, and started reading a book she found on a shelf in the living room. Kimo didn't own a television, but he had amassed quite a collection of books. He left before she was up in the morning and returned after she'd gone to bed. Melody and Lisa were busy with their own lives and schedules.

At twenty-six, Lisa was the youngest of the group. Her room was upstairs, next door to Melody's. Reading novels and watching television seemed to be her main pastimes. Her family lived nearby, in Maryland, so she went home for the weekend sometimes, and at holidays.

In contrast, Melody's life seemed a whirlwind of activity; she was always on the phone or in a class or away from the house. Caitlin sometimes wondered where she went. She admired Melody's boundless energy and enthusiasm. Caitlin's social life was non-existent; her energy, unpredictable.

By Friday, she was well rested. She rose early and entered the kitchen just as Melody pushed the button on the blender for one last *whirr*. Caitlin greeted her with a smile.

"Good morning."

Melody glanced up. "Hey, Caitlin. Would you like part of my smoothie?"

"No, thanks. Another time, maybe."

Caitlin removed a pitcher of orange juice from the refrigerator and took a clean glass from the dish rack by the sink. She turned around when she heard Melody speak.

"On the counter. Scrambled eggs on a toasted bagel. And an apple for later."

Kimo blithely grabbed a brown paper bag from the countertop and stuffed it into his backpack. "Thanks."

He smiled when he saw Caitlin. "Later," he said as he headed toward the back door.

Caitlin searched for something to say before he was gone. "Be . . . Be careful out there!" was all she could come up with.

She watched through the window above the kitchen sink as Kimo took off on his bicycle. A neighborhood dog started to accompany him down the street, tail wagging.

I'd wag my tail too, if I were a dog.

But she was a cat, and she padded daintily across the floor in her ballet slippers. She removed the newspaper from its plastic wrapper and sat at the table.

"Our morning ritual," Melody said, setting a plate in front of Caitlin. She had scrambled another egg and toasted another bagel.

"Oh, thanks!" Caitlin said, surprised by the gesture.

"Kimo gets up early to do taiji and barely makes it out the door on time," Melody said, sipping her drink.

"I don't have that kinda . . . dis-ci-pline," Caitlin said.

"So I fix him breakfast to go," Melody added.

"That's . . . sweet of you."

To her surprise, Caitlin felt a bit jealous of Kimo and Melody's routine. She and Kimo didn't discuss their love lives. She vaguely remembered him mentioning a girlfriend the time he came to her office at OSP, but that was over three years ago; he hadn't mentioned anyone recently. Caitlin wondered what became of the girlfriend. She winced when she recalled her mother's remark that she was too preoccupied with herself and silently vowed to show more interest in other people.

"It's the least I can do for him," Melody was saying, "after all he's done for me."

"Yeah? Like what?"

"Kimo? Gosh, everything from tuning my bike to giving me a home to come back to. I've been back and forth between here and Santa Fe a lot the last few years."

Melody stood by the counter and finished her drink. "He's been able to flow with me in a way few people can. I come and go and it all seems to be okay with him."

Kimo had been an easygoing travel companion in Ireland, from what Caitlin remembered. She set aside the newspaper. After taking a bite of the bagel topped with egg, her mouth felt like it was on fire. She reached for the glass of orange juice.

"What's . . . in this?" she sputtered between gulps of juice.

"Oh, are the chili peppers too hot for you? Southwestern style."

Eyes tearing, Caitlin drained her glass. "Whew! That sure cleared up my si-nuses!"

Melody glanced at the clock on the wall. "Gosh, I need to get ready. Friday mornings I teach an advanced yoga class at a wellness center. You should come for the beginning—that's when we work with sound."

"O-kay," Caitlin said, her mouth still burning. "How do I get there?"

While Melody drew a map with directions to the center, Caitlin filled her glass with filtered tap water. She returned to the table with a tub of cream cheese from the fridge. Melody left to get ready.

Caitlin spread cream cheese on the bagel after scraping off the eggs. She leafed through the newspaper while she ate. A headline caught her attention:

FLU SHOTS ENCOURAGED

Caitlin read the column, which mentioned the strains of influenza that experts expected to circulate that year and included the usual recommendation to get a flu shot early to be safe. Caitlin remembered researching vaccines months earlier.

"Yeah, why don't you men-tion what else is in that . . . shot!" she said aloud.

The article did not explain that the flu vaccine was formulated based on predictions; it could prove useless in combating the strains that actually spread. Nor were readers informed that the preservative thimerosal was used in flu vaccines.

Disgusted, Caitlin closed the paper and brought her dishes to the sink. Using the phone in the kitchen, she left a message for her lawyer that she was back in town and wanted an update on her case. Then, she changed into her yoga clothes and followed Melody's directions to the wellness center.

Melody sat on the floor facing her students. Dressed in a white cotton tunic and pants, she waited until everyone was seated and silent.

"Let's start with the Indian scale. Call and response. *Sa re ga ma pa dha ni sa,*" she sang as she played a harmonium. Caitlin later learned that Melody had purchased the instrument in India.

Most people in the class were already familiar with the Eastern equivalents of *do re mi* and echoed Melody's notes, which were sung in ascending order.

"Again. *Sa re ga ma pa dha ni sa.*"

Caitlin quietly joined in, listening closely to the people around her as she sounded out the syllables.

"Remember that the breath is the source of your power. Don't be afraid to fully breathe in life and breathe out tension and stress!" Melody demonstrated with a deep inhalation and a loud exhalation.

The group followed her example, letting out audible sounds of release.

Melody set aside the harmonium. "Let's try something a little different today. So many of us have blocks in our voices that keep us from expressing who we really are." She stood up. "Learning to speak our truth is important," she said, "but we also need to have a good time!"

She encouraged everyone to experiment with sound and movement. "Make noise; move around the room. Express yourself!" She demonstrated by flapping her arms and running around in a circle, squawking like a chicken. "Don't worry about whether you look silly!"

Melody leaped into the air and said the group needed to "get loosey-goosey" to dispel any false notions they might have about being "spiritual."

"Don't be afraid of joyful exuberance, if that's what you feel! Wha-hoo!" she whooped as she jiggled around. "Get moving!"

One of the few men in the group practiced his samurai moves and battle cry; other participants crawled and stomped, groaned and roared. A middle-aged woman got everyone's attention with a blood-curdling scream. Caitlin felt awkward but went along. She laughed and cackled and shrieked. She pranced around the room and spun in circles the way she had as a child. Then, she would spin until she got dizzy and collapsed into a heap on the floor. By focusing her attention, she could now spin effortlessly for a long time without feeling dizzy. Soon, everyone was rolling on the floor with laughter.

After they had all returned to their seats, Melody discussed the importance of abdominal breathing and led the class in several exercises that combined breath and sound. Caitlin left when the class moved into advanced yoga postures. She felt light and happy. Sharing the silly and the sacred helped her feel a bond with people she had only just met and sparked an interest in attending Melody's beginning yoga class. The centering and relaxation would be useful as her trial date approached.

Being back in the D.C. area felt strange, she realized as she drove to Kimo's house. She no longer belonged, and she had no reason to stay. Perhaps the time away had helped her disengage enough to be ready to move on to the next phase of her life. But first, she needed to conclude this chapter.

∾ 71 ∾

Caitlin kept busy with books and errands. She took the car for an oil change. She ate at her favorite restaurants—the ones she had missed while she was away. She made follow-up appointments with her doctors and waited to hear from her lawyer.

Being on the other side of the attorney-client relationship was a new—and not altogether positive—experience, but dealing with the insurance industry was an exercise in frustration, and Caitlin was glad to have a knowledgeable ally looking out for her interests. The severity of her injuries had required treatment costing hundreds of thousands of dollars.

She had to stay positive, she reminded herself during a solitary walk beneath the fall foliage, and not get trapped in bitterness and despair. She'd been given many blessings in her life, and she was grateful. Since returning from California, she'd received notice that her application for disability retirement had been approved. Though her monthly allotment wouldn't match her former salary, it would cover the basics. If she was careful, the small profit she'd made from the sale of the townhouse would carry her through until she figured out what she wanted to do for the rest of her life—or, at least, the next portion of it. Her lawyer was confident that she would recover compensatory damages for pain and suffering under the uninsured motorist coverage of her policy, but Caitlin knew that insurance companies didn't stay in business by being charitable.

She tried not to think about the crash that had caused her so much anguish and the driver who had escaped responsibility. The injustice made her furious, but when she wished for vengeance a dark shadow pervaded her spirit, and when she cursed the man's carelessness—for she knew, somehow, that the offender was a man—she felt like a victim. She had no recourse against an unknown perpetrator, so nothing productive could come from her rage. She appreciated the peaceful atmosphere of Kimo's house; staying there helped offset stress from legal proceedings.

When she saw Melody in the kitchen one morning, Caitlin asked about the stiff man who'd been in the meditation group the night she arrived. Melody said that the man, whose name was Bart, had recently been diagnosed with cancer. Caitlin reminded herself that the tapes running in her head were not always accurate reflections of reality. No one could really know another person's experiences. She felt compassion for Bart and decided she would send him healing thoughts whenever he came into her mind.

After nearly two weeks at Kimo's house, Caitlin started to feel lonely and left out. She knew Kimo was busy, but she had thought she would see more of him. She wanted their talks to continue and hoped they might practice taiji together, or go out to dinner. Perhaps she hadn't appreciated how much effort he had made to spend time with her earlier in the year.

On Friday evening, she returned to Arlington after a meeting at her attorney's office in Alexandria. As she walked toward the back entrance of the house, she noticed a Harley-Davidson motorcycle parked in the driveway. Kimo had said that Jack stored his bike in the garage when he was on the road and during the winter. Caitlin was curious about the phantom who kept a room in the basement.

She hung her coat on one of the hooks by the back door and entered the kitchen. Lisa and Melody were setting out plates and utensils. The man sitting at the table was telling a story about the collie lying at his feet.

"So it's my first public appearance—a biker bar in some two-bit town in West Virginia—and there's this damn dog a-howlin' along outside the window," Jack said with a drawl. "I went out back on my break to give him something to eat, hoping that would shut him up. But when I came back at the end of the show, there he was, waitin' for me by my old station wagon."

The man chuckled and puffed on his cigarette before continuing.

"I opened the door and he leapt right in, like he belonged there. Used to travel with me, 'til he got too old. Now he stays with Mama when I'm on the road a lot. But he's still my biggest fan."

Melody crouched down to scratch Max's ears. "You know we're talking about you, don't you Maxie?" Melody cooed.

Kimo was at the stove preparing a stir-fry; he wore the "Kimo's" t-shirt Caitlin had brought from Hawai'i. She walked over to him and placed her hand on his back.

"Smells won-derful. Maybe you should open your own . . . grill!"

Kimo smiled and tossed ingredients into the hot pan. Caitlin set her handbag down and approached the table.

"Caitlin, hi," Melody said as she rose from the floor. "Glad you made it in time for dinner. I don't think you've met Jack yet."

Caitlin smiled and nodded at Jack.

"Caitlin's staying in the back room for a while," Melody explained.

"Come, join us." Reaching forward, Jack pulled out a chair at the end of the table.

Caitlin sat down and regarded him carefully. Dressed in a denim jacket, white v-neck undershirt, jeans, and cowboy boots, he was a scruffy-looking character. His dark, curly hair and moustache were streaked with silver strands. He seemed an unlikely addition to the household. Caitlin glanced over at Kimo, surprised he allowed smoking in the house—especially at the dinner table.

Jack seemed to read her thoughts; he extinguished the cigarette and leaned toward her. "He allows me a few puffs now and then," he said with a wink. He had a wry smile and down-home genuineness that Caitlin liked immediately.

"We all have our . . . indulgen-ces," she said. "I could use a drink after meeting with loyals—*lawyers* all day."

She still felt frustrated and embarrassed about her awkward speech, but Jack's casual manner helped put her at ease. He exaggerated a shudder at the mention of lawyers.

"I can well imagine." He pointed a thumb at his chest. "My Pappy's the founding partner of a big firm. Well—big by Carolina standards."

"And I bet his dream was that his only son would become a musician," Kimo said. He set a tofu-and-vegetable dish on the table and removed his apron.

"The offense wasn't egregious enough to disown me, but he's never come to hear me play either," Jack said.

Lisa brought a large wooden salad bowl to the table and sat next to Caitlin; Melody placed a cruet with her special-recipe raspberry vinaigrette next to the salad and sat in the chair next to Lisa. Kimo brought another dish and presented it to Caitlin. He draped a dish-towel over his arm and bowed like a waiter.

"Beef stir fry for the lady," he said courteously.

Caitlin blushed. "Wow! Why the special treat-ment?"

"Jack will have some too, I reckon," Kimo said, playing off Jack's hillbilly style.

He's in a playful mood, Caitlin thought, recalling that Kimo had been a bit of a clown when she represented him in court. She hadn't taken him seriously for a long time as a result. Now that she knew him better, she appreciated his levity.

"Melody and I are vegetarians," Kimo said, taking his seat at the head of the table, next to Melody and opposite Caitlin. "And you need red meat to rebuild your strength."

Caitlin smiled, but hearing Kimo say "Melody and I" made her feel vaguely uneasy.

"I thought you told me you ate meat," she said.

"I stopped after I discovered my blood type."

Caitlin didn't know what blood type had to do with eating meat, but she knew that asking Kimo about it was likely to elicit a long explanation and she was too tired for that. She turned her attention to Jack.

"What in-stru-ment do you play?"

"I can play 'most anything with strings. But bluegrass guitar is my first pick. Pardon the pun." He took the dish Caitlin passed to him and spooned some beef and broccoli over the rice on his plate. "Now if I'd chosen violin, that might have helped my daddy save face."

"I've been think-ing about digging out my brother's old guitar," Caitlin said. "I think it's still at my family's lake house." She paused for a moment before adding, "In Missouri." She was learning to let others in on her thoughts before her plans were finalized, but she avoided Kimo's gaze. "Maybe you could give me a few . . . pointers, to get me started?" she asked Jack.

"I'd be glad to."

Caitlin had reasons for keeping her plans to herself, and going against her natural tendency felt disconcerting. Would Kimo withdraw from her if he knew she was leaving? How did he feel about her? What did she want from him? Would she stay if he asked her to? No; she knew what she needed to do next, and she needed to do it alone. Before she could move forward and create a new life, she needed to step back into the past.

The dinner-table conversation had lulled, and Caitlin felt uncomfortable with the awkward silence. She cleared her throat. "Ger—Great dinner, Kimo. You can cook for me . . . anytime!"

"Nobody tell her it's the only thing I know how to make," Kimo said.

Melody reached for a second helping. "That's not true!"

Kimo pushed his plate aside and stretched out his legs. "Man, something's gotta give in my schedule; I can't keep up these long days. I may need to think about quitting the firm, unless they'll let me cut back on hours."

"Seems like everyone in this town is con-nected with law in one way or another," Caitlin said. "What do you do, Lisa?" she asked, trying to draw Lisa into the conversation.

"I'm a directress at a Montessori school."

"I have no idea what that is," Caitlin said.

"We aim to create a learning community where kids can go at their own pace. And we encourage cooperation over competition," Lisa said proudly, as if reciting a school mission statement.

"Where do I sign up?" Caitlin joked. "Seems I missed a few steps along the way."

"That's what therapy's for," Melody said.

Caitlin shot a glance at Melody, but she was adding dressing to her salad and didn't look up. Caitlin's eyes met Kimo's; she wondered if he'd noticed the cutting impact of Melody's remark.

"Sounds like our house," he said, winking.

Caitlin regretted having derided his little "commune." She appreciated his efforts to create a sense of community in a city where the desirability of competition went unquestioned. She was happy to be part of his circle of life, to feel the warmth of his caring. He, too, was a sensitive soul.

∽ 72 ∽

After dinner, Kimo left for a night class, Lisa disappeared to her room, and Melody went wherever Melody went. Caitlin helped Jack clean up the kitchen. She was happy to contribute to the household however she could. During her stay at the ashram, she acquired a new perspective on tasks she'd once deemed menial—and appreciation for those who were willing to do them. Working with Jack, the job was completed faster, and it was more fun. When the chores were done, they agreed to meet in the living room in half an hour for Caitlin's first guitar lesson.

She had studied music theory in college and her fingers once flew nimbly across the keys of a piano, but Bobby had been the guitar player in the family. He'd abandoned his guitar when he entered the Coast Guard; Caitlin was pretty sure she had seen it stashed in a closet at the lake house. She wondered what else she might find hidden in those closets.

Jack brought out an extra guitar so Caitlin could follow along. He had just returned from a regional tour and expected to be in town for the rest of the month; he told Caitlin she was free to use the guitar during her stay and offered to monitor her progress. She readily accepted his offer.

Jack showed her how to position her hands and play basic chords. He played a simple tune and said he would teach it to her after she mastered the chords.

"It's an old lullaby my Granny used t' sing to me."

Caitlin liked the melody and promised herself she would practice daily. As a child, she had practiced playing the piano for the same reason she had done her homework: it was required of her. She was free now to play or not play, based on her interest and desire. With a live-in teacher to answer questions and offer encouragement, she had no excuses.

She also vowed to attend the beginning yoga classes Melody held at the house on Tuesday mornings and Thursday evenings. At the opening of the first class, Caitlin learned about toning.

"Inhale deeply, and as you exhale, hold each tone for as long as you can, like this: *Aaaaaaaaaaaaa.*" Melody sounded a low note for an extended out-breath. "Now you try."

Melody toned along with the group and led them through a series—*ee, ah, aw, o* and *ooh,* with a different pitch for each sound.

"You're not singing," she said, "so don't try to sound pretty. You're treating yourself to a vocal massage. Sounds can actually help break up blockages. There are numerous instances of dedicated practitioners who healed themselves of serious diseases using only the power of the voice, coupled with intention. Try it again, and see if you can locate places in your body where the sound is vibrating."

Caitlin felt some tones vibrating through her chest and abdomen; others she felt most strongly in her throat or jaw.

When they had finished with the last tone, Melody introduced the first set of yoga postures, or *asanas*. Caitlin discovered how tight and underutilized some of her muscles were as she struggled to follow along and position her body correctly. She wanted to give up more than once but knew the exercises would get easier if she stayed with them. Stretching felt good; she just needed to pace herself.

At the end of the class, everyone stood in a circle. Joining hands, they sounded a long tone that incorporated all the sounds in the series, and then each person turned and massaged the shoulders of the person next to him or her. Caitlin walked away feeling refreshed and recharged. As promised, Melody had given her some sound healing tools; now it was up to her to use them. She felt empowered by all she was learning from Melody, Kimo, and Jack and wished she had a gift or skill she could share in return.

As she headed for the shower, she wondered if Kimo was avoiding her. She didn't want to complain; he'd been so generous, sharing his time and knowledge, his home and friends. His bedroom door was open. Caitlin peered inside. Kimo was sitting at his desk.

"Whatchya workin' on?"

Kimo glanced up. "Calligraphy."

"Can I see?"

"Yeah, sure. Come on in."

Caitlin looked over Kimo's shoulder at the Chinese character he was painting and noticed the discards of several other attempts.

"That's . . . beautiful, Kimo. A man of many talents!"

"This one's 'Hope.' I'm doing a set for my future office." He gestured to two framed works on the wall.

Caitlin walked closer to examine the large black inscriptions tinged with red and gold paint. One was titled "Inspiration" and the other, "Joy."

"Wow," Caitlin said. "You're really into this . . . Chi-nese stuff, aren't you?"

"Taiji, feng shui, qigong, acupuncture—it's all about the movement of energy. How to flow and dance with the *tao*," Kimo replied, still intent on his work. "It's an energy universe we live in." He tacked the calligraphy on the wall and studied it.

Caitlin sat on the edge of the bed. "Ac-tually, it's a . . . *holo-graphic* universe."

Kimo looked at her and smiled.

"I've been reading some of your books," Caitlin said. She glanced around the room while Kimo put away his paint supplies. "How come you don't teach taiji here, like Melody does with yoga?"

"Between work and school, there's not time for much else."

"I guess not," Caitlin said glumly. She probably shouldn't interpret Kimo's lack of availability as lack of interest. Still, the fact remained: she was not a priority. There was no reason she should be, but she was beginning to feel the need to be important to someone, and Kimo's unavailability was likely to continue for some time. Now he was focused on school; later, establishing a practice would require his time and energy. Caitlin reminded herself to be grateful for all they had shared and not expect more than Kimo could give her—or she'd be disappointed.

"Kimo . . . I probably don't tell you often enough. I really approach—ap-pre-ci-ate your friendship. Knowing you has added a whole new dimension to my life."

"You know there isn't anything I wouldn't do for you, Cait."

"Let's hope I don't put you to the test on that one!"

Caitlin leaned over and kissed Kimo's cheek before moving away, embarrassed about her sweaty workout clothes. Noticing a book on the nightstand, *Recovery from Substance Abuse*, she was reminded that he too had his trials. He couldn't solve her problems any more than she could solve his.

"'night," she said.

Kimo met her gaze. "Goodnight," he said softly.

Caitlin showered and got ready for bed, aware of the wall that kept her and Kimo from having a closer relationship. Was it up to her to make the first move if she wanted their friendship to shift to a new level—or would getting involved ruin their friendship? Wouldn't Kimo have initiated physical intimacy by now if he wanted that?

She knew how to be assertive; what she needed to develop was the discernment to know when to act, when to be patient, and when to let go completely.

❧ 73 ❧

The next morning, Caitlin lingered in bed trying to recall a dream. She remembered something about a cat and a bonfire and a group making crazy sounds—a bit like Melody's class, only Melody wasn't there. She sensed that Kimo was there, but the details were hazy. Hunger finally motivated her to crawl slowly out of bed, her muscles sore from yoga. After dressing in soft corduroy pants and a sweater, she went to the kitchen in search of breakfast. Kimo was there, packing containers of food into a small cooler.

"Morning, sleepyhead," he said.

Caitlin yawned loudly as she reached for a glass. In the Rose household, sleeping in when one wasn't ill was a sure sign of shirking responsibilities, but Caitlin heard no judgment in Kimo's teasing. She relaxed her shoulders and poured some juice. How nice it was to feel okay about being herself!

"I borrowed Jack's bike," Kimo said. "I'm heading out to Shenandoah." He grabbed an ice pack from the freezer and added it to the cooler. "Wanna come? The leaves are peaking."

Caitlin had heard that the drive along the crest of the Blue Ridge Mountains near Charlottesville offered spectacular views of the autumn colors. She grinned, nodded, and quickly finished drinking her juice.

❧

Breathless from the bracing wind, Caitlin held on as Kimo zoomed through the colorful landscape. When they arrived at Shenandoah National Park, they removed their helmets and coasted along, looking for a place to stop. Kimo steered the bike into a parking zone. Caitlin rested her head against his soft leather jacket, welcoming the warmth of the sun on her face.

After stretching their legs, they walked to a secluded area and spread a blanket. Kimo unpacked the cooler and his backpack. Caitlin rubbed her hands together for warmth.

"What's for lunch?"

"Always thinking about food! Now if you'd only learn to cook it."

"I'm not . . . the domest-ic type," Caitlin said. She looked around for a place to walk so she could generate some heat. She spotted a wild turkey and walked toward it to get a closer look.

"You might surprise yourself," she heard Kimo say.

As she approached the turkey, Caitlin saw that it was a mother with a half dozen young. When she got too close for their comfort, they ran for cover.

Caitlin laughed. She wasn't so different herself! She resisted closeness as much as she craved it. Could she experience freedom within a relationship, she wondered, or were all men just looking for sex on demand and a wife to take care of them?

She kicked at a pile of leaves, sending a few scattering. She'd loved Jayson, and she'd felt betrayed by him; trusting again was hard. Maybe she would be ready when she found the right partner. She was still learning what she needed in a relationship. She'd love to share life's journey with a man who could allow her to have an identity apart from him, but anyone who wanted to pour her into a mold of his own design should spare them both the heartache.

She looked over at Kimo; he was sitting on the blanket, reading. She liked his easygoing nature, but she wasn't sure how he felt about her. She knew he cared for her—but did he *desire* her?

Of course, chemistry alone wasn't enough—she and Neil had no shortage of fireworks. She also needed to feel love and respect and interest and belonging, not to mention commitment. Perhaps the problem wasn't uncertainty about how Kimo felt, but about whether *she* wanted a commitment from *him*. All she knew was: she would never again think about marrying a man unless all of the essential ingredients were present. Why was she thinking about marriage, anyway? She wasn't even dating anyone, and after her harrowing experience with Sam, she was in no rush.

Wanting a little more time alone, she followed the trail a short distance, still hoping to catch sight of the wild turkeys. Benjamin Franklin had nominated the turkey as the nation's emblematic bird, Caitlin recalled, but the majestic eagle won out.

History hadn't interested her much until she moved to Virginia. The region abounded with landmarks and memorials, making the nation's past hard to ignore. Virginia, one of the original thirteen colonies, was the birthplace of eight presidents, she'd learned. It was also the site of more battles during the Civil War than any other state, and its capital, Richmond, had been the capital of the Confederacy. Animosities between North and South, black and white, still persisted, but no longer threatened to rip apart the Union that President Lincoln had worked so hard to preserve.

Remembering that Lincoln's foreboding dreams seemed to predict his demise, Caitlin wondered what to make of her own dreams. Was her subconscious mind trying to tell her something? How could she know when a dream "meant something" beyond the jumbled images that reflected wishes and anxieties and daily occurrences?

She collected a few colorful leaves and wandered back toward Kimo and his picnic, eager to find out what he'd brought for lunch. He had introduced her to a variety of new foods—cooked grains like amaranth, millet, and quinoa, bread made from spelt and wraps made from teff, vegetables like sunchokes and kohlrabi, and raw juices.

"Different foods produce different effects in our bodies," he'd said recently. "Foods can be warming or cooling, acidic or alkaline. Some foods are energizing, while others make us sleepy."

Kimo had also introduced her to a new way of seeing . . . *everything*, Caitlin realized.

"All of life is interconnected," he'd told her on the flight from Dublin to London. "The basic principles and laws that govern the universe affect the way foods grow, the orbits of solar systems and atoms, the relationship between the human and the divine—and between men and women. When you understand the laws, you can see how they apply in different areas. Seemingly diverse theories and practices suddenly fit into a pattern that makes sense. A new paradigm."

A new paradigm. Those words had stayed in her mind for days—until she met Dru, her delightful distraction from all that had occurred in Ireland. And now, as hard as she tried, Caitlin couldn't remember what had happened at the Shannon Pot—but she knew it was significant.

When she returned to the blanket, Kimo put down the book he was reading and handed her a plate and utensils. He took the lids off containers of hommos, dolmades, and feta-cucumber salad.

"There's a whole philosophy of eating for energy enhancement," he said while removing several slices of pita bread from a plastic bag.

"Of course there is," Caitlin said, smiling. She spread a spoonful of hommos on a sliver of pita and sat next to Kimo on the blanket. "I'm listening."

"Like *yin* and *yang*," he said. "Yin is the expansive principle. It's soft and watery, moving outward and upward. It's considered a feminine aspect while yang, the masculine counterpart, is contracting and descending, moving inward. It's hard and concentrated. Tropical fruits like mango and papaya are more yin, while dense and concentrated foods like eggs and nuts are more yang."

"Okay. So how does that relate to energy?"

"Being out of harmony with the environment creates stress on many levels. Different climates and seasons have different proportions of yin and yang. If the environment is yang and you eat yang, you're going to get too yang; you need to bring in more yin in order to attain balance. Food is one way of doing that, but the same principles can apply to anything," Kimo said. "Marijuana, amphetamines, LSD—'mind-expanding' elements—are yin. Meat, poultry, and wild game are dense and concentrated, hence, yang. Oxygen and nitrogen are more yin; hydrogen and carbon, more yang. Everything has elements of both, and the balance is constantly changing."

"Like the balance of daylight and dark-ness changes throughout the year," Caitlin said.

"You got it," Kimo said. "On a cool day like today, eating a stew or warm, cooked foods would be better than cold salads, but these were easier to bring for a picnic." He popped a dolmade into his mouth before continuing.

"Of course, before modern methods of food storage and transportation, people naturally ate the foods that were in season and grown locally. They were dependent upon the land for survival and celebrated the harvest, honoring the gods—and goddesses—with rituals and offerings. Fertility rites were common throughout Sumer, Egypt, Greece, and some of the Celtic lands."

"Gotta keep those gods happy."

"In ancient Greece, the Eleusinian mysteries were celebrated for hundreds of years. Almost everyone was allowed to participate in the lesser mysteries, but months of preparation were required for initiation into the greater mysteries. Performance of the rites was considered essential for the continuation of humanity."

"Well, yeah, fertility is important. A society needs people and food in order to . . . continue."

"In some traditions, the king was sacrificed to ensure survival of the group. In others, the death of the king required sacrifices: his attendants accompanied him into the afterlife. Egyptian rites helped deceased pharaohs make the transition. Later, a symbolic drama was enacted in the temples for initiates who wanted to achieve resurrection in the body."

Caitlin reached for a napkin. "Dar—Drama—like a play?"

"In a sense. It was a ritual. Candidates for initiation assumed the role of 'the Osiris'—the star of the drama—and were put through a simulated death experience and then revived: awakened."

"Sim-ulated death?"

"Sometimes coma was induced, much as aboriginal peoples invited sacred visions through the use of hallucinogens."

"That doesn't sound so . . . sym-bolic to me!"

"People who master the physical body can control their own heart rates and other functions that, for most of us, are automatic.

They can put themselves into a trance so deep that, unless you had modern instruments to measure brain waves and other indicators, you'd think they were dead."

"And then it would seem like they were raised from the dead when they emerged from the . . . trance."

"John's Gospel—the most mystical of the four—says Jesus died soon after he was given a vinegar drink with a sponge on hyssop," Kimo said. "Hyssop twigs were used for sprinkling blood and water in purification rites in the Old Testament, like when Moses directed the Israelites in Egypt to take a bunch of hyssop and sprinkle their entrances with lamb's blood to prepare for the Passover."

"And Jesus was the Lamb of God."

"Whose death takes away the sins of the world. Typical scapegoat archetype. Blood sacrifice was believed to be necessary for salvation. In Jesus's time, animals were still being sacrificed in the Temple in Jerusalem as offerings."

"And Jesus was called 'king,' so that fits with what you were sayin' about the sac-ri-fice of the king."

"In John's Gospel, when Jesus's hour had come, he said that a grain of wheat has to fall to the ground and die in order to bring forth fruit. Wheat becomes the 'bread of life'—and Bethlehem means 'house of bread.'"

"Is that why Jesus was said to be born in Beth-le-hem?"

"Maybe partly. King David was from Bethlehem, and certain passages of the Old Testament were interpreted to mean that the Messiah would come from the line of David."

"I see what you're sayin' about the sym-bol-ism."

"The Gospel writers had a rich tradition to draw upon. The writer we call Mark probably wrote the earliest of the synoptic Gospels in Alexandria, Egypt—which had a large Jewish population, some of whom had to have been familiar with Neoplatonic ideas and the mythologies of the region. Missionaries and itinerant preachers, armies, and traders spread new ideas and customs. Languages evolved and incorporated foreign words, just as they do today."

"The Gospel of Mark was written in Egypt? In Greek? Didn't Jesus speak Aramaic?"

"Probably, but Greek was the *lingua franca* of the region after the conquests of Alexander the Great. Alexandria was the capital of Egypt, a center of commerce, and second only to Rome in importance. Moses, of course, was raised in Pharaoh's court and later dispensed the law to the Israelites. The Joseph we know from the Old Testament was said to be one of the sons of Jacob, but he also had an Egyptian name: Zaphnathpaaneah. The Bible says he was given the daughter of one of the priests of On in marriage."

"So? Lots of cul-tures have used m-marriage to . . . cement alliances between different nations."

"*On* was the Coptic name for Heliopolis, the main center for the cult of Osiris, the god of rebirth."

"What's Cop-tic?"

"The language used by the early Christian Church in Egypt, after hieroglyphics were no longer used. Coptic was based on the Greek alphabet. Heliopolis was the Greek name for 'city of the sun'; the Egyptian name was Annu. The sun, of course, descends out of sight each evening, into the darkness or underworld, and then it rises again—a perfect symbol of rebirth."

Caitlin watched as a squirrel nibbled on a nut and then scurried up a tree. "The Gospel of Luke says Mary and Joseph fled to Egypt after they went to Beth-le-hem. Do you think Jesus was in-flu-enced by Egyp-tian traditions?"

"His story, anyway."

Kimo dipped a hunk of pita bread into the hommos and took a bite before continuing. "John's Gospel says that when Jesus went to Bethany, he told his disciples he was going to wake Lazarus out of sleep. When he got there, he found Mary and Martha weeping for their dead brother. The whole story is very similar to the Osirian rites where Horus—the Son—wakes Osiris—who is only sleeping— and Osiris's sisters, Isis and Nepthys, are weeping. Remember the prophets, like Ezekiel, complaining about the Pagans reverting to 'weeping for Tammuz'?"

Caitlin nodded.

"Tammuz was the Aramaic name for the Sumerian shepherd-god Dumu-zid—Inanna's consort. Different versions of this same myth have been around for a long, long time. When Jerome visited the Holy Land in the fourth century, the cult of Tammuz had a strong following at Bethlehem."

"So what's the weeping about if nobody died?"

"It's part of the ritual," Kimo said. "Osiris's brother, Set, killed him and scattered his dismembered body parts around Egypt. Isis and Nepthys went in search of the pieces, mourning and lamenting."

"So O-siris did die."

"No, he went to sleep! There *is* no death—that's the point. Death and rebirth are part of the same cycle. These rites were performed annually and linked to the equinoxes and the solstices—decline and death after the harvest, the return of life-giving sun and rains. The Nile flooded annually—until the 1960s, when a dam was built."

Kimo paused to take a drink of water, and then continued.

"When Isis had gathered all the parts of Osiris—except for his phallus; she had to improvise there—she anointed Osiris's body and he was resurrected long enough to sire Horus. Then Osiris ascended into the starry skies. A separate ritual was performed to acknowledge that the Son, Horus, was now assuming the role of Osiris."

"Are you sayin' that the story of Jesus's res—resur-rection is the Jewish equivalent of these other death-rebirth . . . myths?"

"The parallels are undeniable. Early Church commentators couldn't avoid the comparisons—so they said the Pagan religions stole from Christianity!"

"Seriously?"

"The Christians said the Pagan versions were fables at best and demonic imitations prompted by the devil at worst. By incorporating the Old Testament—a choice opposed by some early Christian leaders—the new religion was able to claim that its god-man was the fulfillment of the prophets, the final word. New cults were suspect, and in Rome they were sometimes forbidden. Jewish beliefs and practices had developed over centuries and were influenced by surrounding cultures. The Jews used a lunar calendar, like the Babylonians, but they wrapped bodies for burial, like the Egyptians."

"They didn't mum-mify people, though," Caitlin said.

"No, and they didn't cremate them either, like the Greeks and

Romans. They prepared bodies with oils and spices, like the Egyptians. Jesus spoke of his anointing as being in preparation for his burial. All four Gospels talk about Jesus being anointed at Bethany, which was supposedly near where he later ascended. No town called Bethany is mentioned in the Old Testament—but the name means 'house of misery.'"

Caitlin sighed. "The weeping again."

"The modern Arab town is called El Azariyeh, 'the Place of Lazarus.' 'Asar' was another name for Osiris. And there's probably a link with the name Beth-Any and the Egyptian name for Heliopolis which, as I said, was Annu."

"House of Annu . . . I think I follow what you're saying," Caitlin said, "but I'm not sure what the point is."

Kimo selected a piece of baklava and offered the rest to Caitlin. "Some teachers say that stories like the trials of Job and Hercules are allegories about the stages in the initiation process," he said.

"Ini-ti-ation into what, though?"

"Into the mysteries of the kingdom of God. In the ancient world, traditions were passed orally and through rituals. Baptism, for example, is an ancient rite, going back to Sumer."

"So John initiated Jesus when he bap-tized him?"

"Some Gnostics might say that's the symbolism of the dove descending from heaven," Kimo said. "Though, Mark's text says the Spirit was *like* a dove descending upon Jesus."

"So there was no dove?"

"No dove."

"And the voice?"

"The voice said, 'thou art my beloved Son in whom I am well pleased,'" Kimo said. "The language parallels Old Testament coronation ceremonies."

"The king theme again."

"The Church perpetuates the idea that Jesus was born divine. But setting him apart from the rest of humanity prevents us from recognizing the Christ in each person. If you really believed that each human soul was the temple of the Living God, how could you ever knowingly harm another?"

Caitlin paused a moment to reflect. "Hmm. So . . . are you saying Jesus wasn't born more dov—divine than the rest of us?"

"We each have a human personality and a divine Higher Self; that's why twin symbolism was often used for heroes like Heracles, or Hercules. He was the son of a god but his twin had a mortal father."

"So . . . sometimes we act from purely selfish motives . . . and sometimes we 'rise above' our petty con-cerns and act for a greater good," said Caitlin.

"Most people operate out of their programming—whether it's genetic or conditioned—and ignore the call of their souls. Some souls may be more highly evolved than others. But being special at birth is not enough. What if Jesus had declined his mission? We have free will, after all. Innate gifts have to be cultivated. There is a path to mastery, and degrees of initiation. The initiate must be *perfected* to unite with God—because God is perfect. It's more than being sorry for your sins. It's being sinless."

Caitlin brushed aside a few leaves that the breeze blew onto the blanket. "Sounds like a long road."

"Lifetimes. The stories describe the trials as well as the payoff at the end: enlightenment, gnosis—knowledge of God. One becomes a Christ or a Buddha."

"Yeah?"

"Those are titles that acknowledge a state that's been achieved. 'Buddha' is from the Sanskrit root *budh*, to know reality, to be awake. Christ is from the Greek *christos*; it means 'anointed.' Jesus spoke in parables to the public. The secret teachings were only revealed to those closest to him."

"That makes sense, that more advanced teachings would be given to disciples who have made a commitment to follow . . . a par-tic-ular path."

"Following a spiritual path creates a bridge between the human and the divine so there is unity, alignment—'I and the Father are one.' Then the personal will becomes the same as God's will. That's the reason the Gnostics believed they were above man's laws, a position that outraged orthodox Christians. Initiates are not bound by nationality or ethnicity; they have a more universal outlook. Saint Paul said he became all things to all people so that he could reach them. When he was with the Jews, he was a Jew; when he was with those still under the law—the uninitiated—he submitted to the law, even though he was free from it."

"Did he think he was free from civil laws too?"

"Those who have become one with God can do no wrong—because they follow God's law at all times," Kimo said. "We have to respect man's laws, but when there's a conflict, God's laws must take precedence. Even when nobody else understands. Even at great sacrifice, in human terms."

Caitlin silently pondered Kimo's ideas about laws. She thought about Mohandas Gandhi and Martin Luther King Jr. and the changes they helped bring about through nonviolent resistance. Like Abraham Lincoln, they paid for their efforts with their lives.

"And init-i-ation leads to this unity?" she asked.

"We're given new understandings when we're ready to handle the increased responsibility. Only the most advanced initiates were admitted into the highest mysteries. Paul said he spoke wisdom only with 'the perfect'—and then only in secret. He says in a letter to the Roman church that he wants to come and share a 'pneumatic charisma' so they wouldn't remain ignorant. These things weren't written down, so they were lost when the Pagan centers were closed. There was a Pythagorean community in southern Italy—"

"Hold on. Are you saying Jesus was an init-i-ate in a secret *Pagan* reli-gion?"

"The description of Jesus is that of a faith healer and possibly a magus. Exorcisms, casting out demons—it was all part of the role. Some of the earliest depictions we know of show a figure using a wand to perform miracles—turning water into wine, like Dionysus, or multiplying the loaves and fishes."

Caitlin put up her hand. "Stop, please—I've heard enough."

She was stunned. Was "The Greatest Story Ever Told" just that—a story?

"Can we go?" she asked. She could feel the color draining from her face.

Kimo nodded. They folded the blanket, discarded the trash in a bin at the parking lot, and headed back to Arlington. Riding behind Kimo on the motorcycle, Caitlin felt utterly lost and confused. She didn't know what to think, who to trust. She was grateful Kimo couldn't see her tears.

The wind seemed to slap her in the face, as if to say, "Wake up!" Had she been living in a dream world? Everything she had believed to be true about life was crumbling. She had lost her father, her fiancé, her career, her home. Now she was losing her religion, too. Reality felt cold and harsh and desolate.

What else could she be stripped of?

∽ 74 ∽

Caitlin walked into the living room and chose a spot by the French doors that opened to the backyard. Kimo's once-thriving garden had been neglected in recent months. Caitlin had raked some of the leaves the day before to help tidy up the yard.

She unrolled her yoga mat. The first to arrive, she did some gentle stretches and enjoyed the quietude of the morning.

Meditation had helped her understand the importance of being fully present. If her mind was busy chattering about fears and other imaginary scenarios—if she was brooding over the past or daydreaming about the future—her attention was diverted from what was happening *now*. During times of boredom, escape had once seemed like an attractive option, but she was beginning to understand how much information is available in every moment—information she didn't want to miss.

"Think about the potential contained within an atom," Kimo had said during one of their talks, "and how much power it releases, once accessed. Imagine how much power every human being innately possesses. Every moment of time is filled with potential waiting to be manifested. Every moment is ideal for something, though it might not be what we want it to be."

Discerning what actions were in harmony with the times required the ability to listen deeply; following through required the willingness to change course. Practices like yoga and meditation helped develop flexibility in body and mind.

Caitlin hoped that some of the meditation techniques she was learning could help her access forgotten memories. Practicing mindfulness had to be a good thing, in any case. Her new mantra, she decided, would be: "Pay attention!"

Perhaps if she'd been paying attention, she might have noticed her father's decline, or the changes in her relationship with Jayson. The signs had probably been present from the start with Sam. Agonizing over regrets and mistakes wouldn't change the past; the important point was to learn something, and change. The next time she saw red flags, she hoped she would heed the indications that she was entering a danger zone and not just gape at the pretty shade of red.

She'd been going to both of Melody's weekly yoga classes at the house; the repetition helped her establish a regular practice and reinforced what she was learning. She also attended the Sunday evening meditations. Already, after several weeks of yoga and meditation, she was becoming aware of subtle qualities that had always been present around her but she had previously failed to notice. The idea that she could learn to develop and express more of her own potential motivated her to continue.

Every moment is, indeed, a new opportunity. As some astute person had observed, stepping into the same river twice is impossible. *Kimo would probably know who said that,* Caitlin thought as she leaned forward into the child's pose, but she didn't really care—the wisdom was what mattered. She pressed her forehead against the mat. *Maybe that was his point about Jesus.*

Maybe incorporating the teachings—what Kimo called "the ageless wisdom"—into one's own life was what mattered, not the ability to recite them. What better way to honor a teacher than to emulate him?

Don't shoot the messenger—but don't deify him, either.

The "my god is better than your god" routine seemed almost childish. If she really wanted to know truth, she had to stay open to new ideas and be willing to question old beliefs.

Kimo wasn't saying there is no God—just that the Christian understanding of God is incomplete.

Maybe in losing her conception of Jesus she was gaining . . . something.

Melody arrived, chatting with one of her students. Others filtered in, and soon the class was ready to begin.

Following Melody's instructions, Caitlin chose a note to tone repeatedly as she walked slowly around the room, weaving around the other members of the class, who were all doing the same thing. She felt like she was swimming in a sea of notes and delighted in listening to the sound of each person who came near. Sometimes, the combination of her tone and the other person's produced a brief, harmonious effect until they parted ways and continued moving through the stream.

The yoga positions were more challenging. Her body held the memories of trauma as well as the residues of pesticides and other chemicals she had been exposed to as part of modern living. Kimo had started her on a detoxification program to help cleanse her liver and kidneys and eliminate heavy metals. As much as Caitlin appreciated all the help Kimo and Melody were giving her, she was eager to take these new tools and develop her own practice.

Melody demonstrated a standing tree pose for the class and then walked around the room checking her students' postures. Caitlin wobbled on one leg in the back of the class. Her balance had improved since she'd started practicing taiji, but she still felt unsteady on her feet at times. She recalled the tree meditation from that first night at Kimo's house and remembered how the thought of being rooted made her uneasy. Stability was something she could benefit from, especially now. Perhaps she had not yet found a favorable climate and fertile soil where she could thrive.

"Keep your shoulders down," Melody told one woman, pushing down on her shoulders. She returned to the front of the room to demonstrate the cat pose. "Inhale coming down; exhale as you arch your back like a cat."

Caitlin slowly arched her back as she leaned into the mat on hands and knees. Flexing her spine felt good; once again, her body responded to her directions. Tears of gratitude welled up in her eyes as she thought about how far she had come on this healing journey. A few teardrops fell onto the mat.

Melody came over and gently placed a hand on Caitlin's back. "You okay?"

Caitlin nodded. She came out of the pose and sat cross-legged. "Yeah," she said, overcome with emotion. "I am!"

Melody smiled knowingly and walked to a corner of the room, returning with a box of tissues. She handed the box to Caitlin and then returned to the front of the class, turning on soothing music for the closing period of relaxation.

I really am okay! Caitlin thought as she lay on her back on the mat.

Healing was a mysterious process. Kimo had explained Hering's Law of Cure, named for the father of American homeopathy, Constantine Hering, M.D., who recognized that symptoms recur in the reverse order from their onset. Recent symptoms generally resolved first, with more longstanding imbalances correcting in later stages of healing. As each layer cleared, deeper disorders surfaced. The body, in its wisdom, knew it couldn't manage everything at one time. Symptoms were the body's language and pointed to the nature of the problem—and the cure.

"Ya gotta feel it to heal it!" Kimo said whenever Caitlin complained about feeling pain, whether physical or emotional. "The psyche also manifests symptoms—to call attention to unresolved complexes. When the root cause of an imbalance is corrected, the problem will go away for good."

Root. There was that word again. Caitlin was ready to start planning her trip west. At the lake house, she could take as much time as she needed to reconnect with the past she'd left behind.

She glanced inside Kimo's room on her way to the shower, though she knew he was at school. They hadn't spoken much since their trip to Shenandoah National Park. Caitlin was still pondering Kimo's shocking view of Jesus's life and mission. Kimo believed that ideas like reincarnation and astrology had been part of the teachings given to advanced initiates in ancient mystery religions.

Saint Paul said he put away childish things once he was no longer a child, Caitlin thought as the warm water beat down on her sore muscles. For some adults, Jesus functioned as a grown-up version of Santa Claus. He would say the magic words and take away their sins if only they prayed hard enough. *Perhaps growing up means letting go of illusions.*

She dried off with a towel and chose a gray wool suit to wear to her appointment with her lawyer. *In Alexandria.*

"There's no such thing as an accident," Kimo had said more than once.

Caitlin thought he sometimes overestimated the importance of symbolism and coincidences. That she and Jayson had lived in Alexandria, Virginia, did not mean they had once lived in Alexandria, Egypt! But could she be certain they *hadn't?* What would it be like to return to a place where she had lived before, in another lifetime?

Her old life in Alexandria *was* another time; she hardly felt like the same woman who had held a position of responsibility, been part of a loving relationship, and set ambitious goals for herself.

She unclasped a strand of pearls and draped it around her neck, wondering again where the necklace her father had given her was hidden; it hadn't surfaced when she packed up her belongings for storage. Could her mother have stashed it somewhere, all those years ago?

Caitlin's only goal now was concluding these legal matters. The insurance companies had reached an agreement; her medical insurance policy would pay for covered charges that exceeded the limits of her auto insurance policy. If the car insurance company would agree to a reasonable settlement for damages, Caitlin would be free to leave. She put her palms together, praying for a favorable outcome, and then drove to Alexandria to meet her lawyer.

∽ 75 ∽

The house was dark when Caitlin returned. Noticing the open door to the basement, she walked down the stairs.

The lower level had been made into a comfortable lounge with wood paneling and bamboo flooring. The main area included an entertainment center with a stereo system, a couch, and a few chairs. The small room where Jack slept was located in a back corner of the basement, with an adjoining bathroom large enough for a shower, toilet, and sink. A washing machine and dryer were nearby, along with a clothesline for items that could be air dried. In another corner, Kimo had set up a small desk with a computer and printer; these were available for everyone in the house to use. Kimo was working at the computer when Caitlin approached.

"Hey," she said. "I met with my lawyer today."

Kimo continued typing. "Yeah? How was that?"

"My in-surance company is ready to settle."

"Did you get a good offer?"

"Good enough. I'm ready to get on with my life."

"You'll be leaving, then."

"Yeah. I need some time on my own, to sort things out. I haven't really had that since . . . since the ac-cident. I wasn't ready to be alone before."

"I hope you'll stay for our Hallowe'en party," Kimo said. He turned toward her and grinned mischievously. "We throw awesome parties."

"I'll bet you do," Caitlin said. Kimo's house, she knew, served as the hub for a number of intertwining circles. "When is it?"

"Friday. I was just making up the invitations." He turned on the printer and waited for the first invitation to print. He glanced at it before handing it to Caitlin. "Costumes required."

"Nice," Caitlin said, impressed by the innovative design. "What are you going as?"

"That's for me to know and you to come and find out." He winked at her and then opened a package of colored paper that he added to the printer tray. "This year, Hallowe'en falls on the same day as the new moon."

"So?"

"So Melody's new moon group will have to finish up early. I'm sure you'd be welcome to go. They meet down here. Melody will have lots of fun combining the two."

"You think she'll come as a . . . w-witch?"

Kimo chuckled, but Caitlin was only half joking. She had often wondered if Melody was a witch, but she'd never dared to ask.

"Is she?"

"Is she a witch?" Kimo stifled a laugh. "There is a bona fide religion called Wicca, you know. Members gather in covens and call themselves witches. But, no, Melody doesn't belong to one. As far as I know. I've never been to her women's group, for obvious reasons. Maybe you should go and report back."

"Do they use . . . spells?" Caitlin spoke in a whisper, as if she feared that talking openly about such matters would somehow invite unwanted spirits. "The witches, I mean." She had never known a real witch, so she had no basis for knowing how much of the stereotype was true and how much was bad press.

"Yes, and so do many people who don't openly identify themselves with the dark arts. Advertising and political propaganda are designed to manipulate people. Most of what you call spells are more akin to prayers, invocations, and intentions to create favorable conditions—health, peace, prosperity, love—the things we all wish for. Right speech coupled with intention can be very powerful, especially when the objective serves the highest good of all concerned. It's only the black lodges that attempt to interfere with free will."

"And what if you're the . . . vic-tim of forces that others use against you?"

"Most people are afraid of power, and with good reason. But avoiding the issue keeps you stuck and powerless. When a person abdicates his power, he's more susceptible to being used by others. Alchemy, yoga, shamanism—a lot of paths aim for mastery. You have to learn how to use power wisely. Once you've mastered yourself, then you're in a position to influence others—for good or for ill."

"So . . . offense is the best defense?"

"Sun Tzu said you have to know yourself and your enemy, and know when to fight—and when not to."

"Sounds like good ad-vice."

"The best battle is the one never waged. Thwart the enemy before he can launch an attack."

"Which requires awareness of what your . . . en-emy is up to."

"Vigilance is the price of liberty. And power must be exercised responsibly. Energy is a force; it's not good or bad. Its use, however, can be beneficial or harmful."

"Cre-a-tion or de-struc-tion," Caitlin said, recalling their previous discussions about good and evil.

Kimo nodded. "Even with the best intentions, actions can have unintended consequences. So—are you coming?"

He collected the invitations from the printer and inserted sheets of labels to print addresses from his mailing list.

"Oh . . . the party. Okay, I'll stay—if you'll come to dinner with me on Saturday." Caitlin smiled sweetly.

"Are we into bargaining now?"

"Well, you're not the devil, are you?"

"Bargaining is only fair when both parties have all the facts. Look at what happened to Native Americans."

"Well, I wanted to surprise you, but . . . I thought I'd make a reser-va-tion at Paula's Table. Of course, if you don't wanna go . . ."

"Ooh, gourmet organic. You must have gotten a good offer! All right—you're on," Kimo said, extending his hand for her to shake on the deal.

Caitlin laughed and shook Kimo's hand. "You'll have to wear a cos-tume too," she said. "A suit!"

"I can handle that, on occasion. And this does sound like an occasion."

❧

Caitlin fretted over what to wear to the party and searched for a low-cost, no-fuss costume. She spotted a bird's nest lying on a shelf in the garage and asked Kimo if she could borrow it. He gave her a puzzled look, but shrugged and said "Sure."

By pinning the colorful leaves she'd collected at Shenandoah to brown corduroy pants and a long-sleeved brown cashmere sweater, Caitlin put together a simple tree costume that was warm and comfortable. Using brown socks to cover an assortment of empty cardboard tubes from rolls of toilet paper and paper towels, she fashioned two sets of roots that she attached to Velcro strips and wrapped around her ankles.

It wasn't the most glamorous costume, but the tree was symbolic. Caitlin suspected that her resistance to planting deep roots had something to do with her experience of family life. Healing her relationship with her mother would be a long-term process, and her views about her father were changing as well.

She tied twigs to her arms with ribbons and then placed a handkerchief on top of her head, followed by a small dried wreath she'd picked up at a farmers market. The colorful sprigs of lavender gave off a fragrant aroma. Caitlin clipped the wreath to her hair and carefully placed the nest inside. After checking to make sure it was securely attached, she left her room and walked toward the basement.

She had waited until the last minute before deciding to attend the new moon gathering and had no idea what to expect. As she arrived at the doorway at the top of the stairs, the clock in the living room chimed seven times. A woman with gray hair handed her an unlit candle and locked the door behind her, barring further entrants.

Candles lit the stairs and surrounded the circle of women who were gathered in the basement. The furniture had been pushed aside to create more space. Caitlin waited for her eyesight to adjust to the dim light and then approached the circle. The sight of fifteen women wearing costumes sent a chill up her spine. She didn't see Lisa but recognized several women from Melody's yoga classes. She took a deep breath and stood directly across from Melody.

Dressed as a cat, Melody looked svelte and sexy, with black leg-gings and bare shoulders and cute ears and whiskers. Her tail was long and slender, like the black satin gloves that had been painted to look like paws.

But of course—the witch's companion!

Caitlin realized that some of her fears were illusory, but her experience with Sam had been a potent reminder that, like anger, fear was part of an innate warning system. Learning to distinguish real threats from imaginary ones was important; she didn't want to distrust people, but she didn't want to put herself in danger either.

Melody struck a chime and then paused, allowing the sound to reverberate before she spoke. For the benefit of newcomers, she explained that goddesses represent aspects of the feminine principle. By learning about goddesses that different cultures had honored, they could reclaim lost traditions and restore the proper balance of nature so that all peoples might live together in peace. Together, the women would envision life-enhancing qualities manifesting in their lives and communities. For this new moon celebration, Melody had chosen the story of Demeter and Persephone.

"In ancient Greece, Demeter's initiation rites were part of the Eleusinian Mysteries. Like Isis in Egypt, Demeter was the Grain Mother who brought life and ruled death; her daughter, Persephone, was the Grain Maiden."

Caitlin's eyes widened. *How odd—Kimo was just talking all this, at Shenandoah!*

Believing there must be a message for her in the Demeter myth, Caitlin paid close attention to what Melody said. She was beginning to see the Intelligence at work in life and the universe. Something had drawn her to be present at this gathering.

Melody told the group that the new moon in Scorpio had con-joined the sun at approximately five o'clock that morning. When the sun travels through the constellation Scorpio, she explained, the veil that separates the worlds becomes thinner, allowing a greater flow of energies to pass between different dimensions. Scorpio and its plan-etary ruler, Pluto, were the keepers of the archetypal energies of death and rebirth, symbolic of the descent into the underworld and the resurrection—the phoenix rising from the ashes after being purified in the fires of transformation.

"This is the season of the Day of the Dead in Mexico and All Hallows' Eve in Western cultures," Melody said. "It's a good time for meditating on the outworn habits and qualities we each wish to let pass away. All new moons initiate a new cycle, so it's also a time for declaring an intention for the upcoming moon cycle—a seed that might come to fruition at the full moon. Death and birth. What's falling away? What's beginning anew?"

Cycles within cycles, Caitlin thought.

She felt sad that her life in Washington was dying. By the time the moon was full, she would be in Missouri, at the Ozark lake where her family vacationed when she was young, at the house where her father had died. Before she could think of an intention, a woman named Charlotte started reading the myth of Demeter and Persephone.

"In some versions," Charlotte said, "Persephone was abducted by Hades as his unwilling bride; in others, she felt compelled to go when she heard the desperate pleas of departed spirits and chose to serve as their queen. Either way, down she went, with a torch to light her way."

While Charlotte spoke, another woman, Rita, walked around the circle lighting the candles they each had been given when they entered the space.

"As queen of the underworld, Persephone functioned like a priestess. She welcomed new souls and embraced them into the realm of the dead," Charlotte read.

Melody assumed the role of priestess. She stood beside a table covered with a black cloth; a silver bowl contained pomegranate juice. As each woman approached, Melody dipped her finger into the juice and then marked the woman's forehead with a symbol shaped like a semicircular bowl atop a cross. Then, Melody embraced the woman, welcoming her by name into the circle.

"Meanwhile," Charlotte continued, "Demeter roamed among the living as one half dead, awaiting the return of her fair daughter. Fields were barren, crops and trees and flowers withered, until, finally, one day Persephone returned and tender green shoots sprang forth from the ground below. All rejoiced in the miracle of life renewed."

By the time Charlotte finished reading, each woman had returned to her place in the circle.

Melody held up her candle. "As we descend into the darkness of winter, carry a light to warm and guide you. May you emerge in spring with renewed passion and a sense of joy and purpose." She blew out the candle to mark the end of the ceremony, and the other women followed her example.

Caitlin thought of the many trials she and her mother had endured. They had each gained new understanding, but now Caitlin must prepare for the journey ahead—on her own.

The remainder of the evening passed swiftly. Caitlin felt at ease; nothing about the gathering seemed especially "witchy." Melody encouraged the women to write an intention for the month on a slip of paper; these were all placed in the silver bowl, which had been emptied and cleaned. In this way, they could support each other's hopes and dreams. The group sang a song to bring courage on dark nights, and each woman was given a stone of remembrance by Allison, an energy healer who worked with gems and crystals.

Each month, Allison said, she selected a different stone by intuiting the qualities that would balance and support the women during the upcoming cycle. This month she'd chosen amber, not really a stone but hardened resin, which would bring a warm glow on cold winter nights.

Rita turned on the lights, and the women shared hugs and laughter before climbing the stairs to join the other guests who were arriving for the party.

As the house filled with people, the atmosphere grew festive. Kimo was serious about the costume requirement and turned away a few people who had come in street clothes. He had prepared all of the food; Melody and Lisa had decorated the house. Jack had supplied most of the beverages. Caitlin had been busy getting ready for her upcoming trip but contributed generously to the expenses.

She took the amber and the candle to her room, pausing to notice the way the house had been transformed. A jack-o'-lantern outside the front door greeted guests; black plastic spiders hung from doorways; a glow-in-the-dark skeleton danced in the guest bathroom. In the living room, a pointed black hat and black cape lay next to a broomstick on the floor, reminiscent of the melted Wicked Witch of the West in *The Wizard of Oz*. In the hallway, a green light bulb cast an eerie glow.

Caitlin peeked inside Kimo's room as she passed by. He had mentioned digging out a few novelty items from an old trunk. Tacked to the wall was a black light poster of a cloaked Grim Reaper standing in a graveyard and holding a skull in one hand and a scythe in the other. Illuminated by a black light bulb, the ghoulish figure glowed amidst the surrounding darkness. On the nightstand, a lava lamp oozed blobs of ever-changing waxy formations.

Caitlin laughed, delighted by the retro trip back into the 1960s, Kimo style. Her mother never would have allowed such things in her bedroom or even in Bobby's room. The walls of her room had been painted in pastel colors and were adorned with cute illustrations of puppies and seashells and, later, posters from theatrical productions and postcards from faraway places Caitlin wanted to visit someday. Her bookshelf had been filled with yearbooks, adventure novels, biographies, fashion magazines, and some of the classics. The sports theme in her brother's room changed over the years according to Bobby's interests, shifting from baseball to soccer to football and basketball; his bookshelf was lined with comic books.

Eager to see Kimo in his costume, Caitlin joined the party. She mingled with the guests but quickly tired of small talk with strangers. She wasn't interested in meeting new people; she wanted to spend her remaining time with the friends she had come to love. She looked around for an escape from a man who wanted to know why she was leaving the area.

"What's wrong with Washington?"

"There's nothing wrong with Washing-ton," Caitlin replied curtly. "Well, no more than anywhere else."

Every place—perhaps every thing in the manifest world—had

its good points and its down side; the secret lay in discovering what was needed at any given time. Washington might have been perfect for her before, but no longer.

"It's just . . . time for me to go."

She didn't need to explain or justify her actions—especially to someone she would probably never see again. If he didn't understand, she didn't really care. She drifted over to Melody and her lover, Matt.

"Wanna see my tree pose?"

Melody watched as Caitlin demonstrated her ability to balance on one leg.

"Even with woo—roots for feet," she said, looking down at her limbs.

She spotted a man with a shaved head and thought of Bart; he was undergoing chemotherapy, Caitlin had overheard at the start of a yoga class. His doctor was interested in the new field of psycho-neuroimmunology and had suggested he learn visualization techniques to support his body's innate ability to heal. A friend had recommended Melody's classes.

"What do you hear about Bart?" Caitlin asked Melody.

"His treatments are going well," Melody said. "Kimo looks *chic*," she said, looking past Caitlin.

Caitlin turned and saw Kimo, dressed as a sheik, serving a cup of punch to an attractive woman wearing a mermaid costume. Looking around the room, she saw Lisa, who was dressed as a belly dancer.

"The wallflower has found her calling."

Kimo snuck up on them from behind. Taking Caitlin's hand, he spun her around to face him.

"Dance with me!" he demanded, playing his role like he was part vampire and part suave ladies' man.

Caitlin blushed. "Oh! Kimo, I—"

Kimo was insistent. "Dance with me," he repeated.

He led Caitlin to the adjoining room, where a karaoke machine and small stage had been set up. Several couples were dancing to "Desperado," sung by a woman wearing a bright red jacket covered in sequins. Caitlin tripped over her roots and unfastened the straps from around her ankles.

"The crown will have to go too," Kimo said as he gently removed the wreath from Caitlin's head, "unless you want to poke my eyes out."

He took her in his arms.

Caitlin glanced at the vocalist. "She's not bad."

"Shhh!" Kimo whispered.

"Huh?"

"Don't talk," he murmured. "Dance."

Caitlin was beginning to relax into Kimo's embrace when the song ended. She gazed into his eyes. He leaned down as if to kiss her. The lights brightened and Jack announced that judging for the best costumes was about to begin. Jolted out of the moment, Caitlin stiffened.

"Uh—thanks . . . for the d-dance," she said nervously and moved away.

She said goodnight to Melody, thanked Jack for the lessons and the use of his guitar, and retreated to her room.

What am I so afraid of? she wondered as she removed the twigs from her arms. Intimacy? Taking off the mask? Being truly seen?

Caitlin sensed that Kimo could see into her soul in a way no one else could—and that was scarier than any haunted house.

∽ 76 ∽

Kimo said goodbye to the guests who had stayed to help clean up and then walked through the house looking for stray dishes and glassware that might have been missed. He found a few pieces in odd places.

What were they thinking? He sighed. *They weren't.*

When the dishwasher finished its cycle, he put away the clean dishes. Putting things in order helped him order his thoughts. He'd rather finish the chores now and wake up to a clean house. Tomorrow, he might want to sleep late.

He popped the top off a bottle of beer that had been left on the kitchen counter. He'd given himself permission to enjoy the fresh beer in Ireland, but he'd stayed away from alcohol since. Escaping into a drunken stupor might be a good way to dull the ache in his heart. Soon Caitlin would be gone, along with his chance to win her affections. Did she have any idea how hard saying goodbye to her was for him? He raised the bottle to his lips, but stopped.

No, of course she didn't. She'd lost her memory of the Shannon Pot. And until she regained it, his cause was hopeless. His very presence seemed to threaten her. She wasn't ready to remember.

A line from Rumi came into his head: *"Don't go back to sleep."* Alcohol might temporarily numb his pain, but it wouldn't solve his problems, and he would probably feel worse the next day. He'd learned that lesson the hard way.

She's not worth that, he thought, and poured the beer down the drain. He would stay the course.

The tug of addiction never completely disappeared; that was why he continued with AA and his other practices. Continuing awareness was necessary to keep from sliding into unconscious choices. He wasn't willing to let alcohol control his life. He didn't intend to completely avoid the stuff, but the only way he could enjoy it—even in moderation—was by not *needing* it.

Maybe that was true about Caitlin, too.

He turned off the lights and went to bed.

∞ 77 ∞

Caitlin put on her best pair of black leather pumps and looked at her reflection in the full-length mirror. She couldn't remember the last time she'd worn high heels. They matched her purse and complemented her silk dress nicely, but now they seemed silly and possibly even unsafe.

Who designs this stuff anyway?

As she walked down the hall, she remembered her first steps away from the wheelchair on Easter morning, when she'd fallen into Kimo's arms. She felt grateful for his support and friendship. He wouldn't be there to catch her in the future, or to teach her about nutrition, or to lead her in taiji. She would find other teachers, make new friends. But there would never be another Kimo. He was one of a kind.

She took a deep breath before knocking on his door. She'd told him to wear a suit, but Kimo was unpredictable and lived by his own rules. She hoped she wouldn't be embarrassed to be seen with him, but she was completely unprepared for what she saw when he opened the door: he had cut his hair and shaved off his goatee. Dressed in a sharp suit, he looked like a model off the pages of *GQ*. Caitlin stared at him, speechless.

"Ready?" he asked casually.

She nodded and followed him to his car. She nearly cried when he held her door open until she was safely inside. They had both come a long way since Ireland.

As they walked to the restaurant from the parking garage, Caitlin took Kimo's arm for support. She watched the fog that formed in the cold night air when she exhaled.

She had never heard of Paula's Table until Kimo mentioned that he wanted to go there someday. With selections like wild game and Norwegian salmon, he guessed the prices would be "obscene." She was glad she could treat him to something he'd be sure to enjoy.

Inside, a welcoming fireplace near the front entrance provided warmth and atmosphere. While they waited to be seated, Caitlin glanced around, admiring the modern decor. Floral arrangements dotted the room; expensive art adorned the walls.

The hostess ushered them to their table, where a waiter lit a candle and recited the dinner specials. The menu featured unique entrées with exotic seasonings; fresh salads, select wines, hearty soups, and creative desserts filled out the experience. "Trendy" was Caitlin's assessment. Everything had a name attached to it: Paula's signature moules, free-range chickens from Olney, Maryland, humanely raised veal from the Templeton Farm, and organic vegetables from the local farmers market. Caitlin enjoyed a nice meal—especially if she didn't have to cook it—but she wasn't as particular as Kimo about its origins. She was always appreciative, however, of elegance and style.

For a starter, Kimo ordered nori rolls stuffed with rice and tempura vegetables. Caitlin dipped a few pieces into the miso-based sauce that accompanied the appetizer. Trying something different made for a nice change, but she preferred the tiny puff pastries stuffed with crab and cream cheese that she had ordered. Kimo tasted one but said it was too rich for his system.

He raved about the vegetarian special he'd ordered as his main entrée: grilled tempeh with a savory sauce, accompanied by roasted root vegetables and a seaweed salad. "Mmm—this is my idea of good food."

"And I like the atom—at-mos-phere," Caitlin said. She had chosen the Madeira roast pheasant with sage cornbread stuffing and yams glazed with sake. "At last, we find a common ground between your world . . . and mine."

She offered Kimo a taste of her Australian white wine. He took a sip before responding.

"Yeah, as you're heading out the door."

"I'll be thinking of you as I prac-tice all the things you taught me," she said, raising her glass to him.

"When will you be back?" he asked before taking a drink of Perrier.

Caitlin paused before answering. "I . . . I'm not sure I will be. I don't know how long I'll stay in Miz—Mis-sou-ri . . . or which way I'll head after that."

She looked down at her plate. She wanted to study Kimo's new look but felt embarrassed and shy. She drank some more wine.

"Anyway, I'm grateful for a second chance, to make . . . different choices."

"Every choice contains a yes to one thing and a no to something else," Kimo said.

"I guess," Caitlin murmured.

She was tired of Kimo's veiled references and wished he would come right out and say that he didn't want her to go, or that he hoped for something more between them—if he felt that way. She was never entirely sure, and though she liked his calm acceptance and low-key manner, his passivity confused her.

Maybe she needed to accept that they would never be more than friends, she thought as she took a bite of pheasant. Their differences had been apparent from the start. But couldn't some differences enhance a relationship?

"What's happening with the vaccines?" Kimo asked.

Caitlin welcomed a new direction for her thoughts—but not that one, not another area where she felt she'd failed.

"I heard NIH is gonna fund a study . . . to see if there's any de-mon-stra-ble link between . . . thy—thi-me-ro-sal and . . . autism."

"At least someone in the government is taking the issue seriously."

"Yeah . . . they'll study it for five years and then issue a report saying the results are in-con-clu-sive."

"The pharmaceutical companies are out to vaccinate and medicate the whole world."

"Meanwhile, rates of autism are skyrocketing and nobody seems to know why. I don't know if thy—thimerosal causes autism, but you know as well as I do that mercury is talk—toxic. Add the amount in vaccines to what we already get exposed to in fish and dental amal-gams and . . . it can't be a good thing."

Kimo smiled. He pushed away his plate and rested his arms on the table. "Do you realize how much more aware you are now than when we were in Ireland?"

Caitlin sipped her wine. "Am I?"

He gave her a look that said, "Come on, don't you see it?"

She giggled. "Yeah, I guess I am. What'd you do—hyp-notize me or something?"

"You did it all yourself."

"I had some help. But I can't go back to a 'normal' life—is that what you're saying?"

"It wasn't what I was thinking, but there's probably some truth to it." Kimo reached for the dessert menu the waiter had left. "You know, the whole basis for immunization is similar to the homeo-pathic principle that 'like heals like.' America's first national medical society was the American Institute of Homeopathy, organized in 1844. The movement was so successful, a rival group formed in 1847: the American Medical Association."

Caitlin smiled politely, but she would have preferred talking about something more personal. She often felt that Kimo was trying to educate her or sway her, rather than sharing a dialogue *with* her. She wanted connection, and the distance between them left her feeling sad and lonely. She slowly ate the last of her meal while he continued talking.

"Now the pharmaceutical companies target consumers directly and tell them to go *ask* for particular drugs from their physicians. Convince people there's a need and then charge a lot of money for the solution. Of course, the government and the media help out. And it's not only this country that has a problem."

"I, for one, am laying down my sword," Caitlin said, setting down her knife and fork. "I need to look out for myself for awhile. I can't save the world."

"Sometimes there are more effective ways to bring about change than by fighting," Kimo said. "When you resist something, you stay stuck in polarity with it. That's the beauty of natural medicine. It works with the forces of nature rather than against them."

"I'm sure glad I got off the pills," Caitlin said. "I never knew home—ho-me-opa-thy and herbs could be so . . . effective."

"That's part of the reason orthodox medicine has had such animosity toward natural healers. The witch hunts aren't confined to religion, you know. The AMA campaigned to have homeopathic physicians excluded from medical societies, which meant they couldn't get licensed and were subject to arrest for practicing medicine without a license."

Their waiter returned to see if they wanted dessert. Caitlin decided on the truffle cake with raspberry coulis. Kimo ordered apple and peach cobbler with amaretto ice cream.

"What will you do once you have your . . . license?" Caitlin asked.

"There's not much to keep me here," Kimo said. "Especially with you and Melody both leaving. I'll see what my options are when the time comes."

"Where are your parents?"

"California."

"Were you an only child?"

"Yep. I came along pretty late. Unexpected."

Caitlin wanted to say, "That fits," but held her tongue.

Their desserts arrived promptly.

"My parents were actors. Activists during the McCarthy era," Kimo said. "It wasn't much of a home life. Summer stock, dinner theaters—we were all over the place. I made up my mind that my life would be more stable. Of course, I fell in with the wrong crowd for a while."

He took a bite of the cobbler. "This is really good. Try a taste." He held a spoonful out to Caitlin.

She leaned toward him and opened her mouth, appreciating the intimacy of the gesture. "Nice," she said.

Kimo's blue-grey eyes danced with animation as he recounted exploits from his surfer days. Caitlin liked hearing about his life, his hopes and dreams, his feelings. She reached over and squeezed his hand.

"I'm sure you'll help a lot of people. I know you've helped me. And I'll . . . I'll al-ways be grateful."

His eyes fastened upon her. Caitlin looked away and took another sip of wine. Kimo's stares were so intense. Whenever he gave her his undivided attention, she felt flustered.

She realized that every time he approached, she pulled away. Was she the one sending mixed signals? She wanted to get closer— but how much closer?

✑ 78 ✑

Kimo drove around to the front of the restaurant and parked behind an expensive sports car. Caitlin was standing in the street, talking with the driver. She feigned surprise when she saw Kimo pull up and sauntered over to his car. She leaned down to speak to him. He opened the window.

"And how much are *you* of-fering, sir?"

"Uh—Blank check."

He watched her hips sway as she walked back to the other car and said goodbye to the driver. The car sped off. Caitlin scurried back to Kimo's car, giddy and cold.

He drove across the Key Bridge into Virginia and they admired the view of Washington from the other side of the Potomac River. Kimo longed to park the car and snuggle close to Caitlin, but he feared that if he dared to kiss her, he could never let her go. He drove on to Arlington.

The house was quiet when they entered. They hung their coats by the door, and Caitlin stumbled down the hall, laughing as she recounted the episode outside the restaurant. She was standing on the corner when the car stopped in front of her, she said. The driver was talking to her but she couldn't understand what he was saying. He motioned to her to come around to his side of the car. The passenger window was broken, he said. She was stunned when he propositioned her but decided to play along, knowing Kimo would soon arrive on the scene.

"Maybe it was my fur coat."

"You're lucky he wasn't an undercover cop," Kimo said as he loosened the tie around his neck. "How would that look—'former Justice Department attorney arrested for prostitution,'" he said, reading the imaginary headlines.

Caitlin looked around, as if worried someone might hear. "Shhh! Keep your voice down!" she said, even as she laughed uncontrollably. She steadied herself against the wall and tried to catch her breath. Kimo stood facing her. She grabbed both ends of his loosened necktie and pulled him closer.

"It's all your fault," she said, giggling. "I never used to do things like that. My friends warmed—*warned* me about you!"

Their faces were close. Caitlin stopped laughing and looked into Kimo's eyes. He kissed her tenderly. She didn't pull away. He kissed her again, more passionately. She touched his face; her touch intoxicated him. He was ready to devour her with kisses and carry her off to his bedroom—but stopped.

Making mad love to her would surely be a night to remember. But where—on his twin bed? With Melody in the house? No, it wasn't going to happen that way. He searched Caitlin's eyes for a clue to her feelings. He saw desire there; that was enough for him, for now.

He smiled and said, "Something to remember me by." Then, he turned and walked confidently to his room.

He wasn't trying to tease her, just as his sullen behavior in Ireland hadn't been deliberate. He didn't resent her liaisons in Scotland and Hawai'i; he had no right to expect fidelity, or anything else, from her. He didn't feel intimidated by her or fear her rejection, and he was no longer worried about blowing his chances. He was totally in love with her, and he was in control of himself.

That's an accomplishment, he thought as he closed the door to his bedroom. He was making progress.

His relationship with Melody had been a wild ride. Lots of drama and excitement—and tension. He never knew what she'd do next. Were they off or on? During their many separations, she never wasted much time before finding his replacement. He didn't consider himself a jealous man, but life with Melody had made him crazy. He'd lost all respect for himself. Then the addictions took over. The dark side of their lifestyle possessed them both.

Kimo was the first to break free. Never again would he be drawn to the party scene. He didn't miss a thing about it; the temptation had been burned clean out of him. Melody, too, had come a long way in her recovery. She and Caitlin were alike in some ways—they were both fiery, impulsive, and dramatic—but Melody was often flighty and irresponsible. Caitlin was solid in her core. Seeing her tipsy from alcohol didn't diminish Kimo's respect for her. He enjoyed watching her loosen up and have fun. But he wanted more than one night with her.

He removed his jacket and hung it in the closet. The evening was worth the price of a new suit.

The next day, Kimo and Caitlin practiced taiji together one last time, and then Caitlin focused on packing. Kimo fixed a special dinner for the two of them. Jack was on the road again, Lisa was visiting family for the day, and Melody was with Matt. Goodbye hung in the air.

Caitlin was polite but cool. Kimo wished he knew how she was feeling in the clear light of day. He wanted to reassure her that he hadn't rejected her, but he couldn't find the words. She thanked him for the meal and said she wanted to get to bed early so she wouldn't fall asleep at the wheel the following day.

On Monday morning, Kimo watched from the dining room window as Caitlin loaded the last items into her car. She seemed so self-sufficient, so capable of handling everything on her own. She didn't need him. Maybe that was a good thing. But would she ever *choose* him?

Melody walked up and handed him a small brown paper bag. "Caitlin made it."

His lunch. He looked into Melody's eyes. She'd known him for a long time; they'd weathered many seasons together. Could she tell how lost he felt in that moment? Soon, she'd be gone again too—and this time might be the last.

"Hmm" was all he said. He returned to staring out the window.

Melody looked from the scene outside to Kimo. "You just gonna let her leave?"

He hadn't slept all night, smoldering with desire. Her sensual invitation, beckoning him, replayed in his head. He wanted nothing more than to go to her room—she was so close by he could hardly stand it. Maybe Melody hadn't even been in the house; she sometimes stayed with her boyfriend and returned early in the morning. Kimo's room, Caitlin's room, the living room floor, the kitchen table—what did it matter? He wanted her, anywhere and everywhere. But one glorious night wouldn't change what was to be, and it would only make him ache for her more after she'd gone.

"Yep."

"Does she know you and I used to . . ."

Kimo turned to look at her. She gave him a "you know what I mean" glance.

"I've never said anything," he said.

"Me neither."

He returned to watching Caitlin.

"Does she know how you feel?"

"She doesn't even know how *she* feels." He stuffed the brown bag into his backpack and walked outside.

He strapped a flat package wrapped in brown paper onto the rack on his bicycle. Although he was curious what was inside, he didn't ask. Caitlin had asked him to deliver it to her old office building; whatever it was, it couldn't be very interesting. It wasn't heavy, just awkward, but being a courier, he'd learned many tricks for transporting odd things.

He opened the garage door. He'd picked up a little gift for Caitlin the day before and had been keeping it safe in the garage. He placed the plastic carrier inside a large cardboard box and carried the box over to Caitlin's car.

"All set?"

"Almost." She set a small cooler onto the floor on the passenger side of her car.

Kimo peered inside and saw maps, a water bottle, and a sweater on the passenger seat—nothing that couldn't be moved easily.

"I got you a little something for your travels. Okay if I set it here?" He moved Caitlin's things aside and placed the box on the seat.

"Um—yeah, I guess. What is it?"

"You can open it after I leave." He walked over to his bike and swung a leg over the bar.

Caitlin gestured toward the package and asked, "You know where to . . . to take that?"

Kimo strapped on his helmet. "Yep."

"Thanks . . . for deli-ver-ing it."

"It's on my way. Look, I don't like long goodbyes," he said, looking away. "So you be safe and well and give a call sometime."

He leaned over and kissed her forehead, and then pulled on his gloves and rode away.

⋘ 79 ⋙

Caitlin stood in the driveway with her hands on her hips and watched Kimo ride away.

Just like London!

Once again, when she'd started to feel close to him, he'd pulled away, leaving her feeling confused, disappointed, and frustrated.

She walked back to her car and peered at the top of the plastic container protruding from the cardboard box he'd left on the seat. It looked almost like a cooler, she thought. Maybe he had fixed her lunch, as she had done for him—like a scene from an O. Henry story. She pulled on the handle and lifted a pet carrier out of the box. She nearly dropped it when she saw a small gray kitten with white markings on its breast and forehead looking up at her through the wire grate. It meowed.

"Oh my—" She turned and shouted, "Kimo, wait! I'm aller-gic to—" He was too far away to hear. "Cats."

Staring at the tiny creature, Caitlin realized she was not only allergic to cats—she was also afraid of them.

She unfolded a handwritten note she found inside the box. "It's only a kitten," it read. "Take the homeopathic formula. By the time he's a cat, your allergy will be history."

Caitlin glanced inside the carrier and noticed a dropper bottle as well as small bags of cat food and kitty litter.

"He'll probably appreciate it if you let him out of his cage as much as possible," the note continued. It ended with a query: "Have you ever wondered *why* you're allergic to cats?"

Caitlin crumpled the paper and threw it into the box. No, she had not analyzed why she had allergies! As a child she'd suffered from hay fever; was she supposed to wonder about that too? Weren't allergies like brown hair or blue eyes—some people just had them?

She tossed the empty box onto the pavement and placed the carrier on the passenger seat.

"All right," she murmured. She'd take it with her. After all, it was a gift from Kimo.

She closed the door and turned around, nearly bumping into Melody, who stood watching her with folded arms.

"Caitlin, you know I love you, but I think you're making a huge mistake."

Caitlin was hardly in the mood for a lecture. She picked up the box and carried it to the trash can. "Keeping the cat?"

"Leaving! Don't you know Kimo's in love with you?"

Caitlin felt her face flush. Did she know that? She'd wondered at times, but she'd certainly given him plenty of openings. Saturday night she'd practically pulled him on top of her and still, nothing.

"Did . . . Did he tell you that?"

"Not in those words. You know he won't ask you to stay. Even if he wants to."

Caitlin knew that was true; it wasn't Kimo's way. She also knew she couldn't stay, even if he asked.

"Kimo doesn't have time for a . . . relationship."

"That will change."

"And so will we," Caitlin said. She'd already considered all the arguments and angles. Who knew whether any of them would meet up again?

"I can't just hang out and wait. I've got my own path to follow. I don't know where it leads. But I'm learning to be okay with . . . not knowing."

"I guess I can't argue with that," Melody said.

"I thought you'd understand."

"Well, then. Stay in touch. I guess there's no way to reach you?"

"There's no phone . . . where I'm going. My mail's being forwarded to my mother. She'll send it on to me." Caitlin lowered her voice. "I don't wanna sound . . . paranoid," she confided, "but sometimes . . . I feel like I'm being *watched*."

Since her last encounter with Neil, her termination papers had been processed. She'd had no further dealings with OSP, but the silence felt eerie, not comforting. She hadn't heard from Patrice, either, after leaving the vase at the office for her.

"Ask for protection," Melody suggested. "You'll be fine. You're always welcome to come and visit me in Santa Fe. I hope to be there by the end of the year."

"Thanks, Mel," Caitlin said, embracing her warmly. "I've learned a lot from you."

"Keep up the voice work," Melody said. "It'll make a difference. You'll see."

"It already has."

She checked to make sure the chunk of amber from the new moon ceremony was in her pocket and waved to Melody as she drove away from the house. "Wild World," an old Cat Stevens song, played on the radio.

Caitlin prayed for a safe trip. She refused to allow fears of what might happen out on the road to prevent her from enjoying the journey. Melody once said that people attract whatever they focus on; if Caitlin wanted good, positive people and experiences in her life, she shouldn't continually dwell on the negative. Being alone so much of the time, she'd found plenty of opportunities to practice changing her thoughts when she caught herself slipping into old habit patterns.

The landscape changed from urban to rural as Caitlin drove west. She knew she was leaving behind a career that she had worked hard to build. She felt a mixture of sadness and hopeful anticipation. She'd wanted to leave Washington after the Ireland trip, and she was finally doing it. Only now, she wasn't taking a sabbatical from law to explore other options. She *had* to find another way of life.

She glanced at the clock and wondered if Kimo had delivered the painting. Would Neil remember the remark he'd made to her the day he talked her out of resigning?

"What are you gonna do—go paint daffodils?"

Caitlin remembered. *Maybe so, Neil,* she thought. *Maybe so. And roses, too.*

She hoped she wasn't stirring up trouble by contacting him. Remembering his detective work when she was in Scotland with

Dru, she had taken precautions to make tracing her whereabouts more difficult. As much as possible, she planned to use cash instead of credit cards. Utility bills from the lake house went to her mother, who visited the property infrequently. Life in the Ozarks would be quiet. Caitlin planned to do little to attract attention to herself and anticipated a peaceful retreat—a time to slow down and examine her innermost reality, to put life on "pause."

"Ain't that right, Paws?" she said, glancing over at the cat carrier. *That could be a catchy idea for a song.*

The highway narrowed from four lanes to two as she drove farther away from the metropolitan area. The road spread before her like a canvas waiting to be painted, a blank page awaiting a new story.

❧ 80 ❧

Kimo rode his bike down the trail along the river. His thoughts were all on Caitlin. She would remain in his heart forever, regardless of where she wandered. He wished she'd stay, but if he loved her he had to let her go find out for herself what she wanted and needed in her life. If she found her way back to him, great. He'd be there; he'd welcome her home. But he wasn't going to chase after her.

He paused, breathing hard, and gazed out at the Potomac. Why did he always feel his loved ones were abandoning him when they departed? Losses left hollow craters in his heart. When he was young, he'd sometimes stayed with his maternal grandparents at their farm when his parents' showbiz career couldn't accommodate a child. Maybe that explained his fear that the life force would drain out of him through the spaces that once were filled with love and laughter.

Or maybe the patterns of his life echoed a distant time—a time he'd glimpsed during his plunge into the magical waters of the Shannon Pot. He mustn't let loss or failure destroy him again. Caitlin was learning to be strong enough to risk vulnerability, to surrender control. He was learning to be strong enough to take control, to lead. Being harsh and unfeeling didn't make a leader great, he knew. Staying true to his convictions, having courage and confidence, being honest and faithful, following through on promises—these were some of the qualities that distinguished a man of integrity.

He continued along the trail, haunted by the lyrics of a song from the 1980s about letting go of a lover and then finding each other again. His mother used to play it, over and over, when Kimo was fifteen; he remembered because it was on the radio right after they settled in California. He didn't have any friends yet, so he was hanging around the house a lot. He'd hated the song and cringed every time he heard it. But now the words had meaning for him. Maybe, someday, Caitlin would realize she belonged with *him*.

He hadn't been home for a while; maybe it was time to plan a visit.

Mom will be thrilled.

✎ 81 ✎

Neil tore the paper wrapper off the package addressed to him and stared at a painting of yellow daffodils.

Caitlin.

His eyes scanned the artwork; the initials "CR" were in the bottom right corner. He looked for a note. *Nothing . . .*

He laid the painting flat on his desk and dialed Caitlin's home number.

"This number has been disconnected or—"

Neil hung up the phone and opened the door.

"Find out whether Caitlin Rose left any forwarding information," he told Betty. "And send Patrice in," he barked.

Sam Burns had disappeared and now, it seemed, Caitlin was about to. Was there a connection? Did something happen between Sam and Caitlin that Burns never divulged? Neil paced the floor, as if doing so was doing *something*.

Before long, Patrice showed up. As usual, she didn't know anything. She'd been away on her long-delayed honeymoon and was still writing thank-you notes in her spare time.

Wedded bliss. He must lack the gene for that capability. He told Patrice she could go.

"And send Betty in. Please."

He knew he'd been testy and hard to work with this last year. His legislation had been shot down after some liberal grassroots organization initiated a letter-writing campaign; his reputation suffered. He'd lost his confident stride and shuffled around, despondent. He no longer needed to worry about Caitlin meddling in his affairs, unless Sam had said something stupid.

He turned out to be a big disappointment.

Betty reported that Caitlin's forwarding information listed a Kansas address; she handed Neil a note with the information. He sat behind his desk, listless.

"Will that be all?" Betty asked timidly.

Neil nodded.

Hard to picture Caitlin being happy in Kansas. The accident must have changed her. He knew it had changed him.

He ran his hands through his hair and rubbed his temples. He had to snap out of this stupor. What was the pivotal moment when his luck had abandoned him?

He thought about his visit to the hospital. It was a Friday; he'd stopped by after work—told the nurse he was Caitlin's attorney and pulled out his Bar ID card. Said he needed to see what condition she was in. "Litigation purposes." It wasn't much of a lie; he was an attorney, and he did need to see Caitlin. He needed to see for himself what had happened to her.

His heart sank when he saw her. It was then he realized that knowing her had made him a better man; that without her in his life, he would never aspire to improve his character. He felt her judgment when he strayed too far from behaving like a decent human being. She sparked some latent impulse to be honorable that he hadn't even been aware he possessed.

A tear came to his eye; he quickly wiped it away. Flowers were not allowed in the Intensive Care Unit, a large sign informed him. He looked around to make sure no one was watching and removed a yellow rose from his briefcase. He set it on the narrow ledge beside her door. He'd noticed a yellow rose dangling from the rearview mirror of her car and guessed it was her favorite flower. Then, he left.

He looked again at the painting. Not bad, for a beginner. He was no expert when it came to art. He wasn't sentimental, but he'd hang it on the wall. It would brighten up the drab office. As Caitlin had.

PART SEVEN

REFLECTIONS

☞ 82 ☞

Feeling drowsy, Caitlin stopped at a rest area in West Virginia. According to the digital display inside the car, the outside temperature was 47°F. Caitlin searched the stacks of bedding and towels she had piled onto the back seat and pulled out a Mexican serape, a souvenir from a spring break trip to Acapulco that she and Jayson had taken during their last year in law school.

Closest thing to a honeymoon we ever had . . .

She chose a picnic table in the sun and used the blanket to cushion the cold, hard bench. She'd packed the same foods for herself that she'd given to Kimo: an assortment of fresh vegetables she'd sautéed that morning, a multigrain roll, a chunk of Manchego cheese, and a slice of carrot cake—Kimo's favorite dessert—that she'd picked up from the bakery at the natural foods store the day before. She ate part of the cake and saved the rest for a bedtime snack. After discarding her trash, she walked the grounds.

The last brilliant flash of autumn color was gone. A few leaves fluttered in the breeze, tenuously attached to their source of life. Withered and brown, the leaves would not survive winter's freeze— but the trees would.

Caitlin sat cross-legged on the blanket beneath a large oak tree. She closed her eyes and focused on her breathing, a practice Kimo

403

had suggested. He told her to notice thoughts and feelings without trying to change them. When she realized that she was neither her thoughts nor her feelings, she would gain greater detachment and objectivity, a key to not taking everything so seriously. Then, she would be free to respond to changing conditions in appropriate ways rather than reacting automatically when old wounds were aggravated or emotional patterns were triggered.

She was keyed up about the trip, she'd told him at breakfast on Sunday, and had a lot on her mind.

"Remember the movements we did in taiji," he said. Taking her by the hand, Kimo led her into the living room. He closed his eyes, inhaled deeply, and took a moment to feel his center of gravity, the *dantian*, before starting the taiji sequence, moving out from his center and returning there to rest. Caitlin followed along, as she'd become accustomed to doing, and felt calmer at the end of the routine.

"You can achieve a similar result in a sitting or standing position," Kimo said. "Find your center and then follow your breath, in and out." He closed his eyes and demonstrated the movement of his breath with hand motions.

Caitlin closed her eyes and tried to set aside her worries as she focused on her breathing. These practices seemed easier when she did them with a guide than when she tried them on her own. Now, her mind was chattering with plans and concerns. Was the kitten still dozing in the front seat? What if he was cold or hungry—or peeing on the upholstery! What if the homeopathy didn't work; what would she do then?

She inhaled deeply and imagined a golden ball of energy below her navel—an exercise she'd learned from Melody—but she felt silly trying to meditate in such a public place. She wasn't going to get enlightened today; all she was going to get was a cold butt. She looked up at the tree, as if hoping for sympathy or advice, and then picked herself up and walked toward the car, pausing to view a display about the plant and animal species that were native to the region.

The *arborvitae*, or "tree of life," was believed to be the first North American tree planted in Europe, Caitlin read. Native peoples had taught French explorers how to make a potent tea from the leaves and bark of the *l'arbor de vie.*

Caitlin recalled learning about the arbor vitae of the brain, the cerebellum, so called because of its treelike white matter. One of her therapists had given her a journal article about the effect of head injuries on brain function. Caitlin had experienced the effect; she didn't need to read about it. But if the article helped the therapist understand her condition, she appreciated the interest.

Continuing on to the car, she thought about the significance of the Tree of Life in various traditions and how it contrasted with that other tree in the Garden of Eden, the Tree of Knowledge of Good and Evil. She and Kimo had started talking about good and evil the night before, during dinner. Still feeling confused and humiliated after her forward behavior the previous night, Caitlin had steered the conversation away from anything personal.

Kimo said that good and evil are dualities inherent in the world of form; only in the nondual, formless state could one find eternal life.

"When we die, you mean," Caitlin had said.

"No," Kimo said, "mystics would say true reality is only found on the inner planes; everything else is illusory. Illumination requires contacting the Spirit that is the Source of everything, allowing the soul to guide the personality. That's the resurrection, the rebirth they all speak of. Nirvana, bliss, oneness—the ultimate purpose of life is to reach that stage in the body. Consciousness is the only thing you can take with you. Karma that was created here has to be addressed here; after death is too late."

Caitlin remembered waking from the coma with the sense that consciousness transcends the body and the brain. That conviction stayed with her, even as other thoughts and experiences faded.

Death is not the end of awareness. The soul is eternal.

But the Christian notion of an afterlife—a final destination where punishments and rewards were meted out—didn't quite fit her new understanding that material form helps us experience the consequences of our thoughts in tangible ways.

If heaven is a state of being, maybe the point is to create heaven here on earth.

Was that done by eating from the Tree of Knowledge and achieving gnosis? Or did the knowledge of good and evil create a split that could only be healed by embracing life as a whole, without labeling anything "good" or "bad"—just accepting "what is"?

Maybe the answer to both questions is yes.

She thought again about the nature of light. Studies in quantum physics had shown that light could behave as a particle or as a wave. The ability to accept paradox seemed to be a hallmark of unified consciousness. Carl Jung had talked about holding the tension of the opposites. People described the still point in different ways— the quiet place in the eye of the hurricane, the centered state accessed in meditation, the middle way passing between Scylla and Charybdis—but maybe they were all teaching the same lesson: identify with the Source of Being, which is eternal, and not with the ephemeral things of this transient world. Don't take sides, or get pulled to either side.

Caitlin found the kitten sitting in the driver's seat, licking a paw. She scooted him over to the passenger side and located her next stop on the map. She and Jayson had traveled from St. Louis to Alexandria in one day when they moved to Virginia. Without a companion to share the driving, Caitlin needed to break the trip up into manageable segments.

Her life in Washington hadn't gone the way she had planned— which meant she'd had expectations, an agenda. She had to let go of expectations, she reminded herself. *Living means adapting to change. Moment to moment.*

Caitlin exited the highway at dusk and drove to a rural lodge a mile down the road. The accommodations guide listed an in-house restaurant, but it was closed for the season. The hostess-owner offered to improvise a meal, but Caitlin was more tired than hungry.

An owl hooted as she carried her things from her car to her room. Looking up at the waxing crescent moon in the darkening sky, she remembered her mother's attempts to see the Hale-Bopp comet through a pair of binoculars she'd brought with her to Virginia for bird watching. The comet's closest approach to Earth had occurred shortly before Easter, but Caitlin hadn't taken an interest until after her outing with Kimo on Easter Sunday.

When he took her to lunch in Chinatown, Kimo told Caitlin about a doomsday cult in California. The bodies of thirty-nine members had been discovered several days earlier; they had given up their lives in the belief that a spacecraft was trailing the comet and would provide escape to the next level. Before their deaths, they had purchased alien abduction insurance—something even Kimo considered "wacky."

Caitlin understood the need to believe in and look forward to something, the importance of hope and belonging. The care and concern shown by Kimo and her mother had helped her survive the dark days that followed her hospitalization. But blind faith was a dangerous game, and beliefs often bore no relationship to truth—or reality.

Kimo said that faith and devotion were prominent features of the Piscean Age. The Aquarian Age would be characterized by logic and reason, and science would come into its own.

"You can see this in the clashes between science and religion—the Scopes Monkey Trial and the like. And it's not just disagreements about evolution and creation. New discoveries are being made all the time that deepen our understanding about the origins of life and the universe, but some people interpret the Bible literally and refuse to accept scientific evidence of human existence—or even the existence of the planet—prior to the dates given in the Bible."

The transition from one age to another takes hundreds of years, Kimo explained. He predicted that generations to come would have little use for outworn traditions; if something didn't make sense, it would be discarded.

"Little Spocklets," Caitlin had said.

Kimo laughed. "Spocklets; that's cute."

Already, Caitlin missed him. She fed the cat from the supplies he had given her and set up a makeshift litter box in the bathroom. Calling her mother would have to wait. Saying goodbye to her life in Washington had stirred enough emotions for one day.

After snacking on trail mix and eating the rest of the carrot cake, Caitlin turned off the light, welcoming a chance to close her eyes and rest. Before long, she felt a small weight land on the bed. Startled, she turned on the light.

"Let's get something start—straight right now. The bed is off-limits!"

She deposited the kitten onto the floor and then ran to the bathroom to wash her hands. Too late; her eyes itched, her throat felt scratchy, and she started sneezing.

"Oh, where's that . . . for-mu-la Kimo gave me?" she asked aloud, searching her overnight bag. She put on her coat and walked out to the car to find the small dropper bottle with the homeopathic remedy.

Why did I ever agree to this? she wondered as she returned to the room, sneezing.

After reading the directions on the label, she squeezed fifteen drops under her tongue and turned off the light.

After a while, the sneezing stopped and Caitlin began to drift toward sleep. She heard the kitten clawing at the drapes and covered her head with a pillow. When he jumped onto the bed again, Caitlin locked him in the bathroom. He scratched at the door and mewed piteously; she sneezed. Aware that no other guests were staying at the lodge that night, Caitlin let him whine. Eventually, they both quieted down and went to sleep.

The sky was gray when Caitlin began the second day of her journey. She looked at her reflection in the rearview mirror. Her eyes were puffy; her nose was red. The cat slept peacefully on the seat.

"Sure. Now ya sleep. You're lucky I didn't let—leave you back there!"

She yawned and took another dose of the homeopathic remedy. Why *was* she allergic to cats? Why did some people react violently to substances that were not harmful to others? She'd read about people with multiple personality disorder who suffered from allergies as one personality but not as another. Were allergies psychological as well as physical? She wished she understood more about the mind-body connection.

Back on the highway, Caitlin listened to CDs of her favorite music. The cat stretched and started scratching the upholstered seat. Caitlin dangled a toy Kimo had sent along.

"Kimo thicks—thinks I have an 'issue' with cats, doesn't he? He thinks every-thing has meaning."

Maybe some things just are. *Or have multiple meanings, depending on who is supplying the meaning.*

Like tastes and temperaments, values and priorities differed from person to person. But that didn't mean freedom of choice was an unlimited right; it didn't mean exploitation was okay. Some people's tastes and choices were taking up too much space and using too many resources, not leaving enough for others to even survive, Caitlin thought as she passed a slow-moving logging truck loaded with trees. Natural habitats were being destroyed at an alarming rate, but by the time anyone took the problem seriously, it might be too late to avert widespread disaster—which wouldn't benefit anyone.

What would be the point in ruling the world if everyone was sick and dying? Who would be impressed by your beauty or wealth or achievements? Who would supply your food and manage your empire? There wouldn't be anyone left to conquer and exploit—or talk to.

When the kitten tried jumping on top of the dashboard, Caitlin pulled over to the side of the road and put him back in his crate. She stopped at the nearest gas station, filled the tank and washed her hands, and continued on her way.

After another sleepless night in a budget motel, the weary pair finally arrived in the Ozarks. The kitten disliked being caged, and Caitlin had a headache from listening to its incessant mewing. She sounded out different tones to keep calm while she drove the final stretch of the journey. To her surprise, the exercise helped.

She turned into the parking lot at the general store, remembering the many times she and Bobby had ridden their bikes there to buy an ice cream treat. So many family vacations had been spent at the lake house; being back in the area, Caitlin couldn't help but be reminded of her childhood. She bought food for herself and the cat and then called her mother from the pay phone outside the store.

"Hi Mom," Caitlin said cheerfully when her mother answered. She was happy to hear a familiar voice.

"Caitlin honey! Where are you?"

Caitlin waited for the loud rumble of an old pickup truck to cease before she said, "I'm . . . al-most to the lake house."

"Really? You ought to come here for the holidays."

"Oh—I don't wanna think about going anywhere for a while," Caitlin said. She paused before adding, "Listen, if, uh, anyone's looking for me . . . you don't know anything. Okay?"

"Are you in some kind of trouble?"

"Nah, it's nothin' like that. I just . . . don't wanna be dust—*disturbed.*"

"You're not isolating yourself again, are you, dear? It's not healthy, you know."

Caitlin bared her teeth and formed her hand into a claw before sweetly responding. "I just want some time alone. Maybe I'll get inspired by the old piano." She knew the mention of the piano would placate her mother.

"Oh, it must be terribly out of tune. It hasn't been used in years."

"It's okay, Mom—I'll take car—care of it," Caitlin said, aware that her patience was diminishing along with the balance on her phone card.

"We were down there a few weeks ago, closing up the place for winter. Be sure and check the gauge on the propane tank. You may need to have it refilled if you plan to be there a while. The phone numbers are all there in the kitchen."

Legally, the lake house now belonged to Caitlin and Bobby, but for all practical purposes, Martha had taken possession.

"Okay. Is the key still . . . I guess I've forgotten."

"It's under the flower pot, right where it's always been. The phone service has been shut off, you know, so I won't be able to reach you—unless you want it turned on again."

"Nah, I don't sus—*ex*-pect I'll be making a lot of calls."

"All right, well—call now and then and let us know how you are."

"Okay," Caitlin said, ready to flee.

"Promise?"

Caitlin closed her eyes and tugged on her hair with her free hand. *Why must everything be so difficult?*

"Yes, I pom—prom-ise. I gotta go now. Bye."

Caitlin replaced the receiver and returned to the car, muttering, "I just didn't say *when* I'd call."

Several miles down the road, she reached the entrance to the Laughing Lake, as she'd named the small lake many years before. During the drive from Olathe, her father had told her and Bobby about the loughs in Ireland. Caitlin's seven-year-old mind was already confused by the inconsistent rules of the English language; she couldn't grasp why *gh* was silent in words like "night" yet sounded like *f* in words like "laugh." Then there was *ghost*, and now, here was yet another pronunciation for *lough*, which sounded almost like "lock"! How was she supposed to know which sound went with which words? The best solution to insoluble riddles, she'd decided, was to make up a joke or game.

No wonder I never learned a foreign language.

After Bobby told her about the Loch Ness Monster and convinced her that a dangerous creature lurked within the depths of the lake beside their vacation spot, Caitlin refused to go swimming—until Charlie transformed the beast into a benign Bessie who blew bubbles that created frothy foam at the water's edge and laughed so hard that waves rippled upon the surface of the lake. Bessie guarded a golden treasure and only little girls who were brave and smart had any chance of finding it. Caitlin became an excellent swimmer and, later, scuba diver because of her eagerness to find the treasure that, even then, she knew had less to do with Bessie and more to do with her father's approval.

She drove across the low-water bridge and followed the gravel road a short distance. Only a few summer homes had been built around the lake; each was surrounded by a large acreage. Caitlin had not been back since her move to Virginia. She felt a combination of joy, relief, and sorrow and said a short prayer of thanks for a safe journey.

The sun was setting as she parked the car in front of the small frame house. She found the key to the front door and carried the cat inside. Shivering, she turned on the baseboard heaters in each room. After unloading the car, she plugged in the refrigerator, put away the groceries, and filled a teakettle with tap water.

While the water heated on the old gas stove, Caitlin headed to the bathroom, eager to start filling the tub so she could take a hot bath in chlorine-free well water. The tub looked clean, but when Caitlin turned on the water, brown rusty sediment spewed from the faucet before the water turned clear. Not surprisingly, it was cold.

Caitlin growled and then hunted for a flashlight. She turned up the temperature on the water heater; she would take a hot shower in the morning.

Returning to the kitchen, she opened a box of herbal tea and dropped a tea bag into a mug. She fed a spoonful of vanilla yogurt to the cat before eating the rest herself. She filled the mug with steaming water and then hurried into the bedroom, closing the door to keep the heat in—and the cat out. After quickly undressing, she crawled into the bed where her father had slept. The hot tea warmed her. Burrowed under a down comforter, she soon fell into a deep and restful sleep.

✑ 83 ✑

Caitlin woke with the sun and started cleaning. She removed the sheets that were draped over the furniture and added them to her laundry basket. She started a list of things to do when she went to town for groceries; "find a Laundromat" was at the top.

Her father had never invested in a washer and dryer for the lake house. He took his laundry to a service in town until he injured his back; then, he hired Mrs. Peterson. She brought his clean laundry every week when she came to clean the house. She was the one who had found his lifeless body.

Caitlin found Bobby's guitar in the hall closet when she was looking for a broom. She carried the case to the living room and continued with her chores. She vacuumed the rugs, mopped the kitchen and bathroom floors, scoured the bathtub and sinks, and dusted the lamps. When she had finished, she sat down and listed everything she thought she would need to survive the winter.

She walked outside to check the gauge on the propane tank; it was low. The woodpile was low, too; she would need to stock up on logs to burn in the fireplace. When she went back inside, the reality of being completely alone suddenly registered, and she panicked.

She had never liked being alone. When she was hurting or bored or excited, she wanted to share her feelings with someone, not retreat. Solitary confinement was a hardship to endure until she could find something more interesting to do. *Maybe that's why I felt compassion toward those inmates in the Supermax units.* Her soul would wither and die if she were held captive like an animal.

Unpleasant things happened when she was by herself. When she was in first grade, she'd left her piano teacher's house after a lesson and started to walk home alone. Her mother usually walked with her, but on this particular day, she had to go to an appointment. Caitlin wasn't worried; she knew the way. But her teacher's neighbor kept a large, aggressive dog chained in the front yard. The dog always barked when Caitlin walked by; this time, he broke loose and knocked her to the ground. She screamed. Her teacher's husband, Mr. Davis, arrived home from work earlier than usual and came to her aid. He drove her home. She was unhurt, but shaken.

Who would she call now if she needed help? She didn't even have telephone service. She felt faint and anxious. What was she thinking, coming out here alone? Distressed, she walked outside without a coat. She wanted to run away, but where? This was the place she had run to.

"Stop!" she yelled.

The brisk air felt invigorating; the sunlight warmed her face. She looked around. No animals were attacking; no intruders threatened her safety. It was a bright, sunny day. She had shelter; she had food. What did she have to fear? The uncertainties of the future? *Bah!*

Mr. Davis had shown up at the right time; she had to trust that others would, too, whenever she needed help.

She went back inside, brewed a cup of tea, and then sat in her father's favorite chair in the living room. Feeling the warmth spread through her body as she drank the tea, she thought of Melody's visualization exercises and imagined the area around her body filling with light. She would change her habits of thought, she vowed, just as she had changed her eating habits. She would replace worries about distressing potentialities—the dreaded what-ifs—with positive imagery and discard useless, self-defeating thoughts the same way she had given away the possessions that had been cluttering her house. She needed to take stock of her life; that was why she had come here.

She gazed out the window at the fields and lake behind the house. The place held so many memories. Catching fireflies with Bobby. Outdoor barbecues. Swimming and canoeing. Family outings. Jayson.

The porch swing was where Jayson had proposed, finally, on the way to Virginia. Wanting everything to be proper and formal, he'd asked her father's permission. What father wouldn't approve of Jayson? He was handsome, intelligent, athletic, had a bright future ahead of him—and he loved Caitlin. She wondered if she would ever be loved that way again.

The cat jumped into her lap; Caitlin scratched behind his ears. "But Jayson never would have stuck by me through . . . all this," she said. "Not like—well, *you* know who." Her heart ached for the men she was missing.

She scooped up the cat and walked over to the old upright piano her father had moved from the house in Kansas City when he and Martha separated. *She's probably got a baby grand in her house in Overland Park.* This piano, Caitlin knew, was meant for her.

She had dusted the framed photos that lined the top of the piano, but she hadn't taken the time to really look at the pictures. She picked up a photo of her and Jayson, taken the day he proposed. They both looked so happy and hopeful. Caitlin turned the picture face down.

"Isn't it strange," she said, "you think you know someone, that you have your life fic—figured out. That you'll . . . have babies together—maybe even a cat."

She stroked the cat before releasing him and then pulled out the piano bench. "I don't even know . . . what Jayson's life is like now."

Caitlin sat on the bench and plunked out a tune as she sang, "Won-der what he's doin' now, since we said our last goodbyes." She liked what she heard and, suddenly, she had an idea for a song.

She found paper and a pencil in a drawer and drew a five-line musical staff for her first composition. Working first on the lyrics and then on the music, she jotted down ideas until darkness forced her to stop and turn on a light. She fixed a quick sandwich, fed the cat, and continued working until midnight, afraid she might lose the inspiration if she quit. When she was satisfied with the song, she went to bed.

The following morning, Caitlin looked over her shopping list. She planned to keep working on her song and made a note to look for lined paper so she could properly notate her composition. She also wanted to improve her guitar skills and would look for a how-to book. *And maybe a book about caring for a cat . . .*

She hadn't planned for a cat and had no idea how much food to give him or how much kitty litter he would need. Assuming they survived each other, this one would be an indoor-outdoor cat, Caitlin decided. She didn't want any prissy house cats claiming rights of dominion. He would learn to fend for himself in the wild—just as she would.

Away from restaurants and take-out food, Caitlin knew she would have no choice but to cook for herself. She planned to eat as many fresh foods as possible, with supplies of frozen foods to see her through stretches when she couldn't get out to shop. In an emergency, she could fall back on canned and boxed foods. After scanning the shelves in the pantry, she put the list in her purse, filled the cat's water dish, and headed for town.

The nearest town was fifteen miles in the opposite direction from the general store. The rural flavor of the area had changed little since Caitlin's last visit. "Bar-b-q" restaurants—shacks, really—were still popular. The seasonal businesses that catered to tourists were closed now. Several cars were parked outside the veterinary clinic, but local craftsmen and other year-round establishments had few customers. Long stretches of road separated clusters of houses, trailers, and A-frames.

Caitlin found a composition book at a music store and stopped by the library to register for a card so she could check out a few books. While she was there, she called a piano tuner who also taught music at the town's high school.

Next, she stocked up on groceries at the supermarket. Eyeing the frozen turkeys, she considered treating herself to Thanksgiving dinner at one of the resorts in the area. She quickly dismissed the idea; the thought of being surrounded by feasting families while she dined alone was too depressing.

This is ridiculous. I'm making myself miserable. Over what—an idea? Surely I can come up with a more cheerful idea!

She took a deep breath and thought of a title for her song while waiting in the checkout lane.

"Wonderin' Fool." That's me, all right!

On the drive back to the house, she thought about possible names for the cat. She hadn't yet accepted him as a permanent addition to her life. Like any other arranged match, they would have to see whether they could adjust to living together and whether they were compatible—or even liked each other. But if she kept him, continuing to shout "Here, kitty kitty" would be an insult to his pride and a poor reflection of her creative abilities.

He was a typical kitten, Caitlin guessed; he liked to climb up and hide under and get into whatever he could. He liked sitting in her lap and being stroked, and he liked playtime. Caitlin had thought about calling him Mercury because of the way he dashed about the house like a fleet-footed silver streak, but the toxic effects of quicksilver were too unpleasant to think about. The cat's green-gold eyes were similar in color to hers, but the popular notion of green eyes being linked to jealousy made that feature less attractive. She had tried calling him Lynx because of his tufted ears, but the name was difficult for her to pronounce, and she felt frustrated every time she said it.

She walked in the front door and called out to him. "Hey, Stinker, where are you?"

After setting the packages on the kitchen table, Caitlin walked through the house looking for the cat. She expected to find him curled up in a warm spot somewhere, not wet and shivering in a corner of the bathroom. The toilet paper was completely unrolled. Caitlin had left the toilet seat up. She'd have to remember to close the bathroom door in the future.

"You really are a stick—stinker, you know that?" She reached for a towel to wrap around him. "You're lucky I've acquired some . . . patience, or you'd be out in the cold about now."

She gave the cat a treat and then put away the groceries. When she checked the receipt from the grocery store, she noticed she had been charged twice for one item. *Should have been paying attention to what was going on and not thinking about song titles!*

She walked into the living room to watch the sunset. The pictures on top of the piano had been knocked over; the photo of her and Jayson had fallen to the floor. Caitlin stooped to pick it up. The glass was broken.

Probably time to put away reminders of him anyway.

She swept up the shards of glass before fixing dinner.

Caitlin was in the kitchen early the next morning, determined to discover the trick to making perfect round golden pancakes. Earlier attempts had yielded pale buckwheat discs and burned buttermilk discards. Following one of her mother's recipes, Caitlin combined flour, salt, and baking powder and set aside the large mixing bowl. She was cracking an egg when she heard a pint-sized sneeze. She turned to see the kitten in the bowl, nose and paws covered in white. He froze momentarily when he saw Caitlin approaching.

"Git! Get your paws . . . outta there!" She moved toward him, holding a spoon in her upraised hand.

The kitten leapt off the counter, upsetting the bowl in the process. The powdery mixture spilled onto the counter and the floor and formed a cloud of dust. Caitlin coughed and waved her hands to clear the air.

She watched the cat speed across the dining room table and then race toward the bedroom. She followed, still brandishing the spoon, but he had hidden under the bed, out of reach.

"Where are you—playing with the . . . dust bunnies?"

Caitlin got down on her hands and knees and stared into the cat's shining eyes as he peered out from his refuge.

"Lemme tell you about curi-os-ity and cats," she said. "And stay off my counters!"

She stood up, muttering "You're lucky I don't—" and realized she'd found his name. "Hmm. *Lucky.*"

Caitlin went back to the kitchen to clean up the mess—and made a bigger one. When she dumped what was left of the flour mixture into the sink and turned on the water, a thick, pasty mass clogged the drain.

"Uh-oh."

She turned on the garbage disposal, but it quickly went silent.

"Now what?"

She reached inside and scooped out as much of the paste as she could. Afraid to touch anything until she had a plan, she stood still and wondered what to do.

She couldn't call anyone, so she concentrated on remembering the household tips her mother had passed her way over the years. Baking soda and vinegar had worked when she was a teen and her hair clogged up the bathtub drain. Caitlin poured some of both into the sink and stepped back when the concoction started to foam. She turned on the hot water, but the sink quickly filled with sludge.

Jayson had installed a disposal at their townhouse in Alexandria. Wasn't there something like a reset button? Caitlin retrieved the flashlight from the bedroom—taking a moment to shine it on the cat—and returned to the kitchen.

The water had drained through the sludge; that was a good sign. Caitlin looked under the sink and pressed a red button on the bottom of the disposer. She stood up and flipped the switch. This time, it worked. Caitlin smiled. She'd found a solution.

She would keep Lucky the Cat, she decided as she measured more flour; she was glad for the company. Her allergy symptoms hadn't completely disappeared, but she could manage as long as she kept the house relatively free of cat hair and washed her hands frequently. Luck was only one of the many gifts Kimo had given her.

Caitlin made another batch of pancakes and brought a plate to the dining room. She laughed when she saw the trail of white paw prints dotted across the dark tablecloth.

She topped the pancakes with butter and maple syrup. The trick, she'd finally discovered, was heating the griddle to the right temperature and pouring the right amount of batter. Great cooking was an art, but the simple rules even she could learn.

She thought about the ripe apple Kimo had given her in Dublin. Finding the perfect moment—for anything—was an art, and one she intended to cultivate. By paying attention to nuances, by listening to her intuition, by following the impulses of her body, she would find the right moment to speak or act, to call her mother— or to flip a pancake.

The right timing is essential—in life and in music.

Looking at the paw prints on the tablecloth, Caitlin remembered the song idea she'd thought of during the drive from Virginia, about putting her life on pause by coming to the Ozarks. She jotted down some lyrics and tentatively titled the piece "Pause."

She planned to spend some time at the piano each day and also to continue practicing the guitar, but scheduling a specific time— the way she had practiced piano in childhood—soon became boring. Instead, Caitlin waited for inspiration. By heeding her inner rhythm, she worked and played when she felt called to a task, and soon everything in her day took on a musical quality.

After the piano was tuned, the music sounded sublime. As a warm-up exercise, Caitlin played the classical pieces she had learned in her youth. The long, tedious hours of practice, years before, had laid the foundation that made her newfound joy and spontaneity possible. Without an agenda, mistakes were impossible. Caitlin became one with the instrument; the music played her.

Sometimes she stumbled upon an original phrase and wrote down the notes for later use in a song. She recalled reading that Mozart received his compositions whole and simply transcribed them onto paper. Caitlin knew she was no genius. Pop music was her poetry.

Years before, she had played popular songs for her friends if they were near a piano. She'd sung in the high school choir. She'd danced to music on the radio and attended as many concerts as she could. She'd acquired an intuitive sense of structure that she drew upon now as she imagined how a composition would sound when different instruments were played together.

She sat at the piano, trying out various notes and chords, until the sound came close to the music she heard in her head. Later, she would look for an arranger to turn her rudimentary scribbles into a finished work that other musicians could follow, but the act of creating felt enlivening. Being consumed by music was a mysterious, even mystical, experience that, for those precious moments, overshadowed all else. Hours passed, during which she forgot the time, the season, her hunger, herself. Then, Lucky would come along and demand food or drop a toy at her feet and invite her to play. He forced her to pay attention to him. Giving herself over to a project was fine, but she still needed to attend to the necessities of daily life.

With practice, Caitlin mastered basic cooking skills and improved her yoga postures, taiji movements, and vocal quality. In the morning, she recorded her nightly adventures in a dream journal. In the evening, she read the books she'd brought from Virginia. When she finally turned out the light by the bed, she could no longer distract herself from her sorrows, and she cried. A heavy fog seemed to permeate the property; whether her father's depression lingered in the atmosphere or her own grief was responsible for her malaise, Caitlin couldn't say.

She relied on music to lift her spirits. Did music convey emotion, she wondered, such that a listener absorbs the mood of the composition, or was music a stimulus that evoked an emotional response that was subjective and varied from person to person?

Probably both, Caitlin thought; the effect was interactive. No two people would hear the same musical composition—or watch the same sunset—and experience it in exactly the same way.

"No one *makes* you angry or happy or disappointed," Kimo had said. "You allow yourself to experience those states. Remember: detachment."

Only she possessed the power to transform her experience, Caitlin realized; she needed only to claim it.

"Start from where you are," Kimo had often told her. "There's no time *but* the present."

Emotions surged and subsided as Caitlin recalled people and places from her past. It didn't seem to matter whether the memory was happy or sad; an overwhelming sense of loss engulfed her. Feeling utterly disconsolate, she sobbed uncontrollably. She was grateful for the opportunity to finally release long-held tensions and frozen feelings, but her isolation was so complete that, at times, she feared she would go mad or drown in a sea of tears. When the pain became unbearable, she had nary a friend to hold her hand or offer a comforting hug. But she did have Luck, and Caitlin grew to appreciate the cat's playful affection.

Occasionally, she felt blessed by small miracles of grace—a sense of peace and lightness came over her and brightened her mood. Sometimes, after being plunged into the black depths of despair, she was given the inspiration for a new composition. Refining it into a finished song, though, seemed like an endless process. She settled on the lyrics and experimented with the music, only to find melodies she liked better; then, she altered the lyrics to fit her new conception of the piece.

She thought about stereotypes of suffering artists and wondered if deep inner work was a prerequisite for experiencing the divine bliss spoken about by mystics. Did some universal law demand balance, so that the higher she wished to soar, the further into the abyss she must be willing to venture? When she felt pulled back into the shadows of the underworld, she comforted herself with the notion that she was mining for gold.

This too shall pass.

✍ 84 ✍

On Christmas morning, a foot of snow blanketed the ground. Caitlin sat by the window looking out at the gently falling flakes while water heated on the stove. She wished she knew even one friend to invite over. No one could reach her; she'd made sure of that.

I chose this, she reminded herself.

She drank a cup of a special holiday blend of tea, and then she finished decorating the small tree she had picked up at a lot near the general store. The tradition gave her solace, though she knew no presents would magically appear beneath the branches. She'd found a few ornaments stashed in a closet and hung them high on the tree; a toy mouse she'd bought for the cat to bat dangled from a low branch.

Thanksgiving had passed uneventfully; a sandwich made of smoked turkey from the deli was the extent of Caitlin's feasting. She promised herself she'd do better for Christmas and spent Christmas Eve day preparing Grandmother Clayton's sweet potato casserole topped with chopped pecans, green beans amandine, roasted chicken, and a hearty salad. She enjoyed a nice dinner, and the leftovers would last for several days.

She hadn't made a dessert, though, and thought longingly of the pies that were surely baking in her mother's oven. A year earlier, Martha had suggested that Ray join the two of them for Christmas in Virginia, but Caitlin had adamantly opposed the idea. Now, she was willing to consider visiting her mother and Ray in Overland Park. *Someday.*

She sang a Christmas carol to cheer herself and then carried in more logs for the fire. Sitting alone on the couch, she sobbed tears of loneliness, shame, and gratitude. Her refusal to accept Ray as her mother's partner had been a futile attempt to deny that her father was gone; she felt ashamed of her selfishness and immaturity. Her mother had never turned away from her; she'd always been there, ready to embrace her. Caitlin wished she could call her and pour out her heart. Now that they'd had some time apart, she felt ready to connect and share.

Totally on her own, with no one to blame or defy, she realized how much of her behavior had been a reaction to something or other. She had no one to fight against now—and no one to love. She had taken so much for granted all those years, when she thought time was unlimited, when she thought her parents would always be around and she yearned for independence. She had freedom now, and she cherished everyone who had ever been important to her. Through confronting her own mortality, she'd realized: *it's all good.*

She promised herself she'd write her mother regularly. She didn't want her to worry. Maybe she'd make a card for her; Martha would like that. Gazing out at the lake from the living room window, Caitlin decided to paint the view of the landscape. Maybe creating something beautiful would help transform her pain.

She went to the closet in the hall where she'd found Bobby's guitar, the box of ornaments, and an old quilt that had belonged to Grandmother Clayton. She had seen her father's golf clubs and her brother's old football jersey when she was looking for Christmas decorations, and she wondered what else her mother had left there. Standing on a chair, Caitlin found an old cigar box on a high shelf. It was filled with keepsakes—things that had, obviously, meant something to her father: his wedding ring, a hideous tie Caitlin had given him when she was nine, a photo of Charlie and Bobby showing off a good catch after a day of fishing. Caitlin brought the box to the family room and sat by the fire.

Among a stack of cards, she found an envelope addressed to her. Opening it, she saw the card her father had given her on her sixteenth birthday. Inside, he'd written: *"My little girl is all grown up! And what a beautiful young woman she has become. I remain, your biggest fan, Da."*

Caitlin gasped and stared at her father's handwriting. When she recovered from the shock, she searched the cigar box until she found it: a narrow white gift box. She removed the top. Resting on a cushion of cotton was the silver necklace that had belonged to Katie Moran. Overcome with emotion, Caitlin carefully removed the tarnished keepsake and held it in her hands. Acquainted now with Irish designs, she recognized the pattern as a Celtic knot, symbol of eternity. She'd received a Christmas gift after all.

She returned the cigar box to the shelf in the closet and set the necklace on the dining room table, where she could admire it. It would go well with the silver ring she'd bought while in Ireland, she thought. But first she wanted to have it professionally cleaned and appraised.

She thought of Kimo and wondered where he was spending the holidays. When they were at Paula's Table, he said he was thinking about visiting his parents. Then he started talking about the history and significance of the season and launched into one of his monologues.

The birth of the divine child was originally celebrated in the spring, he said; it wasn't until the fourth century, during the papacy of Julius, that the twenty-fifth of December was chosen, melding Pagan traditions with Christian beliefs.

"Most of the Christmas traditions people follow today have nothing to do with Jesus. They were adopted over the years as Christianity spread to different lands and local Pagan customs were absorbed. After the winter solstice—the longest night—the amount of daylight gradually increases. The rebirth of light signified the conquest of the forces of light over the forces of darkness."

The Roman Empire had long enjoyed festivals at the winter solstice, Kimo said. Roman emperors embraced the sun as a symbol of unconquered victory; they adopted radiant solar imagery for their coins and dedicated temples to the sun. The shift from Sun God to Son of God was a mere change in title for the common folk, who probably had little understanding of theological distinctions.

Caitlin went to the kitchen to prepare lunch. She would never again feel the magic of the Christmas holiday the way she had as a child. She'd lost the innocence of youth and had not yet attained the wisdom of old age. She thought of the story of the Magi—the three "wise men from the East" who had traveled by the stars to witness the divine birth. Kimo said they were probably Persian astrologers.

"Although, some people think they were from India, where wise men also read the stars, and where gifts of gold, frankincense, and myrrh were traditionally presented to new parents."

The parallels between the story of Jesus's birth and that of Lord Krishna added some credence to the idea, Kimo said.

"According to legend, Krishna's parents were imprisoned because of prophecies that a child of theirs would slay the evil King Kansa, Krishna's uncle. As in Matthew's story about Herod, Kansa ordered the murder of all newborns in his kingdom in a desperate attempt to try and prevent the prediction from coming true. Kansa killed each child his sister bore—until Krishna's birth, when the gates of the prison miraculously opened and the holy family was able to escape."

Matthew's Gospel stated that Jesus's birth occurred during the reign of King Herod, but no reports of a brutal massacre of infants by Herod had been recorded, Kimo said. According to Luke's Gospel, Jesus was supposedly born in the year of the Roman census, and that had taken place during the reign of Quirinius—after Herod's death. Kimo thought that both versions contained fictional embellishments.

"Bethlehem had to figure into the nativity story for those who expected the messianic prophecies to be fulfilled, and Matthew was writing for a Jewish audience."

Kimo said that an Ebionite version of the Gospel of Matthew had been written in Aramaic—and made no mention of a virgin birth.

"In the ancient world, oracles and seers looked for signs and omens of impending doom or likelihood of success when practicing the art of divination. People believed that prophets delivered messages from on high, so warnings were taken seriously. In Egypt, the prophecy predicted that Isis would conceive a divine child who would one day defeat Set—that was why Set murdered Osiris, in an

effort to prevent the conception. And, of course, in the Old
Testament story, Pharaoh ordered the death of all newborn males
after Moses was born," Kimo said. "The coming of an enlightened
being threatens the established order and shakes up the prevailing
power structure. The birth heralds a new age and signals the end of
the old regime. The reigning authorities usually don't surrender
without a fight."

Caitlin remembered her response to Kimo that night, before
she'd drunk two glasses of wine: "Okay, I get that a lot of what
Christians believe is extraneous to the real message Jesus taught.
Nonetheless, his story has influenced countless lives for two thousand years."

"The question is: could the story have had that effect if there
never was such a character in 'real life'?"

"Maybe. Christian beliefs vary widely."

"Exactly," Kimo said. "Nobody knows who Jesus really was. To
the Jews, he was a magician and sorcerer. To the Gnostics, he was an
enlightened master. The synoptic Gospels describe him as a healer
and miracle worker. For Matthew, especially, he was the fulfillment
of the prophecies. For John, he was the incarnation of the *Logos*. The
Mandæans considered Isu, or Jesus, a false prophet. Jesus was either
unknown to historians of his time or too insignificant to mention.
The proponents of the Christian religion, centuries later, are the
ones who made him into a mythological figure."

Caitlin wondered what went on in Kimo's head and, even more,
in his heart. He'd shared so much of his knowledge and understanding, and yet, she often felt he was holding something back. Maybe
her yearning was for something that no other person could give her;
maybe it was divine discontent.

She had asked Kimo what he believed about the historical Jesus
while they waited for their server to bring the bill. "So do you think
he really lived?"

"I don't think the Jesus that modern Christians worship ever
existed, but there were undoubtedly charismatic teachers and holy
men who were healers and prophets. I think the gospels were
intended as teaching tools. If you take out all the contrived elements

that were meant to prove a point—whether it was creating legitimacy in the Roman Empire, or attracting new converts from Judaism and from Pagan cults, or explaining why *the* Son of God would suffer such atrocities—you're left with teachings about how to live. I think the story of what happened to Jesus is representative of the stages of initiation. And I think there is a Spirit that we can each contact—call it 'Christ' if you will. I'm all for the message in the teachings, I just don't go along with the 'Jesus died for your sins' routine."

"Clearly, some people were convinced of the truth of the tales. Enough to be willing to die as martyrs," Caitlin had said.

"That's still true of suicide bombers and followers of other religions who are convinced they'll go straight to Paradise as a result of their misguided acts. Belief is a powerful force, and people who feel desperate and oppressed are often driven to extreme behavior."

"True," Caitlin conceded.

"At the start of the Christian era, mystics and schools of learning had already existed for centuries. The Jesus story spoke to the people of the time—and still speaks to many. Maybe he was a gifted healer who traveled about like the Egyptian Therapeutæ. His emphasis on moral teachings was characteristic of Buddhism. Maybe he was a Jewish rebel who threatened to upset the status quo and was, in fact, crucified by the Romans. Maybe he was a mystic who saw the universal truths among the sacred traditions of different cultures and sought to bring peace and understanding, a ray of hope, to the people, who were so often excluded from teachings that were jealously guarded by the priests in power. Plato and Pythagoras were said to have been conceived immaculately; maybe Jesus was an advanced soul and his stature was expressed in the way people of that time and place honored exceptional people—by granting them divine status and an impressive human pedigree linking them to prominent figures from the past. Alexander the Great, for example, supposedly traced his lineage back to the god-man Heracles."

Caitlin sat by the window awhile after she finished eating her lunch. She believed in a Supreme Being, but she wasn't sure what to believe about the teachings of Christianity. Jesus left no writings of his own, and no original copies of any of the gospels had survived.

Perhaps the true story would remain a mystery, or perhaps, in time, new information would be revealed.

Stories about enlightened beings who possess special powers had persisted into the modern era. The idea that these stories describe a journey that any of us can take—a spiritual journey that is not dependent upon religion—was intriguing to Caitlin. Did the process of enlightenment upset 'the established order' of ordinary life and ego control? Were similar truths revealed in stories that arose during different times, in different places?

Kimo seemed to think so. He had shown her the power and importance of myth; her new understanding helped ease the transition to a new way of looking at the world and at religion. Even if the Jesus story was only a myth, the divine Spirit waited to be birthed in each human heart. *Someone* had taught that the kingdom of God was to be found within; others had spread the teaching. Greek sages, too, advised the seeker to "know thyself." The way of the world had changed radically in two thousand years; the way to God had not.

But why did the Church attempt to prevent this gnosis? How pure were its aims, as evidenced by its behavior over centuries? What better place for pernicious motives to hide than behind a cloak of piety? Who dared question men of the priestly caste—even when their actions were motivated by greed or lust for power, even when their harsh punishments, ostensibly designed to save sinners from damnation, were punitive and inhumane? Where were the qualities like compassion, tolerance, acceptance and brotherly love that adherents of the faith were supposed to cultivate and practice?

Kimo said the idea of a divine trinity was not new; Krishna was an incarnation of Vishnu, the second aspect of the Hindu trinity.

"The Hindus have a whole system of spiritual cycles marked out," he'd said. "They expect periodic incarnations of exceptional beings that light the way for the coming age. You could say that Jesus was the avatar of the Piscean Age. But now we're entering the Aquarian Age. There will be a new expression, a new dispensation that shows humanity the next stage of our spiritual evolution. For those with eyes to see and ears to hear."

Lucky jumped into Caitlin's lap and purred with appreciation when she petted him. Then, he curled into a compact ball and fell asleep. Caitlin hated to disturb him, but darkness was encroaching and she needed to add logs to the fire.

As the new millennium approached, she was comforted to think the world wasn't ending—as some of the doomsday prophecies foretold—only the age. What changes would the advent of the Aquarian Age introduce? Could the world look forward to a more inclusive era, or would the ages-old power struggles simply continue in a new guise?

Thank God for light, Caitlin thought as she warmed her hands by the fire. *It brightens even the darkest nights.*

"Yes, you do too, fur-ball," she told Lucky when he rubbed against her legs.

✑ 85 ✑

Caitlin looked at the frozen lake outside her back door and wondered who decided to begin the calendar year in the dead of winter. *Kimo would probably know the answer,* she thought with a smile. He'd crawled under her skin; his ideas echoed in her mind.

"In agrarian cultures, the new year began with the spring equinox," she imagined him saying.

Melody said that the spring equinox marks the start of the astrological year. The first sign of the zodiac, Aries, represents the fiery surge that's necessary for new life to burst forth.

"That's why we Arians are so headstrong," she'd told Caitlin.

Dynamic and impatient, people born in the sign of the ram were thought to be pioneers. Self-starters and initiators, they were supposedly good at forging new paths.

"Not like Capricornian goats, who are plodding and methodical," Melody said with some disdain.

"And Leo?" Caitlin had asked.

"Another fire sign. That's why you and I get along so well. The same element is always compatible with its own kind. It's a harmonious flow of energy called a *trine.*"

Caitlin thought that Melody tossed around definitive words like "always" and "certainly" a little too casually. She found more gray areas to ponder and questioned how a system like astrology could possibly have meaning. She learned from Melody that the zodiac is much more comprehensive than the brief descriptions of sun signs listed in the newspaper.

"A complete astrological chart would tell you where Jupiter and Venus and all the other planets were located at the moment of your birth," Melody said.

Caitlin understood that the moon influences the earth's tides and women's cycles. But how could anyone say with certainty that the motions of Mercury or Uranus have a recognizable influence upon events and lives on earth? Still, Caitlin realized that her lack of knowledge didn't mean something wasn't knowable; it just meant *she* didn't know it.

She wondered if Melody was settled into her new life in Santa Fe, the place she'd most wanted to be. Melody said the community of kindred spirits there helped her keep sight of her life's purpose. When she was away too long, she became self-indulgent and lax in her practice. Then, she scattered her abundant energies.

Caitlin relaxed with a cup of hot cocoa, wishing she could find that kind of place—a place where she could pursue her dreams. Not so long ago, she had considered herself an urban yuppie, but now her only home was here, at the lake.

Wondering what opportunities the new year would bring, she thought about her travels during 1997. From a lush tropical island to the arid desert, from metropolitan Washington to rural Missouri—location didn't seem to matter much; she was mostly left alone with her thoughts. Each place had offered a gift and a challenge; each step of her journey was part of a transformation that was gradually unfolding. Caitlin had no idea where her next move would take her, and thinking about the state of her life only made her anxious.

She'd been good at making things happen when she knew what needed to be done. She'd been accepted into the schools she'd wanted to attend; she'd won the lead role in a school play; she'd found her way into the Office of Special Projects. Without a plan, she felt lost. But she was learning to listen and observe and follow rather than forcing everyone to comply with her agenda, to be guided by her body's rhythms and needs rather than automatically following her mind's programming about when she should eat and sleep or how she should structure her days. This new way felt vague and undefined, like listening to a whisper. Caitlin wasn't quite sure she was hearing it right—or hearing it at all.

Her career had dominated her life for years. She was free now to embrace new ambitions. What did she have the energy, interest, passion, and aptitude for? Did she need to develop a skill, or find new ways to use her training? What she sought seemed intangible—a feeling quality more than a concrete goal; that made it harder to know where to look, how to create the life she wanted.

Being at the lake, Caitlin felt closer to her youth. She thought about the friends she'd known—in high school, in college, in law school; they'd all fallen away. She didn't miss anyone in particular, but she missed being part of a team and hoped the next phase of her journey would bring new people and projects into her life. She wrote her mother regularly, as she had done during the few summers that she'd gone away to camp. Her journal had become her best friend; passages about her frustration and longing were interspersed with ideas for songs she wanted to write.

She went to the easel to resume her painting of the lake. She worked on it at the same time each day so the lighting would be consistent. She hoped that by the time the painting was finished, she would have answers to some of her questions about the direction her life was headed.

She remembered Melody speaking about the importance of intention. Painting, journaling, recording her dreams, playing guitar and piano—even walking and cooking and eating—became meditative acts when they were done with intention and awareness, Caitlin had found. She didn't need to sit in a special position with her hands held a particular way for answers to be revealed; she just needed to listen and respond. She knew she would stay at the lake until she felt inspired to leave. Drifting aimlessly would be pointless, the opposite extreme of being too goal-oriented.

Nights were hard now—cold and long. Caitlin wrestled with her demons: loneliness and fear, sorrow and regret. Depression lay outside her door like a predator ready to pounce at the first sign of weakness and vulnerability. The roots of beliefs and expectations ran deep, and painful memories crept into the edges of her awareness. Music gave her solace, and she embraced it like a life preserver.

The fourth day of January marked the anniversary of her father's death. The polished silver necklace, which the jeweler in town guessed must have been crafted in the nineteenth century, gleamed against Caitlin's black sweater. She was grateful that her parents had kept the heirloom safe for her, though she hoped her father hadn't been offended by her lack of interest when she was young. She would cherish the gift for the rest of her life.

Being in her father's space was both comforting and troubling. Caitlin put aside thoughts about the manner of his death, but she couldn't avoid thinking about death. She lit a candle and placed it on the dinner table. In the grand scheme of the cosmos, a lifetime was like a flash of light, a moment of time in which each one of us appeared—for days or months or years—and then departed.

When she'd finished eating, Caitlin blew out the candle. Even if her spirit continued to live on as conscious awareness, her identity as she knew it would not.

She remembered her father's remark: "It's in the blood." The Bible said the sins of the father would be visited upon the generations that followed. Kimo had talked about family karma. But surely good things were also passed along from one generation to the next. Caitlin had studied law like her grandfather. Like her mother, she played the piano. She was adventurous and inquisitive like her father. Grandmother Clayton had liked to sing. Had she inherited any healing or psychic abilities from Katie Moran? Caitlin wondered.

She gazed at her reflection in a mirror, searching her face for her father's features. Her build was similar to Martha's, but her hair color probably came from the Roses, she thought. Who had green eyes? Her mother's eyes were hazel; her father's, blue. Bobby's eyes were also blue. Caitlin's eyes seemed to be all hers.

How much of life was predetermined by heredity or fate or divine design? Did anyone really have free choice, or did each individual's needs and circumstances impel him toward a particular course that would ensure fulfillment of his destiny? Did some people have more choice than others? Could reincarnation be a real phenomenon—the cycle of rebirth that spiritual adepts attempted to transcend?

Jesus said that his disciples would know the truth, and the truth would make them free. Caitlin wondered what following in the steps of an enlightened master would look like today. How would her life be different if she made the pursuit of higher truth her top priority? What did she have to lose?

She understood now what Satchidananda had meant when she said, "Truth is that which remains when illusions fall away." Maybe some people preferred to stay stuck in denial, but Caitlin wanted to know the truth, even when facing it was painful. For if a thing were false, what good could come from it? And if it were true, how could it be wrong?

Caitlin was determined to find what was truly hers and keep it sacred. The rest, she would relinquish. Whenever she felt the desire to grab hold of something that seemed to be slipping away, she would remind herself of her new mantra: *Let the truth guide my way and all that is false fall away.*

If something—or someone—was never really hers, how could she lose it? Her father would always be her father—always a part of her, always alive in her memory.

She thought again about her awareness when she awoke from the coma and her conversations with Kimo. *There's no such thing as death.*

✐ 86 ✐

February 14 is just another date on the calendar, Caitlin told herself, but the Eagles' song "Wasted Time" played inside her head. Had she wasted time in the wrong relationships?

The fear that she would be alone for the rest of her life had been especially acute when she first moved into the townhouse. After living with Jayson for almost three years, Caitlin felt disoriented. They'd been a pair for so long, she felt incomplete on her own, as if she'd left behind some essential part of herself.

She again felt disoriented, but the familiar surroundings helped ground her. She reminded herself how far she had come. She was grateful to be alive—and independent once more. She hoped the time for being with a partner would come around again, but that wasn't likely to happen when the only people she spoke to were in the checkout lane of the grocery store. She'd never dreamed she would be over thirty and unmarried. All those catchy pop songs of her girlhood had promoted a vision of marriage as the only road to happiness and fulfillment. A new composition gave voice to her sadness about broken dreams. Caitlin titled it "Veil of Illusion."

She no longer blamed herself for that fateful Valentine's night with Neil. She'd sought refuge that evening from the dawning awareness that her perfect life with Jayson had cracks in its foundation, fundamental flaws they would never be able to fix. Intuitively, she knew he was with someone else; she hadn't wanted to believe it. She'd hoped that the affair would blow over like March winds, and that spring would find them happy together again. When Jayson left her alone on Valentine's Day, Caitlin could no longer deny the obvious, and facing the truth was painful. She found comfort where she could.

Blaming Jayson or the paralegal or Neil, or even herself, was pointless. What good would come from ruminating over the sequence of events that had transpired? That was the particular way it all fell apart, but it could have happened another way; the result would have been the same. By spring, circumstances forced Caitlin to tell Jayson about Neil. Even if she could have forgiven him, he clearly wasn't going to forgive her. At the beginning of July, she moved out. The last thing she saw as she drove away was the flag he'd hung outside for Independence Day.

Trying to control everything—or, perhaps, *anything*—would also be a waste of time. Acceptance required acknowledging the truth about a situation, seeing things and people as they really were and not as she wanted them to be. Caitlin couldn't make someone love her or treat her well; she couldn't convince anyone to think or feel as she did. Her thoughts and actions were her responsibility, and that was enough; she had to let go of the rest. If she had done the best she could, she would have no regrets. Her mistakes were what plagued her.

She remembered something Kimo had said the night before she left Arlington. "Remember the three monkeys—see no evil, hear no evil, speak no evil? What you focus on becomes your reality. If you look for love, you will find it. If you look for danger, you'll find that. If I tell you not to worry about getting robbed, what are you going to think about? I've put the idea of robbery into your head by calling your attention to it. Maybe you weren't worried about it before, but you are now. Put your attention on what you want to create, not on what you don't want."

"Isn't that denial?" Caitlin had asked.

"I'm not suggesting you ignore unpleasant facts," Kimo said. "Remember the Serenity Prayer from Alcoholics Anonymous: 'Grant me serenity to accept the things I cannot change, courage to change the things I can—'"

"And wisdom, to know the difference."

"If it's in your power to change something, do it! Fungus and parasites and mosquitoes thrive under certain conditions. In order to eradicate the pests, it's necessary to clean up the environment.

That's true with our internal environments as well—our diets and our thoughts contribute to the overall health or dis-ease of our bodies and minds. Constantly dwelling on the negative will make you miserable."

Caitlin understood that when she was angry about an injustice in the world or believed she'd been wronged, she was the one who was experiencing negativity and anger. Her anger wouldn't change the world or affect the person who had wronged her—but it would eat away at her. If the response became habitual, the negativity would begin to affect her physical well-being.

The alternative was to affirmatively choose happiness. She'd often wondered why Thomas Jefferson had described our natural right as the *pursuit* of happiness.

Happiness is a choice. It's not a state we reach and can stay in forever, not without diligence.

Relationships were that way, too. Willingness—to trust, to forgive, to let go of the past—was essential to keeping a relationship alive and healthy. Otherwise, resentments and misunderstandings piled up and meaningful communication ceased.

Love is never wasted. Just because the relationship with Jayson hadn't worked out didn't mean the love hadn't been real.

Lying in bed the following morning, Caitlin felt a sharp pain in her neck when she tried to lift her head off the pillow. She must have strained her neck when she carried wood inside the previous evening, she thought.

Pain shot through her when she attempted to get out of bed and then, panic. No one would come; she was alone, far from help. Only her mother knew where she was. Would she die there? Had she isolated herself too much?

She winced when she tried again to move her head. Her body had suffered so much injury and trauma already—she *must* be more careful. She inhaled deeply and tried to relax, drawing on the different tools she had learned. She visualized a warm glow surrounding her body.

I have the ability to heal myself. I can overcome any challenge.

A doubting inner voice objected, telling her she was foolish to believe such nonsense, and she started to cry. Pushing aside the thought, she began to softly hum and tone soothing sounds.

Lucky watched patiently, waiting for her to get up and feed him. Then he scratched at the bedpost, an activity he knew was forbidden.

"You're not help-ing!" Caitlin yelled.

Maybe, in cat psychology, he thought provoking her would elicit the desired response. Or maybe he sensed she wasn't in any position to chastise him.

Lucky jumped onto the bed and sniffed around Caitlin's face, as if to ask, "You okay?"

After what seemed like an hour, she was able to slide off the bed and maneuver her body into a standing position. She inched her way to the kitchen and opened a can of cat food. She couldn't bend over, so she carefully lowered herself to the floor, hanging onto the refrigerator for support, and set the can near Lucky's food dish. Then, she crawled into the living room and stretched out on the yoga mat.

Bringing her awareness to her breath, Caitlin focused on breathing in relaxation and releasing tension as she exhaled. Inhaling deeply was difficult. She was afraid of making a wrong move, of stepping out of bounds—of *breathing*. Why?

She remembered how stifled she'd felt around her mother and the Claytons, as if every move she made was wrong and likely to bring reproof. Eventually, she'd given up—she stopped trying to engage when she was around them. Shutting down had been the path of least resistance. Maybe that was what they'd wanted all along. Caitlin learned early that her natural exuberance made some people uncomfortable.

Order and control must be maintained.

Feeling anger rising from deep within her, Caitlin sounded a loud tone to move the energy out of her body. She refused to continue inhibiting her natural impulses. People were idiosyncratic; the same gesture or behavior would offend one person and not another. She couldn't spend her life anticipating how people would react to something she did or said. She intended to fully *live*, according to her own nature.

As the pain in her neck eased, she moved slowly and avoided sudden movements. She stretched and crawled and roared, and alternated tensing and relaxing the various muscle groups throughout her body. Finally, she stood upright. She soaked in a hot tub and then gently rubbed massage oil over her body. As the day progressed, the tension subsided.

By evening, Caitlin had nearly forgotten about the pain. She picked up a romance novel she found lying on a bookshelf and fell asleep by the crackling fire. The next morning, she felt fine.

❧ 87 ❧

By late February, Caitlin was restless for change. The gloomy days were wearing on her, and she longed for human companionship. She thought a lot about where she wanted to go next and wondered if she could pursue a career in music. She felt passionate about improving her craft and, brimming with ideas and inspiration, she was eager to step out into the world and see what opportunities awaited her.

She examined the calluses that had formed on her fingers since she'd started playing the guitar. *The days of long, polished fingernails are gone for good!*

The trade-off *was* "for good." Music had given her so much in return for the long hours she had spent practicing and composing; through music, she gave expression to the deepest longings of her soul. She never felt alone when she was playing an instrument or singing a song. Her cares and worries—her sense of herself as separate—disappeared; she melted into the music.

If she could do anything with her life, what would she choose to do? she wondered as she studied her painting of the lake. She needed to finish it before the trees started blooming and the look of the landscape changed.

Like painting, music had been a hobby, a creative outlet that she enjoyed. Recording a song or two in a small independent studio seemed like a realistic goal. She wanted a finished product to claim as her own, a recording she felt proud of and could share with grandchildren someday. She also wanted a demo of her songs.

But where would she find a studio? She recalled a family outing to a hillbilly jamboree in Branson when she was ten. The town wasn't far; she might find a recording studio there, and musicians to join her in a session. Or, she could take a chance and go to Los Angeles. She never did see much of the city during her stay with Sam, and the music scene in L.A. would be much more vibrant and fresh than the family-oriented entertainment and variety shows that had made Branson famous.

Caitlin dabbed at the painting one last time. Satisfied, she cleaned her brushes and packed up her paints.

The first Monday in March, Caitlin took the painting to a frame shop in town. The clerk promised to have it ready by the end of the week.

At the Wash-o-matic, Caitlin separated her laundry into white, colored, and delicate items. After inserting her coins into the slots of the machines, she looked for ways to pass the time.

She called her mother from a pay phone outside. No one answered. Caitlin left a sweet message on the answering machine, fulfilling her promise to call. As she spoke, she realized her speech had returned to normal.

Elated, she dialed Kimo's number. She had written to him several times since arriving at the lake house, and she'd given him Martha's address in case he wanted to write back. He hadn't. She wasn't surprised; she knew he was busy with school. She still missed him, and she was eager to talk to him.

"I was just on my way out," Kimo said when he answered. "Thanks for your letters, by the way. I appreciate knowing you're okay—even if you won't tell me where you are."

"It's not that I don't trust you," Caitlin said. "I'll be leaving here soon anyway. I promise I'll let you know where I go next. How are you?"

"Good. The clinic keeps me busy. I'm glad to be applying what I know, but I'm itching to be out on my own."

"I'm really impressed with what you've accomplished, Kimo," Caitlin said.

"That means a lot, coming from you," he said. "Hey—you sound terrific!"

"Isn't it great? I've been singing a lot—I guess that helped! I was thinking of calling Melody. Do you have her number? I'd like her to hear for herself."

"Yeah, sure. Hang on."

While she waited, Caitlin watched nearby pedestrians. A child with Down's syndrome walked past her, accompanied by an adult. Caitlin thought of Marvin and wondered how he and Jackie were faring. Kimo returned to the phone with Melody's number.

"I'm ready," Caitlin said. She wrote the number in a small notebook she carried in her purse. "Thanks, Kimo. I'll let you know when I land somewhere. Good luck finishing your program."

"It's good to hear from you," Kimo said. "Call anytime."

Caitlin dialed Melody's number and left a message. "I'm gonna go for it, Mel! I've been writing some of my own songs. I think they're pretty good. I'm going to L.A. in a few weeks and Santa Fe is on the way. Well, it could be, anyway. If you've got room, I'd love to see you. Oh, and Mel—you were right. Music was just what I needed!"

Caitlin walked to Main Street and ate a late lunch at the town diner. She saved some bread and tossed it to the ducks in the park. While her clothes were drying, she shopped for groceries at the supermarket. After folding her clean clothes, she headed back to the house to begin preparing for her departure.

The following Sunday, Caitlin was in the bedroom packing her suitcases when she heard a knock at the front door. She looked out the window and saw a white Volvo sedan parked near her wagon. *What's she doing here?*

"Surprise!" Martha said when Caitlin opened the door. She handed Caitlin a potted plant. "It's an Easter lily."

"I—I can see that. Hello, Mother."

"Hello, dear," Martha said, and kissed Caitlin's cheek. She entered the house. "Ray and I were down at Bella Vista for a golf weekend with a couple from the club."

That would be the country club. Martha had entered a whole new social scene since she married Ray. *It suits her,* Caitlin thought, scrutinizing her mother's sporty attire.

Martha looked down when she felt Lucky's tail sweeping against her slacks. "Oh, look—a kitten!" She picked him up but he squirmed so she set him free.

"I won't stay long," Martha said. "But I couldn't be so close by without seeing you."

Bella Vista, Arkansas, must be at least two hours away, Caitlin thought.

Martha noticed the partially packed bags, boxes, and suitcases Caitlin had set near the front door and asked, "Where are you off to now?"

"L.A.," Caitlin said. She brought the lily to the kitchen and set it on the table by the window, where it would get some light. Then, she added water to the kettle, turned on the gas burner, and struck a match.

"My, you are the restless one!" Martha said. She stood in the doorway to the kitchen, looking around. "This old house has held up pretty well, hasn't it?"

"Would you like some tea?" Caitlin asked as she reached for a teacup. "I also have juice." She waited for her mother's reply before selecting another cup.

"Whatever you're having."

Martha wandered over to the piano, where Caitlin had been working on one of her compositions. "How's the music coming?"

"Fine."

"Would you play something for me?"

Caitlin emerged from the kitchen. "Oh, no, I'd really rather not."

She hated to disappoint her mother and quickly added, "Someday. I can show you the painting I just finished. I had it framed."

Caitlin walked into the dining room, picked up the painting, and tore off the brown paper the clerk had wrapped around it.

Martha hardly glanced at it before looking away. "Kind of a bleak scene, isn't it?"

The teakettle whistled; Caitlin set the painting on the floor, leaning it against the wall where she intended to hang it. "It was winter," she said, and went back to the kitchen.

"I just meant it's not bright and cheery like the flowers you were painting before."

Caitlin carried a tray with a ceramic teapot, two cups, and a plate of snickerdoodle cookies she had baked as a snack for her upcoming trip. "I mailed you a card I made. You'll like that better."

They agreed the weather was warm enough to sit outside on the porch.

"We had some good summers here, the four of us," Martha said, admiring the view.

"Yeah, the four of us and the aunts and uncles and cousins and . . ."

"Yes! Those were the best times, when the whole family was here. Less . . . tension."

Caitlin sipped her tea. "Are you angry at Daddy?"

Martha set her cup on the glass tabletop. "No! Of course not. He was as much a victim as I was," she said. "There were good parts too, like you and Bobby."

"I'm angry," Caitlin said.

She wished her father had reached out to her before completely giving up on his life. Not because she thought she could have saved him. Perhaps she would have failed to pick up on his despair; then she would have been left with one more thing to feel guilty about. But she would have liked the chance to tell him what he meant to her, how much she would miss him. Maybe the overdose really was accidental. He was a writer, yet he hadn't written any final words. He hadn't said goodbye. Maybe that was why she was still grieving— because he'd left without telling her goodbye, without telling her what she meant to him.

"Now, Caitlin, don't go switching from being angry at me to being angry at him," Martha said. "It's a lot harder to argue with a ghost."

"Don't tell me how to feel!"

Caitlin rested her head in her hands. She didn't mean to sound hostile, but her mother had shown up without warning—or invitation. Caitlin was happy to see her, but she was not willing to fall back into old patterns of relating. She and her mother needed to find a more satisfying and genuine way of communicating.

After a long pause, Martha picked up her teacup. "I honestly don't know how to talk to you, Caitlin."

"Don't per-*preach*. Just let me be me." She sighed. Her frustration was already affecting her speech.

"Fair enough. I'll try and do better. I'm sure you'll remind me when I mess up."

"And I'll try to bite my tongue instead of you."

Caitlin knew she had to stop overreacting and give her mother a chance. She'd driven several hours out of her way for a brief visit; Caitlin could at least be cordial.

"I don't understand you," Martha said. "But I want my daughter back."

"I want that too," Caitlin said. The loss of her father made her long for a better relationship with her mother. But honesty was essential, and respect had to be reciprocal.

Martha glanced at her watch. "Well, I better get back," she said as she stood up. "Ray and I have a dinner engagement. Drop a line and let us know how you are. *Where* you are!" Catching herself, she added, "When you're ready," and patted Caitlin's cheek.

"I will."

Caitlin walked outside with Martha and gave her a warm hug.

"You look wonderful, by the way," Martha said. She smiled and added, "You sound good, too."

Caitlin nodded. "Thanks."

Lucky slipped out through the open door and sat on the pavement, captivated by the movements of birds and squirrels. Caitlin waved as her mother drove away. Feeling a chill, she returned to the house. She left the door ajar so Lucky could wander back inside. When he was ready.

∽ 88 ∽

Caitlin awoke to the sound of birds chirping. During her time at the lake house, she had become more attuned to noises and sounds that she would have ignored in the past, when she was bombarded on a daily basis with telephones and copy machines and street construction and lawn mowers and traffic. Now, she noticed the occasional sound of snow plows clearing the road after a winter storm, the hum of the refrigerator, Lucky's purring, the wind howling in the night, the gentle patter of rain on the roof, and more. Bird calls, children playing in the park in town, wind rustling a pile of leaves, logs crackling in the fireplace—these sounds were alive and interesting. The mechanized sounds of machinery, the din of traffic, and the annoying beeping of electronic gadgets grated on her nerves. She wondered if she could ever again live in an urban environment.

Like L.A.

Looking out through the kitchen window, Caitlin saw a cardinal perched on a tree branch. She'd been setting out birdseed, but her supply was running low.

She let the cat out for his morning stroll and cooked oatmeal with raisins and walnuts. She was about to sit down to eat when she heard scratching at the front door.

Caitlin opened the door and saw a dead squirrel on the doormat— and a proud cat awaiting her praise. Her stomach turned at the sight of the lifeless body. She patted Lucky on the head while wondering how she could dispose of the rodent.

Rural living has its challenges too.

After several unsettling attempts to go near the carcass, Caitlin found some rope and tied it to a large binder clip. She attached the clip to the doormat and pulled it a good distance away from the house. Maybe feeding the birds wasn't such a good idea; the poor creatures might end up as playthings for her stealthy little hunter.

Believing that she would soon be on her way, she had cleaned out the fireplace and had only bought enough food to last a few days. But a storm moved in, and the power went out. The lights flickered a few times, giving Caitlin ample time to get her supplies ready—candles, flashlights, and a small propane grill. She pulled a down sleeping bag and air mattress out of the hall closet and fixed up a bed by the fireplace, grateful that no ice storms had interrupted service during the winter, when temperatures had dipped into the single digits.

She lit the candle she had saved from the new moon ceremony. She'd spent the winter on an inner journey, exploring the dark caverns of her psyche. Now, the first buds of spring were appearing on the trees. Persephone was ready to emerge from her sojourn in the underworld and begin a new cycle. Caitlin was eager to see which of the seeds that had been germinating were ready to sprout in her life.

She carried the candle into the dining room, singing "Light of the World" from *Godspell*, the Off-Broadway musical based on the Gospel of Matthew. Staring into the flame, she recalled the Greek myth about Icarus, who fashioned wings of wax that melted when he ignored his father's warnings and flew too close to the sun. Caitlin's aspirations were a little less ambitious; she would find out whether or not they were attainable. But she had to at least try. After all, wings were made for flying!

She gazed at the candle until the flame burned out and then walked down to the road to see if any trees had been knocked down by the storm. Branches lay scattered about, and the slab bridge was submerged. Watching the fast-moving water, Caitlin panicked. She was packed and nearly ready to leave. When would she be able to cross the stream? She returned to the house but felt tense and restless so she walked down to the lake and stood on the dock.

On a calm day, the still water reflected the surroundings like a mirror. Today, the wind sent ripples across the surface. Caitlin returned to the house and added logs to the fire. She looked around, wondering what to do. She'd read all the books she'd brought. Her paints were packed. She wasn't in the mood to play an instrument.

She walked into her father's study and saw an old chess board sitting on top of a bookcase. She brought it to the desk and sat in her father's leather swivel chair. He'd had that chair for as long as she could remember. Thinking she might play a game of chess with herself, Caitlin moved a white pawn forward two spaces, but without a worthy opponent the idea quickly lost its appeal.

She pushed aside the board and turned on the radio, hoping to find an update about weather and road conditions. Country music, a local call-in show with items for sale, and religious programming were the only stations with clear reception. After filling in a few answers in a book of crossword puzzles, Caitlin went to bed.

She dreamed she was learning to swim in a shallow cove, an inlet that was safe from storms and protected from sharks and other dangers. The surrounding cliffs were like brilliant towers, with deposits of alabaster, amethyst, and malachite; the turquoise water glowed with a pale luminescence. Helpers were there to teach her how to glide effortlessly through the water. When she awoke the next morning, Caitlin felt exhilarated.

In some theories of dream interpretation, water symbolized emotions. Caitlin's emotions had been dammed for so long that when the floodgates finally opened, she'd feared she would drown in the deluge. Her mother had been an easy target for her frustration and rage, but Martha's steadfast presence had given Caitlin the reassurance she needed to get through the challenges. Somehow, they had navigated stormy seas together and landed in a better place.

Caitlin decided to write a song about the bond she felt with her mother. With nothing to do but wait for the water to recede, she thought the words would flow easily, like the lyrics for the other songs had, but this one came in spurts. Fragments were there, in a sketchy outline, but something was missing. Caitlin felt her attention being pulled in another direction. She still hadn't said goodbye to her father.

She opened the last can of tuna and shared it with Lucky. Before the sun set, she returned to the stream; it looked almost passable. If no more rain fell, she might be able to drive across in the morning. She went back to the house and sat on the porch swing, appreciating the sights and sounds and smells of spring.

The next day, a cool breeze spun the weather vane her father had placed atop the shed that housed a lawn mower and power tools. Caitlin carried the last of her things to the car. She draped a sweater around her shoulders and went to pick flowers. After assembling a nice bouquet, she tied the stems with an old hair ribbon she'd found in the bedroom that she and Bobby had shared when they were young.

"The top bunk's mine, squirt," Bobby announced on their first trip to the lake house.

He was older and bigger and usually got his way. Caitlin remembered the first time she had the room to herself. Bobby had graduated from high school and joined the Coast Guard. But occupying the upper bunk didn't mean anything if no one was beneath her, and Caitlin continued to sleep on the lower bed—except when her cousin Mildred stayed over. Then, Caitlin was in charge, and she wasn't much more gracious to Mildred than Bobby had been to her. *So much for being a good host.*

Caitlin sighed. She was beginning to understand why her mother had said that she only paid attention to her own concerns. But she could change—her growing ability to recognize when she was being selfish was testament to that. The twelve-step programs had the right idea, suggesting an honest self-assessment—and amends toward those who had been harmed during less enlightened phases of one's life.

Walking the property, Caitlin recalled walking along a trail with Kimo. *Was that in Ireland or Virginia?* He'd talked about the challenges of embarking on a spiritual path.

Is that what I'm doing—embarking on a spiritual path?

She'd thought of seekers as people like Satchidananda, who followed a particular guru and tradition and separated themselves from worldly concerns and ambitions. Perhaps in the new age they were entering rejection of the material world would no longer be required to lead a spiritual life. *Perhaps it never was.* Maybe the end of religious indoctrination was the beginning of true spirituality.

After all, her relationship with God was her affair; nobody else could see into her heart and soul and know what was right for her.

In the end, what is there but consciousness? Caitlin thought as she approached one of her father's favorite spots on the property, an open space between two stately oak trees. He'd often talked about putting up a hammock and enjoying an afternoon snooze or a night under the stars.

Caitlin hoped her father had found peace—that he'd gone to a good place. She read the inscription on the stone that marked his grave:

CHARLES STEWART ROSE, b. Nov. 23, 1930, d. Jan. 4, 1992

Caitlin knelt down and said a prayer. The ground felt cold and damp. She placed the flowers on the grave. *He's gone for good.*

After taking a deep breath, she said, "Hi Daddy. I'm going now. It's not the same here, without you. There's so much I want to say . . . so much I'll never know."

Choked up, she waited a few moments before continuing.

"I believed in you, Daddy. And I wanted you to believe in me, to be proud of me. That's why I went into law."

When she rediscovered her passion for music, Caitlin felt herself come alive; only then did she realize how empty her life had become over the years as she gradually abandoned activities that brought her joy and pleasure. She knew her father disapproved of her ambition to be a performer. Pursuing a career in art, music, drama or dance was, in his mind, on a par with becoming a ski bum, a surfer, or a professional student; it might be fun but it wouldn't produce anything of value. Caitlin's desire to win her father's approval had been so strong that she had given up her dreams—and her mother—in the attempt. She'd taken his side, and he'd let her down. Even when she wasn't playing music, the pleasure she derived from listening to it had enriched her life—and that was worth something.

"I guess maybe we didn't know each other so well after all," Caitlin said. "You know what I always wanted to do?"

She threw back her head and raised her arms to the sky. "Sing!"

Slowly, she lowered her arms and bowed her head. "You never

came to my choir's concerts. You weren't there every afternoon when I practiced piano. Mom was."

Caitlin rose to her feet. "I have to live with my choices—and I have to live with yours. I'm hurt, and I'm angry! You've left a big hole . . . in my life and in my heart."

Tears streamed down her face. "Maybe someday I'll be able to forgive you. I know how hopeless that black empty pit feels. I have been there, and back. And I choose life, Daddy! I choose life. I'm gonna make every day count."

Looking up, she noticed an owl watching her from a nearby branch. She turned and walked back to the house.

She put Lucky's travel carrier on the back seat of the car. After returning the key to the flower pot, she started the motor and drove down the long gravel driveway toward the bridge.

When she reached the creek, Caitlin stepped out of the car. The water had receded enough that she thought she could get across without being swept away. She got back in the car, took a deep breath, and charged forward.

∽ 89 ∽

Caitlin drove toward the Arkansas state line. She planned to drive south to Fort Smith; from there, she would pick up Interstate 40 and go west. The motor club had sent a mapped-out route that included updates on highway construction as well as suggestions for lodging along the way.

Driving along a deserted stretch of highway, Caitlin's thoughts returned to the lake house. Had she remembered to turn off all the baseboard heaters?

Touching her hand to the silver necklace, she felt both gratitude and heartache. *I never laid flowers on my father's grave before.*

Maybe writing a song would help her find closure. Something reminiscent of an Irish ballad. A song about letting go, about saying goodbye.

I can finally see the truth. Daddy's gone for good.

She reached for a notebook and scribbled a few notes.

Thinking that she ought to familiarize herself with a variety of musical styles, Caitlin turned on the radio. A catchy tune on a country station got her attention.

"I was on my way to L.A., gonna make it they all tell me, 'til a detour sent me sailin' down where memories are trailin.'"

Suddenly, a front tire blew.

"Shit! Now what?"

Caitlin pulled to the side of the highway and slowly drove to the next exit. She pushed the button to flash the emergency lights and coasted into a Kum and Go gas station near the exit ramp. After parking by a pay phone, she got out to take a look.

Yep, it's flat all right.

She called the motor club from the pay phone. While she waited for help to arrive, she dialed Melody's number.

"Caitlin! Where are you?"

"Somewhere in Arkansas. I ran into an unexpected delay."

"I was so excited to get your message," Melody said. "My house-mate moved out last week so I've got plenty of room. Come on by!"

"Great. I hope to be there sometime tomorrow," Caitlin said. She glanced at the tire. "God willing," she added. "Oh, and Kimo sends his love."

"I should call him," Melody said. "I'll wait 'til you're here. We can call him together."

"If you want."

Caitlin was always happy to talk to Kimo, and he was so hard to reach that the likelihood of catching him at home was slim. But, then, Melody being who she was, well—who knew what magic they might conjure up together.

"I'll call when I'm closer and get directions from you then. You'll be around?"

"I'll make sure of it."

Caitlin rode in the cab while her car was towed to a garage in Fayetteville, where the mechanic told her she was lucky, she wouldn't need a new tire. She smiled, wondering if her feline companion really did bring her luck.

While the tire was being patched, Caitlin looked through the magazines and literature in the waiting area. She noticed a brochure for the Cherokee Heritage Center in Tahlequah, Oklahoma. It wasn't exactly on the way, but it wasn't too much of a detour either.

I may never pass this way again. I might as well enjoy the journey.

She recalled how she'd felt when she returned to Washington from Ireland, when she wanted to resign. She'd wanted to find a different kind of life, outside the bounds of conventional living.

"Now's our chance," she told Lucky as she drove out of the parking lot.

She noticed a sign for a natural foods market and stopped to buy trail mix, fruit, juice, hommos and chips, a salad, and soap. Walking past a display of fresh muffins, Caitlin smiled. She hoped Patrice was happy in her new life with John.

Caitlin sipped the juice as she headed west on Highway 62. The route took her past the Civil War battlefield at Prairie Grove, and soon she was in Oklahoma. She encountered little traffic on the winding road through the scenic foothills of the Ozarks. Level patches of pasture were dotted with horses and cows, but rusted cars, farm machinery, and abandoned shacks marred the beauty of the land.

She had, indeed, been lucky with the flat, Caitlin thought. If something had to go wrong, at least it had happened in a convenient location. She remembered what she'd told Sam when he lost the car keys in Hawai'i: her guardian angels were looking out for her. She smiled and sent a prayer his way.

She passed a sign for the Jaybird Community Church. Thoughts of Jayson no longer made her heart ache; she could appreciate the good times they had shared and let go of the rest. She softly sang a line from a Carly Simon song, "Haven't Got Time for the Pain."

A sign by the road indicated that she was traveling along the Trail of Tears. Benge's Route, Caitlin learned when she arrived at the

Cherokee Heritage Center, was one of four routes by which the Five Tribes—the Cherokee, the Choctaw, the Creeks, or Muscogee, the Seminole, and the Chicasaw—were removed from their southeastern lands under orders from Andrew Jackson.

The brutal treatment of settlers in the West by some natives didn't justify a government policy of exterminating whole tribes, Caitlin thought as she toured the Heritage Center.

She recalled discussions with Kimo about national destiny and national karma. The United States had used various means to eliminate threats from "the savages" and to acquire their lands. Native peoples were driven onto reservations and required to assimilate into the white man's world. They were forbidden to speak their own languages or practice their traditions. Well-meaning missionaries sought to replace native cultures with their own.

What arrogance!

Melody had mentioned that tribal dances and celebrations were held on feast days at pueblos in the Southwest. Caitlin was excited about visiting New Mexico. She knew from listening to Kimo and Melody that Santa Fe was the reputed center of an "energy vortex" that attracted spiritual seekers and holistic practitioners. Melody said that Santa Fe had also become a trendy destination for the L.A. crowd; expensive restaurants and custom homes were the new norm. After so many months with only her own company—and her own cooking—Caitlin was eager to see Melody again and looked forward to sampling some flavorful Southwestern cuisine.

She also wanted to explore the art galleries on Canyon Road. She thought of Dru and their time together in London and Edinburgh. What kind of man would interest her now? she wondered. What kind of man would be interested in her?

When she'd finished touring the Heritage Center, she put Lucky on a leash so he could get some fresh air. Caitlin sat on a picnic table at the campground adjoining the museum grounds and addressed a postcard to her mother.

So many place-names in the U.S. derived from words that white settlers had learned from Native American inhabitants. Minnesota. Idaho. Alaska. Utah. The Dakotas. *Olathe.*

While Lucky rolled around trying to escape from the confining collar, Caitlin closed her eyes and imagined a blanket of peace extending across the country. Someday, she hoped, people would look beyond the superficial differences that separated them and find common ground in their shared humanity.

Caitlin opened her eyes and stared into the nearby fire pit. She poked the blackened charcoal and gray ash with a stick.

What we have here is a two-party system, she thought. *Winners and losers.*

The conquerors and the conquered. Broken treaties, broken spirits. She, too, had played by the rules, only to be left with broken dreams. But that didn't make her a loser.

Can we all live together in peace?

Melody had told Caitlin about a few of her friends in New Mexico. One was an astrologer who had studied the cycles of time. Long periods of turbulence and chaos were cyclically followed by golden ages of peace and innovation, Melody had said. Caitlin hoped that was true. Maybe human ingenuity and technological innovations would solve some of the environmental crises humans had created in a relatively short span of time. If Kimo was right and the Age of Pisces was ending, then perhaps the religious motifs of the last two thousand years were outworn. Humanity could no longer wait for a savior.

We have to save ourselves. We could start by adopting a cooperative model.

Did enough people want to create new models of living and working and relating that were harmonious and sustainable, or would tolerance for greed and aggression continue to overshadow the efforts of a few forward-thinking visionaries who dared to adopt alternative lifestyles?

Feeling inspired, Caitlin returned to the car to get her notebook. She jotted down a few ideas for a song.

"I don't want to play anymore," she wrote, "if promises will only get broken, and dreams turn to dust as soon as they're spoken. From the ashes of love, my body consumed, my phoenix heart cries to the moon. I'll be home soon."

Ideas for her new song, "Phoenix Heart," quietly played in her mind as she departed the site. She would drive west, she decided, until she felt tired and stop for the night wherever she found herself. That would leave plenty of time the following day to reach Santa Fe before dark.

Before she left the lake house, Caitlin had found a card in her father's desk drawer with a long version of "The Serenity Prayer" by Reinhold Niebuhr printed on the front. She planned to send it to Kimo after she arrived in Santa Fe. One verse in particular had struck a chord:

> Living one day at a time
> Enjoying one moment at a time
> Accepting hardships as the pathway to peace

Caitlin had endured hardships; now, moments of joy were emerging like spring flowers.

The coals in the fire pit brought to mind a dream from the previous night. In the dream, she walked a path lined with red-hot coals. She turned and looked behind her; the coals were burned-out ashes. When she stood still, the heat burned her feet. She took a step forward with her right foot and an amazing thing happened: the glowing coal was transformed into a red rose blossom, silky soft between her toes. She moved her left foot and the same thing happened. Enchanted, she stepped again with her right foot, and then her left. Soon the trail was covered with rose petals.

The red rose way.

She would forge her own path, write her own songs. She had found her voice. Words could not express the joy she felt when her spirit was at one with the flow of life. Only music, the universal language, could do that. Music opened her heart and gave her wings.

No wonder angels are often singing and playing.

Back on the road, Caitlin felt awed by the vast expanse of land that stretched for miles.

Road Angel. Sounds like a good idea for a song . . .

End of Volume One

Acknowledgments

Many people have provided advice, feedback, and encouragement during the process of researching and writing *A Moment of Time*, and I am deeply grateful. Special thanks go to Russ Nelson, Seajay Crosson, and Riqua Serebreni for comments on the manuscript, Judy Adelle Hutchins, OTR/L, for reviewing the parts about autism, and Mary Ann Toner, Ph.D., CCC-SLP, for her expertise regarding apraxia of speech and aphasia.

I was also blessed by the unconditional support of my mother, who always believed in me.

About the Author

Jilaine Tarisa is a licensed attorney with a background in psychology (Master of Arts). She is passionate about increasing awareness of alternative methods of dispute resolution, holistic healing, and sustainable communities. Born in Manhattan, she has traveled throughout the United States and enjoys discovering new ways of promoting peace and understanding.

She also likes to sing.

Learn more at jilainetarisa.com

Published by Inspired Creations, LLC

For information about other titles in our catalog and
forthcoming releases, visit www.inspiredcreationsllc.com

Lightning Source UK Ltd.
Milton Keynes UK
UKOW01f2354220217
295110UK00001B/61/P